T0190779

Elizabeth Sails

Kristin Owens

Text copyright © 2024 by Kristin Owens

All rights reserved. For information regarding reproduction in total or in part, contact Rising Action Publishing Co. at http://www.risingactionpublishingco.com

Cover Illustration © Nat Mack
Distributed by Simon & Schuster

ISBN: 978-1-998076-55-0
Ebook: 978-1-998076-57-4

FIC022140 FICTION / Mystery & Detective / Cozy / Holidays & Vacation
FIC044000 FICTION / Women
FIC045000 FICTION / Family Life/General

#ElizabethSails

Follow Rising Action on our socials!
Twitter: @RAPubCollective
Instagram: @risingactionpublishingc
TikTok: @risingactionpublishingco

Elizabeth Sails

Kristin Owens

CHAPTER 1

October 25th

E thel Papadopoulos Lorenzo Birnbaum steered her Go-Go Electric X5 mobility scooter down the ship's passageway, bumping into doorframes along the way. Her sequined beret glinted in the overhead lights and, with red lips pursed, she tried to focus on the task at hand ... but failed miserably. Giggling, she throttled back but not before wedging herself into a corner.

"Oopsie Daisy!" she hooted and collapsed over the handlebars in laughter. After some herky-jerky movements of forward and reverse, she extracted herself and motored on. Her ship's ID card opened the door to cabin #10007. With a practiced movement, she whipped out her cane from the scooter's basket and propped the door open. She rolled inside and the door closed behind her with a muted thud.

Ethel took a deep breath. Too much wine and more tired than usual. Besides a headache coming on, her chest felt constricted and her legs ached too. She felt her age, all eighty plus years of it. But in spite of her ever-growing list of maladies, she giggled again.

Dinner tonight had been a formal affair (a Roaring 20s theme) and guests arrived bedazzled in their finery. Men sported black tuxedos and white ties, while women festooned themselves in sparkles and feathers. Pretending to be someone else, if only for a few hours, indulging their escapist fantasies. The costumes helped—ladies laughed freely, holding champagne flutes while their husbands kissed them more often. Photographers snapped away to commemorate the events and live music added to the low-grade hum of excitement. Ethel smiled. She had attended dozens of parties. Hundreds. Familiar, even routine, but it still never got old ... the feeling of being young again.

She inspected her cabin, her home. It was tidied, as usual, with her bed turned down and a breakfast menu perched on her pillow. *So silly.* Ramie knew her usual order, which never deviated in the past few weeks: two eggs sunny-side up, two strips of bacon and a pot of coffee. Yet, high service criteria dictated the card be placed there nightly. Cunard required exacting standards and uncompromising quality. Ethel loved it.

It was after midnight. Ethel quickly readied herself for bed; she soaked her teeth, removed her makeup, brushed her hair, and placed her jewelry into a chipped *I Love Rome* ash tray. She pulled the covers up to her chin and glanced at the bedside table. A small silver frame held a photo of two young women, each the mirror opposite of the other. One, tall with golden hair and blue eyes, the other short with dark brown and hazel. With their arms squeezed tight around each other, the girls' wide smiles beamed at her. Ethel smiled back, whispered a little prayer and sank immediately into a painless sleep.

Cabin steward Ramie announced himself promptly at eight o'clock the next morning by knocking on the cabin door. Without waiting, he carried the breakfast tray inside, careful not to spill on his crisp, white uniform.

"Madame Birnbaum? Time for breakfast." He placed the tray on the coffee table while surprised to see her still in bed. "Madame Birnbaum?" Ramie sat down next to her on the bed and reached for her hand. It was cold. He sighed, "Oh, madam."

After a few minutes, he rose and went to the safe inside her closet. He punched in the combination. It clicked open. He pushed aside jewelry cases, stacks of cash and found a thick envelope. Ramie read the address. A lawyer in New York City. He stared at the envelope until tears blurred his vision.

CHAPTER 2

"Uh-huh." Beth held the phone in the crook of her neck while dangling a glittery pompom from a string in front of her white cat. Grendel batted it half-heartedly with his one remaining front paw. If asked, he'd rather lounge undisturbed in the sunspot on her desk.

"Uh-huh," Beth repeated. "Governor Sharp, I was going to submit it. Now we'll miss the deadline." She made the cat toy bob and dance, just out of Grendel's reach. "Yes, I know how important your story is ... yes ... yes, I understand."

She groaned silently. The all-important timeline was now doomed with another last-minute change. Her publisher had strategically scheduled Sharp's book for the winter holidays, just in time to support her election campaign the following year. At this rate, it would be next spring before it would see the light of day. The publication date (and Beth's enthusiasm) was getting pushed further and further away with each of the governor's panicked phone calls and her selective memory of past events.

"What *exactly* do you want to add?" Beth reluctantly put down the cat toy. She took notes. After thirty minutes listening to a new angle of a tired old campaign story, she said, "Okay. I'll need to check with Frank. Can I call you back Monday?" She hung up and put her head down on the desk, defeated. Grendel gently tapped her hand with his paw.

This project just wouldn't end.

This book was her third politician this year and Governor Laina Sharp's autobiography had dogged Beth for almost six months. She didn't know how much of Sharp's story was true, embellished, or fictionalized. Beth was a ghostwriter and, thankfully, not a fact-checker. If she got paid by the eye roll, her publisher would owe her a fortune. A typical assignment was exasperating, but Governor Sharp took maddening to a whole new level. Late night phone calls, excessive handholding, the governor's tedious stories beginning with "I" and ending with "me" were routine. Sharp's ego exhausted Beth. So did all the revisions.

Beth sat pouting in the squeaky chair in her office, which was really a corner in the living room in front of the only window. She leaned forward and pressed her nose against the cold glass. The lone tree in the small garden on Fulton Street below had changed from luxe velvety green to brittle gold and brown. By next week, its remaining leaves would be on the ground. Fall had arrived. Another season and she still wrote other people's stories.

She called her editor, Frank, and left the message, "You owe me!" on his voice mail. Then she released a loud, frustrated sigh sounding like a foghorn. Annoyed, Grendel blinked his green eyes and trotted to the kitchen for the comfort of his food bowl.

While she waited for a return call, Beth cleaned up her desk to help temper the unresolved issue. She tucked her hair behind her ears and organized old notes, interviews, and previous drafts of Sharp's manu-script. She shuddered as she backed-up computer files and wondered how politicians ever got elected in the first place. Although premature (and wishful thinking), she shoved Sharp's paperwork into a file drawer labeled COMPLETED.

On one wall hung framed prints of her bestseller book jackets, her name nowhere to be found on the covers. On another wall, hung her college degree. Bachelor of Arts in English, University of Pennsylvania, 2007. Four years of blissful reading and writing. Ghostwriting was not exactly the career Beth expected. But she was good—hell, great—at it, even though she *was* currently losing patience with inane clients.

She ambled to the kitchen, about six steps. The recycling container overflowed with crusty Marie Callender pot pie boxes. The inside of her microwave looked like a Jackson Pollock painting. But her oven was spotless. Next to an empty Wonder Bread bag, she found a rogue twist tie on the counter. She secured it around a messy braid on the left side of her temple. That was better. Her hair now out of her eyes and she could see. Kind of. Her broken glasses sat crooked on her nose. *I really need to get them fixed*, she reminded herself again for the forty-eighth time today. Instead, she got herself a bowl of Cap'n Crunch.

She leaned against a doorframe and slurped her cereal. Her free week-end was now possibly shot. Thank goodness her small one-bedroom apartment was relatively clean. An antique Folger's coffee can with extra chopsticks from Wong Fu's, a couch upholstered in worn purple velvet, and a heavy glass mason jar filled with spare change helped ornament the small room. Her knick-knacks were definitely *not* tchotchke, but rather pleasing objects rescued from flea markets and second-hand stores. One would think from her decorating skills Beth lived from paycheck to paycheck, but most of her well-earned six-figure salary went directly into the bank and retirement accounts. Beth believed her apartment had a warm, lived-in feel. Eclectic. *Yeah, that's the word.*

And don't forget the books! Towers of books stacked from floor to ceiling provided much needed architectural details to her shoe-box-shaped place. The hundreds of paperbacks and hard covers were an extravagance she didn't mind paying full price for. They provided excitement, comfort, and intrigue depending on her mood. Bored? A romp with *Murder on the Orient Express.* Stressed? Soothing *Little House on the Prairie.* Lonely? A used Danielle Steele paperback with the page corners turned down at the good parts. Like a trusted friend, books could ease any troubles with a few familiar words. Plus, they were safe. Re-read a thousand times, she knew all their endings ... no surprises and no cause for alarm.

She took a habitual favorite, a dog-eared copy of *The Hobbit,* from the top of a stack to read later. Beth dumped her cereal bowl in the sink and shuffled back to the office. She checked her phone ... still no message from Frank. With her procrastination dance over, she had no other option except to adjust her broken glasses and revise Governor Sharp's manuscript. Again.

When the sunshine disappeared and dark skies precipitated turning on a floor lamp, Beth pried herself from the office chair and stared at her big toe that had wormed its way out of a hole in her sock. She considered fixing it. Grendel yawned from the back of the couch (his perch) and stretched like a Halloween cat. Beth stretched too while her tummy grumbled.

"Grendel," she said. "Need. Food. Now!"

He blinked at her.

Her fridge offered little inspiration for dinner: a single piece of bologna, a container of suspect yogurt, and some wilted lettuce. An expired Lean Cuisine lay encased in ice in the freezer. Too much work. She considered ordering in (again), but remembered a promise made to herself earlier. Plus, she needed some exercise. Beth blamed Governor Sharp for the extra ten pounds she'd recently accumulated.

Here we go! Going out. Outside. Big doin's. Beth took a deep breath. She inhaled and exhaled for three counts each. In for one ... two ... three. Out for one ... two ... three. Just like Dr. Joan advised her.

"Calm the heart, calm the mind," Beth whispered as a mantra. She repeated her breathing cycle. *Good? Yes. Let's go!*

At the last moment, she looked critically at her grubby sweatshirt, but decided all she really needed was a bra. She announced to Grendel, "I'm putting on a bra. I'm going out. I will be fine," in a loud, authoritative voice. The cat flattened his ears in response to such unexpected hullabaloo. Beth put on the required undergarment, grabbed her wallet, and opened her apartment door. She stepped over a pile of take-out menus, flyers, and last Sunday's *New York Times* which had accumulated in front of her doorstep.

"Here I go! I'm really fine!" she said to no one. She stepped out and the crisp air kissed the inside of her nostrils.

NYC. The Big Apple. The City That Never Sleeps. But for Beth, it was the City of Fabulous Food. Italian, French, Pakistani ... all available with the press of a few buttons on her phone. Thank God for delivery.

The world outside her apartment could be quite unpredictable. But on the rare occasions she ventured out, her local eating establishments never disappointed. Tonight, she selected *Athena* for souvlaki and home-made baklava. In anticipation, she overcame any fear of the unknown and quickened her steps. This would be worth it.

After a few short blocks, the family-owned restaurant appeared. Blue and white Greek flags decorated the neighborhood standby. The door's bells announced Beth's entrance with unwanted fanfare. She seated herself at a blue pleather booth, glanced momentarily at the sticky menu and ordered from memory. While waiting for her food, she played with her braid and realized it still had the twist tie. Then, as she usually did when she was nervous—a calming mechanism, according to Dr. Joan—she made up a fantastical story about the chef. She didn't want to use up *all* her creativity on politicians.

Konstantinos was a woebegone man. He never smiled and his habitually sad eyes made customers (both men and women) want to grab him in a warm embrace, while whispering, "There, there." Long ago, a beautiful woman jilted Konstantinos at the altar. An authentic Greek tragedy. Left bereft and heartbroken, he poured what remained of his fractured soul into cooking. All his raw emotion and unrequited love transferred into the best spanakopita in the city. Customers felt terrible witnessing his watery eyes, but it didn't stop them from ordering his award-winning food. Athena thrived, but alas, now in his forties, Konstantinos still lived with his mother in her basement. He found out through an unfortunate social media post that his ex-fiancée had married a plumber and had six kids. One named Konstantinos.

At least that's the tale Beth came up with.

Her food arrived and it smelled delicious. She attacked the chicken souvlaki and debated whether to order more pita and hummus.

She didn't mind eating alone. The promising high-energy lifestyle that originally attracted her to the big city had never developed. Her social circle remained small and Beth accepted the writing life as a lonely one. Now she embraced it. Fewer friends meant fewer expectations. Her shyness translated into awkwardness, which meant aloof to most people. And whenever a little insecurity got thrown onto the fire, she usually wound up with a big ol' three-alarm anxiety attack. In retrospect, alone was just fine. Plus, her apartment had everything she needed, so why leave?

Her cell phone buzzed in her pocket. She quickly swallowed a mouthful of pita and answered.

"Hi, Frank. You really owe me." She wiped tzatziki sauce off her chin and wondered if there were any Tums left in her medicine cabinet.

A full, soothing bass replied, "Yeah, I know Sharp's a pain. You're taking one for the team. I wish I had ten more like ya, Pussycat." Speaking of cats, Frank's voice could calm a herd of kittens high on catnip. Sometimes Beth would call his voicemail just to feel instantaneous peace. Once she dozed off while he outlined a new book project to her.

"But this is it, right? The last change?"

"I promise. If she asks for more, send her my way. Maybe we should dial back on politicians for a while. Besides, the market's getting saturated. When are you going to write me a *real* book? Something with heart?" Frank had pushed her for years to do something on her own. His recently acquired middle-aged outlook of *it's-never-too-late* sometimes got on her nerves.

"I'll write one when I have something interesting to write about," she said. "Besides, these politicians are taking up all my time ... thanks to *your* assignments." Beth could give him a little sass, since he wasn't just her editor but also a trusted friend.

"Ha ha. Anyway, I have the lovely job of collecting R.S.V.P.'s for the holiday party. Are you coming or not? Apparently, we need to know how many shrimp cocktails to order." The phone practically buzzed from the timbre of his voice. She stalled for time and rubbed hummus off her sweatshirt with a paper napkin, making the stain even worse.

"First, sing to me."

"C'mon, Beth."

"Please? Sing me something."

Frank cleared his throat, then launched into Beth's favorite Barry White song, "You're the First, The Last, My Everything."

Beth giggled.

"Okay? Please come to the party. Paul will be there ... he hasn't seen you in forever."

She sighed. Her publisher's annual party scared the bejeezus out of her. Besides Frank and his husband, who would she talk to? And about what? It took a whole year to buck up the courage to attend and each time her hands would sweat buckets while she tried to be funny and engaging. Plus, on a practical matter, she usually spilled something down her front. Parties equaled dry cleaning which meant she'd have to leave the house *again*. Definitely *not* worth the emotional aftermath.

"Uh ... I'll think about it."

"I'm putting your name down. You can do it, trust me." Frank hung up before she could squirm out of it.

11

Great. There was nothing unstained or size-appropriate in her closet to wear. Deflated, she decided against ordering the extra pitas. She sulked while looking at her dirty plate streaked with dried hummus. Parties weren't fun. Particularly, since small talk was on The List.

Ah ... The List. The List was all-important, even critical, since the items listed on The List were her fears which precipitated anxieties and Beth tried very hard to not place herself in situations listed on The List. She hated The List but respected it. Doctor Joan said Beth needed to start removing things from The List. She was trying.

As Beth paid her bill, she glanced back at Konstantinos who looked moments away from sobbing on a pile of marinating lamb shanks. Maybe she could take him to the holiday party? Quickly deciding no, she scooted out the door.

Beth slumped toward home, burping and lamenting her expanding waistline. It *would* be easier to take someone with her. But who? Men were not only an afterthought but an extinct species in her world. After a college boyfriend grabbed her ass and called her chubby, she never wore bikini underwear or dated again. Now older and wiser, she realized men tended to date women who shopped at Sephora, regularly got pedicures, and didn't need mantras to leave the house. She couldn't compete. Consequently, her makeup-free look and ten-dollar haircut from Stu, the Fulton Street barber became less of an issue. A good time for Beth was binge-watching old Hollywood musicals with a Whitman's Sampler. She hypothesized she was the only single woman in New York City likely to remain single. She was thirty-eight years old.

As she made the last turn, her face brightened. The corner flower shop displayed a bouquet of gladiolas in the window. Spectacular! A crystal vase held tall stalks bursting with color in various shades of red: cherry, scarlet, ruby, tomato. They filled the entire space like an operatic diva on stage. Beth stood and stared. *Wow, how beautiful.* She stepped inside and impulsively bought a dozen to congratulate herself on a successful outing.

She could barely keep her arms around the bunch wrapped in brown paper. A mistake? Where would she even put them? She didn't have a big enough vase at home and they couldn't possibly fit in the coffee can. The three-foot stems blocked her sightline as she unintentionally collided with people on the sidewalk. She exclaimed, "Oh, so sorry," and, "Excuse me," as she ricocheted off pedestrians like a Roomba, trying to find her apartment entryway.

She huffed and puffed up the stairs to the second floor. Damn. *I really need to dust off Mom's Richard Simmons DVD.* She turned the hallway corner to find a man in a dark suit and tie standing outside her door. She squinted. On closer inspection, it was an *attractive* man in an *expensive* suit and tie. Was he an overdressed exterminator? A Christmas caroler with bad timing? A mafia hitman making a huge mistake? Beth felt a tinge of anxiety growing in her stomach, but it could have been the souvlaki. Then the man waved at her. Not just any wave, but a big goofy wave involving his whole hand, arm, and shoulder. For some obscure reason, Beth thought it was funny.

When she got closer, a big smile appeared on his face. Through her broken glasses, Beth could see a chipped front tooth. It would have been distracting on someone else, but it made his handsomeness quirky and more engaging. She was so disconcerted that she stumbled forward. He held out his hand to steady her. After righting both her and the flowers, he peeked around the bouquet and asked hopefully, "Are you Elizabeth Schiff?"

"Yes ... yes, I am," she said out of breath.

"Great! I need you to sign for this." Reaching inside his jacket, he handed her a pen and then offered her a clipboard, like it was a platter full of fancy hors d'oeuvres. She took the nice pen and noticed 'J. J. Watkins & Son' imprinted in gold. She signed next to her typed name and address. The man smiled and handed her an envelope. *Gosh, he smells good.* Immediately, an image clicked in her head, one of pine trees after a fresh Colorado snowfall. Yes, that's exactly how she would describe it. Beth was glad she put on her bra, but immediately regretted the stained sweatshirt. And her hair.

"What's this about?" she asked, trying to be professional when she clearly didn't look the part.

"Miss, I really can't say."

"Why not?" she asked. Cascading Rocky Mountain waterfalls of concern entered her mind as the man shrugged in response. Then he smiled again, waved goodbye—this time with just his hand—and walked down the hallway to the staircase and entryway.

Juggling flowers, the envelope, and her keys, Beth stepped inside her apartment. The odors of last night's Kung Pao chicken still permeated the air. She dropped everything on the kitchen table, took the envelope, and looked at it more carefully. The paper was heavy-weight and good quality. Her name was printed correctly on the front. As Grendel wrapped himself around her ankles, she opened it carefully.

Dear Miss Schiff,
With great sadness, I must report your beloved Aunt, Ethel Birnbaum, passed away last Friday, October 25. My sincerest condolences for your loss.

As Ms. Birnbaum's legal representation, I am responsible for her final wishes. This necessitates communicating many details and requires an in-person conference. Please note, it is not my intention to cause any undue stress; however, your presence is not only advised but imperative to successfully conclude vital business.

Please call to confirm a meeting scheduled for 9:00 a.m. tomorrow, November 5th, at our Manhattan office. Given the short nature of the request, I am hopeful it works with your busy calendar.

Again, my heartfelt sympathies at this sorrowful time.

Your servant,
J.J. Watkins

Crap. Beth folded the letter and placed it carefully back in the envelope. *Aunt Ethel loved gladiolas.*

CHAPTER 3

The admin assistant ushered Beth into a large office covered in dark mahogany paneling, complete with bookcases and heavy furniture. It screamed *lawyer*. The attorney, Mr. Watkins, stood up from his battleship-sized desk and offered a hand in greeting. In a dove-gray flannel suit and aubergine silk tie, he was elegantly attired and looked pleased to see her, as evidenced by the wide smile on his face.

"Sit, please, my dear." He gestured to a tufted leather couch. "My apologies for this last-minute meeting. I hope it didn't cause any scheduling issues?"

Beth shook her head, murmured no, and tried to look confident all at once. Except her mouth turned into a painful grimace due to her old navy-blue suit (which hadn't seen daylight in about a decade) constricting her midsection. Mr. Watkins sat next to her and continued to smile warmly. Reassuringly.

"Now, where to begin? So much to discuss."

Beth glanced around his well-appointed office and watched the admin assistant pour hot tea into beautiful bone china cups. Aunt Ethel wouldn't have had it any differently; she always had the best. Beth looked down at her shoes and tried to buff a smudge off one of the toes against the back of her calf. In her mind, she repeated, *this won't take long. Just breathe.*

Beth wondered if Aunt Ethel left her any money. Over the years, she had amassed a fortune from several generous husbands. But, how much? *This could be really good news ... but knowing Aunt Ethel...* Beth balanced her teacup and saucer on her knee and tried not to fidget.

Mr. Watkins interrupted her thoughts. "First, please accept my condolences. Your aunt was truly a magnificent lady. She was not only a client of mine for, oh, it must be close to ten years now, but also a friend."

"Thank you," Beth replied.

"As you know," he continued, "she was quite a character. Three husbands and she outlived them all. She had some great stories." He laughed and shook his head. "Oh, the stories! What a sense of humor, too. Did she ever tell you about the time she ... oh my, I really shouldn't repeat that one! Anyways, she enjoyed life fully and I'm sorry she's no longer with us. Still, 'Our dead are never dead to us, until we have forgotten them.'"

Beth raised an eyebrow. "George Eliot?"

"Correct," Mr. Watkins beamed.

"How did Aunt Ethel die?" Beth tried tucking her hair behind her ears.

"She had a heart attack. In her sleep. The ship's doctor reported it happened quickly."

"The *ship's* doctor?"

"Yes. She was sailing on the *Queen Mary 2*. She was a permanent guest of Cunard and rotated her stays among the three ships."

"I didn't know she lived on a ship." Beth had regularly received postcards from Aunt Ethel, a monthly occurrence, just like her rent. Greetings arrived from places like Istanbul, St. Petersburg, and Rome. Her irrepressible humor shone through. Never deviating, Ethel always wrote, "Wish You Were Here!!!" on each one.

"Such an outgoing personality," Mr. Watkins continued. "She loved being surrounded by people and traveling to new places. A ship was the perfect way to do it. The staff saw to her needs—food and medical, and really anything she required was available. She was a wealthy woman and could afford to live in style. She was at sea for years."

"Where was she?"

"The *Queen Mary 2* was making a transatlantic crossing from London to New York when your aunt passed. We were able to retrieve the body once the ship arrived. Her wishes were to be cremated and we've seen to that."

A clock ticked loudly. Beth's tea cooled.

Aunt Ethel had attended her college graduation years ago. Wearing a classic Chanel pink suit and ropes of pearls around her neck, Ethel sported a humongous hat with ostrich feathers trimming the brim. She loved hats. She said they should equal your mood. She was obviously over the moon that day with her large flamboyant hat to match her excitement at seeing Beth graduate. Aunt Ethel was Beth's only family there. She never forgot.

After graduation, Beth seldom saw her. They kept in contact with a few phone calls but mostly by old-fashioned letters. Aunt Ethel hated technology. Despised it. "What's the fun in reading cold, impersonal fonts? Don't you dare email me!" she pronounced. "Besides, finding pretty stamps is always *such* fun."

Over time, Beth's letters to Ethel steadily decreased. There was always a project, deadline, or another excuse preventing her from writing more often. Plus, she wrote for a living, which left free time to write for enjoyment unfairly limited. In the past few years, she hadn't sent Aunt Ethel a thing. Not a note, a card, nothing. Yet, Aunt Ethel's postcards arrived like clockwork. She had received one just a few weeks ago from London. Beth placed her half-empty teacup and saucer on the coffee table in front of her. Her head slowly bowed until her chin reached her chest.

Mr. Watkins watched her closely. He leaned forward and tilted his head. "Are you alright, my dear?"

"Yes. I'm just remembering how I lost touch with her. She was always so good to me. I should have stayed more connected. Really, she was my only family."

A sense of woe filled her. The reality was Beth couldn't make it up to her now. She couldn't call, drop a note, and she'd never get another postcard. It was so final. Aunt Ethel had always been there, even when she wasn't. Just the *idea* of her was comforting. Beth suddenly felt alone. Very alone. As tears dripped down her nose, Mr. Watkins handed her a tissue from a box with a fine silver cover from the coffee table.

"Well." He grasped both his hands together and intertwined his fingers. After a few moments of silence which bordered on awkward, he took a breath and continued, "Well, it seems we have a problem and I need your assistance." His eyes narrowed and became serious. "As executors for her estate, we have the responsibility to see to her final wishes ... which are extensive. Over the last year, Ethel and I discussed her requirements in great detail. And, you won't be surprised, but all her assets are designated to charities ... but it seems, well ..." he stopped, searching for the next thing to say. Finally, he shrugged and said, "Her will is missing."

"What?" Beth sat up straight as if goosed from behind.

"We can't find it. Ethel assured us we would have it in time ... before it was needed."

"You're kidding? She didn't think being eighty years old was time?"

Mr. Watkins looked up at Beth's sudden reaction.

"Are you telling me, even with computers, faxes, email, scanners, all of that—you don't even have a copy of it? Anywhere?" Beth's tears skidded to a stop.

He cleared his throat. "We have an *unsigned* draft in our possession. That's the problem. She had the final copy with original signatures. We conducted an extensive search of her cabin and found ... nothing."

Beth leaned back against the couch and closed her eyes. *This is crazy. This doesn't happen in the twenty-first century.* Aunt Ethel was not only wealthy but also exceedingly responsible. Yes, she was goofy, even borderline eccentric. But still. How could she not have a will, properly executed, witnessed, testified, notarized ... whatever! *What was she thinking? How could she be so unreliable? Especially with everything that had happened? Why would she ...?* Beth opened her eyes. Aunt Ethel was nothing but shrewd. A more intelligent and perceptive woman never lived. There had to be more to it.

"Yes, the whole situation is unbelievable," Mr. Watkins said as if he read her mind.

Before Beth could ask her next question, he walked to his desk and returned with a narrow, cream, velvet box. He handed it to her.

"However, this is something we *do* have. And it was very important to her you receive it."

Wow. It could be anything. It could be her ginormous diamond ring, her Colombian emerald earrings, the miles of cultured pearls. Ethel had excellent taste in jewelry, or rather her dead husbands had. Beth adjusted her glasses further down her nose and gingerly opened the box while holding her breath. Inside lay a silver-linked bracelet. No glittering jewels, no precious stones, no embellishments. Just a plain silver bracelet.

"Uh," Beth said after a disappointed exhale. "It's not what I expected."

"Probably not." Mr. Watkins smiled and sat back down, "Now, for another surprise." He handed Beth a fat envelope from the inside of his jacket pocket and explained, "This is your ticket and itinerary. The ship sails the day after tomorrow from Southampton."

The Cunard logo stared back at Beth: bold red letters under a lion with a golden crown.

"I don't understand," she said.

"You're going on a trip. And on this trip, you'll hopefully find the will." Mr. Watkins sat back against the couch, crossed his legs, and called out to his admin assistant for more tea.

CHAPTER 4

Rumble ... thump ... rumble. The dryer, now on the *cool-down* cycle, danced Beth's clothes together like an unchoreographed cha-cha. Purple socks, gray sweatpants, and red panties flipped, somersaulted, and collided. She watched from a metal folding chair, her chin resting in her hands. Laundry was perfect, a mundane chore taking no brain power to achieve. She monopolized multiple washers and dryers instead of jamming her clothes all together. Today, colors and whites had the luxury of separate machines. Unfortunately, her plan backfired. As she watched her clothes monotonously spin, it only left her more time to think. Plus, the smell of bleach sharpened her senses.

She picked at the tape holding her glasses together and replayed the morning spent at Mr. Watkin's office. The meeting had lasted another hour. A long, excruciating hour.

After the new pot of tea arrived and he had hospitably poured her a fresh cup, Mr. Watkins continued in his legalese. "It's crucial to find the signed will. If not, the estate will go to probate, and involve New York State ... let me try to clarify." He took a deep breath and spoke again slowly as Beth twisted her face in confusion. "When Ethel and her last husband Ezekiel married, they combined all their assets—a large portfolio of stocks, property, mutual funds, basically everything they had of value—into a trust."

"I remember. It's like a will, right?"

"Sort of. When Ezekiel died, everything immediately transferred to Ethel ... except the Birnbaum Foundation."

Oh, no. Beth squirmed. This conversation was heading in a very uncomfortable direction.

Mr. Watkins continued, "A few months ago, I worked with her to generate a will of her own; she identified charities and specific causes to support after her own death. The will was sent to her weeks ago to sign. I never received it back. As soon as its located, my firm can disperse the estate according to her wishes." Mr. Watkins took sip of tea.

"And?"

"And the problem is if we *don't* find it, the original trust remains in place and the next of kin inherits everything."

"Who's the next of kin?" Beth asked and instantly regretted it. That persnickety place in her stomach, just south of her already confined waistband, lurched. Constricted. Twisted.

"Ezekiel's son, Max," Mr. Watkins said quietly.

The mention of his name affected her physically. Beth wrapped her arms around herself as if in pain. *This can't be happening, please, not now.* Immediately, a tickling sensation started in her hands and traveled up her arms. She knew she couldn't stop it. Her breathing exercises wouldn't work now. It was all happening too fast.

"Ethel and Ezekiel had, obviously, no children together and Ethel had none of her own. Which means Max, Ezekiel's son from his first wife, is the next of kin. That's not all."

"There's more?" she squeaked.

"We have thirty days from her death to file the will. November twenty-fifth is the deadline, leaving us twenty-one days."

Beth swallowed. Gulped. Tried to stop the tingling from reaching her throat. "Do you know what an awful person he is?" she asked, almost whispering. She couldn't speak his name.

"I know. But Beth, the estate is sizable. Around fifty million."

Car horns from traffic outside punctuated the stillness. Her hands trembled as she reached for her teacup. As she tried to swallow, her throat constricted and she coughed in defiance. *Oh, God. Please don't let this happen in his office.* The tightening continued, forcing her breath into a shallow wheeze. With her hands growing numb, she tried reaching for her purse.

"Beth, I know it's a lot to ask. But here's the situation ... we've already searched Ethel's cabin on the *Queen Mary 2*. We've searched the entire ship and found nothing. A few weeks ago, she was on the *Queen Elizabeth*, so it's the next logical place to look. I'm trying to file a motion with New York State to ask for additional time. But, meanwhile, I need you to fly to London and get on the *Queen Elizabeth* to look for the will."

"What about my job? I can't leave now." Beth wheezed, groping for the bottle of pills inside her purse. She just needed one. One would help everything and then it would be fine.

"I'm sure you can make some kind of arrangement. It's only for a few weeks."

"A few *weeks?*" Borderline frantic, Beth leaned back against the couch, clutching the bottle of pills to her chest. Her waistband tightened even further. She unbuttoned her jacket with unfeeling fingers to breathe. *Unbelievable.* "I don't even know where to begin. I'm trying to finish a project. A big, complicated project. I really don't know how I can go. I have to talk with my publisher to see ..." She tucked back her hair. Beth already knew Frank's answer. Of course, he would say yes. Her grip on the pill bottle lessened ... a little. Frank could finish Governor Sharp's manuscript without her. Thinking ahead to her own next question, she knew he would also gladly watch her cat.

"Excellent!" Mr. Watkins announced. "I knew you'd be up for it. You're a good niece. Just know, I'm here to help you. As you can imagine, leaving my practice wouldn't be a prudent option. I'll be just a phone call away."

"*I never said I'd do it!*" Beth screeched in a high-pitched squeal.

Mr. Watkins' eyebrows shot up in surprise. Beth took off her glasses and wiped her forehead with the back of her shaking hand.

"Can I get you a glass of water?" He nodded towards her pill bottle.

"No. But ... thanks." Her face flamed in embarrassment as she realized the bottle was still firmly clutched to her chest. She put it back in her purse and forced the air out of her lungs to say in a normal pitch, "I'm sorry. Let me get this straight. You want me to fly to London tomorrow night, get on the *Elizabeth,* and try to find the new will which could be anywhere on the ship?" She put her glasses back on.

"Yes, that's right."

"And if I don't find it, *all* the money defaults to Max?" There, she said it. She said his name out loud.

"Yes."

Beth didn't answer, but her brain contradicted her silence with overloading questions. Details needed answering. She spit them out pointedly in rapid-fire succession.

"How do I get there? Where do I buy tickets? Who's paying for it? Where's the ship going? Will there be food? Why me?"

Mr. Watkins reached over to pat her hand reassuringly. "I've overwhelmed you, I'm sorry. Why don't we talk again later? When you had a chance to think about it." He handed her a card from his desk. "My direct cell phone number. Please call me later this afternoon and we'll talk some more." All Beth remembered was nodding blankly at him and her numb hands trying to clutch the card.

BEEP. BEEP. BEEP. The dryer's sixty-minute timer went off. Fifty-nine too wet. Sixty-one too dry. Her morning conversation with Mr. Watkins continued to swirl like her unmatched socks as the dryer came to a final stop. Beth recounted his words, their order, and her corresponding emotions, as she folded dry clothes into a laundry basket, gathered her remaining quarters and detergent, and took the elevator back up to her apartment. Dozens of unresolved questions still raced. A dull throbbing in her head remained. But at least her body felt calmer. Her hands felt like her own, her voice back to normal. She grasped at her victory: she had managed to get home from Mr. Watkin's office without taking a pill.

Doctor Joan had said Beth should start taking the pills. It was okay and totally safe to do so. They weren't *just* for emergencies. But say she *did* take one and *still* had an attack, what then? Beth was stubborn and didn't want medication to be the answer. But just having the fifty small rays of sunshine rattling in her purse made her feel better. Then when she was too far over the edge, when her voice left her completely and the tingling raced from her hands to her head, like a bull to a red cape, the anxiety charged through her body leaving her helpless and shaking on the floor, then and only then did she take one. And within minutes, Beth could feel it all drain away. The tension. The negative images looping in her brain. A pill stopped it all. Like magic. Hope returned.

She placed clean clothes into drawers while Grendel perched himself on the corner of her bed and supervised. She sat next to him and skritched the underside of his chin. He tilted his head and leaned into her hand with eyes squinted together. Happy cat. She smoothed the fur down on his head. Her fingers ran through his dense and warm coat, going against the grain. She rubbed his silky ears while he purred, the rumble emanating through his chest. That helped. It always did. Grendel was her lighthouse in any storm.

What should she do? *Max Birnbaum.* She shuddered. At face-value, Max one of the most attractive people she had ever met. A charming smile and friendly demeanor belied his true personality. He tried desperately to walk in his successful father's footsteps, but wound-up tripping each and every time. He just didn't have the business smarts. Also, Beth knew another side of him, a personal one. Max was a selfish, spoiled man who didn't give a hoot about anyone, even his own family. He went out of his way to hurt Ethel, to sabotage everything Ezekiel had worked for, and more than likely played a role in Beth's unhappiness. How could

Uncle Ezekiel, such a dear man (the favorite of all her "uncles"), how could his own son be such an asshole?

Beth scooped up Grendel and headed to the old velvet couch in the living room. Curled up with him, she closed her eyes and took a deep breath. She counted one, two, three ... and like air escaping from a balloon, she exhaled, tried to relax, and think of something else. Just like Dr. Joan advised. She needed a pleasant thought, something that made her happy.

Cunard. The epitome of luxury ocean liners. Beth remembered the TV commercials growing up. Beautiful sleek white ships with black hulls and red smokestacks. Attractive people who wore party clothes and sipped champagne on deck. A lady tossed her head back and laughed at something amusing her companion said, while her diamonds glinted in the sunshine. A server in the background held a tray of additional champagne flutes—just in case the bubbly ran out. He stood at the ready and beamed at their pleasure.

It was a fantasy for most people. *The Love Boat*, but real. Beth's mom would sigh, "Such luxury, can you imagine?" as she served TV dinners in the living room. Beth remembered burning her tongue on the gooey cherry pie, while watching passengers on TV eat lobster tails in the extravagant dining room, complete with butlers. Desserts served in silver dishes en flambé. Now, she could be on one of those ships. This was *way* outside her comfort zone. She accidentally squeezed Grendel too hard, which prompted him to squeak like a broken accordion.

Beth stood and rummaged in the kitchen pantry. A bottle of port—a so-called Kwanzaa present from Frank last year—or the year before—was pushed toward the back. She used a pancake spatula to maneuver it closer. She opened the bottle and poured a healthy slug into a chipped wine glass. Now back on the couch and with Grendel, she wrapped herself up in a tattered purple afghan. She turned the glass rim's chipped side to the back and sipped tentatively. Warm, smooth, velvety goodness enveloped her tongue.

After six calls to Watkins earlier that afternoon, Beth got more of her questions answered. All travel expenses were covered, including an airline ticket from New York to London, hotels and yes, the cruise. Transfers from London to Southampton were made and confirmed. Her own cabin was booked on the *Queen Elizabeth*. Plus, Mr. Watkins gave her a credit card for incidentals and shopping. How about that? She'd be traveling in grand style. A vacation sailing on a luxury cruise ship. *That's not scary.*

She asked Grendel, "Is it?"

She closed her eyes and tried to think methodically. She viewed the task as a new project. First things first, what are the downsides? It was a wild goose chase. But like Mr. Watkins said, there was lots of money at stake.

But I'd have to leave my apartment.

Now the upsides. Aunt Ethel's new will would transfer all remaining assets to charities. Ethel had recognized good things money *can* buy: financing art galleries, maintaining cancer research, and establishing college scholarships. Even the New York City SPCA would be a grateful recipient. Hundreds, no *thousands*, of people (and cats) would benefit from her generosity. Beth owed Aunt Ethel, who had always been so kind to others. Beth felt guilty about not keeping up her correspondence ... especially after receiving so many postcards. Aunt Ethel had cared enough to send them, which made Beth feel even worse. She *had* to go.

"Plus, there's no way in *hell* I'm going to let *him* have it. Bastard." Beth swallowed another mouthful of port, this time a genuine swig. She sunk further into the couch feeling mellow. Comfy. Warm.

If Frank took over Governor Sharp's book, it may even make the deadline. He wouldn't take any of Sharp's crap. *Oh, wouldn't that be nice?* Beth would never have to deal with the governor again. He could also hold off on Beth's next assignment. She could take a few weeks. Her last vacation was ... Florida? *Geez.* She had visited Gwen, her college roommate, and spent a few days with her kids at Gator World in Tampa. That was years ago. She took another swig. Why had she saved this bottle for so long? This was good stuff!

"Okay ... I'm due. Maybe this isn't such a bad idea," she said out loud. A little too loud. Grendel opened one eye and repositioned himself on her lap. Another drink and hmmm, it was really tasty. The dark liquid coated the inside of Beth's numbed mouth.

Okay, more positives. "Grendel," she leaned into his ear and stage-whispered, "I can see the world. Maybe not *all* of it, but places I never imagined I'd see." Mr. Watkins had also provided the ship's itinerary: twelve days in Portugal and the Canary Islands. With her eyes closed, Beth visualized orange sunsets on the water. Graceful spires soaring from gothic churches. Cobblestone streets. Sandy white beaches. Plates of seafood paella. Tapas. She took another deep sip of port. *Port! Port was made in Spain, right? Or was it Portugal? Yes! No?*

"I like port," Beth declared to no one. A small warm feeling grew in her belly, untying the knots experienced earlier in the day. Was it bona fide excitement or the port? It didn't matter. The result was the same.

Oh, Crap. Beth sat up straight. "Grendel, what am I going to wear?"

The cat stared blankly at her. There was no way *anything* in her closet would work on a luxury cruise. Nothing at all. Not even a pair of shoes. She would need to go shopping. Great. The first shy glass of port defiantly turned into another.

With the second glass, she read over her collection of Aunt Ethel's postcards. There must have been a hundred. Beth wiped her eyes, sniffling. She glanced at a stack of unopened birthday cards held together by a rubber band and placed them off to the side. Next, old family photos found their way out of shoe boxes and decorated the floor. As she shifted through the memorabilia, feelings of nostalgia turned into tears. The drops dotted faded surfaces which she quickly wiped off with her T-shirt hem. Photos from summers on the Jersey shore. Playing on the backyard jungle gym. She sobbed for Aunt Ethel, who had always understood her. Always. With her crazy hats and butterscotch candy stuffed in her designer purses. She had never cared what other people thought of her. She was the most confident person Beth had ever known.

With the third glass, Beth wrapped herself in the fringed purple afghan and serenaded Grendel while dancing to P!nk's epic anthem "So What?" The cat climbed on the back of the couch and looked at her with bemusement as she twirled in circles and punched the air. His front stump twitched to the music as if keeping time. Beth used the empty port bottle as a microphone and ran out of breath during the last refrain. Then she landed in a heap on the floor.

"Grendel, I'm still a rockstar." she said with an uncooperative fat tongue. "People need me. Aunt Ethel is countin' on me. Mista Watkins, too. I can't let 'em down. Know wha? Tha dirty bastard ain't gettin' any mo' money. I'm goin'."

All of a sudden, she felt very important. Large and in charge. Beth stumbled to her desk, pawed through the top drawer, found a pen and paper, and compiled a to-do list. Gleeful eagerness replaced any previous reservations. With exaggerated movements and tongue sticking out the side of her mouth, she composed the following:

1. Cull F
2. By cloths
3. PISSPUTT

The next morning, her tongue felt like it wore a wool sweater and she had a cut on her bottom lip. After she took two aspirin and drank a liter of water, Beth called Frank (#1) and explained the last twenty-four hours using authoritative tones even *she* wasn't used to hearing.

When Frank finally stopped interrupting with, "Are you serious?" "You're funny," and, "Who *is* this?" they agreed to meet in an hour at Barney's (#2).

Her next call was to Mr. Watkins. Once connected, she said with more conviction than she ever thought possible, "I'll go." Then she frantically dug through desk drawers to find her never-used passport (#3).

CHAPTER 5

F rank held up a red Michael Kors evening gown, high enough to prevent the hem from touching the floor. "This is fabulous! Feel the fabric. It's silk. You need to try this on." Beth dutifully reached for the hanger and added it to the pile of clothes she carried, while following Frank through Barney's like a Sherpa.

"I don't have the build for it."

"We'll find out soon enough." He turned back and put an arm around her discouraged shoulders. "Come on. This should be *fun*! How often do you go on a shopping spree?"

"Frank, you know I don't dress, uh..."

"You dress like a homeless person," he finished for her.

"I wouldn't say *that*. But yes, I agree. My clothing choices lack in both style and substance. Just help me find something fast." Beth chewed on a fingernail.

"Think of me as your personal stylist. If I'm any good, I may give up publishing forever. By the way, is that a chip clip in your hair? Honey, we've got work to do." He watched as her face fell into worrisome lines. "Beth, you need to look the part, even if you don't feel it. It's all about confidence. And nice clothes always help. Let me think ... you'll need some day separates ... some dresses ... more formal gowns ... and shoes ..." Frank rattled off a shopping list as he rushed towards accessories.

Beth chased him around the store. She was overwhelmed by choices, but luckily Frank made most decisions for her. Since he'd been on a cruise before (and followed fashion) she considered him an expert. For Beth, shopping was neither a talent nor an enjoyable diversion. It wasn't about spending money (she had plenty) but the effort of going out in public and possibly making a fool out of herself. Amazon had become her best friend. Her go-to philosophy for clothes was, "If it fits, buy three." Maybe in different colors. Style never mattered, just as long as the article of clothing was comfortable ... and had a drawstring.

Now, in a dressing room surrounded by silk, satin, and velvet, she realized zippers were involved. Beth stood in her underwear and grasped rolls of fat around her bellybutton. This was going to be a challenge.

A memory flitted into her head. She was eleven years old shopping with Mom for a dress at Sears for her first (and last) piano recital.

Her mom had called from outside the fitting room curtain, "Beth, what's taking so long?"

She couldn't zip up the pale blue, polyester frock; a junior's size which didn't accommodate her blossoming bosom or hips. She struggled and tried alternately to inchworm the zipper up from behind, but it wouldn't budge. And then it stuck. Tears pricked her eyes in frustration.

"Beth, come *on*!" Her mom, exasperated, pulled open the curtain. There Beth stood on display, like a horrible piece of performance art, defeated, while the dress strangled her.

Quickly her mom said, "Oh, honey … it's okay. We'll look for a different size." She wiggled the zipper and released it from a seam. "Come on, honey. It's okay."

Beth whimpered, "I don't look like the other girls."

"It's because you're growing up sooner than they are. Don't worry, they'll catch up."

"But why me?"

"Because. It's just part of God's plan. Just remember, you're beautiful."

"God's very funny." Beth struggled to escape the dress and kicked it into the corner of the dressing room.

"He does work in mysterious ways. Now come here and give me a big hug." She held out her arms. Beth stepped into them and inhaled her mom's Chloé perfume. They both simultaneously said, "Big hug."

Beth's sister Vicky sprung from her own dressing room, pirouetting in a pair of designer jeans that looked painted on her body.

"Look, Mom! They fit!" she squealed in delight. She turned towards the mirror and posed like a model, springing a hip. "See?"

"Are they on sale?"

"I don't know." Vicky looked over at Beth's tear-stained eyes. "What's the matter with you? Step on a pin?"

"No." Beth sniffed, wiping her nose with the back of her hand.

Mom found Beth's dress in a larger size, just big enough to zip up the back. Still, Beth could hardly move her arms.

Later that night at her piano recital, with elbows glued to her sides, she plunked away at the Beatles' "Let It Be." During the final crescendo, the zipper split up the middle, showing her brand-new bra to hundreds of eyes. The audience twittered with unsuccessful repressed laughter. She even heard her sister giggle. From the corner of her eye, she saw Aunt Ethel clap a hand over Vicky's mouth to shush her. Ever since, Beth hated dressing rooms. And the piano. She never played again.

Now, decades later at Barney's, she looked at the woman in the mirror. Dull brown hair with overgrown bangs that constantly got caught in her eyelashes. Unremarkable hazel eyes behind broken glasses. A figure bordering on pear-shaped. She still had big hips and a jiggly tummy. Her looks didn't make her nervous, just continually disappointed.

Before she tried on any of the clothes, she yelled out, "Frank! Help me fix this!"

"What?" Frank poked his head into her cubicle. "Beth," he shook his head and grinned, "that's *nothing* that Spanx can't help."

After their morning of vigorous power shopping, compliments of Mr. Watson's credit card, Beth and Frank collapsed for a late lunch at a local deli to rejuvenate their blood sugar. Five sundresses, two pairs of linen pants, matching tops, three gowns, and coordinating shoes lay neatly packed into shopping bags at their feet. Plus, she'd purchased a pair of sassy sunglasses and versatile leopard-print tote bag to carry her essentials on the plane. Frank insisted on stylish but functional accessories. Apparently animal print was considered a neutral. Who knew?

"It's a good start," Frank said, "but you still need some cocktail dresses." He wagged a dill pickle at her. "At least three. You'll have to buy more clothes on the ship." He popped the pickle in his mouth. The brown stripe in his dress shirt complemented his skin tone nicely. Hmmm.

Maybe she was learning a few things from his whirlwind tutelage. But what would match her own hue? Tapioca?

"It seems like a lot of clothes." Beth pulled out the ship's itinerary from her purse and ran her finger down the dress code listed for each evening. Twelve days meant four formal evenings and eight informal. Formal required gowns or fancy cocktail dresses for ladies and tuxedos for men. "Who wears this stuff anymore?"

"Passengers on Cunard. Remember, it's the last bastion of civilized society ... and you're going to fit in if it kills me, *or* you." Frank picked up his corned beef sandwich and took a big bite for emphasis. "I have to admit, I'm jealous. I'd kill to go."

"I'd gladly trade places, but I need to do this for Aunt Ethel." Beth slurped her Diet Coke loudly. "Where do I even start? The will could be anywhere on the ship. Do I begin at the front and work my way back?"

"It's called the bow and stern," Frank said.

"Okay, the bow and the stern."

A brochure was included among her trip documents. Apparently, the *Queen Elizabeth* carried fewer than two thousand passengers, boasting a more intimate traveling experience than larger cruise ships. But still, it was the size of three football fields.

"It's as good a plan as any. You'll find it—but if you run into trouble, just ask people for help. It *must* be on the ship. At the end of all this, I hope Aunt Ethel left you something good."

"The only thing she left me is this." Beth held out her right wrist to show the silver bracelet.

They ate the remainder of their sandwiches. Mayonnaise squirted out of Beth's and onto her lap. Frank rolled his eyes at her.

"How's Paul? Does he mind you watching Grendel?" Beth asked with another mouthful.

"A better man never lived. No, he doesn't mind your cat. Christ, he was in *Cats* for five years when he first started out." Frank threw his head back and laughed hard, showing a mercury filling in his back molar.

"What's he doing now?"

"He's casting a new show. Another musical. He keeps crazy hours whenever he starts up a production. I only see the man asleep." Frank shook his head and chuckled softly to himself.

"What?"

"To think we met a karaoke bar, singing until the wee hours. Now we're in bed by nine o'clock. We're officially an old married couple. Okay, let's talk about something fun. Tell me more about the trip. Where are you going?"

Beth glanced at her beat-up Timex; only a few hours before she left. A small smile crept over her face when she realized there wasn't any time for an anxiety attack because it wouldn't fit into the schedule. This *almost* made her laugh. Maybe this trip was a good thing. Maybe it would help. Maybe it was the worst decision she'd ever make. She wiped her mouth and crumpled her napkin onto the plate.

"I must admit the itinerary looks amazing. The ship leaves from Southampton—it's about an hour south of London and we'll have a few days at sea. Then a stop at Madeira, the Grand Canaries, a few more sea days, on to Lisbon, and then back to Southampton. Mr. Watkin's assistant arranged for a car to take me to JFK tonight. I just need to be ready."

"Traveling in style. I like this Mr. Watkins."

Beth nodded. "He's been really nice. I know it's short notice and part of me wants to throw up, but I can't help feeling excited about the whole thing. A *good* excited. You know?"

"Great! You should be," Frank said. "This is a fabulous adventure, Pussycat. You're long overdue. *And* you can handle it. Just remember your breathing exercises."

"Thanks. I hope so. You know, my mom always wanted to travel on Cunard. She just never had the chance. Gosh, she loved those ships ... the three Queens. She even named me after the ship, the *Queen Elizabeth*. Did you know that?"

Of course, Frank knew. Frank knew everything about her. Beth didn't wait for him to respond as she paid the check.

"Once, she even ordered brochures from a travel agent. I remember her showing Dad at the kitchen table. Mom treated each page like it was a piece of fine art. She'd say, "Look, look," at each one. She started saving coins in a big glass jar. But after paying the bills, there was always so little left. I honestly don't know how they ever sent me to college. Then when Dad lost his job, it got even worse. And then ..." Beth took a cold French fry off Frank's plate. "It just doesn't seem fair *I* get to go."

"Maybe this is your aunt's way of making it up to her. Through you."

"Maybe. I never thought of that."

They collected her shopping bags and exited the diner. From the curb, Frank tried to hail a cab back to Beth's apartment so he could pick up Grendel.

"Will you email me? The ship has internet, right? I really want your eyes on Governor Sharp's final draft. Plus, you *have* to keep me posted."

"Of course." She turned to face him. "Frank, thanks for taking over the book, and thanks for your help." She reached for his hand and grasped it. "You're a good friend. If I need to, can I call you? Will you sing to me?"

He smiled. "Of course, but you'll be just fine. Don't forget to send us a postcard." He squeezed back and kissed her on the cheek.

Passport, check.

Tickets, check.

Snazzy new tote bag with wallet, check.

Pills, check to the third power. Absolutely!

The hired car was scheduled to arrive in a few minutes. After the day of shopping and whirlwind preparations, Beth was ready. Or as ready as she'd ever be. She had said a woeful farewell to Grendel, "Be a good boy for Mommy," then kissed him on the nose and shoved him into the cat carrier. "Don't let him get too fat," she threatened Frank.

Now, even though all was accounted for, Beth paced the inside of her apartment doing her deep breathing exercises while butterflies the size of hippos danced in her stomach. *In for one ... two ... three. Out for one ... two ... three.* A calmness came along with the feeling of fresh air in her lungs.

She announced to the empty room, "I'm fine! I'm ready!" She locked her apartment door and thumped her luggage down the stairs to the curb. She continued her pacing and clutched the hem of her T-shirt, which had been laundered so many times it felt like silk. Over it she wore a clean Gator World sweatshirt (only a few stains) and a pair of yoga pants which had never seen a *namaste* in their life. She stood at the curb and shifted her weight from foot to foot as if the pavement was hot. Back and forth. In and out. *Calm the heart; calm the mind.*

Beth couldn't tamp down her excitement, even as twinges of uncertainty continued to catch her off guard and harass her like a middle-school boy on the playground. When a shiny black Lincoln Town Car pulled up to the curb and the driver packed her one bag containing her new wardrobe into the trunk, it all became real. It was really happening. Beth slid into the back seat and felt like royalty.

She gestured grandly and said, "JFK, please!"

The driver responded, "Yes, Ma'am," with a salute and a small chuckle.

It was a smooth ride ... almost too smooth. As the car turned, Beth almost slid back and forth from one window to the other, gliding on the supple leather seat. She hung on to the seatbelt. Less than thirty minutes later, she stood at the JFK departures gate with plenty of time to spare. The large electronic sign indicated her British Airways flight was scheduled to depart on time. She checked her bag. After hearing horror stories from Frank about airport security, Beth found the experience shockingly uneventful and the lines short. The thousands of travelers made her feel safe. She wasn't alone. She could handle this.

Before Beth knew it, she was at her gate. Early. To kill some time, she browsed a gift shop and spontaneously purchased some magazines and an *I (heart) New York* T-shirt. She also treated herself to a fancy double shot espresso mocha with whipped cream. While deep into pages of the latest *The New Yorker*, an electronic voice startled her and announced the flight's boarding. She hoisted her new tote bag onto her shoulder. This is it, no turning back now. Beth took a deep breath and stepped inside the jet way. *Success!* Part of her wanted to call Frank and let him know. She was on the plane!

A flight attendant steered Beth toward coach. The line moved slowly due to several factors: passengers shoved too-large bags under seats, parents helped small children get settled, older people needed help stowing heavy carry-ons in overhead bins. As Beth waited for the line to move, she watched a woman in a center row dole out crayons and coloring books to her little girls, one on either side of her. Each girl had a Ziploc bag of goldfish crackers and a juice box. Mom patted sweat off her forehead with a Kleenex.

"Now girls, I don't want to hear a peep out of you," she said, while adjusting the overhead fan. "Not a peep."

Beth couldn't help but stare. It was as if she had time-traveled back to the early 90s. The woman looked just like her mom. The no-nonsense brown ponytail pulled back. The permanent wrinkle of worry stamped on her forehead. The simple gold hoop earrings. And the girls bent over their coloring books, trying to stay inside the lines. The line shuffled forward and Beth passed the family of three. Her heart lurched in her chest for additional space.

Now, at the back of the plane, she couldn't find her seat assignment. Confused, she uncrinkled her boarding pass and showed it to another flight attendant. Was she on the right plane? Had she blown it already? Her hands began to prickle with invisible electric shocks.

"Oh my, you're in business class," the flight attendant responded, sounding slightly surprised. She led Beth back up toward the front and dramatically parted the heavy blue curtains into a separate compartment.

Ohhh. Large cream-colored leather seats like La-z-boys lined up in pairs on either side of the aisle. A flight attendant in a uniform with a gold braid at her shoulders stood in the aisle and held a tray of wine glasses. Beth found a pillow, folded blanket, and toiletry kit arranged on her seat.

Within minutes, she quickly arrived at the revelation that business class was, well, outstanding. She couldn't dare to dream about first class amenities. What could *they* possibly have? Massages? Tarot card readings? They hadn't even departed and she was already comfortably full of booze and snacks. This was better than her apartment. Way better. If she had any social media accounts, she would've posted a selfie. *Oh, Mr. Watkins, you're making this easy.*

Once airborne, Beth took off her shoes and reclined her seat to full stretch-out mode. That's when she noticed another hole in her sock. *Eeek.* Unfortunately, the flight attendant noticed it too while handing out magazines and newspapers. Beth looked up at her, a little sheepishly and tried to smile.

"Ma'am, would you care for some cabin socks?" The flight attendant was nothing but polite.

"Uh ... sure!"

Within moments, the attendant returned with a pair of blue socks with *British Airways* imprinted on the soles. Okay, free socks, what more could you want? Perfectly content, Beth stretched out again, grasped another Merlot in both hands, wiggled her toes in complimentary socks, and proceeded to watch a movie. *This is living.* What had she been worried about?

After a few hours and a scrumptious dinner served on real china, the woman Beth had observed earlier dashed through the curtains separating coach from business class.

"I'm sorry," she began, "but there's a long line in the back and I couldn't wait any longer." When the woman returned to her seat, she passed by Beth and gave a small smile. The woman's hand went to her hair and she self-consciously smoothed it down. A scent of Chloé followed her. Beth's heart clenched again. This time painfully squeezing without reprieve.

She turned her head toward the window and closed her eyes. It was all about that night. That awful rainy night. The phone call from the police. The hospital. The funerals. Beth winced as tears began to fall. Horrified she'd wake up the passenger across the row, she muffled her cries into her sweatshirt. She didn't want to admit to anyone she really, truly, wasn't okay. It wasn't just her anxiety, but honest to goodness sadness and despair.

The flight attendant walked slowly through the aisles and offered more drinks. Beth pulled the hoodie over her head and faced the window, pretending to be asleep as tears dripped off her nose. New tears for an old tragedy ... one she couldn't forget no matter how many years had passed. The reason for most of her fears. Her pain. She fell into a troubled sleep thinking about the mom and kids seated thirty rows behind her.

At around noon the following day, the plane touched down outside of London. Beth disembarked feeling surprisingly refreshed if not just a little wilted and wrinkled like an old dollar bill. United Kingdom Customs provided her first passport stamp: the word "Gatwick" inside a plane logo in blue ink. A taxi—oops a *cab*—drove her to a quaint hotel—oops a *B&B*—called The Barberry Bramble where she would pick up a bus—oops a *coach*—to Southampton the following day. So far, all was going according to plan. Mr. Watkins had coordinated all the details perfectly.

Beth made it. She looked out her bedroom window from the second floor of the stone cottage. Gentle rain fell on the green Surrey countryside dotted with complacent cows. Mist swirled on top of the pastures like lazy clouds.

And now my adventure begins.

CHAPTER 6

Eighteen Years Ago

R ain fell ferociously. Drops ricocheted off the street, hitting pedestrians and cars like misguided bullets. Gutters swelled into rivers; puddles grew quickly in diameter underfoot. It was inevitable. After waiting a few minutes, the girls decided the storm was not letting up any time soon.

"Do you want to drive?" Beth asked Vicky as they huddled underneath a shared umbrella on the sidewalk. The fringe of her knitted poncho was getting soaked.

"No way. I hate driving in the city. Don't bother parking, just drop me off." Vicky sniffed. "Hurry, let's get out of here. I'm getting drenched." She clutched her coat tighter and flipped the collar up around her face while huddling closer to Beth.

The wedding was over. Both Aunt Ethel and Ezekiel had looked triumphantly radiant. After exchanging brief nuptials, the happy couple had hosted a hundred dinner guests at the Plaza Hotel. A mixed crowd, but all held membership within New York City society's elite; philanthropists, politicians, and bankers mingled under gilded coffered ceilings. Standing in a small huddle in such grand opulence, Beth, Vicky, and their parents felt like turnips that fell off a truck. It was awkward for them, but still, they *were* family. In any case, Aunt Ethel was ecstatic to have them there. She hugged and kissed them each time she floated by. Ezekiel's side of the family, well, that was another matter entirely.

"Aunt Ethel looked pretty. Did you see her hat?" offered Beth as they waited for her car. The beat-up Mazda clunked and shuddered as the valet brought it around. He handed Beth her keys as if they were dirty.

"Let's hope third time's a charm." Vicky laughed as they climbed into the car.

Minutes earlier, the girls had said goodbye to their parents in the hotel lobby. They promised to be home next month for Christmas. Their mom, Mary, with teary eyes, gave each of her daughters a squeeze and said, "Big Hug. I love you," just in case they didn't know. James Schiff had already untied his tie, an ancient polyester with brown and olive stripes. With his sport coat held over one arm, he hugged the girls with the other. He said in a faux-gruff voice, "Now you two, be careful. No hijinks!" and winked at them.

The girls waved as their parent's Plymouth drove away in the rain. The drive from New York City back to Allentown took about two hours, yet the poor weather meant a longer trip ahead for Mary and James. Vicky had a red-eye flight booked to Los Angeles and Beth was driving her to JFK before circling back to the University of Pennsylvania.

"Why didn't Mom and Dad just spend the night in the city?" Beth asked as she pulled out onto the road.

"Probably money. Unemployment checks don't last forever, you know. Plus, they were probably ready to get out of there. There's only so much you can take."

As they waited at a red light, Beth shook her head. "That Max ... I think he may be the most attractive man I ever met."

"Looks will only get you so far. I think they make up for his personality."

"Yeah, he turned out to be nasty piece of work. A real no-goodnik, you know? And his toast ..."

Vicky interrupted, "You sound like you're from the 1930s. What book are you reading now? A Mickey Spillane? College girl." She laughed and fussed with her blonde hair in the mirror. "Yeah, he's a *no-goodnik*," she quipped.

"You're funny. *Really* funny. Seriously, he didn't have to do that. Max went out of his way to embarrass us, especially in front of his fancy friends. Plus, he was mean to Mom and Dad."

"Don't forget Aunt Ethel."

Both girls decided Ezekiel's terribly good-looking, middle-aged son was a jackass. But it had taken them the entire night to figure it out.

After the initial mazel tovs, when Max welcomed Ethel into the family with a wedding toast, the words 'gold' and 'digger' somehow escaped. The sisters had thought he meant it as a joke (several guests laughed), but as the celebration continued, they weren't quite sure.

At cocktail hour, when Max had handed Mom an empty glass and ordered another scotch as if she was hired help, they believed it had been a simple mistake.

At dinner, when Max reached over and fingered James' suit lapel, asking if the material was flammable, they considered he was being friendly, even if in an inappropriate way.

All of this happened with a smile on his face, his perfect teeth gleaming, and icy blue eyes sparkling. But by the end of the night, when he approached Ethel and said, "There's no free ride here. This ridiculous wedding cost a fortune. Where should we send the bill?" they knew Ethel wouldn't be welcomed into the Birnbaum household. Ever.

Ironic, considering Aunt Ethel had plenty of money on her own and his dad, Ezekiel (who was off getting another piece of cake at the time), was one of the nicest guys in the city. A premiere endodontist, Dr. Birnbaum had a coveted clientele list of Manhattan's high society, who trusted him and *only* him with their gums. If a thriving practice with appointments booked years in advance wasn't lucrative enough, lo and behold he discovered a surefire process for quicker and less painful root canals. After patenting the procedure and equipment (known in the ADA world as the "drill & bill"), he earned quite a fortune.

In addition, Ezekiel was a prominent member of the Landmark Preservation Board and Historical Society. He sat on the Apex Savings & Loan board of directors. He established the well-respected Birnbaum Foundation. He adopted rescue dogs. Always one to open his checkbook, he was a popular guest at charity events throughout fundraising season. He was also funny, engaging, and just a nice guy. A mensch. Ethel had met him at an AIDS & the Arts event, while reaching for the same piece of rugelach. Laughing, he immediately took her hand and kissed it. Ethel found a good man. Unfortunately, Ezekiel's only son Max was not.

"I heard some gossip about him," Vicky whispered, despite being alone in the car with Beth.

"Who? Max? Spill it," Beth whispered back.

"I heard he's on an allowance. He can't be trusted with money." Vicky took out a hairbrush from her purse.

"Where'd you hear that?"

"From a guy at the reception. I think he was a banker. He'd had a couple drinks, so he was chatty. He said Max is ... let me think ... 'incompetent.'"

"Uh oh," Beth said, trying to keep her eyes on the road.

Vicky continued while she brushed her hair. "Apparently Max isn't in the family business—he had no interest in scraping tartar. Also, something about germs and blood. Anyways, the guy said Max is always trying to develop some new idea or product and strike it rich like his dad. Except he has no experience in anything. He tries and fails spectacularly. You know what Dad says ... never trust a man with a pinky ring."

"The guy said all that, huh?"

"Yeah, well, he got me a drink, so I was obligated to listen," Vicky said.

The two sisters discussed the wedding details. How happy Aunt Ethel looked. How Ezekiel held her hand the entire evening. How Max stood in the receiving line in an elegant tuxedo, steel grey hair meticulously coiffed, showing off a blue sapphire ring and his third wife, Bernadette.

"And what about her?" Beth ranted. "She just sat during the ceremony and played with her lipstick ... like she couldn't be bothered. And those earrings, my God! Were those diamonds? They were the size of ice cubes."

"Did you hear her talking with Mom? Bernadette asked if she'd ever been to Naples. Mom said she *loved* Florida. Bernadette almost choked on her canapé."

Beth threw her head back and laughed. "Oh ... classic Mom."

"Did you see *Max's* mom? Ezekiel's such a nice guy, he even invited his first wife. But she wasn't very pleasant; when I introduced myself, she just turned her back to me and walked away. What a witch."

"That's not very nice, calling her a witch."

"Well, I'm not feeling very nice right now. Plus, someone pinched my ass. I know it was Max."

"Yeah? How do you know?"

"I know."

"Well, he completely ignored me. I could've been a potted plant." Beth snickered.

"Count yourself lucky. Anyways, I guess he's not thrilled dear old Dad married again. Ezekiel's not exactly a spring chicken. Maybe Max sees Aunt Ethel as a threat ... you know? Less money for him down the road?"

"Aunt Ethel has plenty. Plus, she's the least threatening person alive."

"True, but there's some not-so-nice people out there. Trust me, I know." Vicky now finished with her hair, applied some face powder, and flipped the car mirror back in place. She had lived in L.A. going on four years now and from what she confided to Beth, it wasn't working out as she had hoped. After countless auditions, Vicky had only landed a few minor parts. Beth wondered if she would stay there or eventually move home. Still, her sister was tough ... just as tough as L.A. Beth wondered who would eventually win.

"How are auditions going?" she asked.

"Okay. I have a callback on one, but it's a long shot. A TV series."

"Yeah? But a callback is good, right? Did you tell Mom?" Beth slowed down for another stoplight. The windshield wipers gamely kept up with the unrelenting rain.

"No, I didn't want to get her hopes up. You know how she gets." The raindrops sparkled like crystals in the streetlights, providing more illumination on otherwise dark streets. The traffic picked up as they inched closer to the airport. Beth turned into the departures lane which was uncommonly empty. Vicky buttoned up her coat and took her purse from the floor. "School going okay? Any more of those tuition bills?"

"The bursar said I'm all paid up. It must have been a mistake. I'm applying for internships now. I'll start in March. Cross your fingers I get a publishing house."

"I'll keep them crossed for both of us." Vicky leaned over and kissed her sister on the cheek. "Big Hug." Beth pulled over to the curb.

"Love you."

"Love you, too."

Vicky jumped out of the car and ran inside the nearest entrance, shielding her hair with her purse and grasping a small carry-on. Even in the pouring rain, both men and women stopped and stared at her sister with her long blond hair and shapely legs peeking out from underneath her short trench coat. Beth shook her head and smiled ruefully as she drove back around and toward the Pennsylvania turnpike to school. *That's my sister.*

CHAPTER 7

A graceful, yet authoritative silhouette loomed. From the dock's sidewalk, the ship looked enormous. On a clean, white background *Queen Elizabeth* was scripted in navy along the bow with *Cunard* lettered in red. Beth tilted her head back and tried to commit to memory the parts and pieces which made the ship whole. Portholes lined up in equidistant rows on the bottom half of her hull, balconies and open decks on the top. Shining glass. Polished brass. Teak-stained wooden handrails. The ship was lovingly cared for and her beauty shone. Beth staggered to think of the surprises held inside.

At the Southampton cruise terminal, porters competed for Beth's one piece of luggage; she wouldn't see it again until she arrived at her stateroom. Signs directed her toward an escalator to the second floor for check-in. She took a number and a seat in the pre-departure lounge.

Her outfit—the newly purchased *I (heart) New York* T-shirt and sweatpants—didn't match her surroundings. Her gaze drifted over to other passengers seated nearby, clutching their own numbers. She stuck out big time with her loose ponytail and crooked glasses. This was going to be tough. Maybe she should have worn one of her new outfits?

Focus. Your job is to find the will, not be a fashion icon.

Beth tried not to fidget while she people-watched. If anything, the guests could make good character studies. The passenger demographics varied, but not by much. Directly across sat a well-off, middle-aged couple. The man, dressed in a camel sport coat and slacks, scrutinized a *Wall Street Journal* two inches from his reading glasses. His companion, a younger woman attired in spotless white linen and pearls, casually flipped through a *Vogue Italia*. Next to her, a designer bag chock-full of fashion magazines—*Mondrial, Elle,* and *Bazaar*—were ready for future reading. The couple didn't speak to each other.

An older lady sat on Beth's left. Several bobby pins attempted to harness her curly white hair. A red straw hat lay on the floor by her feet. She wore gold lamé sandals with pedicured toes painted in vibrant fuchsia. Rings flashed and bracelets jangled as she animatedly spoke on her cell phone.

"Darling, I'm waiting to board. Just a few more minutes. Don't fret ... I'll see you soon. Meet me at the bar. No, not that one ... the other one. Kiss-kiss."

An elderly woman sat off to the side in a black dress, black hosiery, and unattractive chunky black loafers. In her lap, she grasped an immense crocodile valise with both hands, as if all her worldly possessions were stowed inside. A tight gray bun stretched the pair of beady eyes blinking behind a pair of rhinestone glasses. She looked like a recent widow. Beth wondered if her dead husband's ashes were inside the valise. Maybe she was going to bury him at sea? The woman's face suddenly pinched as if she smelled something rotten, then she caught Beth's eye and smiled at her, her teeth too perfect to be real.

To the right, two thirty-something-year-old men talked quietly but earnestly. Each sat hunched forward, with his hands clasped. Beth overheard, "But what if they don't like me?"

The other answered, "Don't worry, they'll love you. Just like I do. How could they not?" He grabbed the other man's hand reassuringly.

Beth didn't have long to wait, because "Number A28!" rang out over the intercom. She sprang from her seat, grabbed her new tote bag, and quietly thanked Frank for the nicest thing she owned. Maybe people would see her fabulous tote and think she was a famous person, just dressing down to mingle in with the crowd. Or not. A customer service representative in a red jacket, with "Audrey" pinned to her chest waved Beth over.

"Your name, please?"

"Elizabeth Schiff."

"Welcome, Ms. Schiff. Oh my! Isn't it a coincidence? Your name is just like our ship."

"Yes, it is."

"How interesting. I don't know many Americans who have that name; it's German for *ship* isn't it?"

"Yes." It was obvious the poor woman knew Beth didn't belong. Audrey's small talk was an attempt to make her feel a little better. Or at least that's what Beth deduced. *Talk about customer service.*

"Fancy that." Audrey quickly took Beth's photo and a plastic card spit out from a dispenser on the computer. A form also printed and Audrey confirmed Beth's passport and cabin number.

"Here is your ship's ID card. You'll need it to access your cabin. We are a cashless ship, so onboard credit can be used for any purchases. However, a credit card is required in case you go over that amount ... which is here," Audrey circled a number on the form.

Beth looked down. Her eyes widened. "There must be some mistake. My onboard credit is five thousand dollars? Are you sure?"

"Yes, Ms. Schiff. That's what I have on your account."

"But meals are included, right?" Beth asked in disbelief. Mr. Watkins had never said anything about onboard credit. "What do I use it for?"

Audrey laughed. "You can gamble, do some shopping. But, if it were me," the representative leaned in with a confidential tone, "*I* would book some spa days for while you're at sea; appointments go quickly." Beth shifted from one foot to the other self-consciously. "Also, a wine package. Definitely take some tours ... oh wait, your tours are already booked. Lucky girl, more spa treatments and wine for you!"

Beth reached out for the bulging white envelope offered to her. Tours? Another item Mr. Watkins failed to mention.

"Right then. Those are your tour tickets. If you have any questions or wish to make other arrangements, please see the purser or tour desk. They are both located on Deck 1. Here is a ship's map—which should come in handy. May I help with anything else?"

"Uh ... not now. Thanks."

Beth took her paperwork and stumbled toward the exit door. Feeling confused and fatigued, she repeated in her head, five thousand dollars? She clutched her tote bag tighter with both hands. Her face flushed. Was this jet lag? Whatever it was, she'd never felt anything quite like it before and she was pretty much in tune with her bodily sensations. This new visitor had unfamiliar fingers pulling her eyelids and slowing her footsteps.

After a brief ascent up another escalator, a short walk under a covered gangway led her to the side of the ship. A red carpet sprouted from a dark hole. A young man dressed in a red Cunard uniform and matching red cap greeted her with a genuine smile. *Red, red, red.* Beth stifled a yawn as the man unceremoniously squirted hand sanitizer into her palm.

"Welcome aboard, madam. May I have your ship's ID please?" After a quick swipe and scan, he gave a little bow and gestured for her to enter. Beth clenched her teeth tighter to stop yawning (really, it would be rude) and after a single step, was inside the ship.

The light went dim.

Flowers. The scent of lilies, orchids, and freesia greeted her, lovelier than obnoxious perfume promos stuck inside a magazine's spine. The aroma grew with each step inside. The light intensified and suddenly Beth was on a balcony which overlooked a Grand Lobby. The flowers—an astonishing arrangement the size of a Volkswagen Beetle—sat on a round table in between two curved staircases meeting below. The arrangement would have filled her entire apartment.

The scene jolted her awake. Jet lag now forgotten, Beth stood and stared with wide eyes as she adjusted her glasses. The visuals stunned her. Glass twinkled at every turn. Surfaces gleamed. Rising two stories tall, a world map with inlaid pieces of bronze and wood veneers dominated the lobby. The ship's enormity felt like the scale of her task.

Her sweaty hands gripped the banister. Well-dressed passengers strolled confidently like invited guests to an exclusive party. They greeted each other with friendly smiles and nods. An anticipatory air vibrated throughout and competed with the flowers for attention. The ship practically hummed. How would she *ever* fit in? How would she *ever* find the will? It was overwhelming. Frozen and unable to move, she debated what to do next and received an immediate answer. A photographer snapped her picture. *Great.* Just what she needed.

To her left was a spacious lounge with turquoise velvet sofas and ivory linen chairs grouped for intimate conversations. Heavy embossed drapes framed panoramic windows looking out to the harbor. An embossed sign read "Midships Lounge." Vast silver bowls held champagne bottles swaddled in ice. A server in a white uniform stood with an even whiter linen towel over his arm and a tray of filled flutes.

"Champagne, madam?" he offered while holding out the silver tray.

"Really? Okay." Beth took a glass carefully by the stem and tasted. At least it gave her something to do. Cool, crisp bubbles caught the back of her throat. *Oh, refreshing.* Several passengers did the same. They either sat at small, elegant tables for two, stood at the bar, or leaned over the balcony. But they all sipped glasses of champagne. *My God. It's just like the commercial.* While Beth struggled with keeping her knees from buckling, she realized her mom would have fainted in sheer delight. Beth's mouth unconsciously turned into a smile.

A seated elderly man with a white waxed mustache caught her eye. His own eyes twinkled at her. Dressed in a tweed suit, he clutched a book in his lap. With the other hand, he held out his glass and said, "Cheers, love!"

She had no other choice but to hold her own glass up and shyly return his toast.

Okay. Time to reset. Time to get to business. Beth decided to find her cabin. She unfolded the small map Audrey had given her and turned it right side. She squinted. Deck 6. She found a bank of elevators and quickly got in before the doors closed. Manipulating the map, champagne, and tote bag, she pushed the button for Deck 6. She exited to the left and had four choices. Passageways flanked a staircase and headed both fore and aft. Luckily, staff were posted nearby ready to assist. They quickly directed her to the left and after a few feet, she found her cabin, #6077. Trying to commit the route to memory, she said out loud, "Okay, remember ... exit elevators, go right, then left." She was on the starboard side, the righthand side of the ship (which she learned from the brochure Mr. Watkins had given her). Her ship's ID acted as her key.

Beth stood in the open doorway of her cabin. Her first view was of an expansive window looking out to Southampton. She threw her tote bag down on the bed and beelined to the balcony outside. She slid open the door and found a pair of chairs and table arranged. As the windy sea air tossed her hair about and the sunlight glanced off the water in full force, she shaded her eyes with her hand and looked at the other ships docked at port. How high up was she?

She held tight to her empty champagne glass and took small, hesitant steps to the railing. Why? Because heights were on The List, too.

She ventured a glance downwards at the decks below and the tops of people's heads. Childishly, she thought, *I could spit on them and they would never know it's me.* She retreated quickly before she got dizzy.

Back inside the cabin, a small sofa with a coffee table provided a seating area. An ice bucket held a split of champagne and some fruit arranged on a plate. *Gosh, more champagne?* She refilled her glass after unskillfully wrenching the cork free from the bottle. Opposite the sofa was a desk with a small TV screen and chair. A king-sized bed took up the majority of the room. White linens and a mountain of pillows beckoned. Perfect for bouncing on. Small chests of drawers flanked either side. Lights were operated by several buttons next to the bed. A closet with plenty of hangers and a safe contained a fluffy white robe and slippers. The gold Cunard logo was embroidered on all.

The bathroom was small, which she expected, but the fixtures sparkled. A narrow shower, just enough to turn around in, offered recessed spots for soap and shampoo. An ample, well-lit mirror had shelves for toiletries. Hair products, soaps, even Q-tips were neatly arranged on a tray. Beth opened a bottle of lotion and sniffed. *Nice!* White towels hung inside. Overall, her cabin glistened, ready for a photo shoot.

A brisk knock at the door broke her away from further investigations.

"Madam, your luggage!" a deep voice said from the passageway. Beth opened the door and found a tall young man with her bag. He looked serious, dressed in a pressed white uniform. But then his dark eyes flashed and face lit up with a huge grin when he saw her.

"Hello, Madame Schiff. I'm Roberto, your cabin steward. May I bring in the luggage?"

"Yes, thanks." She moved out of his way.

He hoisted her bag onto a leatherette cover protecting the linens on the bottom half of the bed. His black hair shone with gel or pomade. He acted fully in control, the complete opposite of what Beth felt at the moment. She was glad to see someone who had it together. Maybe he could help her? And as if on cue, the steward pointed to a card angled on the desk.

"This is me. If you need anything, please call this number. I'm here to help."

Beth looked at the small card, neatly printed with ROBERTO in neat block lettering, with a five-digit extension.

"Thanks."

He pointed to a second card positioned on the desk. "Here's your table assignment. You're dining at eight o'clock at Table 8. Is there anything else, Madame Schiff?"

"No. Thanks ... so much." Geez, should she tip him?

"Then have a pleasant evening." Roberto gave a little bow before he exited. "Be sure to go out on deck for the sail-away!"

The door closed. Beth sat gently on the edge of the bed. True, her cabin was splendid ... anyone would be perfectly content here. Yet, a small fissure of anxiety went through her like a low-level electric charge. Dinner. She would be eating dinner with strangers. She should have asked Roberto how many people were at her table. Like it mattered. They would expect her to converse about current events, be witty, and not spill soup down her front. The familiar numbness started in both her hands as her body grew warm and prickly.

Instead of focusing on the physical sensation, she ran a finger over the silver bracelet on her wrist. She felt the texture of the individual links connecting one to the other, the solid and secure clasp. She held it up to the sunlight and watched it sparkle. She shook her wrist to feel the bracelet's heft.

Aunt Ethel would never have felt this way; she'd never be nervous. She would have loved this ... she *did* love this. Ethel loved new experiences in the exact way Beth avoided them. Her head drooped in recognition of this. But really, what was the worst thing that could happen to her on the ship? Eat too much at the buffet? Fall overboard? Honestly, the most likely thing she'd do was make an ass out of herself and she was used to that. Beth figured she'd never see any of these people again. You can't die of embarrassment, can you?

Her only option was to have remained home, locked inside her apartment with no one but Grendel to watch over her. This precipitated another consideration—she could stay in her apartment until she died. Grendel would lick her appendages for food, newspapers and Chinese menus would grow knee-high in the doorway, and the authorities would finally find her once old Mrs. Rosenberg knocked for help to change a light bulb. This was Beth's destiny. Unless she took some chances. Like now.

Beth physically shook herself. Her hair flew back and forth, and her glasses soared from her nose. She stopped and clutched the bed coverlet. She had two choices. She could sit there and work her way into a full-blown anxiety attack, or she could have a good time. Beth had a fabulous cabin—*oh, Frank would just die*! She would see amazing places. Eat terrific food. And she didn't have to pay for *any* of it. Plus, sailing on Cunard was something her mom had dreamed of doing. This was a gift from Aunt Ethel.

With greater conviction than she intended, she said out loud, "Enough!" Some measure of control came back in a small wave. She took immediate advantage of it. She snatched her glasses from off the floor and shouted, "I'm fine! Really, truly, fine!" at herself in the mirror. Then she grabbed her tote bag, ship's ID, and headed out to explore the ship before she could change her mind.

Using her map, Beth found the tour desk and confirmed her tours. Yes, she was indeed booked for a tour at each port stop. Yes, all paid for. At the purser's desk, she inquired about the onboard credit. Yes, it was accurate, too. Running out of housekeeping tasks, she asked Raul, the purser, "Do you recall an Ethel Birnbaum traveling with you? She was my aunt and recently passed away." Beth figured it was as good a time as any to start searching for the misplaced will.

"I know several Birnbaums. Did you say, Ethel?"

"Yes, Ethel. She was around eighty years old ... liked to wear hats?"

"Oh yes, I knew Ethel. I'm sorry to hear she passed. What a lovely lady." Raul was dressed in a navy suit and on his name tag, several international flags represented the foreign languages he spoke. Beth couldn't recognize some of them.

"So, you knew her?"

"Of course, she was one of my favorite guests. Always gave me a piece of candy from her purse ... butterscotch." Raul laughed.

"When was she here?"

"Oh, it was probably a few months ago. I think it was the same itinerary. It didn't matter where the ship was going, she always acted like it was her first time."

"That sounds like her. This is awkward, but I'm trying to find something of hers. I think she may have left it on the ship. Do you know if there's any way that I can check the cabin she was in? Is it occupied?" Beth gnawed at her thumbnail.

"I'm sure our stewards would have found the missing item. How about I check Lost & Found for you?"

"That would be great." Beth left her cabin number with Raul and continued exploring the ship. *Okay, a little progress.*

Outside on Deck 3, she walked—promenaded—around the ship. Wooden lounge chairs were lined up as precisely as soldiers at attention. Most passengers weren't sitting but leaning against the railing and looking downwards. The ship's engines started to rumble below. As Beth tried to peek over the side from a safe distance, monstrous ropes were released from the dock cleats and pulled inside the ship. Thrusters activated and pushed the ship away. Below, the water swirled a frothy white. What a production.

At precisely six-o'clock, the horn blew, *Honnnnnnnnnnnnnnnnk!* The immediate vibration in Beth's chest nearly knocked her off her feet. The passengers on deck laughed at the surprise and waved to the bystanders below. "Goodbye, goodbye!"

"Bon Voyage!" they replied and waved Union Jack flags.

Beth stood on deck and watched it all like a movie. The ship turned gently and majestically took her leave of the harbor. Southampton looked smaller and less important by the minute. Seagulls followed the ship to the channel. Even with a bright autumn sun, the breeze became noticeably cooler. The skies grew darker and early stars flickered. Beth checked her watch; it was almost seven o'clock. Where did the time go? She had lost track of the minutes while watching the waves behind the ship. It was mesmerizing. She loved the ocean with its endless blue and how the setting sun flickered on it. Thank goodness sea sickness wasn't on The List. Yet a small twist in her stomach reminded her. It was inevitable, she had to get dressed for dinner.

CHAPTER 8

As she carefully climbed the staircase to the Britannia Restaurant's second floor, Beth murmured to herself, "Step, together, step, together," in fear of tripping over her dress hem.

She held it gingerly by her fingertips as if it were a hoop skirt, but still, the evening gown was uncooperative. The dress, black chiffon with a bold red flower print, had a matching jacket with fringe on the sleeves. Frank had insisted she could pull off boho-chic, but she felt more like a faux Frida Kahlo.

At the top of the stairs, Beth overcompensated in her new kitten heels and tripped upwards (always the worst) and landed on her knees. She was down for a mere moment, but it felt like hours before the maître d' quickly scooped her up by the elbow. Beth smoothed her dress back down as fringe flapped around her. *What a fool.* Later, she replayed it in her head in slow motion and had to admit it was classic Beth. *Note to self: Frank will find this hilarious. Email him.*

She mumbled her thanks and the maître d' escorted her to Table 8, a large, oval table with seven seats already occupied. A server held out the last empty chair and Beth slid into it sideways. Seven faces turned to her with varying expressions. Everyone was ... old.

"Good evening," Beth squeaked. She cleared her voice and tried again, "Good evening."

"Good evening! Isn't it *nice* to have a young person with us?" an elderly lady with a chipper voice enthusiastically asked the group. "I'm Constance. Delighted to meet you." She put a wrinkled, bejeweled hand on Beth's right arm. Her diamond choker glinted in the low light. Beth recognized her from the cruise terminal lounge but without the red hat. Tonight, she wore sparkly hair pins in her white curls. Her perfume caught Beth's nose. Elegant.

"I'm Madeline," said another lady further down to Beth's right.

"Ian Fitzsimmons. My pleasure to make your acquaintance." The elderly man who had toasted her at the Café Carinthia nodded. He had changed from his earth tone tweeds to a polished blue suit and regimental tie, which had to be from some fancy British college—Oxford? His waxed mustache raised with his smile. He sat to Beth's immediate left.

"We're the Kippermans. Saul and Judy." A couple directly across from her volunteered as they both grinned and showed lots of teeth.

"Bob and Teresa Gunderson." A large man with a noticeable Texas twang pointed to himself and his wife, who looked like a scared rabbit.

"I'm Beth Schiff." *Gulp*. "Nice to meet you all." She grabbed her napkin and wiped her sweaty palms underneath the table. She'd never be able to remember all of their names. Later she'd write them down with the Cunard pen on the Cunard notepad she found in her cabin's desk drawer.

"Oh, just like that actress. The one on the telly. *Legal Briefs* is a jolly good show," Saul said.

"Darling, that was *Victoria* Schiff," his wife corrected him. "Not quite the same." Luckily, before any additional conversation was necessary, the server reappeared. Beth closed her eyes and prayed a silent thank you. She didn't want to go down a potentially disastrous path; she had enough to worry about already.

"My name is Glenn. I'll be your head server for the duration of your voyage. Welcome to the *Queen Elizabeth*." He passed out menus disguised as leather-bound encyclopedias.

A woman dressed in a tailored black suit with a small gold pin on the lapel also introduced herself. "I'm your sommelier, Brigitte, and happy to help with your wine selections." Beth had read about sommeliers but had never met one in person. At least that she knew of.

"Would you care for some wine, madam?" Brigitte handed the wine selections to her. Another hefty tome.

In a low voice, almost whispering, Beth asked, "What do you suggest? I'm kinda out of my element here."

"I think the 2005 Pinot Noir is a nice choice." Brigitte pointed to a selection with her fingertip. Fifty dollars.

"Okay, sounds great." Beth tried to smile confidently as she handed back the list with both hands. *For fifty dollars, it better be awesome.* Wait a minute, she couldn't drink an entire bottle of wine. Would she have to share it? Could she take it back to the cabin with her? Maybe she should ask for just a glass. Is it too late? Will people think she's a fool? She grimaced. Already in a predicament and the food hadn't even arrived yet. Food! She hadn't even ordered. This evening was going from bad to worse.

Nonetheless, the other diners at Table 8 fell into easy conversations chatting with each other. Beth occupied herself by fussing with the fringe on her jacket sleeves. She tried to organize the individual strands in a coherent fashion, but eventually gave up. The time it took also prevented her from making any small talk ... which was her game plan all along.

When she had unpacked her luggage earlier, she found a small toy cat, complete with a missing front paw, its seams carefully stitched closed. Also, a motivational note from Frank: *Good luck, Pussycat*. She wondered what her tablemates would think of a grown woman sleeping with a stuffed animal at night. Still, the idea calmed her. This was the first step to finding the will. Get out there and look. If she couldn't hack it, there was always the buffet.

Beth glanced upwards to take a small peek at the table. Crisp white linens and napkins murmured elegance. Lilies gathered in a small crystal vase in the middle whispered sophistication. Varying stemware and china suggested wealth and the heavy silverware surrounding her on either side, hinted, well, confusion. Frank never mentioned this. The other diners continued their conversations, seemingly to leave Beth alone to stew in her anxiety.

Music drifted above from a small trio on the first floor of the dining room. *Good! A distraction!* To take her mind off the impending chaos called her place setting, she tried tapping her toe to the beat. This proved difficult since harp strings and flutes didn't warrant a consistent baseline. Instead, she swayed her head back and forth. *Look at me! I'm a classical music aficionado.*

"Are you alright, my dear?" Ian Fitzsimmons's bushy eyebrows raised in consternation.

"Uh. Just fine. It's awesome music, huh?"

"Yes. Splendid," he agreed and smiled at her.

Beth immediately returned her gaze back to her lap and safely played with her fringe. Once in a while she'd give a weak smile to the flower arrangement. Her attempts at acting like she belonged at this fancy table with its fancy diners resulted in saying nothing. Better to remain silent and thought a fool than speak up and remove all doubt. *Thanks for the advice, Abe Lincoln.* If things got too rough, she could always try Dr. Joan's deep breathing exercises, but she hoped the others wouldn't think it was a heart attack. And spoken mantras were *definitely* out.

After drinks arrived, Glenn took dinner orders from a menu that read like the American Constitution. Beth scanned the options and silently thanked Glenn, who left her for last. By the time he made his way over, she had finally made her selections. She pointed to an appetizer of chilled cucumber and mint soup with herb sour crème, a mixed gourmet salad of asparagus, and the Beef Wellington with roasted potatoes, glazed vegetables, and périgourdine sauce (whatever that was) for her main course. All a far cry from the leftover Chinese food turning green in her fridge.

Beth took a small sip of the cherry-red wine in front of her. *Ohhh. Delicious. Brigitte can try and stop me, but I'm definitely taking it back to my cabin.*

Then dinner began. Glenn and a team of servers presented each course with the same pomp as the last. Whether a small salad or giant lobster tail, they placed each plate to the left of the diner. They spooned gravies, vinaigrettes, and dressings from sauce bowls. Beth never served herself. She nodded and pointed at what she wanted. Even if she wasn't aware what it was.

The silverware was still overwhelming, as she didn't know what to use when and there were too many plates. A plate for everything, even her roll. Beth didn't *own* this many plates. She wished she knew how things should be done according to tradition. After all, "Knowledge is power," as Aunt Ethel used to say. She watched her table mates carefully for guidance. Beth glanced over at Ian who used a knife (one she didn't have) to cut a piece of fish. Constance took the outermost fork for her salad and winked at Beth when she did the same.

"It's terribly overwhelming, isn't it?" Constance remarked.

Beth nodded.

"Is this your first time on a cruise?"

"Yes."

"Don't worry, all of this will seem silly in a few days." Constance waved her hand over the silverware and smiled.

Beth nodded again and quickly took another sip of her wine. Her cheeks tingled with sudden, comforting warmth. Like a hug.

Two hours later, Table 8's formality had descended into a hilarious uproar. Sharp punctuations of laughter interrupted other diners' meals. It was an all-out cackle fest. The ladies dabbed eyes with napkins, their tears threatening to undo careful makeup applications. The men threw back their heads and laughed heartily until no sound came out. Glenn couldn't help himself either. He propped himself up against a column and held a serving tray to cover his face while his shoulders bounced up and down.

Empty wine bottles littered the table. The diners refused Brigitte's offer to remove them because they wanted to keep count. They were up to seven.

"And *then* I said, don't even *think* about serving me salmon. You know I can't *stand* Alaska!" Constance finished her story as the table roared with laughter. Beth, who had finally relaxed from either the wine or listening to their hysterical stories, shook with the giggles as she tried to serve herself another glass of Pinot Noir. Brigitte rushed to pour it for her.

Dinner, by all accounts, was a smashing success. Even Beth couldn't disagree. During appetizers, brief biographies were exchanged: where everyone lived and how many kids and subsequent grandkids they all had. Over soups and salads, they shared the number of times they'd cruised on Cunard. While enjoying delicious main courses, epic story-telling began. Beth couldn't help but be engaged because this was her specialty. An area she could relate and even contribute to, was how to tell a good story. Plus, she was on her third glass of wine and feeling fine. In fact, she was feeling *mighty* fine.

The two British ladies, Madeline and Constance, had traveled together for years since their respective husbands died decades ago. Ian was a retired professor. The Kippermans were from London and cruised every year, *only* on Cunard. The Gundersons were indeed from Texas; Bob was loud and brash, and even though he frequently waved his big gold watch around for all to notice, had a good sense of humor. His wife never said a word, but laughed along with the rest of the table, especially at his exploding BBQ story. All in all, it was a friendly table, which boded well for the remainder of the trip. An oppressive weight floated off Beth's chiffon-covered shoulders.

As she scanned the rest of the Britannia Restaurant, she acknowledged her terrific luck. Other large tables ate in complete silence; guests studied their salads and glanced over wine glass rims to remote corners of the room. Tables for two were occupied by older couples, who again, sat in silence. Maybe, after all those years, they had run out of things to talk about. How lucky was she to get assigned to this table?

After her worries about being charming and engaging, Beth found it easier to just sit and listen. It was okay with everyone else, as they had plenty to talk about. They didn't push her to share. As other guests began to filter out of the dining room, her table reluctantly disbanded and said good night. They shared kisses and hugs all around, as if they had known each other for years.

That wasn't bad at all. It was actually fun. The food, of course, was delicious. The wine, outstanding (Brigitte offered to cork the little remaining and have it ready for dinner tomorrow). A flourish of satisfaction ran through Beth as she picked up her dress hem and left the dining room to explore the ship. She did it ... she survived dinner.

But.

So many sophisticated people. How could she keep this up for twelve days? Beth squeezed her evening bag and meekly smiled in response to greetings of, "Good Evening," from elegant passengers in elegant surroundings. Some congregated in lounges. Some drank cocktails in the bars. Some shopped at the small boutiques. Some strolled through an art gallery with original paintings and prints. Most were older than her. Okay, *all* were older. But they all looked like they belonged.

She followed the sounds of music to the main ballroom, the Queens Room, and found a comfy chair in a corner. A grand piano sat under a sparkling chandelier. A live orchestra played as couples twirled on the lacquered dance floor. Varying degrees of dance ability didn't preclude anyone from spinning in time to the music. She wished she had a notebook to capture it all. She hated pecking out long sentences on her phone. It made her eyes hurt.

The Kippermans made their way to the dance floor. Saul led Judy in a waltz. His lips moved as he counted one-two-three and began to turn her. Her steps matched his and they sped across the floor like a professional dance team. They circled the entire perimeter and ended where they started just as the music finished, perfectly choreographed. It reminded Beth of the show *Downton Abbey*.

She relaxed and watched the dancers. To her surprise, she was having a good time ... and it wasn't just from the wine. Her dining companions had kicked-off the trip well. She loved listening to their stories. Sure, everyone was twice her age, but it turned out to be a non-issue. She preferred the company of mature people with real experiences; she could have been stuck on a booze cruise with drunk twenty-somethings. Thank goodness Aunt Ethel had good taste in ships. If Beth had to socialize with seventy-year-olds, so be it. She sat up straight in her chair. She hadn't thought about Aunt Ethel or the missing will for several hours. Was that good or bad?

When the orchestra took a break, Beth decided to explore some more. Time to get to work. Time to find the will, right? That's why she was here in the first place. She passed by glass showcases highlighting Cunard's maritime history and stopped. She wondered if the will was inside one of the cases. It would be like Aunt Ethel to hide it.

Cunard had a 184-year history so there was lots to read about. Among the more interesting facts, the original *Queen Elizabeth* sailed from 1946-1968 and her successor, the *Queen Elizabeth 2*, from 1969-2008.

This ship was new, built in 2010, and went back to the original name. There were only three Queens in existence: the *Mary 2, Victoria,* and *Elizabeth.* How ironic.

Old newspapers, menus, and large bronze bells from decommissioned liners were displayed behind the glass. Neatly typed information cards explained that the White Star line, famous for the *Titanic* tragedy, was purchased by Cunard in 1934. Maps, vintage postcards, and photos of famous guests were artistically arranged. The display was a history lesson and a time capsule all in one. Beth wondered if any of it was important to locating the will.

She walked up a smaller staircase and glanced in the shop windows along the Royal Arcade. A jewelry store offered expensive watches and colorful gems. An employee behind a counter smiled as Beth ogled the glittering window displays from outside. Next door was a cosmetics and perfume shop. A clothing boutique and a souvenir shop sat across the way. The scent of flowers wafted to Beth again, but she decided it must be coming from the perfume shop. Emboldened by either the wine or her success surviving dinner, she stepped inside. A young lady with sleek hair, black as a raven's wing, offered assistance.

Beth cleared her throat. "This is going to sound silly, but I smell the flowers from downstairs in the lobby. The ones in the big bouquet? Can you tell me what they are?"

"Ahhh. It must be the jasmine. It's lovely, isn't it?" The lady turned, selected a bottle from a glass shelf and sprayed a narrow piece of white cardstock. "Is this it?"

Beth took the card and inhaled. "Yes! That's it!" A burst of springtime; lilacs and daffodils reminded her of Easter and new plastic shoes. Happiness.

"It's Chanel ... Chance Eau Fráiche." She held out the bottle for Beth to inspect.

Even the bottle was pretty. "How much is it?"

"We have the large size for one hundred or a smaller travel size for fifty."

"Is that dollars, pounds, or Euros?"

"Dollars."

Beth hesitated for a moment, oscillating back and forth on her kitten heels.

"Can I use my onboard credit?"

"Certainly, madam."

If she bought it, she could smell lovely all the time. Maybe happy, too? A little confidence-booster? Finally, fighting the last bit of hesitation, she said, "I'll take the travel size."

"Your ship's ID please?"

With her new purchase tucked safely inside her evening bag, Beth felt like a lady. *Fancy perfume! And French!* But after a mere moment, she realized she should be keeping track of all her expenditures. Even though she had a hefty onboard credit balance, the wine... the perfume... it would add up quickly if she wasn't careful.

She exited the shop and saw tables lining the hallway offering sale items and services. A sommelier offered wine packages. A trainer registered people for yoga and Pilates classes. At the end of the row, a small crowd of eager passengers formed, mostly women. Beth, intrigued, tried to see the vendor. Were they giving away free stuff?

Two women wore white smocks with *Royal Spa* embroidered in turquoise across their left breasts. Beth took a pamphlet, *Rituals of Luxury,* to determine what the hubbub was about. The small book listed services galore ... everything from acupuncture to waxing. Passengers waited (some, not so patiently) for their turn to book appointments. Beth could feel the tension rising even from where she stood outside the throng.

One of the Royal Spa therapists implored the crowd in a Ukrainian accent, "Ladies, we open at eight o'clock in the morning. If you wish to make an appointment, we're happy to see you then," The other, who held a clipboard, tried to organize the women despite being frazzled. Beth smirked and returned the pamphlet to the table. Really. Who knew rich people could be so grabby?

Priorities. Back to work. She continued to explore the ship, looking for Aunt Ethel's will.

She looked in portholes, inside life rafts, and behind buoys strapped to the railings on deck. She peeped into bathrooms. She even snuck a look inside a "Crew Only" doorway and found nothing. Frustrated, she realized the hunt was going to be monumental on a ship this size and she had only searched two decks out of twelve. There were a thousand different places the will could be. Her shoulders sank in acknowledgement.

After a few hours, her feet ached from her new shoes. Plus, she was lost. Every turn confused her since landmarks were yet unknown. She eventually pulled out her ship's map to find her cabin, only to realize she was at the opposite end of the ship. After a small panic, racing down long unfamiliar passageways, Beth found herself outside of #6077. Exhausted, she practically hugged the door in gratitude.

Inside, she immediately kicked off her shoes.

And froze.

Red gladiolas filled her cabin. A dozen vibrant blooms were arranged in a gigantic crystal vase balanced on the small coffee table. An envelope rested against it. Aunt Ethel's bold loopy handwriting greeted her. *What?* Beth's mouth fell open as she tore open the envelope and read,

My sweet Beth,
You are finally here! How absolutely lovely, lovely! I hope you have a glorious time (please have a glorious time!).
Before you get cross with me, know I love you dearly and wish you much success and the Very Best of Luck. But you are a smart and clever girl, so there should be no need for that!
I lived a full and wonderful life. I am thankful for all my experiences. I traveled to exotic locations and learned about many of the world's cultures. I was humbled before great works of art. I dined on marvelous food and tasted delicious wine. I met interesting people and learned about their lives, all the while becoming richer in my own.
I want the same for you. Life is a banquet and most poor suckers are starving to death! Okay, I stole it from the movie **Auntie Mame,** *but it's TRUE! You need to start living to your fullest potential. So, enough! Get off your duff! Take some risks!*
You seek something valuable and I'll help you find it. Solve the clues, complete the tasks, and you'll find more than treasure in the end.
Let's begin with an easy one, just to get the ball rolling.

All my love,
Aunt Ethel

On a small, separate piece of paper, the size of a Chinese cookie fortune, Beth read:

This epic journey
concealed within the dead trees
tests your loyalty

She sat on the bed with a plop. Both pieces of paper fell from her hand and glided to the floor. From outside her balcony door, the waves softly kissed the side of the ship. The *Queen Elizabeth* gently swayed from side to side, in a much needed, soothing way.

Aunt Ethel, that devious old lady, planned this. None of it was by accident. All details were carefully constructed and now, after her death, being dutifully executed. There was no *missing* will. It was all a game.

In bewilderment, Beth tried to piece what little information she had together, attempting to connect non-existent dots. *How could she? Why would she?* Then Beth had the last reaction she ever expected. She laughed.

CHAPTER 9

B eth clutched a new spiral notebook under her arm as she headed
to a late breakfast. Due to limited options in the gift shop, she had
resigned to purchasing a sparkly, pink one with frolicking rabbits. She
made sure the title 'You're No Bunny 'til Some Bunny Loves You' was
turned toward her armpit.

The Lido restaurant spanned almost an entire deck and provided food
twenty-four hours daily. A breakfast buffet as long as a New York City
block offered something for everyone: muesli and fruit for the Germans,
grilled tomatoes and beans for the Brits, and eggs with crispy bacon for
the small contingent of Americans and Canadians.

Beth placed a mug of coffee and a dainty muffin on her tray and found
a coveted seat next to the window. Each table held smiling, enthusiastic
diners, who smacked their lips on food they hadn't had to shop for or
prepare. *God Bless Vacation.*

She yawned into her coffee. After a late-night transatlantic phone call to Mr. Watkins via satellite (how's *that* for an incidental!), Beth hadn't been able to sleep.

The overseas call had taken a few minutes to connect, but once patched through she immediately accused Mr. Watkins with, "You *knew*! Didn't you? Why didn't you tell me it was a game?"

"Who is this?"

"It's Beth. Sorry, Elizabeth Schiff."

"Oh, Beth. Now calm down," Mr. Watkins had said. "If you had known beforehand, would you have agreed to go?"

"Uh ... probably not."

"There you are. Give your aunt some credit. She knows you well." He yawned. "Anyways, I'm glad you called. We heard back from New York State ... they denied our request for an extension. So, it's imperative Ethel's will be found as soon as possible."

"Seriously, you don't know where it is?"

"No, of course not. It's your puzzle to solve. Once you find it, I'll take it from there."

"It's really hidden?"

"Yes, but I'm confident you'll find it. Remember, 'Optimism is the faith that leads to achievement.'"

"Mary Shelley?"

"No, Helen Keller."

"Well, there's nothing left to say but I'll keep you posted. Just promise me there's nothing else up your sleeve. I'm not a big fan of surprises."

"Beth, a lawyer can't promise you anything. And if he does ... run the other way." He hung up the phone while laughing at his own joke.

Afterwards, Beth had tossed and turned in bed thinking about her predicament. A scavenger hunt seemed like fun, but *not* finding the treasure could be disastrous. Plus, Aunt Ethel was certainly having the last laugh. Beth couldn't help it. Long stretches of contemplation were interrupted with unexpected bouts of giggles. *Oh, Aunt Ethel!* The last thing Beth remembered was the digital clock blinking 4:20, mocking her. This, and a smidge of jet lag had resulted in oversleeping this morning. Now, she felt rushed.

Slurping piping hot coffee at the Lido, Beth tried to wake up her brain. She brushed muffin crumbs off her new dress, red with a polka-dot print. Frank insisted it made her look like a 1950s pin-up. After Beth rolled her eyes at him, he had rolled his own back and groaned, "Just wear it." This morning, after she opened the closet door and found her new wardrobe organized by color, it was the first thing to jump out at her. She liked it and hoped she wouldn't spill coffee on it. But she noticed, when crossing her legs, her naked calves looked just like the plump weiß wurst at breakfast.

Okay, where to start? She opened her new notebook and clicked her Cunard pen. She unfolded Aunt Ethel's note on the table in front of her and read it for the seemingly thousandth time.

> This epic journey
> concealed within the dead trees
> tests your loyalty

It was a haiku. And a kinda bad one. But something. Was this the first clue of many? Beth took out the ship's map (which now lived inside her pocket) and unfolded it.

She tried to think logically. 'Dead trees ... dead trees ...' From what, beetle-kill? Global warming? Pollution? Is the *Queen Elizabeth* spilling oil into the ocean? Are toxic gases causing the death of trees? There aren't any trees in the ocean. What the hell? Beth groaned internally, already frustrated, and she hadn't even started.

She got up to refresh her coffee and get a bigger muffin. *Okay, maybe thinking logically wasn't the best plan. Remember it's Aunt Ethel and her sense of humor. I may be over-thinking this.* She sat down and studied the note again.

"Ahoy there!" The Kippermans stood in front of her, with expressions like lost puppies, holding their trays. "Mind terribly if we join you?"

"Uh ... no," Beth said. She quickly folded the clue and placed it into the notebook.

"Looks like you have a project. Are you working? You should be enjoying your vacation," Saul said, placing his full English breakfast plate from the tray onto the table.

"It's just a game."

"Oh, I *love* games," Judy said. "Is it like Sudoku? I can do those for hours sitting by the pool."

"Not really."

Beth took a closer inspection of the Kippermans. Last night, from across the table through broken glasses, she couldn't see well. But now, as the Kippermans ate, Beth observed additional details.

Saul seemed intent on defying old age by coloring his hair. However, jet black wasn't going to fool anyone. He had a long face and even longer chin, which gave him a one-dimensional profile. Saul was tall and awk-wardly skinny. Her dad would have asked him, "How's the weather up there?" When Saul walked, his arms bowed around his sides, gorilla-like. He must have been heavier once, his arms automatically compensating for absent girth. As Saul got up to refresh their coffees and teas, Beth's assumptions were substantiated by his long belt tail with stretched holes. A trophy from his extensive weight-loss? Beth imagined arguments with Judy, who probably said (complete with a wrinkled nose), "Get rid of that nasty old thing."

"Hey, I saw you two dancing last night, you're really terrific!" Beth said, changing the narrative in her head.

Saul grinned. "Just call me twinkle toes."

"Where'd you learn to dance like that?"

Judy smiled and touched Saul's arm. "I think it was for our anniversary … our twentieth or twenty-fifth, I don't remember which one, but I wanted Saul to take me dancing. He couldn't dance, the old sod, so I signed him up for lessons."

"Arthur Murray School," Saul said between mouthfuls of fried eggs. "Best place to learn. Professionals, you know."

"He learned so beautifully, when we went dancing, I felt like an utter fool … I kept stepping on his toes. So, afterwards, I signed myself up, too. We took classes together for about a year." Judy squeezed lemon into her tea.

"Great exercise," Saul said.

Aha! That confirms it.

They continued chatting. Topics ranged from their dinner compan-ions—*all so interesting*, the upcoming port stops—*glorious*, and the *fantastic* evening shows in the Royal Court Theatre according to the

Kippermans. Judy said the ship's entertainment was East End-quality, which translated for Beth into Broadway-caliber. She promised to see a show.

As Judy continued to elaborate, Beth scrutinized her as well. It turned out Judy colored her hair, too. Maybe they got a discount at the salon? Hers was bright red, not so much Emma Stone, but more Julianne Moore. She also favored red and pink clothing, which failed to complement. Another thing Beth learned from Frank: no matchy-matchy. It was as if Judy tried to portray a fiery personality with her color choices, but only managed to get to bubbly. She wore a simple watch and a scarf printed with fuchsia peonies tied around her neck.

"Really, you'll be missing out," Judy admonished as they stood up to depart for their scheduled massages. "The entertainment is excellent, not to be missed! You *must* see the shows." *Great, more things to do.* Beth knew she'd be pushing herself to try new things and experiences (like Aunt Ethel said in her note), which made her automatically poised for unease. She decided, before any new anxieties decided to introduce themselves, to take one day at a time. Moreover, now she had a project—she could focus on solving the clue and keep her mind busy. She'd try her best to keep it together. Then she snickered; who was she kidding?

Beth grabbed her notebook and continued last night's tour of the ship, looking for possible hiding places, this time related to her haiku.

On Deck 9 she found two swimming pools and the Garden Lounge, modelled after an English winter garden. It was decorated with lush green plants, white wicker furniture, and a small piano, which Teresa Gunderson played softly. Beth waved to her, and she returned a shy smile. Further forward was the Royal Spa and fitness center. She found two sophisticated bars on Deck 10; the Yacht Club overlooked the swimming pools and the Commodore Club offered stunning views from the ship's bow. The map became her best friend. How long would it take before she knew her way around?

"About two weeks," a voice answered the question Beth had asked in her head. Surprised, she looked up from the map and saw one of the ladies from Table 8. "It takes about two weeks before the map is no longer required," the woman said, laughing.

Beth couldn't remember her name, so she just said, "Hi."

"Madeline." She stuck out a sweaty hand to Beth. Madeline wore sneakers and soaked athletic clothing. She wiped beads of perspiration from her forehead with the edge of a towel draped around her neck. Her gray hair, knotted into a wonky ponytail, dripped with her recent exertion.

"Hi, Madeline. The ship's big, huh? Did you take a class?" Beth pointed toward the fitness center.

"No ... just thirty minutes on the treadmill. In the mornings, I usually jog around Deck 3, but I got up rather late today ... too many people now. All those *old* people walking slow." She laughed again. "What a lovely time last night! But we didn't have much time to chat. Fancy a drink before dinner? Constance and I always have cocktails beforehand. Say, half-six at the Commodore Club?" She wiped her brow again.

Beth folded her map into the palm of her hand to buy some time. "Half-seven? That's like six thirty?"

"Yes."

"Sure."

"Brilliant! See you tonight," Madeline called out as she jogged toward the staircase, bypassing a convenient bank of elevators.

Wow! I just got invited for drinks. Beth immediately started brainstorming topics to discuss, since she wouldn't be able to sit and play with her fringe again. It would only work with that particular dress. What would she wear tonight?

Down a few flights of stairs to Deck 3, she found herself outside the Britannia Restaurant. She read the evening's dinner menu posted on the door—filet mignon and cheesecake. She peeked inside and saw staff preparing for the lunch service. Over at Table 8, Glenn was already setting their table. *Bingo!* Just who she needed to talk to.

As she walked through the cavernous room, Beth saw a pair of feet sticking out from underneath the tablecloth. Saul Kipperman suddenly crawled out backwards like a hermit crab.

"Saul, what are you doing?" She must have spooked him, because he hit his head on the underside of the table.

"Hi, Beth. Fancy seeing you here. Judy lost an earring last night and I was trying to locate it. A pity. I hope it isn't gone for good." He stood up and rubbed his head.

"I hope you find it. Hey, there's a Lost & Found on the ship—go ask Raul at the purser's desk, he can help."

Saul thanked Beth and left to go and inquire about the lost earring.

Beth turned to the server, grasped her hands together and announced with a serious tone, "Glenn, I need your help."

"Of course, madam. Have you lost something too?"

"Kind of. But that's another story. Here's the thing, I've never sailed on a ship like this before. In fact, I've never sailed at all. Could you show me what to do? I mean like what to use when?" Her words tumbled out while she pointed to the silverware at the place settings. "Last night, I felt kind of stupid."

"You're not stupid; it's just new to you. Please, sit." Glenn held out a chair and waved her to sit.

Over the years, Beth realized that the more she knew about a specific subject, the more her confidence grew. Consequently, she read a lot to fill in knowledge gaps. She familiarized herself with possibilities to help manage expectations. But Dr. Joan had said it couldn't always be the case. Life gets in the way.

"Yes, when one goes parachuting the chutes are *supposed* to open. It doesn't mean they always *will*," Dr. Joan had stated at a session while sitting behind her desk with a half-eaten yogurt and her Birkenstocks resting on top of disorganized papers. "Life is full of surprises and chaos."

Beth shrieked in response, "How does this help me? How much am I paying you to scare me? Not cool, Dr. Joan." When she got back to her apartment, she immediately put 'surprises' on The List and 'chaos.'

But silverware was solvable. Within fifteen minutes, Glenn had given Beth a full tutorial on place settings. She learned, basically, to work her way from the outside in. A salad fork was always first, but if she didn't order salad, Glenn removed it. No need for it. The soup spoon aligned across the top edge of the plate, but again, if she didn't order soup, it would be removed.

"So, you're helping me, taking away the things I don't need," Beth said.

"Correct."

But, on the other hand, if she ordered steak, Glenn would bring her a special steak knife, just like he brought Ian a fish fork last night. With the after-dinner petit fours, she just needed to point. Glenn would always serve the food; he reminded her not to take it herself.

"Otherwise, I'm out of a job," he said.

"Okay, but make me a deal? When you bring a plate could you kinda nod to the right thing to use? It would help. Sometimes I get a little flustered."

"I don't think it's necessary, you'll catch on," he said. Brigitte came over to watch the lesson, which prompted Beth to ask her questions as well.

"I'm not quite sure what you do exactly."

"I help you select wine."

"That's a cool job."

"Yes, it is." Brigitte smiled.

Beth went into interview mode to learn more, a skill she had mastered while writing client's memoirs and autobiographies. Plus, it was easier to ask questions here than at dinner in front of everyone, as she didn't feel as awkward admitting her lack of sophistication.

"What's the biggest mistake people make?" she asked, more so she wouldn't make it herself.

"The biggest faux pas is to smell the cork. Never smell the cork. You look like a beginner." Brigitte shook her finger for emphasis.

"What am I supposed to do with it then? You kinda make a big deal about it."

"The sommelier shows the cork to verify the vintner. In the past, low-quality wineries used to recork their cheap wine in good bottles. By checking the cork against the bottle, you know what you ordered is correct." Brigitte continued. "Plus, don't ever feel intimidated by wine. I'm here to help you select something you like."

"What if I don't *know* what I like?"

"It's not a bad thing. You can spend the entire voyage finding out."

Beth thanked both for their time and lessons and promised to do better that evening. As she began to walk out, she turned and asked, "By the way, did you know my Aunt Ethel? Ethel Birnbaum?" She figured it couldn't hurt to start asking people, especially staff.

Glenn answered, "We meet thousands of people on the ship. It would be hard to place her, Brigitte?"

Brigitte replied, "No, not off the top of my head. Did she drink wine?"

"Probably. She was on this ship a few months ago."

"Glenn and I just arrived on the *Elizabeth*. Cunard likes to rotate the staff among the ships, so it's possible we may have met her and just not have known."

"Well, thanks anyways."

Although a little more assured in her dining skills, Beth was still no closer to solving the haiku. She went back to the Garden Lounge and found a chair tucked away in the potted palms. She took out her notebook and started brainstorming. She re-read the clue. Trees ... dead trees. Maybe it didn't matter what they died from, but where they are now? Are there dead trees on a ship? Wood? There's wood all over ... chairs, tables, paneling.

She tried tucking her hair behind her ears. An ivory and lilac orchid sat on a wicker side table next to her. A small clip anchored the delicate stem to a green stick planted in the pot of dirt. Beth looked around her. No one was watching. She quickly took the clip off the plant and used it to hold back her hair. *Okay. I've sunk to a new low.*

Focus! What's made of trees? Dead trees? Wood. Furniture. What else? Paper. Books. Books! Beth sat up straight. *Books! That's it!* It must be. Where on the ship are there lots of books? She took out her map, which was already starting to get a little ratty around the edges. She moved her finger methodically along Deck 9 and worked her way down the ship. Decks 8, 7, 6, 5, and 4 were all cabins. *Books. Books.* She got to Deck 3 and saw it ... the library.

"They have a library?" she said aloud. She grabbed her notebook and took off running for Deck 3.

The library was a majestic space, as if the *Queen Elizabeth* didn't have enough already. Heavy glass doors opened to a main reception area. Two stories tall, an interior winding mahogany staircase joined Decks 2 and 3 inside. Sheets of crossword and Sudoku puzzles were neatly stacked just inside the entrance for passengers' daily mental calisthenics. Comfy overstuffed chairs rested beside convenient floor lamps. More practical workspaces faced the ocean windows. Hundreds, no thousands, of books were shelved behind locked, beveled glass cabinets.

The librarian explained matter-of-factly, "For when we experience rough seas."

"How do I check out a book?" Beth asked.

"I just need your ship's ID."

Beth thanked her and strolled around to look at the titles. *Ahhh books.* She felt completely relaxed for the first time on the ship. It was like home. The library provided lots of travel books, of course, and many biographies of famous British people. Large, heavy atlases lay displayed on tables. So many. Could Aunt Ethel have hidden the will in a book? If so, which one? Beth grasped her tote bag as she wandered among the stacks.

An electronic bell suddenly echoed throughout the ship. A voice boomed from the heavens. Beth's heart slipped a beat. *Are we sinking?*

"Good afternoon. This is Commodore Pederson. I welcome you to the *Queen Elizabeth*. All of us at Cunard wish you a memorable voyage.

We will do our level best to make it so. At this time, we require your participation in a *mandatory* safety demonstration. We ask all guests kindly return to their cabins and retrieve their life vests. Please locate your muster station and assemble in thirty minutes. This is a mandatory drill. If you have any questions, please do not hesitate to ask any of our staff. Again, this is only a drill. We thank you for your participation."

"Really?" Unenthusiastically, Beth took out her map and hurried to her cabin.

After the mind-numbing drill, which only exacerbated her own anxieties about sinking and a watery death at sea, Beth realized she had missed lunch. The late morning muffins were the last thing she ate. Now starving, she consulted her watch. It was after five o'clock. She had promised to meet the ladies for drinks at six-thirty, so she needed to get ready now. Too late for even a snack! There was no time to go back to the library. Besides, it would take hours to examine the collection of books. *If I only knew which one. Crap!* She reluctantly went back to her cabin and pulled out another dress and matching shoes from the closet.

Drinks with the ladies proved to be a delightful diversion. Beth hadn't a moment to think about books, the library, or bad haikus. Constance and Madeline were a lively pair and provided ample entertainment with raunchy stories about their dead husbands. Beth listened while she commandeered the bowl of crisps set on the table. When the server asked if she'd like more, she mumbled, "Yes," through a salty mouthful.

"There were occasions when he just *pretended* to sleep," Constance said. "But truly, he couldn't keep up with me. Still ... he *was* a doctor and was exhausted most nights anyways. I guess he had a valid excuse."

The ladies also gossiped about other passengers. "Honestly, did you see those earrings—fake by a mile!" And made suggestions on upcoming port calls, "Definitely tour Madeira, oodles to see. But Las Palmas ... just beaches, dear."

"Do you travel a lot on cruise ships?" Beth asked.

"Beth, don't ever refer to Cunard's ships as *cruise* ships. They are *luxury liners*," Madeline explained.

Beth nodded. "It's my first time."

"I'm sure it won't be your last," Constance said, raising her glass for a toast. "It's a glorious way to see the world."

Madeline agreed and grabbed Constance's free hand. "But imagine if we could have done this when we were younger?" Then she looked at Beth. "Us old birds have a hard time maneuvering sometimes."

Constance slapped her hand away. "Madeline, you have more crap than a Christmas goose." She leaned over to Beth as if telling a secret in a not-so-hushed voice, "This 'old bird' ran the London marathon last year. Don't believe a word she says." She took a big swallow of her wine and glared at her friend.

"Anyways," harrumphed Madeline, "I do envy you, dear. I spent my entire youth listening to my husband ... I'm almost glad he's gone."

Beth's eyebrows shot up in surprise.

Constance remarked, "You're a nasty old thing."

"Aren't I though?" Madeline cackled and she ordered another round of drinks.

Later, at Table 8, Beth resisted the urge to wipe her sweaty hands on her new dress (a pretty rose-colored silk with cap sleeves, no fringe) and remembered her earlier lessons with Glenn and Brigitte. She had squirted a hefty dose of her new perfume behind her ears, neck, and wrists like she'd seen her mom do years ago. Now, she could smell the fragrance as she handled her silverware and it gave her more confidence. Just like she had hoped.

She focused on her food. After only two days, she would never be able to eat a Hot Pocket again. And, what a show! She watched the staff perform their roles in a perfectly rehearsed play known as dinner. Appetizers, first course, second course, entrée, desserts, and petit fours ... no wonder it took over two hours to eat. It was all coordinated with drinks: pre-dinner cocktails, sparkling water, wine, coffee, and post-dinner digestives. Beth tried it all. And loved everything. Especially the coconut macaroon petit fours with chocolate drizzled over the top—her new favorite.

Sated, she leaned back in her chair. Fortunately, the conversation at Table 8 never waned, continuing its lively clip from the night before. The guests had plenty to discuss about their first day at sea. The Kippermans and Gundersons had relaxed by the pool and lamented their trouble finding deck chairs positioned in the cool November sun. Ian and the ladies voiced their dilemma about finding deck chairs in the shade. The other diners' conversations played like background music. Beth tuned most of it out, while she recited the haiku over like a chant in her head.

Which book could it be in? How many books would she need to read to find it?

"Nobody cares how many calories these have, do they?" asked Saul as he popped another petit four in his mouth. "Nobody—that's my name." Then he rubbed his eye.

Beth stopped her internal recitations. She stared at Saul as he licked his fingers free of chocolate. Suddenly, words began to click and fall into an organized pattern. Epic ... journey ... tests ... loyalty ... A glimmer of hope, a spark of possibility, formed in her mind. Her heart started beating wildly in her chest, but in a good way. An exciting, terrific way.

Beth quickly turned to Constance sitting next to her and asked, "What time does the library close?"

"I believe nine o'clock."

Crap. It was almost ten.

The evening ended after coffee and Beth said goodnight to her table-mates. Disappointed and frustrated, she stomped back to her cabin. She undressed, put on her *I (heart) New York* T-shirt, and stewed at her desk. She planned to be at the library as soon as it opened, which, according to a phone call with Raul the purser, was eight o'clock. What if her hypothesis was wrong? Then what? Not much she could do about it tonight.

She doodled on the Cunard memo pad. Then she jotted down her tablemates' names and a brief description to help her remember. Admittedly, it would get easier since she ate with them every night. Besides, they were all such characters.

She wrote:

Saul – very tall
Judy – wears lots of pink and red
Bob – loud and funny
Teresa – doesn't speak?
Constance – nice jewelry
Madeline – athletic and raunchy
Ian – proper English gentleman

She stretched and yawned, remembering her poor sleep from the evening before. The comfy bed beckoned. Beth crawled into it and arranged the massive marshmallow-looking pillows around her body. With the light switched off, she listened to the waves crashing against the side of the ship. What was missing? Grendel's low-level purrs punctuated by his occasional snorts. *Wait!* She squirmed out of her cocoon, grabbed the mini-Grendel from her underwear drawer, and jumped back into bed. Before Beth could think of another thing or consider an additional worry, the *Elizabeth* rocked her lovingly like a newborn and she immediately fell into a deep, dreamless sleep.

CHAPTER 10

Only five more minutes. Beth stood outside the ship's library and, with hands shielding her eyes from the glare of the overhead lights, she squinted to see where fiction was housed. Her nose made a smudge on the locked glass doors. She stepped back and tapped her foot impatiently, arms crossed. Inside, the librarian tidied newspapers and shelved books from the previous day's patrons.

Come on ... come on ...

After an early wake up (such a lovely sleep), brief shower (super nice shampoo), and wolfing down her breakfast (more than a muffin), Beth, like a racehorse in the blocks, was ready to sprint. The librarian finally came over to the doors and smiled at her through the glass.

"Good morning!" she said after unlocking both doors and propping them open.

"Morning. Can you tell me where fiction is?"

"My, you're an early bird! What can I help you find?"

"It's one my favorites. I hope you have it. *The Odyssey* by Homer?"

"Of course! You're in luck. It was returned yesterday. I really should order another copy." The librarian walked to the left corner of the room and plucked a book from the bottom row. "It's a classic. Anything else?"

"No, this is great. Thanks."

Beth took the book and sat down in an oversized chair facing a window with ocean views. Excitement trickled through her and made her heart flutter a little faster.

She inspected the book. The pages' edges were dusted in gold. A handsome edition, which is why a dust jacket protected it. She flipped open the cover to find 'Property of The Queen Elizabeth' stamped inside. The pages were heavy and crisp.

Beth paged through it expertly and found the reference she was searching for in chapter 9.408.

So, you ask me the name I'm known by, Cyclops?

I will tell you. But first you must give me a guest-gift as you've promised.

Nobody – that's my name.

Nobody – so my mother and father call me, all my friends.

But he boomed back at me from his ruthless heart,

'Nobody? I'll eat Nobody last of all his friends –

I'll eat the others first! That's my gift to you!"

Without Saul referring to himself as "Nobody" last night, Beth would have never guessed Homer. Even though it completely made sense. Then when he rubbed his eye? Ding-ding-ding! We have a winner! The answer *had* to be the heroic Greek poem of Odysseus sailing back home fighting challenges along the way. An original quest story if there ever was one. Beth hoped she wouldn't have as many dangers to face. Cyclops, Circe, and deadly sirens? *No thanks.*

She flipped through the rest of the book. Nothing. She didn't see any writing in the margins, no notes. Nothing stuck in between pages.

She closed the book and sat with it in her lap. The adrenaline from finding it continued to shoot through her corpuscles. Her hands stroked the outside cover and its binding. How many times had she read *The Odyssey*? Aunt Ethel had given Beth her first copy, a collector's edition in blue leather, when she was eleven. Yet most of Aunt Ethel's presents were in the shape of experiences or 'adventures' as she'd like to say. Trips to the zoo to make faces at the monkeys, a book signing with a famous author, volunteering at a cat shelter. "Just think, all these poor pusses have no home," Ethel had said, forever imprinting it into Beth's memory for when she picked out her own cat. She had chosen the one least likely to find a family, Grendel.

Okay Homer, I'm here. Help me find Aunt Ethel's will. It had to be here. She held the book to her chest and hugged it. It just had to be.

More memories of Aunt Ethel. How she always wanted the best for Beth and Vicky. Her desperation to keep her family together, even when it trickled down to two. But Beth's singular memory of Aunt Ethel was her laugh. A big cackling laugh for everything: a joke (even bad ones), when she embarrassed herself (which was often), or unfamiliar situations (seldom, but who would know?). Beth had asked her why she laughed so much once, and she replied, "It makes others happy, too." Beth agreed. You couldn't help but laugh *at* or even *with* Aunt Ethel. Beth wished she had that ability. There were lots of things Beth wished she could do, mostly everything on the ever-expanding List.

She looked down, disappointed in herself. Between the spine and the book's dust jacket was a flash of red. Something was wedged inside. She opened the book to give the cover more leeway and shook it. Nothing.

She carefully removed the dust jacket and turned the spine toward her. A miniature red envelope, the size of an extra-large postage stamp, was taped securely to the edge.

Oh! Oh! Oh! It was like finding a carefully hidden, plastic Easter egg. Or better yet, finding one in the heat of the summer, long forgotten, with a quarter still inside. Beth quickly, but carefully, unstuck the envelope from the spine. She slid her fingernail under the flap to open it.

Inside she found two things: a tiny metal ship and a small piece of paper folded in half. On the paper was itsy-bitsy writing ... so small Beth couldn't read it. She squinted and held it up to the light. Three lines of text, but she couldn't make out any of the words. She removed her glasses. Still nothing. She reassembled the book, zipped both the ship and the paper carefully in a compartment of her tote bag, and looked out the window at the ocean.

She'd found it. Not the will—but something. Flutters of elation in her belly made her take a few quick breaths. This was exciting. A good exciting. She rose and approached the librarian at the front counter.

"Do you have a magnifying glass?" she asked.

"I do, for maps." She handed it over from a drawer in her desk. Beth took it back to the chair, retrieved the note from her bag and tried to read it again. Still too small. She returned the magnifying glass back to the desk and left the library. After a few steps, she had an idea. In her wanderings about the ship last night, she had found someone who may be able to help.

Passing by the Queens Room, Beth paused briefly to watch a ballroom dance lesson. Two professional dance instructors patiently led a pack of over-eager students through carefully controlled movements of the tango.

"Gentlemen, you are the matadors. Ladies, you are the capes," said the instructor. He demonstrated with large, sweeping arm movements. As the men puffed out their chests, the ladies twittered. Beth watched Bob and Terry Gunderson stumble through the steps. Bob, not entirely ungraceful with his large girth, tried his best to harness Spanish machismo. But Teresa, who moved like a mini-Frankenstein, looked nothing like a cape. All in all, the students made up for their inaccuracies with enthusiasm.

Beth hadn't danced in years. She remembered how, as kids, she and Vicky would grab hands and spin around in a circle while the radio blasted. Vicky would scream, "Don't let go!" as the centrifugal force would throw them into mismatched living room furniture if hands dared unclasp. As they spun, they'd throw their heads back and laugh, hair fanning out behind them. They would have had a field day on this gigantic dance floor with nothing to get in their way. Beth had forgotten they used to dance like that. It was so long ago. Why was she having so many memories on this ship?

She imagined Vicky was now married to a rich man with a paunch and imposing bald spot who sold tech stocks. He probably brought her boxes of fine Belgian truffles while she reclined on a satin chaise watching *Jeopardy* in a pink, faux-fur-trimmed peignoir. Her husband probably loved her. Whatever.

Beth walked by the Golden Lion pub and mentally noted a lunch option for later. A flight of stairs led up to the shops. Standing outside the jewelry store, she recognized the employee from last night. With distinguished gray hair at his temples and impeccably dressed in a tailored black suit, starched white shirt, and silver tie, the man was helping an older couple at the counter. Beth entered the store, pretended to browse, and simultaneously eavesdropped.

"Madam, it looks like you're in danger of losing a stone," the man explained. The couple turned toward each other with grave concern.

"Really? Which one? Not the *big* one?" The woman was dressed in a drab gray pantsuit and looked like a small battleship. Her husband was unusually tall and lanky. Standing next to each other, they looked like the number ten.

"It's a simple repair. I can adjust the prong on the center stone. If you don't mind waiting?"

"Of course not! I would *hate* to lose my emerald," she said loudly. "We bought it in Colombia. It's a treasure!" As she clasped her hands to her chest in dramatic fashion, the sparkle of colorful stones set in additional rings catching the overhead lights. Other customers glared at her from the corners of the store, as if her unseemly volume disturbed their shopping for luxury items.

"It should only be moment," he replied.

Beth watched as he took out a velvet pad and placed it on the glass counter. Then he opened a drawer and removed a pair of pliers and a jeweler's loupe. He placed the loupe in his right eye and squinted. The pressure held the loupe in place as he held the ring with one hand and the pliers in the other. In less than a minute, he was finished.

He cleaned the ring with a soft cloth and handed it back to her. "Madam, it's ready."

"Oh Daniel, you glorious man! How wonderful! I would have been devastated, just *devastated* to lose the stone."

Her husband murmured, "Devastated."

"My pleasure, madam." Daniel lowered his eyes and Beth watched him struggle not to show an unintended smile creeping at the corners of his mouth.

"Now, we'll just have to come back and visit that ruby bracelet later, won't we?" she asked her husband as they exited. "It looked so lonely."

The door closed behind them and Beth made her way to the counter.

"Hi. I don't have a Columbian emerald, but I have something I'd like you to look at." She took out the red envelope and removed the small metal ship.

"What would you like to know?"

"If it's valuable. I'm Beth by the way."

"Daniel, and it's my pleasure to assist you." He looked at the ship with the jeweler's loupe and pronounced, "It's genuine sterling silver. Not rare. It's a *Queen Elizabeth* souvenir charm. We used to sell them onboard."

"You don't sell them now?"

He shook his head. "Nowadays it's all about Pandora. Charm bracelets were popular a few decades ago. Just like the one you're wearing."

"Really, is that what this is?" Beth looked down at her right wrist. She shook the bracelet. Links glinted.

"Yes, the open links make it easy to attach charms. But yours looks quite empty. May I attach this charm for you?"

"Oh! Could you?" Beth wondered if more charms were in her future. How many more clues would she have to find? She watched Daniel take out his pliers again and a small plastic box filled with jewelry findings. He selected a small, silver ring and quickly attached the charm to ring and ring to bracelet.

"There. I would recommend having the ring soldered when you return to the States."

"How do you know I'm from the States?" Beth asked.

"Your accent."

Beth laughed. "Okay, I'm sure it gives me away. Hey, can I borrow that magnifying glass for a minute?"

She pulled out the itty-bitty note, placed the loupe in her own eye, and tried to read the writing on the paper.

"Beth, you have it backward." Daniel took the loupe from her eye and flipped it around, "Try it this way."

Beth squinted, trying to keep the loupe in place as she read. Neatly hand-written on the paper she could make out the following:

Madeira, so fine.
try Oliveira's and sing
loudly, "I LOVE WINE!"

"Well," muttered Beth, "at least this one rhymes."

"Pardon?"

"It's a little game my aunt is playing. Kind of like a treasure hunt. How much do I owe you?"

"No charge, it was my pleasure," Daniel said, his eyes now fully crinkled in the corners.

"Thanks." Beth left the shop and backtracked to the pub for lunch and to mull over her next clue.

The Golden Lion was fashioned as a traditional British pub with forest green patterned carpet throughout. Heavy wood and brass chandeliers swung from low tin ceilings. The leather club chairs and booths with dark wood tables were almost completely full of passengers. Beth found an empty table for two and sat down. From her vantage point, she saw a well-stocked bar complete with scotch, whisky and ales, all originating from the UK. For the Brits, it was a refuge. For Beth, it was a glimpse of British tradition playing itself out.

A small stage was located in the front for entertainment. Beth had heard music the previous night, but this afternoon a trivia contest was underway. The entertainment director read questions over a microphone. Teams penciled in their best guesses on slips of paper while they ate lunch and sipped their dusty ales.

"Okay folks. Here's number five. Question number five. From the hit show in the 1970s, what were the names of the *Charlie's Angels*?" The lunch crowd discussed with each other before committing answers to the game form. Some were loud enough for other competitors to hear.

Sabrina, Jill, and Kelly, thought Beth. *I've watched enough reruns.* In a quiet corner, Constance and Ian ate lunch together. They had pints of red ale at the ready. While Beth waited to place her order, she observed their mannerisms and expressions as they sat deep in conversation.

Constance sparkled in a variety of ways. First, her smile. Always happy, Beth never saw a frown or grimace on her face. If you needed cheering up, just sit down next to Constance. Spinning tales, all side-crackingly funny and most at her own expense, Constance had the gift of a seasoned storyteller. Her clothes were a jumble of fashion; expensive designer jeans paired with a Beatles T-shirt (but then again it was probably vintage and worth a fortune), but her jewelry was grand, ostentatious, and glorious to admire. In the last few days, Constance had worn a huge blue sapphire pendant the size of a baseball, a diamond cocktail ring surrounded by multicolored gems, and a pair of antique jade earrings from the Shang dynasty that China was probably still pissed about.

Beth made up a backstory for her. Call it an occupational hazard, but she couldn't help but fill in the blanks.

Constance's husband had gifted her a piece of exquisite jewelry on each of their anniversaries. Though he has been deceased for the past two decades, it still pains her to speak of him. But not how you'd think. Her collection of jewels represent terrible memories of their life together. A marriage fraught with undeserving reproaches. Awful and hurtful. Yes ... he criticized her cooking. Should Yorkshire pudding require a straw? Are these mashed potatoes or wall spackle? Such an awful spouse, he bought her jewelry to apologize. Whenever she looked down at her rings, she considered pawning them to buy a gun. And her bracelets, a bottle of poison ... or maybe ... okay stop. She's a nice lady, don't ruin it.

Someone cleared his throat. A server stood next to her with his order book and tray. He explained the pub offered three lunch options, all traditional British fare. On his recommendation, Beth ordered the fish and chips and an Old Speckled Hen.

After the waiter left, Beth imagined Ian's story.

He was a tenured literary professor who eschewed the Booker Prize and collected fifteenth-century erotic poetry written by women named Virginia. But on Friday afternoons, Ian's academic compatriots congregated at his old stone cottage in Yorkshire, for tea and scones while they bantered over seminal works of literature. On the weekends, he would go for a constitution with his terrier (named Shakespeare) down a cobblestone lane, swing his distinguished walking stick, and tip his hat to passers-by. At the end of the block, Ian would meet Bob Cratchett and they would complain about terrible working conditions for the poor ...

Her meal arrived. She glanced over at Constance and Ian; they had ordered the exact same lunch. Constance saw her and waved. Beth waved back. She felt a little sheepish, making up implausible stories, so she stopped her musings and listened to the trivia contest instead.

"Number ten," the announcer said. "Question number ten. Our final question. Who was the author of *Jane Eyre*? Come on folks, it's a classic." Collective groans arrived from all corners of the pub. The guesses were mostly wrong. *Ian should know this one.* But it didn't look like he was playing, as he was still deep in conversation with Constance.

It's Charlotte Brontë, Beth answered silently as she shoveled mushy peas into her mouth. Kind of interesting. The fish was good too, nicely breaded and deep-fried to a golden color. Her French fries—okay, *chips*—were salted and extra crispy. She tried some malt vinegar, sprinkling it over the chips as the other diners did, and decided she had a new favorite meal—authentic UK fish and chips. Not surprisingly, with all the glorious food she was tasting, her favorite meal changed by the day. However, her ale was flat and warm.

An inconvenient shadow covered her plate. Beth looked up from her lunch. A small person stood in front of her. It was the elderly lady dressed in black from the pre-departure lounge in Southampton. Was she wearing the same dress? With one hand, she leaned on an ebony cane with a silver handle, the other on the chair in front of Beth.

"Is this seat occupied?" Her voice sounded like an angel's, sweet and melodious.

"Uh, no. I was just finishing up." Beth wiped her mouth with a napkin.

"You don't need to leave; we can get to know one another." The lady pulled back the chair and sat with a determined plop. She hooked her cane on the tabletop. It swung back and forth as if it were a large metronome. "My name is Mabel." Her eyes sparkled from behind her rhinestone glasses.

"Hi, Mabel. I'm Beth." She reached out her hand.

Mabel shook Beth's fingertips. "Beth, you say? Is that short for Elizabeth?"

"Yes."

"You should use your given name. It's such a pretty one." Mabel reached for a menu and reviewed it like a promising tax return. "Where's your home?"

"New York."

"Traveling alone?"

"Yes, I'm on vacation. And you?"

"The same. I try to find ways to amuse myself, even at my old age," Mabel replied. She put down the menu and looked at Beth directly, who picked at the tape on the sides of her glasses.

The announcer interrupted their conversation to give answers to the trivia questions. The crowd either celebrated or booed, based on whether they answered correctly. Beth got the *Charlie's Angels* right.

But when he got to question ten, a small disagreement broke out.

A persistent group of participants claimed it was Emily Brontë, not Charlotte. One guest tried to be comical and said it was J.K. Rowling. The announcer looked flustered and continued to point at his answers. He looked over to Ian, sitting in his corner and appealed to him. Ian, stood up, straightened his tweed vest, smoothed his mustache and pronounced with great authority, as if he were presenting in a lecture hall, that yes, the answer was indeed Charlotte Brontë. Some people hissed, most clapped. Nonplussed, Ian gave a dignified bow and sat back in his chair. Beth laughed, watching.

"Games are fun, aren't they," Mabel said as a statement rather than a question.

Beth nodded in agreement. She took a bite of fish and promptly coughed. And coughed. And coughed. Then she sneezed. People glanced over at their table. She was creating quite the ruckus.

"Are you alright?" Mabel patted her arm.

Beth grabbed a glass of water and drained it and coughed again. "I must have eaten some pepper or something." She wiped her lips. Warmth spread from her throat to her face. Her face flushed. She patted her forehead with a napkin.

Mabel continued, "You're not sick, are you? Poor, dear. You don't have Covid, do you? It's extremely contagious." Several more heads turned to witness Beth's answer. Whispers of, "Covid," begin to swirl around the room.

"No, I'm not *sick*. It's just something I ate." Then she started coughing again.

"Well, that's how it starts. With coughing. It could be *Covid*," Mabel said even louder. Conversations became frenzied, chairs scraped the floor as people headed toward the pub's exit, which promptly clogged. What was going on? Was it a bomb scare?

The server suddenly reappeared at Beth's side. In his hand, he held a cell phone.

"Ma'am, I need you to come with me," he said. "Immediately."

CHAPTER 11

"This is insane." Beth hurried to catch up with the server's long strides out of the pub and into an elevator. "Where are you taking me?"

He turned to her and whispered, "It's just that ... even if there's a *mention* of COVID ... we take precautions. It's ship's policy."

"Are you kidding? I just swallowed some pepper."

"I'm sorry." He shrugged his shoulders apologetically. "The whole ship can be quarantined." The look on the server's face convinced Beth. With his eyes wide and brow crinkled into worrisome wrinkles, he wasn't kidding. "I could lose my job." He pushed Deck 0.

Down in the ship's bowels, the server stopped in front of a white steel door with a red cross painted on it. He practically pushed Beth inside the utilitarian medical office.

"I called ahead," the server said before rushing away.

A nurse asked Beth to fill out a questionnaire while she waited for the doctor.

Chills? No.

Headache? No.

Muscle aches? No.

Fatigue? "Well, I'm still jetlagged," Beth mumbled with a thermometer in her mouth. She checked off response boxes to questions they really had no business asking and handed the clipboard back to the nurse. Cunard travel brochures were stacked on a table. Maybe these were left strategically for passengers to book their next cruise? They wouldn't make her leave the ship, would they? If so, how? Would she have to swim home?

Finally, the doctor came out, dressed in mask and gown as if suited up for an Ebola virus outbreak. He led her inside an exam room, careful not to touch her. After an awkward fifteen-minute interview concerning Beth's intimate bodily functions, he cleared her of any possible plague.

"If you start feeling poorly, in *any* way, please come back. If a virus ever runs through the ship, it could be disastrous: ports of call re-routed, guests quarantined in their staterooms, even dinner cancelled," he said.

"Really, you'd cancel dinner?" Geez. She was duly warned. On top of everything, the physician made her sign a form before she could leave.

While she waited for the elevator, Beth realized how important it was to be on her game. She couldn't get sick or hurt. She had to find the next clue. She had to find the will. Beth looked down and shook the new charm on her bracelet and wondered what awaited her in Madeira. She hoped they didn't over-pepper their food.

"Summertime, and the livin' is easy. Fish are jumpin' and the cotton is high. Oh, your daddy's rich and your ma is good-lookin'. So, hush little baby, don't you cry."

The baritone inside cabin #6077 sang not only richly, but with feeling. Beth stood outside and waited for him to finish. She contemplated applauding, but Roberto suddenly opened the cabin door. His face turned a bright pink as he wheeled a vacuum cleaner outside.

"Roberto, that was amazing! I didn't know you could sing."

"Madam is too kind." He glanced downward. His black hair shone like oiled steel in the overhead lights.

"Seriously, how do you know *Summertime*?"

"My mama got a record player from Goodwill. The records that came with it were all musicals. I grew up listening to them." He shrugged matter-of-factly.

"Where are you from?"

"The Philippines. My family is still there."

"I live in New York City and I've seen lots of Broadway shows. You're just as good."

Roberto blushed again, but this time, a smile crept over his face.

"You should think about auditioning there."

"Oh, I don't think so." He went back inside the cabin to exchange dirty towels for clean ones.

She followed him inside. "Hey, Roberto ... what do you know about Covid?"

He immediately turned and reached past her to close the door behind them. "*Shhhh* ... don't say that word!"

"Tell me about it; I was just interrogated in the infirmary because I coughed at lunch. I'm not sick."

"I know. I'd be the first to find out." Roberto nodded toward the bathroom. "We have to let our supervisors know if we see anything ... uh ..."

"Suspicious?" Beth answered for him while wrinkling her nose.

"That's it."

"I definitely don't want your job."

He laughed. "There *are* days ..." Then he held up last night's evening dress draped over the back of the desk chair. "Is this soup?" He pointed accusingly to a stain on the front of the gown.

"Yes."

"I'll take care of it." Roberto took the dress with him and closed the cabin door.

After her infirmary debacle, Beth had made a quick stop at the sundry shop. Her complimentary British Air toothpaste was empty and she needed aspirin (no, not for Covid). Also, what the hell, a bright red lipstick called *Harlot*. Beth stowed her small bag of purchases in the bathroom and placed the aspirin next to her unopened Zoloft.

Back to business. She took out the new clue and copied it into her notebook. But as much as she tried to tease out the haiku's meaning, one word kept troubling her: sing. *Oh please, no.* Aunt Ethel wouldn't do that to her, would she? Particularly, since singing was on The List. She wasn't sure what it all meant, but maybe her booked tour in Madeira was part of it.

She took the Cunard envelope containing her tour tickets from the desk drawer, sat outside on the balcony, and patted her stomach contentedly. Yum. Fish and chips ... with mushy peas. The Golden Lion pub really delivered an excellent lunch. Could she go back? Would they remember her? How embarrassing. She should probably play it safe and stick with the Lido buffet.

Tomorrow was another day at sea. Beth decided she could be at sea forever. She sat on the balcony and studied the varying shades of blue. The azure sky, the sapphire ocean, the cobalt waves. So many hues. Occasionally, another ship would be off in the distance, typically a cargo ship or oil freighter. But for the most part, the *Queen Elizabeth* was alone on the never-ending ocean. Beth's cabin was on the starboard side, which meant glorious afternoon sun. She propped her feet up on the second chair, tilted her head back toward the sunshine, and breathed in salty warm air.

She closed her eyes.

It wasn't lost on her she hadn't felt the oh-so-familiar twinges of an impending anxiety attack since she boarded the ship. Maybe all the activities and distractions kept them at bay. Although that was a reason to celebrate, an anticipatory feeling made her pause. It was inevitable, but when? She almost wished it would happen, just so she could get it over with. Regardless, she allowed her thoughts to meander pleasantly, without any prescribed direction or medication.

About an hour later, Beth woke up with a start. Seagulls cried and called from below. She stood up and stretched as the birds circled. Suddenly, small round shapes appeared beneath the water. Then fins. Yikes, were those sharks? Beth leaned carefully over the balcony railing (as far as she was capable) to see closer. With an explosion of white water, several dolphins leapt from the sea. One after another, they took turns hurdling in and out of the waves as they swam parallel to the ship.

"Dolphins, look dolphins!" Beth cried and pointed. She dropped the forgotten envelope from her hands and watched as it fell below. *Holy Crap.*

She leaned gingerly over the railing to see the balcony beneath her. A man rubbed the top of his blond head. He looked upwards.

"Ahoy, there!" he said, "Missing something?" He held up her envelope.

"I'm so sorry! I'll be right down. Wait ... what cabin are you in?"

"5077."

"Just a second!"

What a nincompoop! She left her cabin, ran down the stairs to Deck 5, and found the cabin directly below hers. The door opened before she could knock.

"Hi." A sandy-haired man with blue eyes welcomed her inside. "I think this may be yours? I'm Mike."

"Thanks! I'm Beth." They shook hands. "Those are my tour tickets."

"Now, that would've been a shame." He handed the envelope to her. "This is my partner, Alex." He motioned to a man seated on a couch stacked with empty luggage. Beth recognized both men from the Cunard pre-departure lounge in Southampton. She also noted their cabin was identical to hers, except for the artwork over the couch. A different seascape but painted in similar nautical colors. Clothing was strewn about as if they were still unpacking. Shoes littered the floor and ties hung from a floor lamp.

"Hi." She tried to think of something interesting and engaging to say, but only came up with the standard, "Are you enjoying the cruise so far?"

"After tonight we will." Mike laughed. "We're getting married. So, nerves are a little frayed right now."

"Congratulations! Do you have family here to celebrate?"

"My new in-laws-to-be," Alex answered.

"Which is *plenty*," Mike said. They all chuckled. Each man was in his late thirties, handsome and fit. Dressed in khaki pants and polo shirts, they looked like a Macy's ad.

"Are you with someone?" Mike asked.

"Like a person? Oh, no." Beth's face began to burn.

"Lucky. You get the whole cabin to yourself."

Alex rolled his eyes. "Keep talking like that mister and *you'll* have the whole cabin to yourself!" He gestured to the piles of clothing. "I'm marrying a slob."

"Yes, but I'm *your* slob," Mike said, reaching out to grab Alex's hand.

Beth smiled. "Well, I hope you have a nice day."

"Thanks. Hey, we're having a little party at the Yacht Club tonight—you should stop by for a drink. We don't know anyone on-board and we're practically neighbors!" Mike said.

Without thinking too much, Beth said, "Okay. I will. Good luck ... and congratulations again." She left the cabin and headed back upstairs.

Wow. In two days, she'd been invited for drinks and now a party. She considered using her phone's calendar app to keep it all straight. Instead, she sat at her desk and organized her social engagements, business-like, by writing in her notebook: *Mike and Alex's wedding reception at Yacht Club tonight*.

It was only day three of the cruise, but it didn't escape Beth that Cunard excelled at organization, which she appreciated. She liked routines and order. Each evening, she found an activities program for the following day, a summary of world news events (complete with American football scores), and a brochure detailing upcoming ports, all artfully arranged on her bed. Plus, the morning breakfast menu and a chocolate. Beth decided to have breakfast in her cabin tomorrow. She ticked off her choices: coffee, orange juice, eggs, bacon, and a blueberry muffin. On second thought, she scratched off the muffin.

She glanced over at the bed. It looked like a cloud. A big cloud. A big, fluffy cloud. Roberto had tucked the mini-Grendel in amongst the pillows, like a rajah.

Now lounging across the king-size bed, propped up with multiple pillows, Beth spread out the tickets from the rescued envelope. Much better. Madeira, La Palma, Tenerife, Grand Canaria, and Lisbon ... five ports of call. She wondered if there would be five more clues to find or riddles to solve.

The day after tomorrow, the *Queen Elizabeth* would dock in Madeira, Portugal. *How exciting!* Another passport stamp to add to Beth's grow-ing collection of one. She found the Madeira brochure and read the one-page summary regarding its history, exports, and tourist activities.

Madeira was an island, colonized by the Portuguese in the 1400s. The ship would dock at Funchal, its main harbor, for the day. Her tour, 'Es-sential Madeira,' was rated *active* on the activity scale, which translated to plenty of walking. For six hours, an English-speaking tour guide would lead a small group to see Funchal's highlights: the Botanical Gardens, a cable car ride, Santa Clara Monastery, some cathedrals, and Madeira wine tasting at ... Oliveira's Wine Bar.

Jackpot! How easy was this going to be? Aunt Ethel had this complete-ly organized.

The instructions were very clear; the tour group would meet at 8:30 a.m. in the Queens Room and return to the ship at 4:30 p.m. The ship sailed at five o'clock sharp. Cunard recommended leaving passports in cabin safes. Her ship's ID was the only thing required to re-board. *Crap.* That meant no passport stamp.

And still ... there was singing involved.

Okay, singing wasn't *specifically* on The List, but it fell under the sub-header of anything-to-do-with-embarrassing-her-self-in-front-of-a-large-group-of-people. Which she should've been used to by now and it's not like she hadn't humiliated herself already on the ship. Falling up the stairs at dinner. Not knowing what silverware to use. Being sent to the infirmary like a school child. But when it was purposeful, knowing she would make herself look like a bonafide fool? *No thanks.*

Yet, Beth felt a small bit of relief because she wouldn't have to search the entire ship. All she needed to do was show up for her tour and she'd get the next clue. Since tomorrow was another full day at sea, she figured she could enjoy the ship a little more. Maybe go to the pool? Get a book from the library? It could be a *real* vacation. She said a little thanks to her aunt for making this relatively painless, even though this whole fiasco was Ethel's fault to begin with.

She wanted to call Mr. Watkins and give him an update but remembered that phoning New York six time zones away would be rude this early. She pulled out the ship's map. An internet café, Connexions, was on Deck 1 by the purser's desk. Perfect. She wouldn't have to peck out coherent sentences on her phone.

She found it easily and used her onboard credit for an internet plan. The small room held ten individual computer stations. Most passengers were updating their social media accounts. Madeline sat in the corner with reading glasses balanced at the end of her nose, typing furiously like it was her dissertation. Besides a helpful tech person, a large scanner in the room also doubled as a photocopier. Beth found a free computer station and sat down to write some emails.

Hi Mr. Watkins,

I'm now officially on the scavenger hunt. I found the first clue in the ship's library. My next clue is in Madeira. But I'm sure you know all this. Just keeping you posted, AS I PROMISED.

Thanks!

Beth

There was no email from Frank. She assumed he was hard at work finishing Governor Sharp's book. She felt a little (just a little) guilty about dumping it on him. Instead, she wrote:

Hey Frank,

How's Grendel?

Beth

And a note to her college roommate:

Gwennie!

How are you and the girls?

It's been way too long and we really need to get together soon. I'm feeling like I can do another trip, maybe Disney this time?

Love and hugs,

Beth

And a message to her counselor:

Hi Dr. Joan,

I'm going to miss next week's appointment because I'm on a ship! Now heading to the Mediterranean! Surprised? Yeah, me too.

It's a long story, but I'm taking lots of notes so I can tell you all about it later. Also, guess what? I haven't had to take a pill. Not one! Aren't you proud of me?

You can email me, but I wouldn't call because it's really expensive.

Best Wishes,

Beth

———

At dinner that night, Constance showcased a new hair style, which received compliments by the Table 8 diners. Her silver hair was styled into a fancy twist, intricately balanced at the top of her head. The braided coils shone like snake scales in the low light.

She patted the up-do appreciatively and remarked, "Olga is amazing. A magician!"

Beth wore an amethyst dress with silver flowers attached to the shoulder straps. The crystals centered in each flower sparkled when she moved. The dress cinched at the waist and the full skirt had oodles of pleats. *Perfect for twirling later on the Yacht Club's dance floor.* Optimistically, she straightened her glasses on her nose and selected her dinner courses with more authority. Practice makes perfect. She placed her napkin in her lap.

Over the main course, the table's conversation turned to previous travels. Best cities, most memorable museums, great restaurants—it seemed as if everyone had a story to share.

Constance looked at Madeline. "Remember Baden-Baden?"

Madeline raised her eyes to the heavens and shook her head.

"Oh, that was memorable," she groaned.

"Trust me, I'll never look at you the same way again," Constance said. The two ladies cackled.

"Okay, now you're going to have to tell us the story," Beth requested.

"Well," Constance took a sip of wine before starting, "the two of us were on a Rhine River cruise. It was lovely. Castles on either side of the river, beautiful vineyards climbing from the water up the sides of mountains. We were on a smaller ship of course, maybe a hundred passengers. Afterwards, we decided to spend a few days in Baden-Baden before we flew home. I had read about it being a restorative spa town with healthy waters ... a place to go to rejuvenate and feel young again. How could one miss *that* opportunity?"

Madeline interjected, "Rubbish. It was all your bloody idea. I had nothing to do with it."

Constance sipped her wine and paused, glancing at her captured audience. "On the first day, we visited the bath house—the Friedrichsbad. We arrived and the front desk informs us it's a 'mixed' day. I thought it meant the water would be hot AND cold. But noooo ..." She stopped. Madeline laughed so loud Constance had to increase the volume of her story.

"It meant men and women *together*. Of course, we didn't find out until *after* we paid and realized it was a *naked* spa. We couldn't wear our bathing togs. It was *verboten*."

Glenn appeared to clear plates and his eyes widened. Everyone at the table tossed their heads backward and laughed. Bob even spit out some of his wine.

"What did you do?" Beth asked.

"We got naked. It turns out after four hours bathing in seventeen different pools, I got used to it. Besides, I looked pretty good for my age, considering the other people I saw. Ironically, my self-confidence shot up a few notches." Constance finished the story with the last swallow of her wine.

"I agree, you never really know who your friends are until they see you naked," Madeline said. Beth was glad she didn't have that many friends. Glenn refilled their glasses and left as quickly as he could without sprinting.

"Then you know they're *true* friends," Constance said, "for life." She toasted her friend with another full glass of wine.

After dinner, Beth said goodnight to Table 8 and took an elevator up to Deck 10. As soon as the doors opened, dance tunes boomed from inside the Yacht Club. Outside, a classy sign proclaimed "Private Party" in fanciful script. She tiptoed inside the dark room and squinted to see a bar, small dance floor, upholstered chairs and couches scattered throughout. The happy couple greeted guests as they entered.

"Beth, you made it!" Mike said. He grabbed her in a bear hug.

"How'd it go?" she said into his shoulder before he released her.

"We're married! I can't believe it. I was so nervous, but now I'm over the moon!" He showed her the ring on his left hand.

"Old married couple now!" said Alex. Smiling, he showed Beth his ring, too. "And by a Commodore, no less!" They both looked handsome in their spiffy tuxedos.

"Here, have a drink." Mike motioned a server over. "We have martinis and daquiris, take your pick. Mom, Dad, this is Beth. Our upstairs neighbor."

Beth took a daiquiri off the tray and turned to say hello to Mike's parents. "You must be very proud. A wedding at sea ... what a memorable way to get married."

Mike's parents smiled woodenly in response and stood as stiff as Quakers sipping lemonade from straws. Mom was dressed in a long, matronly chiffon gown, melon-colored, with sleeves to her wrists. Dad wore a tan polyester suit. They looked like the cast for a *Little House on the Prairie* reunion. It seemed their mouths couldn't shape into smiles. Beth found out later, they weren't Quakers, but Mormon.

The Backstreet Boys' "Larger Than Life" blared from the speakers and more guests got up to dance. It was a much younger crowd in the Yacht Club, more fifty and sixty-year-olds versus the septuagenarians waltzing in the Queens Room a few decks below. Plus, the disc jockey took requests from this century.

Somehow, both Ian and Madeline had finagled an invite. They sat at a couch for two, their heads bowed toward each other and tried to talk over the loud music. *Ian sure gets around.* Beth watched as she stood next to Mike's parents and nursed her drink. But she stopped when the next song came on.

An electric guitar. A simple thudding drumbeat.

"Na-na-na-na, na-na, na ..." P!nk's voice exploded from the speakers. *Oh no.*

"Na-na-na-na, na-na ..."

The dance floor got crowded, but everyone kept their elbows in check while they danced and sang along to P!nk's rousing "So What." Beth could hear Ian exclaim, "Stupendous!" as he held Madeline in a close foxtrot.

Crap, the chorus ... not the chorus.

Now everyone was dancing except for Beth and Mike's parents. Then *they* left to dance. Beth stood all alone next to the DJ.

"C'mon Beth!" Alex shouted over the din. He waved at her.

I'm alright ...

People pumped their fists in the air and hopped up and down.

I'm just fine ...

Should she go? Would anyone realize she couldn't dance at all, but just spin? Would it be rude to ignore Alex? Maybe she could pretend she didn't hear him. The prickly feeling started in her hands.

"Beth, c'mon!" Alex yelled again from the dance floor.

People shouted the lyrics at the top of their lungs.

P!nk wouldn't stay back. P!nk would dance. P!nk's a bad ass.

Beth finished the rest of her drink in one swallow and put her empty glass down on a side table. Then she bowed her head and bee-lined into the dancing fray. No one knew her anyways.

Hours and hours later, the DJ seemed to have exhausted his entire 90s repertoire and transitioned back in time to the 80s. The bass thumped so loud, wine glasses hanging behind the bar clinked together in rhythm. Mike's parents disappeared sometime in between Joan Jett's "Do You Wanna Touch?" and Madonna's "Like a Virgin." It must have been too much to handle. Everyone else partied like it was 1999.

After a few too many daiquiris, Beth's enthusiastic spinning made her dress fan out like a demented flower. During the extended mix of "You Spin Me 'Round," her glasses flew off her nose into a silver bowl of mixed nuts at a nearby table. A good-looking bartender found some tape and hastily repaired the temple to the frame. Now both sides had tape affixed at the corners, which gave her the look of a comical, horn-rimmed owl. Which apparently the bartender found attractive because he asked if she was traveling solo.

At around two in the morning, Beth pawed through the pile of discarded shoes heaped in the middle of the dance floor to find her own pair. Sweaty and tired, she said goodnight to her hosts. *How much fun was that?* Not to mention, she could cross out an item from The List: dancing in public. She *was* a rockstar! Dr. Joan would be so proud.

"What a great wedding day!" Alex said as he kissed Beth's moist cheek before she left, "Thanks for coming."

Mike waved from a chair, feet propped up on another, bow tie undone. He blew her a kiss.

Beth hobbled barefoot back to her cabin. The passageways were eerily quiet; most passengers had turned in hours ago. She didn't see a soul.

Outside the cabin door, she found a plain envelope and a shiny gold card wedged behind the numbered acrylic sign. "The Royal Spa invites you with an exclusive offer ..." It was a promotion advertising salon and spa services during tomorrow's day at sea.

Beth opened her door, threw her shoes inside, and looked in the bathroom mirror. She removed her dilapidated glasses. Her hazel eyes scrutinized her features. Nice lips, good eyebrows, clear skin. She had some redeeming qualities. Maybe they just needed some freshening up. As if on cue, her hair flopped into her eyes. *Maybe it's time for some professional help.*

She sat on the bed and opened the envelope. Written on a piece of Cunard note paper, it read:

GO TO HELL

What a shitty way to end a lovely evening.

CHAPTER 12

Eighteen Years Ago

B eth sat alone in the reception area of the New Jersey state police department just outside greater Newark. With her head resting in her hands, water drops pinged the floor as if there was a leaky pipe somewhere. A constant drip ... drip ... drip. Water trickled from her hair and made small puddles, one surrounding each shoe. The back of the plastic chair squeaked whenever she moved. So, she stopped moving.

At first, Beth had considered Lieutenant Bloom's call a prank, someone's idea of a terrible joke. She was almost a quarter way back to school when her cell phone went off. It startled her because no one ever called it and she only kept it for emergencies. She pulled onto the shoulder of I-95 (not an easy feat) and answered it. As she listened, her emotions escalated from anger, to confusion, and then eventually shock. She hung up.

A few silent minutes passed.

She exited, turned the car around and blindly headed north toward Newark. She found the police department after stopping at an all-night gas station to ask for directions.

Now dripping on the precinct's floor, she sat frozen. Not from cold, but from fear.

"Elizabeth Schiff?" An officer arrived in the doorway with a clipboard.

"Yes?" She stood up, grateful for the activity.

"Follow me, please."

Inside a patrol room, desks, file cabinets, and uniformed police officers were organized haphazardly. Phones rang, people yelled, and a photocopier hummed loudly in the background. A TV, hung high on the wall with chains, played the local news. Beth smelled burned coffee from an old Mr. Coffee maker on a table littered with Styrofoam cups, packets of sugar, and plastic creamers.

The officer led Beth to an office with "Lt. Marvin Bloom" stenciled on the door. Flecks of gold paint had chipped off so it read like "Marvi B oom." He motioned for her to sit in the chair across from the desk. Papers sat stacked high and organized into neat piles on the desk blotter. A pencil cup was filled with chewed Ticonderogas. The officer closed the door behind him.

It was quiet except for the staccato ticking of an industrial clock. Beth watched as both its hands came together and nestled one on top of the other. After a few minutes, an older officer with additional stripes on his uniform entered. He introduced himself as Lieutenant Bloom. He removed his hat. Raindrops dotted the plastic cover.

He verified Beth's name and address in a calm, monotone voice. Then he told her a story. One she didn't want to hear. Since she already knew the ending, the middle was really of no consequence. And the details—extraneous. But still, he tried to explain. It was, after all, his duty to communicate the facts.

At approximately 9:00 p.m., multiple New Jersey State patrol cars responded to an accident on I-78 heading west. Officers found a late-model Plymouth Acclaim crumpled on its roof in the median of the road. Two ambulances were called to the scene.

"What were they doing in Newark?" Lieutenant Bloom asked. He grasped a newly sharpened pencil in his hand to record Beth's answers.

"We went to my aunt's wedding in New York. They were driving back home."

"Where's home?"

"Allentown."

"Why weren't you with them?"

"I was going back to school. I needed my car."

"Where's school?"

"Philadelphia. University of Pennsylvania."

School. How would she go to school on Monday? Beth sat, rigid, with hands clasped tightly in her lap, each finger indented into the other. If she moved, she would shatter into a million pieces. Thoughts and emotions that had blown feverishly inside her head only an hour earlier now trickled to one at a time, as if her brain could process a single, solitary concept. It was all she was capable of.

Lieutenant Bloom, an experienced investigator, kept his meeting short. There would be more opportunities to get additional details. Tonight wasn't the time. He recognized Beth was in shock, so, he only said, "The injured party is at the hospital. The deceased has been transported to the coroner's office."

She closed her eyes. She bowed her head back into her hands and sobbed. It just couldn't be any worse. And then it was.

Bloom let her cry for a few moments. She was entitled. He closed the file in front of him and put down the pencil. He handed her a box of tissues from his desk.

"Ms. Schiff, is there anyone we can call for you? Anyone you can stay with tonight?"

Beth looked up with wet eyes. "Not anymore."

"Do you have any other family? Anyone who can help?"

"My sister is on a plane to L.A. There's my Aunt Ethel. I can call her ... but what happens now?" Beth wiped her nose. Her eyes looked to Bloom for help. They pleaded, *anything really, I'll take whatever you can give me.*

Lieutenant Bloom shuffled some paperwork on his desk, trying to find a suitable answer. He cleared his throat. "We'll be conducting a thorough investigation. A *thorough* investigation, I can assure you. But for now, we'll let you know when the coroner's office releases the body so you can make arrangements."

"Arrangements?" Fresh tears arrived. She brought the wet tissue up to her face. Her throat closed, making it difficult to speak. What was happening? She whispered, "I can't do this alone. I *can't.*"

Bloom contemplated for a moment. But all he said was, "Ms. Schiff ... Elizabeth ... I'm truly sorry for your loss."

CHAPTER 13

As the ship continued its voyage south, smart passengers took advantage of the warmer temperatures to sunbathe before port stops began the following day. Thank goodness the two swimming pools were located on opposite ends of the ship, otherwise, the *Queen Elizabeth* would be in danger of listing toward one end and sinking to the bottom of the sea.

The chaise lounges were filled at maximum capacity. Bodies of all shapes and sizes were splayed out like beached flounder. Sunbathers either napped, read, or worked on Sudoku and crossword puzzles. Few actually swam in the pool and when they did, they didn't swim, but bobbed. Like a stew bubbling away in a crockpot, white-haired bathers bounced up and down in the water. Even fewer exercised by walking slow-motion-like back and forth in the water, as if jogging on the moon.

Nearby carts supplied warm towels. Several servers stood within snapping distance for drink orders. Quiet conversation permeated. Not loud, but pleasant. Just enough to remind passengers they weren't alone.

It was just before lunch time. Beth leaned against a railing and squinted, waiting for a spot to vacate. Before she left for the pool, she had written Roberto a note and asked how to get her glasses fixed. The tragic pieces were piled next to the vase of gladiolas. Without them, Beth had to strain to see distant shapes. Staring too long made her feel unbalanced. She hoped to get through the day without accidentally falling overboard.

An elderly man vacated a chair next to the hot tub and Beth scurried to claim it. She plunked down her tote bag filled with magazines and notebook and settled into her spot. Without her glasses, features were blurry, but she recognized Mabel from the Golden Lion pub. Still completely dressed in black, Mabel stood out among the tropical prints and oiled bronze skin. Poolside, people wore a variety of outfits. Most had bathing suits, others regular clothing, and one lady ... her underwear: a black bra, structured like plated armor, paired with a black industrial girdle. Even squinting, Beth knew it couldn't pass as a bikini. The woman either didn't care or was oblivious to her own faux pas. In any case, she snored with her mouth open.

Beth removed her improvised cover up, the *I (heart) New York* T-shirt. Although her skin was pale, it was smooth compared to the wrinkles surrounding her. The older crowd sure liked their sun. Brown patches, liver spots, and suspect moles were on display. Her red bathing suit was more modest than most. Women with much bigger curves unabashedly sported two-piece bikinis. Although generously-sized, the suits didn't leave much to the imagination. Older men, older *non-athletic* men, wore small speedos, which required Beth to shift glances elsewhere. Geez. *That's a sight not going away soon.* Yet all the passengers were smiling, laughing, and having a fine time at the pool. Maybe their looks didn't bother them. So, why should they bother her?

Beth put on her fashionable cat-eye sunglasses and tried to focus on a magazine. A small wind blew up and tossed her bangs about. *Hey, I can see!* A small feeling of euphoria shot through her. Her new hair cut was perfect. And yes, Olga *was* a magician. Earlier that morning she called the Royal Spa and inquired about Olga's availability. The receptionist informed her Olga had a nine o'clock cancellation. Beth took it.

"Madam needs a new look, yes?" Olga had sorted through Beth's hair as she picked and pulled pieces in interesting shapes and directions. Beth looked in the mirror and unconsciously made faces.

"Yes. It always gets in my eyes. I'm considering bangs. What do you think?" Beth was open to any professional advice. Sitting with a cape fastened around her neck, she was now committed. Olga took the front of Beth's hair and folded it underneath itself, patterning the look of bangs.

"Hmmm. I think you are correct. Look at the eyes ... they pop! Yes, you can carry off a heavy bang ... very chic."

After a luxurious wash, tingling scalp treatment and something called a gloss "guaranteed to make hair silky and shiny," Beth sat relaxed in the styling chair as Olga confidently wielded a pair of scissors like a Japanese Samurai. Two inches off the back, a few layers cut into the crown for volume, and finally the bangs. Snip, snip, snip. Olga trimmed as Beth closed her eyes.

"Mmm ... not enough," Olga declared and went back to work. Snip, snip, snip. "There. Perfect." After a quick blow out, Beth heard, "Open your eyes, madam."

Beth squinted at herself in the mirror ... or rather someone who could be her. It was a better version. Stylish. She looked *finished*.

"Wow. It's really, um, amazing." Her new bangs framed her face. Her eyes were huge. Her hair *was* silky and shiny and when she tossed her head, strands moved and fell magically back in place. "You *are* a magician!"

Olga shrugged. "I do what I can."

Now, lying in the sunshine onboard a luxury cruise ship, Beth felt a rare surge confidence. Was it because she looked different? Better? She wondered if others would notice the change. But in all honesty, do looks really matter? She had to admit, they did to her. More so, she liked looking at her new 'do in the mirror. Was that wrong?

She settled back in the chaise lounge, crossed her legs, and read her magazine. *Gosh, this is nice.* No laundry to do, no work to think about. She considered going swimming later, but her hair looked too good. Plus, her head still pounded from last night. She hadn't danced that much since she boycotted her high school prom and went to the midnight showing of *The Rocky Horror Picture Show* instead. Just too much fun, she remembered.

Then she recalled last night's (this morning's?) not-so-nice-note. Who would have put it on her door? Maybe a passenger was mad about the whole Covid incident? Ordinarily, Beth would have spent half the night stewing about it, but after the fun dancing, the free cocktails, and generally awesome evening, she fell into bed exhausted. This surprised her. Normally, her default emotions of worry and fear would have superseded any sleep. But after considering Aunt Ethel's letter encouraging her to 'Live, live, live!' she felt no remorse. When she found the note again this morning, she tore it up in two and threw it in the trash.

After an hour of flipping through magazines, she decided a drink was in order, an iced tea since she drank enough alcohol last night to fill a bathtub. Servers were busy elsewhere, but the pool bar was only a few steps away. She left her items on her chair and rationalized it was a safe bet no one would steal anything. As Beth passed loungers reading or post-lunch napping, she avoided making eye contact with anyone.

And tripped.

In spectacular fashion.

Beth sprawled forward on top of a cart stacked with pool towels. She fell to the deck as the cart skidded out from her weight. Towels exploded everywhere. Some provided her a soft landing, but most flew onto unsuspecting passengers nearby. This, itself, would have been humiliating, but Beth also clipped a server on her way down ... a server leaving the pool bar with a full tray of drinks. Pink paper parasols, pineapple wedges, and other assorted fruit garnishes showered surrounding guests. Some unfortunate nappers woke up to a rain of ice cubes and deluge of toppled beverages. A confusing fracas ensued.

"Are you okay?" a man asked as he removed towels from Beth as she lay face-down, stunned and immobile. People unfolded themselves from lounge chairs to help. The server apologized and offered napkins to the doused passengers as he plucked ice cubes from their hair. A bartender came over to provide assistance and napkins. In general, it made for interesting drama for the sunbathers. It was guaranteed to be a topic of conversation at many dinner tables later that night.

"I'm okay," Beth said in a quivering voice as she rolled over to stand up. A bruise on her arm was already starting to develop. "No broken bones, just my pride," she said and tried to laugh. Talk about making a fool out of herself.

The man who had helped her held on to her elbow. "Are you sure? You took a frightful fall."

"I'm sure." Beth rubbed her arm, "Just a bruise."

"You're very lucky. You could have been seriously injured." He patted her gently on the back.

A janitorial crew was summoned to mop up the mess. The server refilled drinks for the disrupted guests. A pool attendant rearranged the fallen cart and restocked it. Beth tried to help fold them, but the staff politely brushed her away.

Beth gathered herself together at the bar. A lady, dressed in a colorful muumuu, sat on a stool and smoked at one end. She motioned Beth over with a small flip of her fingers. Beth limped toward her.

"You okay, hon?" The lady exhaled. Smoked plumed around her large straw hat. She looked like she was on fire.

"Yes, thanks. More embarrassed than anything else."

"Here, you look like you need a drink." The lady motioned to the bartender and held up two fingers, then patted the adjacent bar stool. Beth sat down. Within moments, the bartender placed two small glasses of amber liquid in front of them. The lady pushed one over toward Beth and commanded, "Drink up."

Beth took the drink in one swallow, which resulted in a harsh cough immediately following. *Yikes, whisky.* She felt the liquor travel down her throat and into her belly, burning her insides along the way.

"It wasn't your fault, you know." The lady sipped from her own glass.

"What?"

"It wasn't your fault," she repeated.

"Clumsy is my middle name."

"Someone tripped you." She flipped cigarette ash into the ashtray.

Beth raised her eyebrows. "It must have been an accident."

"I don't think so. I was watching her. She stuck out her cane as you walked by." The woman sipped her drink and placed it in front of her, making watery swirls on the bar with the glass. "I think she did it on purpose."

Beth looked over at the empty chair where Mabel had sat only minutes before.

"Someone doesn't like you. Be careful, hon," the lady said in a soft tone.

Beth gulped and murmured, "Thanks for the drink."

Then Beth walked (carefully) back to her lounge chair. A crew member brought her an ice pack for her arm, but she insisted it was fine.

Beth couldn't believe she had been purposely tripped. People on Cunard were much too refined for roguish behavior and an old lady? Maybe she was jealous of Beth's snazzy new tote bag ... or her sexy haircut ... or more likely Beth's missing glasses prompted her to trip and fall. She replayed the scene in her head. She hadn't seen a cane, but the lady at the bar did. Why would she make it up? Beth had noted a second, empty whiskey glass in front of her; maybe she had a few too many. Then she remembered the nasty note from last night.

She ruminated as a server came by with an iced tea from the man who had helped her up. That was nice of him. She sipped her drink and tried to stop thinking about the note, tried to stop the worry-loop from playing in her brain. She focused on getting back to her relaxed state and concentrated on the sun. It felt fantastic and tingled her skin. She felt like a big cat. The gentle sea breeze cooled away any excessive heat. She looked down at her toes. Maybe Olga did pedicures too?

Six minutes later, screeches and screams announced the arrival of three small children. Two harried parents followed, carrying a variety of floaties, pool noodles, and water wings.

"Michelle, slow down! Jimmy, stop it *this minute!*" Mom, already exasperated, was losing patience. "No, do *not* go into the pool until I get there!" she yelled after them. The kids excitedly discarded clothing and shoes along the way. Dad silently picked up the items and dutifully followed.

The kids raced to the end of the pool and when they reached Beth's chair, abruptly stopped. All three heads looked up. A miniature pool located three stairs up had ... bubbles! Lots of bubbles! When they commandeered the hot tub, about two hundred sunbathers glared with silent objection as one.

Fortunately, kids have short attention spans because only minutes later Mom announced it was lunch time and, "If you kids are good, you can have ice cream." The kids sprang from the hot tub and hooted as they ran toward the familiar Lido Buffet. Mom followed and picked up wet towels. Dad, who never got a chance to sit down, gathered the remaining debris left in their wake.

A woman to Beth's right, put down her book and groaned in relief, "Oh, thank God."

Her husband snorted from behind his newspaper, "Ours were like that too, once."

"Yes, but we never considered taking them on a cruise. It's just bonkers."

The man held up his paper, the *New York Post*, and started reading again. On the front page, a familiar-looking name got Beth's attention.

She leaned over, but without her glasses, it was just too far away. The man suddenly announced he was hungry and wanted lunch.

"Give me a few more minutes ... I want to finish this chapter," his wife said.

"You take forever. I'll see you inside." As he walked toward the Lido, he tossed the paper on a side table next to Beth, who grabbed it and read:

Shitty's Kicks Out Kitties & Titties!

Max Birnbaum Enterprises announced a proposal to purchase property located at 2nd and East 58th, currently occupied by the New York SPCA and Cindy Lou's Secret Banana Drag Revue.

Plans include razing present structures and replacing with a 15,000 square foot, multi-level themed restaurant named 'Shitty's' offering, "All the bad foods you love to eat." Preliminary menu items include blooming onions, chili dogs and funnel cakes. Carnival rides for kids and adults, including a tilt-a-whirl in the works.

Birnbaum Enterprises suffered large financial losses over the last six quarters, yet sources remain confident purchase will be made. Wall Street investors and financial experts question, where is the capital? Birnbaum's public relations staff didn't respond to our request for additional information.

"That bastard!" Beth said aloud.

"Tell me about it. I've been married to him for forty years." The woman shook her head and went back to her book.

CHAPTER 14

That night at dinner, Constance extracted a small, bejeweled flashlight from her handbag. She clicked it on to read the menu in the dim light. While studying options, she would discuss her selections with Beth and essentially volunteered *foie gras* was really duck liver and caviar. Beth was familiar with these dishes (she had edited a cookbook once), but she still wrinkled her nose.

"Don't judge before you try," warned Constance, "You never know. Once I *swore* I'd never eat squid, but when I found out it was calamari ... well, I *adore* calamari. Beth, is that a new haircut? Olga?"

"Yes. She had an opening and I grabbed it."

"Good girl. We need to treat ourselves once in a while." Constance touched new tourmaline and diamond earrings, smiled, and winked conspiratorially.

"Did you buy those on the ship?"

"Yes. A pleasant man named Daniel helped me decide. I just couldn't make up my mind."

"Oh, I know Daniel. He's nice, isn't he?"

"Everyone who works on Cunard is pleasant. I imagine it's part of the hiring process. I've never met anyone onboard who wasn't."

"I've met some passengers who aren't." Beth reflected back to her note and earlier mishap at the pool.

"In that case, you're correct. I find whenever there are more than ten people in a room, one of them is bound to be a stinker. On a ship this size, it means ... over a hundred. We just need to stick together, that's all," Constance said squeezing Beth's arm.

Conversations naturally broke off into sidebars during the dinner courses. Beth chatted with Ian about books, a topic she felt confident discussing. Besides being an expert in the classics, Ian was well-informed about new titles. They discussed publishing trends and the public's unending infatuation with the dystopian genre. He proclaimed the lack of creativity in plot lines and the *New York Times* Best Seller list consistently unsettled him.

"Rubbish!" he exclaimed, "I fancy it's all political."

The conversation was so engrossing, Beth had unconsciously unclenched the napkin in her lap.

Before she knew it, appetizers were completed and Glenn placed her entrée in front of her. *Yum, New York strip steak and mashed potatoes with garlic.* Ironically, she had to be on a cruise ship sailing to Portugal to eat a New York strip. It was perfectly grilled, medium rare with a tasty char on the outside. The potatoes were fluffy and butter dripped off her fork as she spooned them into her mouth. She closed her eyes and groaned silently. She finished the last half glass of wine remaining in her bottle and wondered if she should order another.

As people tucked into their meals, Beth watched the other diners, which gave her something else to do besides eat. She wasn't being critical. Her ability to self-assess led her to easily recognize shortcomings in others as well. Okay, maybe not shortcomings, but differences. Beth may have looked like a fish out of water to others more sophisticated than she, but at least she was an observant one, even without her glasses.

From across the table, she squinted at Bob and Teresa Gunderson and couldn't help but imagine their character backstories. They looked self-made. There were little hints. For one thing, they were overly pleasant to the Cunard staff, remembered all their names, and while she couldn't be one hundred percent positive, she thought Bob had slipped folded bills to both Glenn and Brigitte on day one.

Beth noticed Bob carefully reviewed prices of wine. *He scrutinized price points, which came off as being 'selective' to others. But maybe what he was really doing—even subconsciously—was acting cautiously. The Gundersons weren't like the other diners: affluent passengers who had decades of practice spending oodles of money. The Gunderson's wealth could disappear in the next fiscal crisis. Which meant they didn't have it long enough to feel confident, or even comfortable, even with an extra zero. They were still learning the age-old lesson: the rich only get richer. It would take years for them not to count change or rationalize extravagant purchases.* Which is maybe why Bob always looked down at his gold watch ... just to confirm he hadn't pawned it.

Teresa looked like a ravenous bird. Her thin neck struggled to hold up her well-styled hair. Her collarbones stuck out, but nevertheless her small frame belied the fact she ate like three lumberjacks. She always finished everything on her plate—including the garnish—and sometimes Bob's. *After working at Harry's Hamburgers for years and earning pathetic tip money to feed her family, Teresa now made up for a rumbling tummy with all the food presented to her on a silver platter. It was a challenge, but she purposefully reigned herself in and tried to eat daintily, like a lady, when she really wanted to use both hands and slap away anyone who dared sample off her plate. But if it was a hamburger ... they were welcome to it.*

Or so Beth believed. They could be cousins to British royalty for all she knew.

Dessert was three flavors of simple sorbet. The petit fours arrived promptly with coffee. Beth pointed to two she liked and Glenn placed them on her plate with a small pair of silver tongs, while he gave her a little smile. *Fantastic.* Beth congratulated herself. She didn't spill anything, she talked to people, and didn't eat too much. Tonight, she scored herself a solid B-.

Music from a string quartet wafted upwards from the first floor of the dining room. As they exited, the Table 8 diners glanced over the railing to see down below. The commodore's table sat next to the music. Maybe so he didn't have to talk to the guests? He was probably sick of hearing about grandchildren. Beth couldn't imagine having to talk to strangers each and every night.

Commodore Pederson looked just like Beth envisioned, a distinguished man with a full head of white air and trimmed goatee. Though he was seated, Beth could tell he was tall, and a chest full of ribbons decorated his uniform. At his exclusive table sat Mabel, still wearing her conventional black dress. However, tonight she added an accessory, some kind of a hat. It had feathers and looked like a dead bird on her head. Maybe it was her formal wear? Beth imagined she didn't have a lot of money, since she'd been wearing the same dress for days.

"Ian, how do you get invited to the commodore's table?" Beth asked as they walked out of the restaurant together.

"It's been my experience that Club Level passengers are invited. Or if they're famous celebrities. Or diamond-level members. Needless to say, the selection isn't a perfect algorithm," he replied.

"Have you ever eaten there?"

"Of course." Then like a perfect gentleman, he bent, kissed her hand, and said goodnight.

Beth opted for a stroll on deck. The sky was wrapped in gray velvet and a soft breeze coaxing couples to walk closer together, arm and arm, to keep warm. Beth glanced up at the stars, but clouds began covering the evening sky. Whenever the moon tried to peek out, shadows enveloped, which proved difficult to determine where the sea and sky met on the horizon. Small whitecaps flashed as waves rolled over in a choreographed sequence, but darkness reigned.

Beth leaned against the railing and wondered what Table 8 thought about her. A mysterious single woman looking for a Latin lover in the Bay of Biscay? An heiress lamenting her excessive fortune? A doctor with a cure for ingrown toenails sailing to collect the Nobel Prize in medicine?

Little did they know she grew up in the shadow of a gorgeous, talented sister, days could pass without her exchanging a word to anyone and her best friend was a three-legged cat who judged. Whatever Table 8 believed; it was probably wrong. Beth just needed to get through the next week without making too big of an ass out of herself.

I hope they keep being nice to me.

Another visit to the sundry store resulted in a purchase of aloe vera for her sunburned nose and SPF 30. Earlier at the pool, the sun hadn't felt *that* hot. Beth walked around the ship and swung her little shopping bag. The Queens Room was filled with ballroom dancers again. Tonight, the music sounded upbeat and the dancing resembled a foxtrot. Couples hopped up and down like popcorn kernels in a pot of hot oil while they bopped across the parquet floor. That took some talent. At the shopping arcade, tables were organized for a sale on evening bags, gloves, and sparkly things. Beth looked at the accessories but didn't buy anything.

She went to Connexions and sent out another email to Mr. Watkins. Mainly, to ask him about the *New York Post* article. The paper was dated a week ago; it must have come via London when the ship first sailed.

Over the years, Beth couldn't help but follow Max's failures in the news. She experienced a certain schadenfreude as she watched his business ventures crash: Post-It note wallpaper he'd neglected to ask 3M to approve which resulted in a costly legal battle, a costume jewelry collection made with metal sourced from Chernobyl (he had gotten a *great* deal), a hair salon franchise guaranteeing blowouts in ten minutes … the list was endless. He even filed for bankruptcy, not once but twice. For his latest endeavor, did he need Aunt Ethel's fifty million? Of all things, a restaurant was an even riskier investment; even Beth knew that. She chewed on her fingernail. In any case, it seemed Max believed he was getting money soon.

"Bastard," she said under her breath. She needed to find the new will because it would certainly write him out. But she didn't understand why Aunt Ethel made it so complicated. Why didn't she just sign the will and send it back to Mr. Watkins? Why the scavenger hunt? Why her? Why not Vicky? She was the clever one. Beth had no answers.

She checked her email once more before signing off. Still no word from Frank on the book. She hoped he wasn't having a problem with it. Or with Governor Sharp. Beth had to admit she hadn't really given it much consideration in the last few days.

But she did receive an email from Dr. Joan.

Dear Beth,

Color me flabbergasted! Thank God I'm sitting down or you would have knocked me on my ass with your news.

I can't wait to hear how all this came about (like how did anyone ever convince you to get on a ship?) but I'm certain this must feel very unsettling to you. Please remember what I've said in past sessions: TAKE YOUR MEDICATION. You're not winning any awards for bravery by not taking it. Also, remember your breathing exercises and mantra.

If you run into any problems, just email me.

When should we reschedule?

Best,

Dr. Joan

Back at her cabin, Beth was surprised to see Roberto sitting at her desk. With a pair of glasses perched on his nose and a loupe clipped to one lens, he was gluing her glasses back together. He looked up at her with a magnified eyeball.

"Please, don't touch these," he requested. "They need an hour to dry."

"Oh, thank you! I promise."

"The fix is only temporary. You'll need to get a new pair. There are plenty of shops at the ports." He handed her a note written on the Cunard memo pad. "You got a message."

"Someone called? Who?"

"Barry White."

"Barry White's dead. It must have been Frank." Beth took the note which simply said: *Book Finished*. "That's it?"

"He said he'd email you." Roberto packed up his supplies from the desk and said good night.

Beth looked at the glasses and didn't touch them, even though she was tempted to try them on. She tried to hang her nice clothes away properly as she undressed. In the closet, Roberto had organized her shoes. After she brushed her teeth and washed her face, she put on her nightgown, which was an old Dave Matthews concert T-shirt.

She set aside the tour ticket for tomorrow's Madeira trip and felt a little giddy. An overture of excitement hit her. *Tomorrow, I'll be in Portugal!* She would see churches and cobblestones and ships. She would eat fresh fish and drink more wine. Or port? And she'd get the next clue! She'd be one step closer to finding the will.

Then she remembered Governor Sharp's book was completed.

She couldn't help herself.

Beth lost all sense of the ship's decorum and proceeded to jump up and down on the big luxurious bed with unabandoned glee.

CHAPTER 15

F unchal, Madeira's main port, greeted the ship with outstretched arms. The sides of the port narrowed to a central point showcasing a small boat harbor and a main square perched on the waterfront complete with palm trees. The dock was located on a manufactured spit of land on the port side. A new roadway ran from the dock, alongside the spit and back into a town, making a sideways U. Taxicabs stood at the ready and waited for customers with British pounds, Euros, and/or American dollars. Atop a large, stone tower waved the Portuguese flag, its red and green colors flapping lazily in the breeze. The *Queen Elizabeth* pivoted on her axis, slowly circled like the point of a compass, and cautiously backed into her berth.

After three days of continuous eating and napping, passengers were eager for adventure. Or at least some shopping and picture taking. They queued enthusiastically by the gangplanks ready to disembark. Those participating in tours followed guides to buses lined up with military precision parked next to the ship.

Over the public-address system, the Commodore provided a warm welcome to Madeira and gently reminded his passengers, "The *Queen Elizabeth* sails with the tides at five o'clock. For your added enjoyment, we have provided sunny weather in the mid-seventies for our American guests and mid-twenties for everyone else."

Beth sat on a tour bus marked 'Red 5,' which matched a sticker stuck on the strap of her sundress. She recognized familiar faces among the group of twenty passengers: Ian, dressed in a smart linen jacket and the Gundersons, with Bob in a loud Hawaiian print shirt with cargo shorts and Teresa in turquoise capris pants and matching top with a sequined whale. Through the bus window, Beth saw their tour guide talking with Mabel, who looked lost. The tour guide took her hand briefly and guided her to another bus. Beth felt bad for Mabel. She couldn't imagine the challenges of traveling alone at that age.

While waiting for the bus to leave, Beth made up her own story about Mabel.

Mabel had a terrible, poverty-stricken childhood. Whenever the ice cream truck jingled by, her parents never bought her a cone. Her only toys were empty tuna fish cans scavenged from the garbage. But her voice, her sweet voice, elevated her to the opera stage, where she became an overnight world sensation. She met a tuba player in the orchestra pit and fell madly in love. Alas, musicians aren't very good at math and he lost all their money in a Ponzi scheme. In retaliation, Mabel went out of her way to make his life insufferable. She burned his toast. Put hemorrhoid cream on his toothbrush. Superglued his credit card inside his wallet. Maybe she killed him. Maybe his ashes were in that big black valise.

The tour bus finally rumbled to life, backed up, and headed toward the main square. At the front of the bus, their guide, a tall, attractive woman with tanned skin introduced herself. Her sleek, brown hair fell past her shoulders and as she spoke in a thick accent, she turned her head back and forth so it fanned out like a curtain of silk. *I bet she uses a lot of conditioner.*

"Ladies and gentlemen, my name is Constancia. I am your guide for this tour. Please ask me any questions and I will answer. We have many lovely stops today. I will describe each. Please, before we go ... I have rules. Stay with me and don't get lost! Most importantly, don't miss the bus! I'll show you the toilets and shopping too. It's a lovely day for us!" Her enthusiastic use of hands and eyebrows made up for her less-than-perfect English. She proceeded to detail their itinerary over a microphone.

Beth's attention wandered elsewhere. Hopefully, Mr. Watkins would email her back soon. Hopefully, they'd get to Oliveira's on time. Hopefully, she wouldn't have to shave her legs again in the tiny shower stall.

"Now, we go to a lovely garden. A beautiful garden," announced Constancia over the crackling microphone.

Beth wound up chatting with Ian who volunteered that Portuguese literature started with troubadours. "Yes, they were heavily influenced by the French in the twelfth century," he said. "They sang their poetry." Who knew?

The bus sputtered up a hillside, its clutch making obscene noises. It stopped with a sudden lurch and the passengers exited, taking the stairs carefully while they organized fanny packs, unnecessary rain jackets, and canes. They dutifully followed Constancia, who led them with a bright yellow scarf tied to the end of a stick.

The Madeira Botanical Garden was situated on a hill overlooking the rest of the island. Large palm trees shaded the sun. Small water features dotted the park. Fountains shot water that splashed down onto rocks into small pools with koi. Intricate topiaries lined the main walkways and separated the riot of colors planted in manicured flower beds.

Constancia explained the colors were brighter a month earlier, "These now, they die." Still, Beth was amazed at all the colors and the new smells. It was lovely and a far cry from the steel grey of New York buildings and streets. From the garden, they could see the ship off in the distance. The group snapped many photos and bought souvenirs at the gift shop.

At an ice cream stand, Bob began to panic. Apparently, he misplaced his wallet, so he dashed back inside the gift shop to look for it. A minute later, he exited, triumphant, with it held above his head. Teresa shook her head and rolled her eyes. Besides that incident and Beth realizing her new sandals squeaked with every step, nothing very exciting happened.

A bee buzzed next to her and landed inside a hot pink flower bursting with sweet scent. Beth was almost tempted to stick her nose in it, except for the bee.

Constancia waived her yellow flag stick and gently announced, "Back on the bus, please!" She herded the group like a mother hen as they headed off to the next attraction.

No sooner were the tourists back in their seats, then the bus turned into another parking lot and they exited again. Monte Cable Cars hung and swung on steel cables spanning from the top of the island to Funchal's main square below. Groups of eight wedged themselves into the glass cars which plummeted down the mountainside at an alarmingly fast rate. Trees and tile roofs whizzed by. By the time the group rummaged through purses and backpacks to find cameras, they were already at the bottom. Panoramic views went undocumented. Beth hadn't a moment to panic about the heights. It was all over before she could lament, "The List!"

"Back on the bus, please!" Constancia smiled and ushered her brood on board.

Beth sat across the aisle from Bob and Teresa. His blue eyes twinkled as he shared funny stories about forgetting his wallet and/or losing his camera on previous trips.

"Only in the best places," he remarked.

Bob and Teresa sat together and held hands like high school sweethearts. Bob must have been a heartbreaker thirty years and thirty pounds ago. He wore his silver hair cut short at the temples and his fingernails were buffed. Up close, smoker's lines on his face framed the corners of his lips. His skin, although damaged by the sun (freckled and patchy) had a nice glow to it. Facials? At times, he would glance down at Teresa, smile, and squeeze her hand. She'd answer back with a huge grin.

After the roller coaster ride down the mountain, the tour kicked into high gear with a whirlwind of churches: Igreja do Colegio Sao Joao Evangelista, Santa Clara Monastery, and Sé Cathedral. Nondescript exterior stucco walls with terracotta roofs contradicted gilded interiors. Numerous statues of saints prayed to the heavens. Altars decorated in gems, gold-leaf, and rich paintings detailed the journey of Christ or Mary or John or whichever patron saint was major-duomo of the current structure. Votive candles requested money to flicker.

The churches' cool interiors provided a respite from the sun's heat. A chill radiated from the stone walls that had stood for centuries. How many people had prayed here? Got married here? Beth looked down at the worn stone floors, at the undulating patterns carved from ancient footsteps. *So many people.* It made her feel small. That and the soaring roofs with domes and stained-glass windows casting rainbow light across her face. *How beautiful.* Almost inspirational.

Yet, after the third one, the churches began to look similar and individual specificities became intertwined with the last. As fatigue set in, Beth's concentration waned. Constancia's tour group slid into pews, not to pray, but to rest their aching feet. Ian sat in a pew and fanned himself with his hat. Beth's new sandals rubbed uncomfortably against her right pinky toe, creating a blister. Consequently, she sat in an empty pew and deleted unflattering photos from her phone. As she waited patiently for the tour group, she wondered, how many photos of a cross could you take?

She was hungry. Starving, in fact. While on the ship, passengers normally adhered to regular mealtimes. It helped provide a sense of routine: wake up, eat, read, eat, nap, eat, sleep ... repeat. It was already past two o'clock. This was borderline abuse. Now back on the bus, Beth and the rest of the group began to compose some unkind comments for the end-of-tour evaluation. They quietly took a vote the next stop would either be food or a mutiny. When Constancia took the microphone and announced lunch was next, the participants breathed a collective sigh of gratitude.

As the bus drove off from the last church, Ian gave a thumbs-up to a statue of a saint flanking the front door and said, "Thank you for answering my prayers."

"Now, we have a favorite treat," pledged Constancia after giving directions to the driver. "Madeira is most famous for wine. Special wine. Aged wine. We're going to a famous wine place to have lunch and we all try it." Attitudes on the bus buoyed and passengers gave a small cheer. Within ten minutes, the bus pulled up to a bland building.

Inside the winery were small tables and matching chairs made from old wine barrels. Helpful staff greeted the guests and sat them quickly.

A faint odor of grapes permeated the cool room, which gave Beth even greater hunger pangs. She followed Bob's eyes to an enticing buffet by the bar. He whimpered in anticipation. Fresh-baked bread and small twisted rolls, cheeses, and meats sat on the table amidst grilled vegetables, olives, and sliced fruit. When given the go-ahead, the tour group descended upon the buffet as if it were their last supper and made quick work of the food. Frenzied people worried there would be nothing left. Beth's empty stomach won over any hesitation and she selected some tender fish in a decadent cream sauce with wafer-thin sliced potatoes. Bob said it was cod. *Delicious!*

"Try this pork sliced with passion fruit, it's magnificent!" Ian exclaimed.

After thirty minutes of oinking, the diners slowed down and relaxed. With stomachs now sated, they were eager for the main event: wine.

Beth realized she couldn't procrastinate much longer ... it was time to get the next clue. But then Bob asked her to take a picture of him and Teresa, since he'd left his camera on the bus. They posed and smiled in front of large wine barrels while Beth took photos on her phone. Next, Ian asked for some photos to be taken, too. She was stalling. But when should she do it? When should she sing? Should she wait for a drum roll? As Beth started to fret, the manager stood up to address the guests.

"We at Blandy's Wine Lodge welcome you!" The manager opened her arms wide in a large gesture of greeting. "We have several wines for you to try. But first, some history ..." As she began to explain the fermentation process, staff brought out cordial-sized glasses filled with a golden honey-colored liquid.

"What did she say?" Beth was seated with the Gundersons. Bob sat back contentedly and munched on a toothpick while reaching for a glass.

The manager continued her educational speech. "We start with a seco, or a dry wine. This is aged five years ..."

"Where are we?" Beth questioned. "What did she say the name of this place was?"

"Then, the wine is aged in dark bottles and racked on lees to ..."

"Blandy's. It's world famous," Bob answered between sips. He pointed to a pamphlet on the table, lying next to a wine price list. Teresa sipped appreciatively from her glass, making little sounds like mews.

Beth stared at the brochure. "Blandy's? Oh crap! I'm in the wrong place. This is supposed to be Oliveira's!"

She looked around the room for Constancia, who was at the bar in deep conversation with the bartender. A well-deserved, large glass of wine sat in front of her. Beth trotted over to her. "Constancia, is this Oliveira's?"

"No, Blandy's"

"Why aren't we at Oliveira's? It said Oliveira's." Beth reached into her tote bag and pulled out the brochure as evidence.

Constancia shrugged tanned shoulders. "Blandy's is very nice. The wine is good here."

Beth took a deep breath. "Okay, how do I get to Oliveira's? It's really important!"

"You take a taxi—not far, up the road a few miles. But we're going back on bus soon. The ship is leaving at 4:30."

Beth hurried back to her table and told the Gundersons she had to go.

Bob looked from side to side. He looked down at the pamphlet and rubbed his forehead. "Don't you want to try the wine?"

"I can't stay. I'm at the wrong place. I'll explain later at dinner." She ran out the front door. This was *not* supposed to happen. She clutched the wrinkled brochure.

On the shady, tree-covered street, Beth looked up and down the block for a taxi. Several passed by already occupied. She jumped up and waved her hands in the air. A cab turned the corner and pulled up alongside the curb. She opened the door and slid inside.

"Por favor ... necessito .... vamos a ... Oliveira's?" Beth faltered. "Muy rapido. Yo tengo Euros! Mucho Euros!" She looked at her watch... 3:45. "No tiempo!"

The young driver turned to her and said, "This is Portugal, not Spain."

"Sorry."

"We speak Portuguese here. Not Spanish."

"So sorry."

"I speak English. You want to go somewhere else? Why not stay here? Blandy's is the best."

"I need to pick something up at Oliveira's and get back to the ship before it sails at 4:30."

"Oh."

"When we get there, will you wait for me?"

"Sure, you said you have Euros."

He sped off and after a few quick turns, he pulled up to another long, white building on top of a hill, just past the University of Madeira. The ride took less than five minutes.

"Please wait for me," Beth yelled as she sprinted out of the car and slammed the door closed.

After she passed through a small, wooden door, a great open hall appeared. Enormous barrels of wine lay on their side. Thousands of dusty black bottles with thick white printing rested on shelves lining the walls. Similar to Blandy's, old wine barrels were fashioned as tables and chairs for tastings. But there was one huge difference. It was chock full of tourists, well over a hundred people. Maybe two hundred. Three?

Beth checked her watch again. 4:00.

She hurried toward an empty chair smack in the middle of the room. She tripped over shopping bags on the floor and bumped tourists' elbows as they tried to sample wine.

"Bitte, nehmen Sie ein Platz." An old man who looked like Santa Claus offered her the chair. He raised his glass to her. "Prost!" He held his white beard with one hand and sampled the wine with the other. "Das ist lecker. Gut, ja ... sehr gut." Blue eyes sparkled as his tablemates nodded in agreement.

What's he saying? Beth wondered. *Do I have food on my face? Gosh, it's warm in here.*

The tourists laughed and talked loudly as they sampled different shades of wine. The noise was deafening. A server hurriedly placed a wicker basket of crackers and refreshed a water pitcher at her table.

Beth's watch said 4:10. She was running out of time. She sat perched in her barrel chair and looked about. How should she do it?

"Diese ist besser. Süss, ja?" Santa held up a darker wine to the light. With his homburg tipped to one side, it gave him a rakish look. Beth gave him a terrified smile.

The room grew warmer and sweat trickled down her back. She took out her notebook and fanned it in front of her face. She re-read the clue.

Madeira, so fine.
try Oliveira's and sing
loudly, "I LOVE WINE!"

She poured some water from the pitcher into a glass and gulped it quickly. Her scalp prickled. Her hands sweat. The familiar feeling of anxiety beckoned with a cold, uncaring finger. The process started. Too late to take a pill. *I can't believe I didn't take one.*

No time for deep breathing exercises. Screw the mantra. *Do it.* She'd miss the ship. *Do it. Do it!*

Either from the threat of impending doom or emboldened by the benevolent smile on Santa's face directly in front of her, Beth's meager courage won over. It was now or never. She climbed on top of her barrel chair.

With arms above her head for emphasis, she sang to everyone in the hall, "I LOVE WINE!" at the top of her voice.

The tinkling of glasses and loud conversations skidded to stop. After ten seconds of complete silence—which felt like ten minutes—an explosion of laughter rocked the building and century-old barrels were in danger of rolling off their wooden trestles. Hundreds of tourists whooped and clapped.

Beth crawled from the top of her stool and sat down. The rush of anxiety over, her face flushed with embarrassment. She took another big gulp of water as she tried to hide inside the glass.

Santa reached over and grabbed her shoulder with affection. "Ich liebe Wein auch!"

His friends laughed and clapped Beth on the back good naturedly. The harried server reappeared at the table and presented Beth a small red satin bag.

"For you," she said.

"Really? Oh, thank you. Thank you!" Beth hugged the waitress and zipped the red bag into her tote. She waved goodbye to the Germans and sprinted out the door. It was 4:20.

The cab was gone.

Crap! He said he'd wait! Beth looked up and down the street. A car squealed around a corner and pulled up alongside her, almost running over her foot. She backed away quickly.

"The police made me move—get in!" The taxi driver yelled out the open window.

As soon as she closed the door, it took off in another squeal. Beth was thrown from one side of the seat to the other.

"Like James Bond, right?" The driver laughed and sped toward the harbor. Not able to buckle it, Beth held on to the end of a seatbelt for leverage. As they drove down the hill, a ship's horn blew in the distance.

"Oh, faster please!"

The taxi raced along the roadway and reached the dock at precisely 4:30. The *Queen Elizabeth's* engines were running, water whipped up from below. Crew members began to dismantle the gangplank, roll up the red carpet, and remove the hand sanitizing stations.

About a hundred feet away, the taxi screeched to a stop in front of a security gate erected to prevent unauthorized cars from reaching the ship. Beth threw a fifty-euro bill to the taxi driver and yelled, "Thaaaank youuuuuu," as she took off running. She scrambled to show her ship's ID to the security guard as he waved her quickly through.

Her legs churned, arms flailed, and her tote bag smacked her hip as she ran toward the ship. *Thwack. Thwack. Thwack.* A wall of sound enveloped her. She glanced up. Passengers stood on the port-side balconies and decks. They cheered, "Go, go, go!" "You can do it!" and "Run faster!" from above.

Oh, my God, it's not even remotely possible to be more embarrassed. Two thousand people are watching me.

But she didn't stop.

As she continued to run, her face turned red, her ears prickled, and her armpits slicked with sweat. Her sun dress flew up over her knees as a cramp pinched her ribcage. The blister on her toe split open, the raw skin rubbed against the leather of the sandal. She bit the inside of her cheek.

So close. Keep moving. Almost there.

Thunderous applause met her when she finally reached the gangplank. The *Queen Elizabeth's* passengers clapped and cheered. Beth stopped and caught her breath while bent over the gangplank's railing. She stood upright and wiped the sweat off her forehead. And with as much dignity as she could muster, gave a dramatic bow to her audience.

Chapter 16

I nside her cabin, Beth collapsed backward on the bed, arms stretched
out overhead and legs wide, like a jumping jack caught in midair. The
coolness of the cotton comforter and breeze from the open patio door
helped her compose her body and pride. She lay spent for a few minutes
until her heartrate slowed to normal. Then she sat up, opened the red
satin bag, and shook the contents out. A piece of folded paper and a silver
charm in the shape of a wineglass fell into her lap. Very funny.

She read the next clue.

> Breathe deeply for air
> in turquoise blue waters fair.
> of sharks, please beware!

Seriously? Sharks? Beth hung her head in disbelief. Humiliation is fine,
but death?

She kicked off her sandals, got some water out of the fridge, and
guzzled it directly from the bottle. She peeled off her sweat-stained dress

and threw it into a laundry bag in the closet. Then she jumped into the shower and stood under the spray. The cool water stabbed her raw blister like an ice pick. She leaned against the shower wall. The low water pressure streamed down over her head as she ruminated. Acting like an idiot in front of a ship full of strangers was one thing; being eaten by sharks was another entirely.

Too many questions. How much did Aunt Ethel expect of her? How difficult was this game going to be? Today was supposed to be easy, yet it was close to an epic failure. And almost missing the ship–she would never live it down. Beth was dubious, not just in her capacity to solve additional clues and perform future tasks, but in her ability to save any self-respect in the process. With this next clue, it was almost as if Aunt Ethel knew what was on The List. How would she ever go underwater? And swim with sharks? It had to be a joke.

Now, sitting on the balcony in her Cunard robe and slippers, Beth watched as Madeira disappeared from view. She visualized herself in the taxi as it careened down the hill through town. She replayed the scene of running toward the ship. Okay. It *was* kind of funny. In fact, if it hadn't been her, she would have laughed her ass off, too. But still.

Maybe she should email Dr. Joan for help? Except she already knew what her response would be: "Good for you, Beth!" "See, you *can* do uncomfortable things." "You didn't die." *Yeah, yeah.* Beth knew all of this on an academic level. Just try explaining it to her heartrate and sweaty palms.

She moved inside to the desk and copied the new clue into her notebook along with the others. A burgeoning collection. Roberto had removed some of the dead gladiola blooms from the vase on the coffee table. The existing stems were trimmed shorter. Seven gladiolas remained and provided a reminder of how many days Beth had left to solve the game. *At this rate, the flowers may outlast me.*

Tonight was a formal dinner night. That meant fancy. After she spent an hour futzing with her hair and applying her makeup, Beth stood in front of the closet and weighed her options. She pulled out the beautiful red silk dress Frank insisted she buy. She also removed her Spanx from a drawer.

Here goes nothing!

She squeegeed her way into the shapewear, starting at her feet and working upwards. It was military-grade spandex; anything extra had to go somewhere, so it pushed body parts northward, which gave her an impressive bosom. Where did *these* come from?

Okay, now the shoes. She sat on the bed to buckle her new gold evening sandals. The Spanx limited her range of motion and prevented her from bending over. She propped her feet on a chair but still couldn't reach her shoes.

Exasperated, she peeled off the Spanx and buckled her shoes. She wiggled into the Spanx again. Now sweaty, she hobbled to the bathroom for another layer of deodorant. She gently patted tiny beads of sweat off her forehead and tried not to smear her makeup. She used the hair dryer on additional sweaty parts.

Beth picked up the red dress carefully by the straps and attempted to step into it. It wouldn't go past her hips. She stepped back out of it, trying not to catch her heels in the long hem. She sat back on the bed and tested putting it over her head. She got most of it over her shoulders, until it stuck. Now, with her arms raised over her head, she stood up and wobbled. Her head was now stuck inside the dress, like a blind mummy in formal wear.

Crap! Beth wiggled. Beth shimmied. Beth contorted in every way possible, but the dress wouldn't budge. Side-stepping carefully to the desk, she leaned over in a badly performed yoga pose for the phone. She punched in five numbers with her free hand. Within moments someone knocked on the door.

"Come in ... hurry!" she pleaded. "Okay, I'm really embarrassed, but I need your help." Laughter erupted from the door frame. "It's *not* funny, Roberto!"

"Yes, it is. Sorry. Here, I'll help you." Roberto turned her around and gently eased the dress from her head over her backside until the hem hit the floor.

"Now, I'll zip. Okay?"

"You think it will zip?"

"Of course, Spanx fixes everything."

Zipped up, Beth turned to the mirror and smoothed out any wrinkles. "Not bad," she said.

Cunard formal nights meant a little extra of everything. Photographers set up cameras at the base of the Grand Staircase to capture dramatic descents. Harpists played in the corner of the Carinthia Club. The art gallery boasted a new show with a visiting artist, who specialized in oil paintings of über-blond children cavorting on beaches. This necessitated a *By Invitation Only* sign embossed in gold lettering on the easel outside, which prevented any riff-raff from entering. Guests lingered longer in the bars and had an extra cocktail. Even the flowers smelled more fragrant.

On the way to dinner, Beth visited Daniel at the jewelry store and asked him to attach her new charm.

"Your bracelet is growing," he observed. Beth jingled the two charms on her wrist.

They discussed the next port stop, La Palma and agreed the weather should be fine. She spent more time chatting with him than intended and arrived at dinner a few minutes late. As she approached Table 8, her dining companions broke out in applause.

"Fine show, my girl," Saul said.

"You're faster than you look," Bob said.

"Now, now," Constance admonished. "She's probably heard enough already. Darling, you look *divine*."

"Thank you." Beth sat down stiffly in her seat. Glenn helped push her chair in and draped a napkin in her lap.

"Wine, madam?" Brigitte asked, as she held out the wine bible.

"Yes, please." Together, Beth and Brigitte selected a 2017 Medoc. Its description promised dark fruits with a sensual plum note. They also discussed the merits of new versus old world, while the other diners selected their entrees. After that important business concluded, Beth took a sip of water and congratulated herself silently for pulling off the conversation without bursting into giggles. At the very least, she was learning a lot.

"What happened?" Constance asked impatiently while smacking her fork on the table. "I heard you almost missed the ship." Ruby earrings the size of gumballs swung from her ears.

"It's a long story. Basically, I needed to pick something up at Oliveira's and just ran out of time." Beth took a roll and buttered it She decided not to say anything more.

"I hope you got it. You're lucky to have made the ship," Bob said. "Poor girl. You were in a pickle, that's for sure! I just can't believe you ran out before trying any of the wine. Such a shame."

For her entrée, Beth ordered roast rack of lamb with ratatouille and rosemary au jus and Grand Marnier soufflé with vanilla custard for dessert. Unfortunately, her dress groaned by the end of the salad course.

To try and prevent any further discussion about the day's mishap, Beth leaned over to her left and asked Ian more details about his job.

"I'm a retired literature professor from Oxford," he said.

Ha! I was right. "Do you miss it?"

"No. Now I get to read for pleasure," Ian answered. "Plus, I've escaped grading essays. A brutal job."

As their conversation snowballed, the rest of the table volunteered their pre-retirement professions.

Saul offered, "I was an engineer, very boring. Judy had the more exciting job."

Judy laughed and said, "I was a part-time teacher's aide. Everyday there was always a crisis of sorts ... tantrums ... tears ... and that was just the parents!" The table chuckled in response.

"What about you, Bob? What did you do?" Beth asked. Bob mumbled something about the oil and gas industry. Then he pointed to Teresa and said she stayed at home to raise their three kids but taught piano lessons part-time. Teresa smiled as she shyly pulled out a photo of her grown kids from her evening bag. Constance had managed a small London art gallery and had been married to a doctor. Madeline used to be a travel agent, but it was before the internet "basically killed all the jobs with personal customer service," she exclaimed.

Beth offered she was taking a vacation from her job, which led to explaining what a ghostwriter was.

"I help famous people write their autobiographies," she said. "Cleaning up after bad writers was not my dream job, but at least I'm gainfully employed." Beth explained her senior year internship at college turned into a steady editing job, which morphed into writing for a big-five publishing house. She was lucky, as most of her fellow graduates never got half as far. "I write for a lot of politicians. It seems everyone running for a political office needs a book to tout their accomplishments. Or at least embellish them a bit." Beth took a sip of wine. Plummy. Definitely plummy.

"Oh, how exciting! Who have you written for?" Judy asked in between bites of her Chateaubriand.

"I'm mostly assigned American politicians. I can't get into too many details, but ... have you heard of Pat Moldrund from Las Vegas?"

"Oh, my goodness!" Madeline exclaimed. "Of course, we know him. You mean you actually had to *talk* to that man?" She patted some sauce from her lip.

"Yes. And I'm glad *that* project is over with." Beth heaped creamy potato au gratin onto her fork as if someone would steal them off her plate. After swallowing, she continued, "He was *not* a nice man and it's really hard to write for someone you don't respect. His arrogance was blinding."

"What was the name of the book?" Judy asked.

"*It's All About Me.*" Beth suddenly broke out into giggles. "Oh, it feels so good to laugh about it now. For months, I never thought I would. Or could. I really shouldn't have told you. He will probably sue me."

"Wasn't it a best seller?" Ian asked.

"Yes." Beth scraped any residue of potatoes cleanly from her plate.

Madeline summed up everyone's thinking and said, "Well, you *must* be good."

Bob caught Brigitte's attention and ordered two bottles of Madeira wine to share with the table over dessert.

"We can't have you in Madeira without tasting the wine," he explained to Beth. They all agreed it was sweet, maybe too sweet for a main course. But with the soufflé for dessert, it paired exceptionally well.

Table 8 voted it was the best dinner yet, but they all ate too much. Beth agreed and decided afterwards she would walk the decks a bit. Ian called it, "A digestion constitutional."

Most passengers from the late seating were doing the same. The ship sailed slowly, so the outside decks were windless and pleasant. No jacket required.

Beth walked Deck 3 twice. Slowly in her gown, she took shuffling baby steps not to trip. Not to mention, her blister was still cranky. As Beth made her rounds, other passengers nodded toward her in recognition of the afternoon's sprint to the ship. *Oh great, now I'm famous.* Dr. Joan's voice murmured in her head, *and you didn't die.* Frank's echoed with, *you go, girl!*

As she strolled, Beth thought back to the conversation at dinner. Her tablemates had held various occupations and were now making the most of their retirement. She considered her own job. As a ghostwriter for the past fifteen years, she clarified ideas, revised metaphors, and deleted clichés. Her clients were happy to have a professional on their side. Her publisher was thrilled she met deadlines. Her career was stable. Beth realized, not for the first time, how other people's crazy, interesting lives provided for her own. She had money tucked into a retirement account. She was lucky not to have any student loans. Wealthy? No. Comfortable? Yes. She could pay her astronomical New York City rent. *You know, I'm doing okay.* She just wondered what she'd be doing thirty years from now.

As she turned a corner, she came across Mike and Alex standing at the railing. Alex was adjusting his cummerbund.

"Too much to eat?" Beth asked.

"You know it. Thank God, this cruise is only twelve days. I've already gained five pounds," Alex said.

"Yes, but we have the *Mary* to worry about." Mike sighed and unbuttoned his own jacket. "We have to get home, you know."

"You're taking the *Queen Mary 2* home? From Southampton?"

"Yes. The ships' itineraries lined up. Instead of flying from London, we opted to take a ship back to New York. Call it an extended honeymoon," Mike explained.

"How romantic," Beth said. "Are your parents coming, too?"

"Very funny. No, they're staying in London to see some museums, then flying back," Mike said.

"We're going to the show tonight, want to join us?" Alex pointed toward the bow of the ship. "You look fabulous, by the way."

Beth blushed as she thanked him for the compliment.

They made their way to the Royal Court Theatre to see the late show. As she sat in a crimson velvet seat, Beth stared in awe at her surroundings. With the gilded stage, complete with curly-que façade and heavy curtains, and the walls lined in red silk, the theater imitated a massive jewelry box. The large auditorium seated several hundred guests in two tiers and was mostly full. It even had balconies and opera boxes. It was amazing it was on a ship. Just incredible. Mike agreed and ordered three glasses of champagne.

Forty-five minutes later, Beth had forgotten most of the day's worries: the embarrassment from the afternoon and Roberto seeing her in Spanx. The production's singing, dancing, and music fully entertained her. The extravagant costumes and sets were top-notch. The Kippermans were right. The young cast sang and danced as if it was the last night on the *Titanic* and this was their *second* show of the evening, Beth marveled. They must be exhausted.

She thanked Alex and Mike for the invitation and hummed, "You Must Be Swinging on a Star" back to her cabin. The crazy adventures of her day now seemed comical and trite. Most importantly, she got through them without much trouble. Not *too* much. Her mood shifted and she enthusiastically looked forward to La Palma. Maybe that's why Aunt Ethel loved to travel—there was always something new to look forward to, something new to experience.

Then she stopped. *Oh crap, I forgot about the sharks.*

CHAPTER 17

I mposing mountains sprang from the ocean, their peaks towered overhead. Lush tropical hillsides rose to jagged volcanic craters. Endless clear blue skies provided a contrasting backdrop to their dark rocky profiles. In the water, just off the coast of La Palma Island, a small boat pitched wildly as a series of waves unbalanced the passengers. Eight scuba divers and a dive master clutched the rails. It was like a small-town carnival ride, only the passengers weren't quite sure when it would end. Or how.

Thankfully, Maria of Maria's Underwater Adventures was a patient person and she never lost a diver yet, which she repeated several times. Maria gamely stood and showed the group, again, how to adjust their masks, regulators, and weight belts. The dive master enunciated clearly, "To clear out your mask, just spit and swirl," and advised, "Get comfortable now, because in the water, you have limited mobility."

Beth couldn't imagine being more *uncomfortable* than at present.

Her tour ticket not only included transportation to and from La Palma Island but, surprise, an undersea scuba diving extravaganza, complete with a one-hour training. Craters littered the volcanic island like that of an apocalyptic landscape and most of the ship's passengers booked Jeep tours to view the wildness and peer inside defunct volcanoes. Beth would have been fine with great photo ops. But no, her ticket was for scuba diving. And the tour was not just for one dive, but two. *Twice the agony,* she lamented. *Geez, Aunt Ethel.* She clutched a Zoloft in the palm of her sweaty hand.

Long ago, when she was a kid, she used to love to swim. Loved it! Her family would take beach vacations to the Jersey shore every summer. She and Vicky practically lived in the ocean. But when Beth's fears began to surface, swimming became one more casualty on The List. There was really no explanation, just one more thing. It was beginning to make her angry. She remembered receiving a postcard from Capri with Aunt Ethel's loopy handwriting: *Dear Beth, I feel like a dog's rubber chew toy. But being underwater is really the* only *way to see earth's big blue sea. You MUST try this! Bellissima!* Of course, Beth never did. She'd rather scratch her eyes out with a pasta server.

But here she was. On a boat. Nearly falling into the ocean with each wave. She held onto the rail as if it were a buoy while the boat plunged forward. She'd never get through it. Can a person die hyperventilating into a dive mask? If this wasn't the ideal scenario to pop a pill, what was?

"I can't believe I'm doing this!" Beth yelled in Madeline's ear over the screaming motor.

"Oh, it's so much fun, darling. You'll love it!" Madeline yelled back.

Surprise—Ian was there, too. The British gentlemen, who normally favored tweed vests, sat next to her and beamed in his own dive suit.

"Glorious day, simply glorious!" he yelled. Beth wondered if his waxed mustache would wilt when it got wet.

The boat zoomed further out to sea and slowed down as they approached a small reef. The captain killed the engine. Finally, blessed silence. Maria explained more safety information and reminded them of what they learned in the practice pool only an hour ago. Apparently, tourists had limited memories while on vacation, so everything was repeated at least twice. With her nerves stretched, Beth couldn't remember her own phone number.

"Don't forget ... if you see any nurse sharks, assume the meatball position," Maria warned. Beth immediately recalled how to pull in both her arms and legs. According to Maria, the nurse sharks populating the warm coastline were harmless, but still, "If they're hungry, they may be tempted."

Seriously? Beth looked over at Ian. Her hands began to tingle. Before she could ask if they preferred to chomp on chubby women over elderly men with mustaches, Maria continued her instructions, "Remember your dive buddy."

Beth instinctively grabbed Madeline's arm. It was only twenty minutes under water. How bad would it be? Bad, Beth decided. But getting the next clue was too important. She couldn't negotiate herself out of this one ... List or not. After yesterday's debacle, she didn't want to become even more infamous than she already was on the ship. The tingling began spreading up her arms to her face. *You win.* She reached over for a water bottle and swallowed the pill.

"When we get in the water, make sure to signal you're okay. Touch your head with your hand, don't make the thumbs-up sign—that's something different," Maria said. Also, she explained, because of the sunny day, there'd be more opportunities to see colorful fish.

Would the fish touch her? If they even rubbed up against her, Beth would lose her mind. Slimy fish scales. Fins flicking. Big buggy eyes blinking. *Ewww.* The panic-level increased ... the familiar choking, she could feel it even inside the wetsuit. It was getting claustrophobic. The tightly zipped-up neck was cutting off her ability to take a deep breath.

Oh, please Zoloft. Do your thing. Fast.

Maria took charge. "Okay, everyone ready? Let's get started. Just lean forward and step off the back platform."

A few ambitious souls stood ready to get in the water. Beth had found it challenging just walking in her flippers, how would she swim with the rest of this equipment? A buoyancy-control-device—BCD—was fastened around her chest with an attached regulator. A mask with a snorkel encircled her head and oh yeah, a thirty-pound tank was strapped to her back. She looked ready for an expedition to Mars. She didn't know if she could even stand up. Waves of anxiety started to fall over her again.

Please. Please, work.

"Beth, I'm your buddy," Madeline said reassuringly. "I've done this many times."

"Thanks, Madeline," Beth squeaked. The anxiety must have shown on her face.

Just go. Happy thoughts. Calm the heart, calm the mind.

Madeline squeezed her hand before jumping in.

Beth stood up and announced, "I'm ready! I'm fine!" But with her regulator, it sounded like "Um eddy! Um ine!"

She was the last one remaining. Madeline bobbed in the water in front of her and encouraged her to just step off. Maria was telling her the same from behind. Even the captain yelled, "Just jump!" Beth, embarrassed by all the attention, took a deep breath, and stepped off the platform with her eyes closed. She may have peed a little in her wetsuit.

Whoosh. She plunged into the water and then shot back up like a cork. Thinking back to the recent lesson, she adjusted her BCD and slowly sunk, her eyes still squeezed together tight and mouth pursed around her regulator.

Then silence.

Can I breathe?

A hand gripped her arm. She opened her eyes. Madeline's mask was inches in front of her, her eyes crinkled into a smile. Madeline made an okay sign, her pointer finger circled with her thumb, followed by a questionable shrug.

Beth gauged her situation. Her normal senses shut down as the water supported her. Underwater currents jostled her slightly, her limbs outstretched involuntarily to steady herself. There was nothing to hold on to. Her own heavy breathing panted over the regulator. Besides some slight pressure in her ear drums, she couldn't hear anything. The regulator in her mouth tasted like rubber. Water encircled them while the other divers adjusted their equipment. Then suddenly a bright yellow fish swam past her, as if lost, looking for its school. Beth made eye contact with Madeline and gave her an okay back.

Her heart slowed to a normal rhythm, her mind and body suddenly awash with ease. She didn't swim, but merely hovered over the ocean floor and watched scenes unfold around her. Beth saw wondrous things. On her left, giant rocks formed a natural habitat for all kinds of undersea creatures. Electric blue fish with yellow stripes the size of her pinky finger swam in and out of the crevices. Orange puffy creatures with prickly spines hovered past her mask, with eyes blinking at her. Long sea eels darted in and out of holes in the rocks and coral. A playground in the ocean. She had never seen so many fish. And such color, like a box of new crayons.

Beth got more courageous. She gently swished her flippers to get closer to some coral and saw little crabs scuttle on the sand below. Bright green plants danced lethargically in the water as the current massaged them to and fro. The scene brought on a very Zen feeling. Beth relaxed her mouth to form a softer "o" on her regulator.

Madeline pointed to a stingray on the ocean floor a few feet below them. Almost completely camouflaged, its fins flapped in the sand as it made a cloudy getaway. It floated along the bottom, propelling itself until it rested again about ten feet from its original hiding spot. Sand settled back over it until the next diver disrupted its peace.

A school of silvery, gray fish swam toward her and when the sun glinted on their scales, they looked like toy knights dressed in metallic armor. As if by magic, they split into two groups and parted around Beth. Astonishingly, they never touched her. Never came close. Beth watched as the school halved itself down the middle and reconvened on the other side, a well-coordinated, choreographed movement. *That's impressive.*

Madeline grabbed Beth by the hand and pointed to her watch. Time. *It couldn't be!* They just got here. She hadn't even looked for the clue. The other divers swam toward the ladder above, which hung from the boat. She followed, slowly, until it was her turn to get out. She popped her head out of the water, spit out the regulator, and reluctantly handed her flippers to the captain. He grabbed the back of her tank to help.

"Oh my God," Beth said to no one in particular. "Did you see all that?"

As the captain removed her tank and stowed it, the other divers talked animatedly about what they witnessed below. Madeline boasted about the stingray. Apparently, the others didn't see it. Ian was disappointed there were no sharks.

I forgot all about sharks. Being underwater and experiencing an undiscovered environment was euphoric. She couldn't talk fast enough. Her effusiveness made her stumble over words and stutter, "Did anyone have a camera? Did anyone take pictures? Why don't people do this all the time? Where are we going next?"

Maria congratulated everyone on a successful dive and pulled out a cooler full of Dorada beer, brewed especially in the Canary Islands. Each diver sat with a beer in their hand and now, with their shared experience, the group of strangers talked nonstop.

Madeline explained to Beth that scuba diving was different everywhere you go. Some fish are brighter, some fish larger, sometimes there are no fish at all. "But every time, it's a new opportunity ... you just never know what you're going to see. I guess that's why I love it so. The adventure. Every time I come here, I see something new."

"You've been here before?" Beth swallowed her cold beer from the can.

"Ah, no. I meant the Canaries. So much to see in the Canaries."

"I can see why."

After a second beer, Madeline playfully slapped Ian's knee and said, "Oh, you scamp!" They had discovered they both belonged to the same golf club back in East Sussex and were discussing the merits of woods over irons.

The waves had calmed enough for lunch to be served picnic style on the boat. Each diver got an individual box with a sandwich, cookie, and an apple. The group munched with dripping dive suits half-unzipped around their waists. The sunshine was so bright, it was almost painful. Everyone had to dig around to find their sunglasses because of rays ricocheting harshly off the water. It didn't take long before the group began talking about previous scuba adventures. Fiji—absolutely. Australia's Great Barrier Reef—disappointing. Hawaii—no color left, all bleached out.

Beth listened with fascination. So many places to visit and see more ... do more. She could now understand why Aunt Ethel loved to travel. For as many wonderful places there were to visit and experience new food, people, art—there was always more to see. Aunt Ethel never settled, just like with her husbands. When her first one died, Aunt Ethel remarried. After the second died, she remarried again. Either an eternal optimist, or she believed there was always more. Love? Beth envied Aunt Ethel's ability to move on, move forward, even in the face of defeat. Beth couldn't do that.

But this afternoon was different. *She* was different. She couldn't help but wonder if it was the Zoloft. Had it really helped that much? The tingling was certainly gone. Beth sat contentedly, ate her lunch, and smiled. At times, she glanced up and looked toward the mountains on the island. Beautiful. *I'm in the Canary Islands—who'd've thought? Oh, if Frank could see me now!* She found her phone in a dry bag and took a selfie to send to him. Her chest squeezed tight, not with anxiety but with joy. A happy squeeze. As if something was hugging her heart.

After lunch, the captain revved up the engine and the boat scooted across the water for the second and final dive. This time, Beth was far less concerned about jumping in. Even excited.

As she sunk towards the bottom, she remembered the clue. It had to be underwater. It had to be on this tour. Where else would Aunt Ethel hide it? Beth got more active in her search. Instead of watching the fish, she looked under some rocks. She peered around an old anchor decaying in the salt water. She investigated a big coral outcrop. Nothing. Maybe it was on the first dive and she had missed it? Could they go back? She was running out of time.

About twenty feet past the boat's anchor line, she saw something out of place. Something red and waving. Are there friendly red fish? Beth quickly swam toward it, while Madeline took photos of an eel with an underwater camera. Beth didn't want her dive buddy to see her. She quickly flipped her flippers towards the object. As Beth got closer, she recognized a small red flag floating about five feet from the bottom. It was attached to a rock. No, it wasn't a rock. It was a treasure chest, just like ones found in a pet store for an aquarium. It was small, less than a foot, but it was painted gold, with fake jewels on it.

It was honest to goodness treasure! Beth would have laughed except for the regulator wedged inside her mouth.

A dark shadow appeared on her right side. A long fish, a *very* long fish came up from behind her. But it wasn't a fish. The shark swam slowly toward the treasure chest. Beth froze—which was hard to do underwater. She quickly pulled in her arms and legs, trying to make herself as small as possible. She could feel the shark's motion as it passed alongside her. The displaced current made her tilt to one side. *Oh please, please don't bite me.* If she believed in God, she would have prayed. Then stillness. She turned her head and opened her eyes. All she could see was a tail passing her. *Yikes, he's big!*

Zoloft or not, she focused on normalizing her breath. In for one ... two ... three. Out for one ... two ... three. After taking stock of her vitals, Beth turned her focus back to the treasure chest and hurried before another shark decided to visit.

She quickly swam up to it. She reached down and opened the latch which secured the lid. Inside, a red bag broke free and hit her in the goggles. She grabbed it by a drawstring before it floated past her. There was nothing else inside the treasure chest. No gold coins or pirate booty. Was Madeline watching? Nope. She was still snapping photos.

Beth took the bag and unzipped the neck of her wetsuit a few inches. She wedged the bag inside. It was tight, but she managed to shove it in for safe keeping. Then she rezipped it and almost caught her chin in the zipper. She looked for more sharks. Free and clear.

She closed the treasure chest and swam quickly back to Madeline, her grin stretched wide inside of her mask.

I did it! I did it!

Madeline turned around and patted Beth's arm while gesturing to the surface. Time had run out.

Once all were safely onboard, Beth told everyone about her shark encounter. The other divers, mesmerized, made her repeat the story at least three times. Of course, Ian wanted full and descriptive details. How big was it? Did she see its teeth? Was she scared? Beth just laughed and said it was the first and last shark she ever hoped to see.

The boat headed for shore. On the return, the waves weren't as rough, which provided an enjoyable journey back. With the scuba experience complete and the clue found, Beth was free to enjoy the ride. The sea spray misted her cheeks refreshingly. The warm sun kissed her face with affection. She couldn't help but smile into the breeze. Beth almost felt like singing. Out loud.

Back at the dive shop, they unloaded all the gear from the boat. Beth unzipped her wetsuit and quickly removed the damp red bag. Then she peeled the wetsuit from her shoulders and folded it to her waist. She sat on a bench to remove the rest. Like with a pair of too small tights, she rolled off the wetsuit and extracted a foot. Then the other. She sat in her bathing suit on the wooden bench and wondered, who planted the treasure chest? Who placed the red bag inside? How ...

Madeline was watching her.

"Are you okay?" Madeline asked. "You look wankered."

"Just fine," Beth replied. She smiled and tried to look nonchalant as she tucked the red bag inside her tote. She would look at it later. But still, a little piece of her wanted to jump up and down and scream, "Yippee!"

Madeline extracted herself from her own dive suit revealing a skimpy black bikini beneath. Beth's red one-piece looked positively matronly in comparison.

"Damn, Madeline."

Madeline turned and struck a model's pose, with a hand on her hip. "Not bad for an old bird, huh?"

Beth could only wish for a body that athletic, let alone when she was in her seventies. Madeline's physique was slender but toned. She wasn't skinny. Madeline didn't get this way from diet, facials, or massage, but exercise. She was always brisk and energetic with her actions and didn't slouch. She couldn't picture Madeline lounging on the couch watching TV eating a pint of ice cream. It just wasn't, well, her style. She was more likely to go paragliding, bungee jumping, or surfing—just for kicks.

As Beth packed up her gear, she watched Madeline expertly disassemble her own equipment like someone a third her age. Her mouth clenched tightly as she worked. She was finished before anyone else, as if it were a competition. *Where does she get the energy? It's probably how her husband died ... trying to keep up with her. Hiking the Andes. Biking the Rocky Mountains. Swimming the English Channel. Competing in Kona at the World Ironman Championship. He probably keeled over from physical exhaustion.* Beth decided if the *Queen Elizabeth* ever went down, she'd want Madeline in her lifeboat.

The wetsuits were hung to dry on a rack. The divers tossed masks and snorkels into a large tub of fresh water to rinse off the salt. The air was chilly against her wet skin, so Beth bought a hooded sweatshirt from the gift shop to add to her collection. 'Get Tanked, Go Diving!' was imprinted across the front and exotic multicolored fish swam up the sleeves. She also bought a postcard of a shark. She placed her wet bathing suit in a plastic bag, she pulled her new sweatshirt over her sundress and gathered wet hair back into a ponytail. Outside, a shuttle bus idled. She climbed onboard. It killed her not to open the red bag, but she didn't want to explain things to Madeline, who sat next to her.

"Buy something at the gift shop?" Madeline asked.

"Just this sweatshirt and a postcard."

"Yes, they don't have much. They need some new souvenirs." Madeline wiped her nose with a tissue.

———

Nowhere on the La Palma tour brochure did it say scuba diving—even for forty minutes—made you exhausted. When Beth returned to the ship, she took a hot shower and decided to crawl into bed for a small afternoon nap. The cat nap turned into a full-blown snooze fest. Two hours later, the ship's horn woke her. *Queen Elizabeth* was leaving La Palma and sailing to the next port stop, Tenerife—another island in the Canaries.

Groggy and disoriented, Beth stumbled out of bed. In the mirror, her damp hair was plastered to one side of her head. She drank some water and contemplated dinner options. Eating at Table 8 was always available, but she didn't feel like dressing up. The Lido Buffet? But even the thought of putting on pants was just too daunting. She was happy and comfy in her Cunard robe.

Beth picked up the phone, pressed the button for room service, and ordered a grilled cheese sandwich. As she waited, she sat cross-legged on the bed and re-opened the red bag to peek inside again. A silver fish charm fell out and she held it up to the bedside lamp. Light caught the diamond cut marks and made the scales sparkle. Now, she had three charms. She unfolded the note (thoughtfully written on waterproof paper) and re-read it.

Tall and mighty strong,
but without a stitch to wear.
Courage! Grab a pair.

A pair of what? Shoes? Dice? Tomorrow's tour brochure described Tenerife's highlights, but nothing looked obvious for her next clue. Are they famous for shoes? Do they have a casino? Beth read through the itinerary again but couldn't find anything resembling a logical hiding place. Her tour outlined another full agenda of sightseeing, which meant another long day. *I better pack some band-aids.*

She took out her postcard. Who should she send it to? Without much consideration or planning, she grabbed a pen and wrote:

Dear Aunt Ethel,
Today I did something new. I went scuba diving! I not only saw lots of colorful fish and a stingray, but a real shark. And no, I wasn't scared ... much. It was wonderful. Thanks for the push.
Love, Beth

Her dinner arrived quickly. She ate in bed, swilled a Heineken from the mini bar, and watched *Lethal Weapon* in French. Still exhausted, she couldn't shake her sleepiness. Her eyes felt heavy and her limbs like chunks of cement. By eight o'clock, she was fast asleep. She dreamed of angel fish serenading her with gospel music in the deep blue ocean. *Hallelujah ... Hallelujah ...*

CHAPTER 18

Seventeen Years and Nine Months Ago

Philadelphia's Our Lady of Victory hospital smelled like disinfectant spray with an unwelcome undertone of bleach. Fluorescent overhead lights cast harsh yellow shadows onto items below, including the patients. Nursing staff moved efficiently from room to room, returning to their stations to record data discovered on their travels. A profusion of numbers listed on paper: oxygen levels, temperatures, beats-per-minute. Patterns emerged over time; they either increased or decreased.

For the past three months, Mary Schiff had slept in Room Twelve attached to hoses, tubes, and wires. Except, her numbers never changed. The car accident caused extensive internal damage, much beyond repair. Yet, the coma provided *some* comfort. Her husband James had died at the scene of the accident. She didn't know.

A white cotton blanket was pulled up to her armpits and folded neatly across her chest. It rose and fell with the ventilator's assisted breath, the sound of inhales and exhales automated in rhythm. Her mouth pulled to one side to accommodate the tube, so her lips were cracked and dry. Beth took out a Chapstick and applied it.

"Hey, Mom." Beth took hold of one of her hands. She squeezed it tenderly, just adding the smallest bit of pressure, to let her know there was a change of state. "I'm here. It's Beth." The ventilator provided a steady tempo. It was almost soothing.

"Your hair looks nice. Did you just get a bath?" She leaned over and smoothed the brown silky strands from Mary's forehead. She tucked some behind her ears. No response. Beth knew better, but still. One day, maybe, there would be a reaction, just a small one. She needed to be there to see it.

In the meantime, she organized the few items on the bedside table. It didn't take long. A box of tissues, a tube of hand lotion. Her mom's watch, a Timex, lay ticking. In a willow basket, sprigs of delicate edelweiss were arranged with a card from Aunt Ethel reading, *My dearest sister, please wake up.*

"Let me tell you what happened at school this week." For the next half hour, Beth provided a detailed report of her classes, assignments, and papers. It was her last semester prior to graduation, so there was lots to talk about. "And Mom, the best news of all ... I have an internship in New York City for six weeks. I'm going to be an editor! Okay, a *junior* editor. A junior *junior* editor. Who knows, if they like me, I may even get a job offer! Isn't that great?" Beth leaned over and squeezed Mary's hand again.

The Timex continued to tick, filling up the empty space. Beth tried to think of something else to talk about. However, ever since her dad's memorial service, happy options were limited.

As with any organized program on grief, it had started as a sad affair with plenty of tissues. Beth felt untethered looking at a photo of her dad framed at the front of the room, while thinking about her mom in a coma. Vicky had grasped her hand tightly and never let go throughout the service. Friends and co-workers told touching stories about James: how he helped jumpstart a car in a blizzard, ate shrimp at the company picnic and immediately had to be taken to the ER for an allergic reaction, fell off a ladder and broke his toe which resulted in wearing a flip flop for a month. Tears evolved into laughter. But instead of ending on lovely tributes, it was punctuated by shock.

Courtesy of Max Birnbaum.

While Vicky and Beth listened to the wonderful stories about their dad, small buoyant bubbles of happiness filled their hearts hearing how he had been so loved and respected. Ethel was last in the program and shared a sweet story of when Mary met James. The service ended on a happier note.

But when guests began to exit, Max must have felt left out of the program and decided he had his own words to say. In an abnormally loud whisper to Bernadette, Max said, "We're probably paying for this, too." He nodded toward Ethel. "At least it's cheaper than their wedding."

Ethel, standing two feet away, glared. "What did you say?" Beth had never seen Ethel so incensed. The black feathers in her hat shook with anger. Ezekiel immediately put his arm around Ethel as if either to protect her or hold her back.

Max and Bernadette made their way toward the exit. Ezekiel blanched and quickly hurried after them. Beth never knew what happened after that. But Vicky had clenched her hand even harder and left fingernail marks in her palm. They could and would *never* forget what Max said. The look on Aunt Ethel's face would haunt her for years.

Vicky. Vicky would make things better; she always did.

Now Beth looked down at her mom. "I almost forgot. Vicky's coming to visit! The show is filming at City Hall in a few months. Cool, huh? She promised to stop by, but she's not sure of her schedule yet. But you'll be home by then anyways. She's been really busy ... press tours and stuff ... isn't it exciting? She can tell us all about Hollywood."

No response from Mary, not even a flicker in her standard tranquil expression. Beth glanced up at the TV and checked the clock.

"Hey, the show's on right now. We can watch it together." She took the remote and switched on the TV. *Legal Briefs* was a new prime-time show, a network sit-com, and Vicky's big break. She played a ditzy sec-retary and the butt of most jokes. Critics railed against the outdated stereotypes and tropes—it was comedy at its lowest brow. But for some magical, nonsensical reason, the public loved it. Who could forecast viewers' interest? Already, there was talk about being picked up for a second season. After only three episodes, it was a bona fide hit.

There she was. Vicky, but not really. Full overblown makeup and big sprayed hair. She wore a short, tight skirt and low-cut blouse, her cleavage on display for millions of viewers. Beth watched as Vicky trotted in five-inch heels around a reception desk to dramatically pick up a piece of paper that fell to the floor, her bottom raised high and pointed toward the camera. As one of the lawyers watched her, he tossed another piece of paper to the floor. The laugh track sang with giggles and guffaws.

"Ohhh ... fiddlesticks!" Vicky squeaked. "You're just a clumsy one, Mr. Johnson!" She batted her eyes and handed him the paper as her hips sashayed their way back behind the desk. Beth couldn't help but roll her eyes. The whole thing was a farce. The show wouldn't win any dramatic awards, but still, it was a huge break for Vicky.

On weekly phone calls to Beth, Vicky had unloaded. L.A. stunk. She hated the lifestyle and fakeness of it all. But she wanted to act and if you want to act, beautiful faces went to L.A. For years, Vicky auditioned and paid her dues waitressing, bartending, and house cleaning. She had also worked as a perfume associate at Neiman-Marcus, the most soul sucking of jobs. It required eternal smiling and spraying expensive scents on cards for potential customers. To Beth, it seemed the worst job ever, but Vicky confessed it was a good way to practice her characters. One day she was delicate and ethereal, the next sophisticated and smart.

"Just like the perfumes," she had joked on the phone to Beth. Vicky tried to stay positive, but it probably took every ounce of her self-confidence.

Then it had happened. Just when she was ready to give up, L.A. finally coughed up a lucrative part. A last-minute audition led to a second and third call-back. Then a reading with the cast and before she knew it, a contract offer. After years of hoping and wishing, the whole process took a month. Regrettably, it was the month of their parents' car accident.

When Vicky called Beth to tell her she had a recurring part in a network show, it was a bright lining in a series of very gray, dismal clouds. Vicky's success was the only piece of good news for the family since they buried their father and both girls grasped at it.

Hours after their dad's funeral in Allentown, Vicky had to fly back to L.A. It was terrible timing. Her contract wasn't signed yet and therefore the deal was still tenuous. Beth understood. The entertainment business was fickle and if Vicky missed a rehearsal or costume fitting, the final contract could never materialize. Plus, her agent would have killed her.

Through tears, Vicky and Beth had clutched each other tightly at the airport, both stuttering, "Big Hug."

"Knock, knock!" a nurse called from the doorway, "Am I interrupting anything?"

"No, come in." Beth released her mom's hand and stood up. "Has there been any change?"

"Not since your last visit." The nurse checked Mary's numbers and wrote them on a clipboard. "She's comfortable." She walked around the bed and straightened the coverlet. "I'm sorry I don't have better news."

Beth sat back down in the chair. She looked up at the TV. Now the scene was just three lawyers in a conference room. Vicky's one scene was over. On her last phone call, Vicky explained even though her part was small, she was trying to make it memorable. She was only signed for one season.

Beth missed her dad. Beth missed her mom. Beth missed Vicky, who was really the only one in her family she could talk to now since Aunt Ethel was a certified mess. Since the accident, Beth couldn't get an intelligible word out of her on the phone. After delaying, Ezekiel had insisted they finally go on their honeymoon to Switzerland, just to get Ethel's mind on something else for a while. Now, the two sisters were really on their own and Vicky wasn't able to help because of her schedule. Beth had to grow up fast. She wasn't sure if she was ready for this kind of responsibility. Or losing another parent so tragically.

She asked the nurse, "Am I being unrealistic? I mean, is there really any hope? I keep thinking one of these weekends I'll walk in and Mom will be eating or reading a book and I'll be able to talk with her again. Is that normal to think?"

"Sure, it's normal. But, it's always more difficult to accept reality. You know it's just a matter of time."

Beth lowered her head and said in a very quiet voice, "I know." She took a tissue from the box and wiped her eyes as they started to leak. "Thanks for making her hair pretty."

CHAPTER 19

At 7:30 a.m. the next morning, while standing in her underwear and scratching her butt, Beth realized her closet was empty. All her new clothes were stuffed inside the laundry bag. The spoils of the shopping spree with Frank had lasted about a week and now only a lonely pair of bleach-stained shorts and flip flops remained. She filled out the laundry form, itemized her clothing articles, and signed her cabin number with a flourish. She left the bag on the bed for Roberto as instructed. Talk about a vacation! No quarters or dryer sheets needed.

Her tour left at nine o'clock, so she skedaddled to Deck 3 wearing her new dive sweatshirt and remaining wardrobe.

On the Royal Arcade, a ladies' boutique held a fashion runway of sparkly dresses and coordinated separates—typical cruise clothing. While Beth quickly flipped through the hangers, she murmured Frank's advice, "Simple, some color, and clean lines ... otherwise you'll look like a lampshade." She pulled out capri pants and a matching tunic blouse in lemon-yellow with sequined dolphins.

191

"May I help you?" the shop attendant asked. Her name tag said 'Adrienne.'

"I didn't bring enough clothes with me. You see, the trip was kind of last-minute," Beth explained, "*and* I have an hour before my tour leaves."

"A challenge! No problem. These items," Adrienne said, pointing to Beth's choices, "may be a little *mature* for you. Let's try something more age appropriate." She selected a pair of white linen pants and a black top. "See?"

In less than thirty minutes, Adrienne zoomed around the boutique and selected ten mix and match outfits and more formal wear. A black and white print dress, a red cardigan with black jet buttons, a proper pool cover-up, a sheer blouse to wear over a striped tank top, and various other options to coordinate easily. She also added some accessories, like a glittery evening bag, a straw hat, and another pair of sandals. Like Frank, Adrienne could coordinate well.

"You're amazing," remarked Beth, her head spinning.

"On a cruise, it's all about options. Each item needs to do at *least* three things," Adrienne explained as she headed toward the cash register, arms full of clothes.

"But what about that?" Beth pointed to a silver sequined dress as Adrienne placed a plastic bag over its hanger. "I'll only wear it once."

"It was on clearance and looked terrific on you. Wear it once for a formal night and you got your money's worth."

The bill added up to almost two thousand dollars. *Wow! I have good taste! Now my onboard credit is really going to dwindle.*

She checked her watch and asked if she could take an outfit with her. Adrienne promised to have the rest of the purchases delivered to her cabin that afternoon. Beth took the white pants, black top, straw hat, and sandals, and hurried back to her cabin. She quickly changed, grabbed her tote bag and the 'Treasures of Tenerife' ticket, and ran down three flights of stairs to the Queens Room to meet the tour group.

On the bus, two tour guides (a middle-aged husband and wife team) presented information like a seasoned comedy duo. One would set up the joke, while the other delivered the punch line. At first, it was clever and the passengers considered it entertaining, even "novel," said Constance. But after about an hour, it became old just like an amateur open-mike night: good intentioned but lacking the skill to sustain. The laughs reduced to giggles and then to half-hearted chuckles. Eventually, the passengers tuned out entirely and looked out the bus windows.

This gave Beth some time to think, which in the past few days, she hadn't had much of. The days were flying by, especially on those she had tours scheduled. The excitement of waking up in the morning surprised her. She couldn't remember the last time she felt excited about anything.

And how items were being crossed off The List. It was unfathomable, subtracting rather than adding. She never imagined it possible. She expressed as much to Dr. Joan in another email last night, this time pecked out on her smartphone with the limited sketchy Wi-Fi in her cabin because she was too lazy to go to Connexions.

Dr. Joan had written back almost immediately:

Beth –

See??? I told you to take your meds. If they work for sharks, imagine what your daily life will be like. Keep me posted.

I'll be in Sedona, Arizona for the Sacred Vortex and You: Living Your Best Life workshop this weekend, but will have access to email in between chanting.

- Dr. Joan

Tenerife was the largest of the Canary Islands and its city, Santa Cruz, was a major port stop for ships. Plenty of tourists roamed the streets. Viewed from the bus window, the local residents shopped, went to the bank, grabbed a coffee, and headed to work—normal things. Instead of the usual red-carpet welcome rolled out to cruise ship passengers (as experienced in previous stops) it was more like being dropped into an average person's everyday life. Less of a small tropical port, more big city. Yet the lush palm trees reminded Beth she wasn't in New York City.

The first scheduled stop was Mount Teide, a dormant volcano situated in the middle of a national park. As she watched hikers bravely climb to the summit, Beth gave silent thanks for the air-conditioned bus. Plus, her blister still hurt from the Madeira debacle. At the peak, tourists gladly stepped off the bus to stretch their legs. They were greeted by a giant, steaming hole.

Beth looked at Constance and said, "I was hoping for rampaging lava."

Constance shrugged. "Righto, rather lackluster. I expected more from this tour." She sniffed and patted her hair after the wind dislodged a strand from her carefully constructed updo.

"Still, it's a nice view and I've never seen a volcano before. I guess if you're going to see one, it may as well be defunct," Beth reasoned.

After taking a required photo, Constance commented, "You see one, you've seen them all," and went into the gift shop to use the free Wi-Fi. Beth followed and bought a postcard for Frank that said, "Blow me."

Next, the bus drove back down the mountainside into town where they saw a large and rather strangely constructed opera house. Besides unattractive to look at, it was unmemorable. Just a big empty building. So far, the 'Treasures of Tenerife' tour was uninspiring and not living up to its promised billing. *Where's the next damn clue?* The sooner she found it, the sooner Beth could relax and have some fun.

The next stop was lunch. Unfortunately, it didn't go well either. The family-run restaurant was unprepared for a busload of hungry tourists. Talk about scrambling! The owners had to practically go out and catch more fish to serve them all. It was chaos, even borderline mayhem just finding a place to sit. Constance and Beth each squeezed a butt cheek onto a chair and shared, since there were none left. Their elbows glued to their sides.

"Oops, sorry," Beth said as she accidentally stabbed Constance in the arm with her fork.

"Dear, I'm frightfully sorry," Constance said as she bumped Beth's arm while she drank a glass of water. Her dress was now splashed with a Rorschach design reminiscent of an octopus. "Let's try to eat in shifts, shall we?" Constance offered to the rest of the table.

There were a lot of wild gestures and raised voices, but in the end, after a gut-busting meal, enthusiastic kisses were placed on everyone's cheeks. Beth wondered if it was just typical for Tenerife ... a lot of smoke, but no fire.

Then that was it. The comedy duo had nothing left to say. They had run out of jokes *and* tour stops. Beth wondered if they should have worked less on their shtick and more on organizational skills they could've seen a lot more. Plus, she hadn't found the clue yet. She had assumed it would be on the booked tour like before. Ultimately the tourists were cut loose on their own, to wander, shop, and stroll through the town. Which suited them just fine. The tour bus would meet them at a designated plaza at five o'clock and then return back to the ship.

Constance and Beth stopped inside a souvenir shop. Inside, they found Ian staring dejectedly at a wall of T-shirts. "Hi, Ian. What are you looking for?" Beth asked.

"Something pink and sparkly."

"For your granddaughter?"

"No, my grandson. He just turned three and has definite opinions. Do you think any of these would fit?" He held up a ladies' large.

"Nope." Beth helped him find a toddler's size in pink with a bedazzled mermaid on it.

"Jolly good," he said, pleased with her selection.

"Are you on a tour?"

"No. I've already been to Tenerife, just getting some souvenirs."

Constance held a shopping basket full of trinkets: a refrigerator magnet, a picture frame with *Memories of Tenerife* emblazoned on it, a wooden back scratcher made from bamboo and a snow globe. "Christmas gifts," she explained. While Constance and Ian ventured back into the clearance racks, Beth said she'd see them later on the bus.

She found a nearby café with shade, plunked herself down in a chair, and ordered a powerful coffee. She drank it from a small cup with an itty-bitty handle. Her pinky couldn't help itself and stuck out unconsciously. She laughed thinking about Ian and his grandson, hoping he would like his gift. Is that what old people did for fun? Buy gifts? They probably had enough stuff of their own. She remembered Aunt Ethel always had a knack of picking out the perfect present—like Beth's treasured *The Odyssey*. Maybe it was because she had no children of her own. But there was one gift, one especially, which stood out from the rest. It had created uncharacteristic chaos in the Schiff household and was the reason they never received any more gifts from Aunt Ethel.

When they were kids, Vicky and Beth had been scanning the Sunday paper and inside a glossy toy store advertisement, they found a jungle gym. Not just *any* jungle gym—but one with a slide, cargo net, climbing wall, *and* club house with ladder. Currently a pile of cardboard boxes lay in their backyard, courtesy of Dad's receiving department at the plant. The wind would blow them around and rain would soften the cardboard over time, yet the girls were creative and had built imaginary homes. Vicky called hers a condo. Beth settled for an apartment. But this jungle gym, correction, *Backyard Discovery Fort*, was beyond spectacular. After needling their parents on its particular attributes, they became very disappointed to hear Mom state, "Absolutely not. It's way too expensive. For God's sake, there's a tire swing you never use."

Dad just shook his head and tried to find the sports section among the paper scattered on the floor.

They didn't give up. The sisters carefully cut out the ad with Mom's good pinking shears, Vicky found a stamp and Beth secretly mailed it to Aunt Ethel at her New York City penthouse. When Christmas arrived, not only did the girls get the surprise of their life, so did their parents.

Mom was furious. She called Aunt Ethel and through clenched teeth told her *never* to do that again. It was too extravagant. She spoiled them. Her girls needed to earn their own way in life. The Schiffs were not a charity case. Ethel tried to negotiate, but in the end, she promised Mary to give the girls neither gifts nor money. Ever.

It was a powerful lesson and the girls were punished for going behind their parents' backs. Ever since, Ethel never bought another thing for them. Only 'experiences,' which in themselves, could be grand affairs. Movies, plays, trips to the art museum. But the girls never forgot: if they needed (or wanted) anything, Aunt Ethel would always come to the rescue. It stayed with Beth her whole life. Also, how many hours of fun they had on that jungle gym. To her recollection, it was still there in her parents' backyard, now probably owned by another family. She wondered if they had kids.

Beth looked down at her empty, teeny cup. She ordered another Americano, which she suspected was espresso. The caffeine kicked in quickly. Beth replayed the clue in her head from memory, *Tall, mighty strong ... without a stitch to wear... grab a pair ...*

After the four-hour bus tour, she didn't see anything resembling her clue. Was Aunt Ethel getting tougher? Beth needed help. She checked her old watch, as it seemed to be running a little slow since the scuba trip. Only two hours left before she had to meet the bus at the waterfront.

Okay, obviously, the next clue was *somewhere* in Tenerife. *Aunt Ethel had booked the tour purposefully, so I need to do something here*, Beth reasoned. She hoped the red bag wasn't back in the volcano. Was it an additional tour option? To attach a rope and scale down inside it?

She quickly left some money on the table and figured the potential for failure outweighed any embarrassment asking strangers for help. She asked a shopkeeper. She asked another. She asked taxi drivers. She asked other tourists on the street. "Do you know where I can find this?" as Beth showed the haiku. Most shook their heads 'no' or raised their hands in the internationally recognized gesture of 'sorry.'

Whether it was a language barrier or simply not knowing, Beth continued to have zero luck in her quest. The temperature rose substantially during her search; it was now midafternoon, the heat of the day. Sweat rolled down her forehead. The soles of her feet stuck like glue to the new leather of her sandals. Frustrated, she looked at her watch. Only an hour left. In the back of her head, Dr. Joan's advice hounded her. *Just take a pill. It will help.*

A touristy hop-on-hop-off bus was parked at the end of Emilio Calzadilla, a main shopping street. For twenty Euros, passengers could see the city quickly on a red double-decker. A perfect option for day-tourists. Two identical young men wearing red vests stood next to the advertising sign with stacks of pamphlets. They tried to solicit cruise passengers as they arrived from the docks. If anyone would know, they would, Beth reasoned.

"I'm guessing it needs to be inside something or someone has it," she explained to them.

In flawless English, one of the young men said, "It's like the TV show, right? Where you travel the world looking for clues?"

"Kind of. But I don't know the town well enough to know where to look. Hey, wait a minute, you're twins right? Does it have something to do with you two?"

They looked at each other.

"No. But we know the area. Let's see it." The young men took the paper and with their dark heads bent over it, started to read. They looked at each other again and laughed, hands held in front of their mouths.

"Should we tell her?" one said finally.

"No. She can figure it out."

"We don't want to give it away, but you're really close. You need to go to Plaza de España, just down the street." They unfolded a tour map and pointed to an open space not far away.

"That's where the bus is meeting me, at this street corner here." Beth pointed to the north end corner of the park.

"Go ahead and walk there, find a bench and face this way." They pointed south. "You can't miss them."

"Them?"

"Yes." The tour guides both started to laugh again. "Here. Good luck!" They gave her a free map.

Beth walked down the street until she arrived at the large square. In the middle was a circular manufactured lake with a fountain shooting water high into the air. The pool itself must have been the size of a football field. It wasn't deep, since many children splashed in it and small toy boats bobbed. The water looked cool and refreshing. Wrought iron park benches encircled the entire pool. Beth flopped onto one of the benches and faced south as suggested. Drips of sweat tumbled down her back. Her hat band was wet with perspiration. She took it off to wipe her forehead with the back of her hand.

She re-read her task.

> Tall and mighty strong,
> but without a stitch to wear.
> Courage! Grab a pair.

In the distance, directly opposite from her on the other side of the pool, she could make out a statue of sorts. It had a tall gray stone pillar in the shape of a cross. Beth looked down at her map. It was the Monumento de los Caidos, a monument to commemorate the victims of the Spanish Civil War. At its base stood two very tall figures. Not just tall, but gigantic. *Hmmm. Did they match? A pair?* To get to the other side necessitated walking around the circumference of the pool.

The shuttle bus left in thirty minutes and an encore of Madeira was out of the question. She got up and walked quickly, her sandals flapping on the ground. The blistering sun continued to bake her whenever she stepped out from underneath the shade of trees and palm fronds. As she got closer to the monument, the two figures came into view. Identical bronze statues approximately fifteen feet tall flanked the monument.

They were naked. Okay, not *completely* naked. Each had a sword grasped in both hands and wore some type of helmet. Also, a fig leaf, a very *small* fig leaf, covered their privates.

"Crap," she said out loud.

She can't mean ... of course, she did. Oh, Aunt Ethel! Her face prickled with future embarrassment. She didn't have a choice.

She went up to a statue and decided, at the very least, she needed to introduce herself. "Hi. Hiya doin'?" She looked up at his face and said, "Sorry about this." She sighed and looked around to see if anyone was watching. *Geez.* This was humiliating. She stood on tiptoe, reached between his legs and fumbled behind his fig leaf.

Oh, please let me find it quickly!

A pair of Japanese girls twittered as they took photos of Beth on their phones. She ignored them, focused on the task, and slid her hand inside. Her fingers grabbed for anything that moved. She found nothing but cold hard bronze.

With her face feeling a glorious glow of red, Beth moved over to the second statue. A group of tourists took pictures, posed on either side of it. They made faces and the peace sign. She impatiently waited for them to finish. Just as the group moved off, another group moved in to do the same and used a selfie stick.

Her watch ticked to fifteen minutes.

Come on!

Finally, the group left. Beth looked from side to side, hopeful no one else would approach. As she reached underneath the fig leaf and wondered if she should ask him to cough, her index finger hooked around a string. She pulled. A red satin bag fell to her feet. *Bingo*!

Beth grabbed it from the ground. She quickly glanced inside to see a silver charm and piece of paper. She zipped it into her tote bag and took off running, as she held her straw hat to her head. She yelled over her shoulder, "Thanks, boys!"

The tour bus idled directly on the other side of the large pool. Passengers with shopping bags were getting on. She reminded herself, the shortest distance between two points is a straight line.

Beth rolled up her new pants. She removed her new sandals and put them in the tote. She waded through the water, amongst kids and their toy boats. She sloshed and splashed to the other side of the pool. At least it was cooler. But the bottom of the pool felt slimly, as if it needed to be cleaned. *Ewww*. She shuffled closer and closer to the bus.

Beth confidently marched forward, taking longer and riskier strides, until she slipped and fell, slow motion into the water. She flipped and wound-up on her backside, her tote bag on her head, as if she were fording the Amazon with all her earthly possessions. She sat in the knee-deep pool, completely soaked. A toy sailboat floated by and mocked her predicament.

Only five feet from the edge of the pool ... she had almost made it. Everyone on the bus looked out the window, faces pressed up against the glass.

There's one good thing ... at least I didn't get my bag wet... or the clue. But then she remembered the red panties she wore under her new white linen pants.

Constance exited the bus with a large shopping bag. "Beth, are you alright?" she called out.

Beth half-heartedly waved from the pool. Then she took a deep breath, stood up, and sloshed the last few feet over to Constance.

"You're entertaining, that's for certain," Constance said as she handed her a beach towel with woven palm trees. "You're in luck. Look what I got on the clearance rack!"

Beth got out of the pool, wrapped the towel around her waist, and squished onto the bus.

Ian and Constance asked what had happened, had she gotten lost?

"No, just preoccupied and forgot the time," Beth responded.

The excuse was getting old, even to her. How many times could she use it? *Really, I've got to get my act together ... I've been cutting it too close.*

Beth sat in her wet clothes and took stock of her recent searches: she almost missed the ship in Madeira, practically forgot about finding the clue while scuba diving yesterday, and now today ... she spent hours searching in a city she'd never been to before only to run out of time. Again.

Maybe she should ask for help. *I can't afford to screw up.* Beth methodically debated a strategy and its possible consequences as she dripped on the bus back to the ship.

CHAPTER 20

A spoon full of crème brûlée paused midway between Madeline's lips and her plate. She stared at Beth with an open mouth, very unladylike.

"... and that's what I'm up to." Beth finished her story and patted her lips with a napkin. Madeline dropped her spoon back to her plate. Table 8 sat surrounded by their desserts, coffee, and digestives. They either looked at Beth or each other with vacant expressions.

"You're pulling our legs, Beth." Saul finally broke the silence. "We know you're a writer—one of those creative types—but really?" He licked his dessert fork and stared.

"Yes, really." Beth added sugar to her coffee. She took the tiny spoon and swirled it clockwise, then counter-clockwise. She knew it was the right thing to do, asking for help. After wrestling with her decision on the bus, it was really the only answer. As much as she hated to admit failure, the risk of not finding the will was too great. Max shouldn't get any more money just to piss it away. No way. She didn't want her stubbornness to be the reason he got it.

"Petit four?" Glenn automatically placed two on Beth's plate without waiting for her answer. Tonight, the lovely little goodies were coconut macaroons with chocolate drizzle. Her favorite. She quickly popped one in her mouth. There was a measured beat, quite a few seconds, before anyone else spoke.

"I knew it!" Constance slapped the table with authority making Table 8 jump. "I *knew* you were up to something! Why else would a young, single girl like yourself go on a cruise with us old fossils?"

"Can you tell us the next clue? Oh, how exciting! Isn't it, everyone? We can help you—just like detectives!" Judy was almost giddy. She squeezed Saul's arm as he tried to take a sip of coffee, which resulted in spilling on his suit lapel.

"Do you really want to help? I mean, it's my puzzle to solve. But honestly, I'll take all the help I can get," Beth said.

"Let's see, shall we?" Madeline asked the other diners. The entire table nodded in enthusiastic agreement.

Beth took out the red satin bag from her evening purse. She opened it and held up the new charm, a fig leaf. The diners laughed as she dangled it from its ring. Then she unfolded the piece of paper and read,

> Relax on the sand
> at Las Canteras, quite grand!
> See Mike for a hand.

"Who's Mike?" Bob asked.

"No idea."

"Tomorrow you're going to Las Canteras beach to look for a guy named Mike?" Saul asked.

"Guess so. I have no tour booked."

Their questions worked themselves around the table like a game show.

"How many clues are there?" Ian asked.

"I don't know."

"How did Ethel leave the clues?" Constance asked.

"Beats me. I'm trying to figure it out. But it's hard to leave clues when you're dead, right?"

The group sat in silence.

"We're not much help, are we?" Ian said. "We have more questions than answers."

"Beth," Bob began slowly, "what happens if you don't find it?"

She hesitated a few moments. "Then I let Aunt Ethel down."

The table lingered. They discussed Beth's predicament quietly. She could hear the silverware clatter from neighboring tables, even some of the other diners' conversations. Table 8, so loud and boisterous, usually blocked all other sounds out. It was if her fellow diners were silently respecting Aunt Ethel and her recent death. Beth waited until someone said something. Anything.

"Such a pretty bracelet," Constance offered.

"Yes." Beth showed her the charms dangling from it and explained again where she found each.

"Isn't that nice ... we really are the sum of our experiences, aren't we?"

"I never really thought about it that way before." Beth wondered about Aunt Ethel's motivations behind the scavenger hunt. Were there more than one?

"Do you have any other family?" Constance asked.

Beth continued to think about Aunt Ethel. After her college graduation, their interactions were brief. A quick lunch date in the city, a short telephone call. She had more vivid memories from her childhood. Beth knew, even from an early age, that Ethel traveled in different circles than her family did. Le Cirque versus TV dinners. Lincoln Continentals versus Chevy Novas. Paris versus Pittsburgh. Certainly, the distinctions between Ethel and her mom ... Ethel would let the girls try on her expensive jewels like they were costume pieces, a ring for every finger, sometimes two. Mom wore a plain wedding band. Ethel laughed and sang and wore crazy hats. Mom washed the kitchen floor.

But the sisters did have something in common, they never scolded except whenever Beth fought with Vicky. They would say, "Remember, she's your only sister," in stern voices. Beth would look up in surprise at their uncharacteristic tones.

Beth answered Constance, "Aunt Ethel was my only family. I have a sister, but we haven't spoken in years."

"That's a shame," Constance said. Her eternal smile unexpectedly turned downward at its corners.

Beth glanced back down at her bracelet.

After dinner, Beth stopped at Connexions on Deck 1 to check email. It had been three days since she last wrote Mr. Watkins and he should have replied by now. When she opened her email account, she had a few messages waiting for her.

Dear Beth,

How wonderful to hear from you. I trust all is well and your adventure at sea is progressing nicely. In some ways, I am envious. To be young and seeing the world, how exciting!

I regret there is not much to report from New York. Yes, Max Birnbaum submitted a proposal to purchase the property referred to in the newspaper article. I have heard, from various reliable sources, that banks are unwilling to finance this latest endeavor, mainly due to his recent financial misfortunes. In short, cash is his only answer. Let's not allow him to get more, shall we?

In addition, it has come to my attention that there may be a complication in your search. A reliable source indicates a potential obstacle, one sent to hinder your efforts. This impediment is in the form of a passenger. I have no additional information to provide. Please be wary and on guard. As Roosevelt would say, "Speak softly and carry a big stick." It would pain me greatly if you were to run into any misfortunes.

Sincerely,

J.J. Watkins

and...

Beth -

So nice of you to check-in. Too busy eating at the Captain's Table? Dancing till dawn? Swilling champagne?

In any case, I hope you're doing well and having fun because you deserve it. We miss you and can't wait to hear all about it.

BTW: Sharp's manuscript is done. It's sitting now with the line editor. That woman was a pain in the ass. She tried adding more (again) but I threw some important-sounding three-syllable words her way and threatened to contact Legal. I should give you a raise. Anyways—worry not. It's on schedule and off both our plates. But you owe me. Diamonds are nice.

Grendel is just dandy and sleeps in between us. Do you know he snores? Grendel, not Paul.

Love you, Pussycat–
Frank

Beth walked slowly across the ship. The Golden Lion pub was in full swing. Music from a small jazz band spilled from its doors into the hallway. The Empire Casino was busy, all seats at the roulette table occupied. Beth watched the wheel spin 'round and tried to guess the winning number. She was wrong on every try. Mabel, busy pushing buttons on a slot machine, waved to her with a free hand. The Queens Room buzzed with music and dancers gamely circled the floor in various capabilities of the waltz.

Guests inspected photographs displayed in the gallery for purchase. All week, the Cunard photographers had taken snaps at cocktail parties and formal nights, which were now organized along the wall like a community college art exhibit. Some were quite good, others, well ... the soft focus really helped. Beth spied the photo of herself when she first arrived onboard in her wonky glasses, with her hair askew, and wearing stained sweatpants. She bought it just so other passengers wouldn't see it.

She strolled past the Royal Arcade and saw a small group of ladies looking at jewelry displayed on a sale table. Different styles of chains were looped around spools. Basically, a customer picked a chain, a length, and the staff would attach a clasp to it. Daniel was inside the jewelry store talking with the couple from the other day. He held up the ruby bracelet, turning it back and forth in the light. *I hope it's no longer lonely.*

Directly across from the bookstore, a pair of heavy double doors led to the Promenade deck. Outside, a small wind kicked up and swirled Beth's amethyst-colored dress around her legs. *There may be a Marilyn Monroe moment if she wasn't careful.* She held the skirt down on either side with her hands, as she shuffled alongside the railing. Thank goodness her clothes had arrived from the laundry, as well as her new clothes from the boutique. At dinner, her new dive sweatshirt would have been, as Ian would say, *Déclassé.*

An empty chair appeared midships and she sat down thankfully. A red fleece blanket draped on the back embroidered with the Cunard logo provided some warmth for her bare knees. Cunard thought of everything. Beth looked out at the stars, which were plentiful. They hung over the water like a sequined net.

Mom would have loved this. "Just once," she had said, "I want to experience it just once." The fancy clothes, the food. Just the ship itself. How everything sparkled and shined. But then, it was all so foreign ... maybe her mom would have felt as unnerved as Beth was. It *was* fun and glamorous, but she couldn't help being intimidated most of the time. Still, the more familiar it became, the less nervous she felt.

On the other hand, Beth knew for a fact her dad would have hated it. Hated it! He would've complained about not finding NFL football—what, no Eagles? What's with all the soccer? What, no Budweiser? What's with this *ale* crap? Beth smiled. He would have been so uncomfortable, like a fish out of water. But he would have done it for Mom. At least one cruise. He knew how important it was to her.

Beth could imagine the entire scenario. Mom would insist on having a photo taken of her and Dad dressed in rigid formal wear, standing on the *Queen Elizabeth*'s grand staircase posed like royalty, just so she could display it on the mantle back in Allentown. She would *so* do that. Beth chuckled. Mom would have been so proud of the photo, showing everyone who ever approached the house. The meter reader ... the Fed-Ex guy ...

Hmmm. Maybe that's why people have photos taken on the ship, so they can look back later and see themselves all tricked-out and scrubbed-up at their best. Maybe all the passengers, every single one of them, really sat around in their sweatpants like she did when they weren't cruising on Cunard. Maybe Beth wasn't alone in her awkwardness. Maybe they were all a collective sham.

Gosh, I miss them so much. I wish I could talk to them again and hear all the stories, even the ones I'd heard a thousand times. Now with Aunt Ethel gone, who would remember their stories once Beth forgot? And without Vicky, her own history was slowly disappearing.

The air had grown colder, the sky even darker. Beth folded the blanket and placed it on the chair. She went back inside.

At the Café Carinthia a few empty seats beckoned at the bar, so she sat at one. When the bartender asked for her order, she surprised herself by responding, "Champagne." She decided to toast her parents if it was the only way they could experience the ship. *Dad got off easy.* She smiled. The bartender sat a crystal flute filled with sparkling bubbles before her. She said silently, *To you, Mom and Dad*, before taking the first sip. A guest took the empty barstool on her right. Beth turned her head to see Mabel.

"Good evening, sweetie," Mabel said. She hooked her cane to the edge of the bar in between them.

"Hi Mabel. Did you win at the casino?"

"Oh, no. I never win; it's becoming a small problem."

Beth laughed. "You're up late."

"There's so much to see and do on the ship. It's never a dull moment. Are you enjoying the cruise so far?"

"Yes. And you?"

"Oh, yes."

Beth sipped her champagne and wondered if she should offer some to Mabel. Maybe she didn't have a lot of onboard credit to spend on booze.

"What are your plans for tomorrow's port stop?" Mabel asked. She inspected Beth through her glasses. Beth always thought it was cliché, but nope, Mabel had beady eyes.

"Just going to a beach. Las Canteras. I hear it's nice. What are you going to do?" Beth decided she should be more empathetic. The woman was probably lonely.

"I'm going to ... oops. Could you pick that up for me?" Mabel's cane had fallen. Beth slid from her barstool, knelt down to retrieve it, and handed it back to Mabel. After she got back on her stool, Beth took another swallow of the frothy champagne and saw the bottom of her glass. So soon?

"If you're going to the beach, you should wear some suntan lotion ... you don't want to burn. Skin cancer, you know."

"I'll certainly do that. What are you going to do?"

"Try to win my money back at the casino."

"Good luck." Beth drained her glass. "I really should go now. I've got an early morning. Have a nice night, Mabel."

In her cabin, Beth found Roberto turning down the bed linens and arranging the various news and brochures for the following day.

"Did you go into port today?" she asked him. "I saw a lot of the crew headed into town."

"Yes, madam. We got some down time. There's free Wi-Fi in cafés. We also know the best places for wine and chocolate."

"You've been to Tenerife before?" Beth yawned. The last few days with all their activity was starting to catch up to her.

"Oh, lots of times." He tilted his head to one side. "Maybe five times now." He shook her pillows so they poofed up and placed her chocolate in the middle.

Beth watched as he moved efficiently in the cabin, hanging up her robe, closing the sheer drapes. Her eyes felt so heavy ... droopy ... it took enormous effort to keep them open.

"Roberto, how long have you worked on the *Queen Elizabeth*?"

"For over a year. But I've worked on the other ships, too. I've been with Cunard for about six years." He efficiently refreshed her towels and removed her trash.

"That's a long time. Do you like it?"

"Yes. It's hard work, but I make good money ... enough to send home to my family. Plus, I get to see the world and really beautiful places."

"What's your favorite city?" Beth yawned so wide her jaw cracked.

He stopped moving, "Hmmm ..." His eyes glanced upwards as if trying to determine the correct answer for a test. "I'd have to say New York City."

"Really? Why?" She leaned against the desk chair, unable to stand up straight.

"It's terrific. Everything you want is there. Great food ... and the music. Incredible. I try to see a show each time we dock."

"Are you going into town tomorrow?" Beth opened the closet, now restocked with clean clothes again and threw her shoes inside. She couldn't wait to get into bed. She was exhausted. She rubbed her eyes, smearing her makeup.

"Yes. The ship gets small. Any chance to get out is good and there's a great paella place on the beach." He smiled wide, showing teeth.

"Hmmm." Beth noticed her gown hanging back in the closet. "Hey, you got the soup stain out of my dress! Thanks, Roberto."

"My pleasure. Good night." He closed the door behind him.

In record time, Beth undressed and slid into bed. She didn't even brush her teeth. She looked over at her gladiolas. Down to five. Before she could factor the math, her eyes slammed shut and she slept so soundly, she snored.

Deep dreams. With crazy images. Sharks drinking champagne. Her mom in the Queens Ballroom square-dancing alone. Her dad, lost somewhere on the ship, calling out for his Phillips screwdriver. Aunt Ethel wearing a French beret, telling her to, "Live, live, live!" while doing a shot of Jägermeister at the Golden Lion Pub. Max Birnbaum sitting on a mountain of gold coins in a dragon's lair. Dr. Joan singing "Three Little Birds" wearing dreadlocks. Vicky running away from her, falling into a dark hole filled with shattered mirrors.

What the hell? At one point, Beth tried to wake herself to reset, but the visions continued in their cirque du soleil fashion. Her eyes felt superglued shut. Her body was pinned to the bed with imaginary tethers. Her only option was to shrug in her sleep with an eyebrow raised in consternation.

CHAPTER 21

While Beth slumbered, the ship arrived early in Grand Canaria. Quietly, like a patient lover, the *Queen Elizabeth* docked with little fanfare and waited for the rest of the world to wake up. When the steady hum of the motors stopped, eager passengers disembarked for shopping and beaches. Inside the ship, cabin staff rolled cleaning carts down passageways to service the rooms. Vacuums roared. Dirty dishes on room service trays rattled.

Throughout the morning's business, Beth continued to sleep. And sleep. And sleep.

At noon, someone knocked on her cabin door.

"Madam? Beth?" Roberto asked from the hallway. He pounded a little heavier.

Beth moaned from inside the sheets, stumbled out of bed and reluctantly opened the door.

"Huh?" She leaned inside the door frame.

"Are you alright? It's late." He walked past her and pulled back the curtains to the balcony. Bright sun blinded her.

"Oh crap, CRAP!" She rushed to find her clothes. "How long did I sleep? What time is it?"

"It's twelve o'clock," Roberto said, trying to stay out of her way. "Here, I'll call room service and order you some breakfast. You get in the shower," he ordered. Beth took his direction.

How could she have slept for fourteen hours? She was now behind schedule. Really behind. She had been dreading the aimless search for a Mike, but now instead of the whole day, she only had a few hours. Beth rushed to wash her hair. Brush her teeth. She spilled blue toothpaste on the Cunard robe. Then the unthinkable happened. In her haste, she snapped off an earpiece on her repaired glasses. *Damn!*

When she tripped out of the bathroom, room service had arrived and Roberto was gone. Beth gulped her morning coffee and shoved a muffin in her maw while standing on the balcony overlooking the port. Bright sunshine and palm trees greeted her bad attitude. A few tall buildings stood in the distance. A shopping center that looked like a giant spaceship faced the right-hand side of the dock. A handful of busses queued in front of the ship for afternoon tours. Her ticket included transfers to and from the town center. No tour. After the past few days, she welcomed the flexibility. She didn't need another day stuck on a bus visiting churches. Thank God.

As Beth quickly dressed, the Cunard TV station played Grand Canaria highlights in the background. Besides parks and churches, beaches were a big draw. Las Palmas (different from the island of La Palma—how confusing!) was the capital of the Grand Canaries and boasted four beaches. Las Canteras was the largest.

Oh, great. It had to be the biggest *beach.*

The town offered plenty of shopping and seafood restaurants for tourists. She learned the island's sister city was San Antonio, Texas—who cares. It had never seen snow—big deal. The most prominent resident was actor Javier Bardem—now *that's* something.

A weather report stated a pleasant seventy-five degrees with ocean breezes and guaranteed it wouldn't be too hot on the beaches. Beth quickly packed sunscreen (thanks, Mabel) and a map she found at the tour office in her tote bag. She wore a sundress over her bathing suit and slid on her sandals. She balanced her glasses on her nose by one remaining earpiece, like a giant pince-nez. Her pinky toe was carefully wrapped in a Band-aid. Ready! Late, but ready.

Beth swiped her ship's ID as she exited the ship. She noted the sign 'We embark Grand Canaria at five p.m. Please return on time!' and remembered, with her face flushing, back to previous days. *I will* not *be late. I will* not *be late today.*

She ran down the gangplank and boarded a bus labeled 'City Center.' As soon as it filled to capacity, the bus drove past the large shopping center and a circular roundabout. Palm trees shaded the streets and walkways to the town center directly in front. Five minutes later, the bus deposited her at the Parque de Santa Catalina on the left. Really? She could have walked there faster. Talk about *more* time wasted.

Her map showed Las Canteras beach directly west of the dock. She found Calle Luis Morote, a direct artery to the beach and marched toward it. The road eventually ended at the Las Canteras beach. Easy, she just needed to stay on it. Shops sold straw hats, T-shirts, and postcards. Others specialized in perfumes and electronics. ATMs were plentiful. As she got closer to the beach, small bodegas offered drinks and Spanish beer. Cafés touted tapas and seafood paella a la English, German, and French on wooden easels propped outside their welcoming doors.

Even though this was her fourth port stop, some of the scenery remained the same. Beth couldn't help but notice (again) how the ship's passengers looked woefully out of place. Ladies with painfully coordinated outfits and large purses window shopped. Men with backpacks and cameras meandered as if lost through town. It looked like a cultural invasion. She could also pick out the ship's crew members. Attired in casual shorts and faded T-shirts, they converged at the electronic shops and used the free Wi-Fi. They spilled outside onto the curbs and with heads bent, concentrated on their phones, texting and emailing as fast as their fingers could fly.

She passed a small supermarket, its wide glass doors open for breezes and noted more crew members buying armfuls of chocolate and wine. Roberto stood in line for the register, almost unrecognizable in a *Star Wars* T-shirt and cut-off shorts. She waved to him. He lifted his chin in acknowledgment and smiled back, wine bottles balanced in his arms. *He's fast.*

A little further down the street was a shop with a giant eyeball in the window. *That's creepy.* A sign touted, "Ojos nuevos! en menos de 30 minutos." It was an optician's office. Peering in the window, eyeglasses were displayed from floor to ceiling on modern white shelves. Different colors, shapes, and sizes; a buffet of eyewear. Beth wondered if she had time. She had at least a few more hours. It wasn't much. But still, here was a golden opportunity.

She hemmed and hawed. She couldn't make up her mind. She shifted from one foot to the other and agonized. *I'm spending more time trying to decide.* Resolved, she stepped off the hot pavement and through the door inside to a cool, air-conditioned office. A bell tinkled.

As promised, less than thirty minutes later, her broken glasses were in the trash and she had plastic discs floating in her eyes. Contacts. Amazingly, she could see both near *and* far. Dr. Manuel, in sexy accented-English, explained bifocal contacts. After a quick eye exam, he outfitted her with a trial pair lasting two weeks, some saline, and a prescription to take back to New York.

Beth skipped out feeling lighter and amazingly brighter. Her bad attitude had all but disappeared. With new motivation, she sallied forth on her pilgrimage to the beach. After she walked for ten minutes, blue water appeared on the horizon. She spilled out of the city's confining tall buildings to a large pedestrian boardwalk running perpendicular to the sea. White puffy clouds hung in the sky. Groups of umbrella stands stood in formation on the sand every few hundred feet. A sign read 'Playa Las Canteras.'

Good. It's the right place. But ... so big.

She walked down the boardwalk. Time to look for a guy named Mike. Where to start? She saw shops. Cafés. Hotels. As she got to the end of the boardwalk, she turned around and headed back. Sweat dripped down her back. Her new sandals pinched her feet. She shifted her tote bag to the other shoulder. She yawned. She needed a game plan; aimless searching wouldn't work.

Up ahead, a café with white plastic tables and chairs called to her. She sat down at the first free chair and ordered a sangria. She unbuckled her sandals and wiggled her toes on the sandy boardwalk. The young server brought a stemmed glass and small pitcher of burgundy liquid chock-full of sliced oranges, limes, and lemons.

"Gracias. Por favor, hablas English?" Beth asked.

"Sí. Of course."

"Great. This is a long shot, but do you know anyone named Mike?"

"No, I don't know anyone named Mike."

"Is there a restaurant, shop, or hotel named Mike? Maybe a street?"

"No. It's not a Spanish name. There's a lot of Miguels though. It's Spanish for Mike."

"That might work. Okay, any places named Miguel?"

"Sure. Lots. Miguel's Pizzeria. Hotel Miguel. Miguel's Nail Palace ... those are the ones I can think of around here, but there's many more on the island."

"Thanks. Can I have your Wi-Fi code?" Beth drank her sangria, chewed on a lemon slice, and re-read her task.

Relax on the sand
at Las Canteras, quite grand!
See Mike for a hand.

She pulled out her phone to Google 'Miguel,' and over twenty places popped up. They ranged from a doctor's office to a liquor store. After searching Google maps and swilling sangria, Beth realized she had lots more walking to do. She was so tired, so she considered a taxi. The server came back and removed the empty sangria pitcher. Beth hiccupped.

"There's also Miguel's beach stand." She pointed to an umbrella stand about a hundred feet from the café. A white wooden beach shack sat below the boardwalk on the beach, surrounded by lounge chairs and closed umbrellas stacked in a pile. On top of the roof was a sign cut out in the shape of a hand with a finger pointing to the water. 'Miguel's Beach Rentals' was painted in red. *Well, that's definitely a hand.* Beth was making things more difficult than they needed to be.

"I think you solved my problem." Beth paid her bill and left a big tip.

She swung her sandals by the straps as she walked on the beach toward the shack. Cool sand soothed the balls of her tired feet. *I should have brought my hat.* The sun's rays bounced off her head.

Inside the shack, a radio played American country western music.

"Hola, Senorita!" a man called out from his plastic chair set in the doorway. He waved a partially-chewed cigar between his fingers. "What you like? A chair? Umbrella? I'll make you good deal." He smiled and winked at her. His curly black hair was plastered to his head with gel. A tight T-shirt stretched across his belly, reading, *Kiss me, I'm Irish*. He was middle-aged, but tried to charm her like he was still twenty in his thick accent.

"Are you Miguel?" Beth asked.

"Sí. What's your name pretty lady?" He tilted his head to the side and squinted in the sun.

"Elizabeth ... Beth."

"Okay Elizabeth-Beth, what do you need?"

"I guess I need 'a hand?'"

"No comprendo. I have chairs, umbrellas. You need one? I'll give you a good deal ... both for ten Euros."

Beth looked around and saw maybe twenty people with chairs and umbrellas. It was not the height of summer season. Only a few kids played in the sand and a trickle of people splashed in the water. It looked cold.

She repeated, "I need a *hand*."

Miguel waved his cigar about and said, "Okay lady, I will help you with the chair and set up the umbrella."

Exasperated, she said, "Okay." *Maybe he's not the right guy?*

He stuck his cigar back in his mouth, got up slowly, and dragged a chaise lounge from the pile next to him to the front of the beach, about fifty feet from the water's edge. He opened an umbrella next to it.

"You have until five," he said, while pointing to his watch.

"I need to be on the ship by five, so I'll be leaving sooner."

"No problemo."

She handed him ten Euros. As Miguel walked back to the shack, he hummed along to Kenny Rogers' "The Gambler" and snapped his fingers in time to the music.

Beth sat down, positioned her tote bag and looked out to the ocean. Now what? She took off her sundress and lotioned-up with SPF. The aloe had helped her previous burn from the pool, but still, she wasn't taking any more chances. Why was she still so tired? She tried to keep her eyes open.

She watched the kids play in the waves. They ran to and fro, trying not to get wet. They squealed and screeched when a wave would crest and hit the sand. Beth remembered doing that with her sister at that age. They would take turns racing back and forth from the shoreline, playing who-could-get-back-to-the-beach-blanket quicker. Vicky's legs were always longer, so she always won.

A summer vacation at the Jersey shore was a welcome reprieve after sweltering in dusty, coal-filled Allentown during August. Her parents had rented an old beach cottage and the four of them would eat pizza, buckets of take-out chicken, and ice cream cones for an entire week. Dad said, "Screw the four food groups." They lived in their bathing suits. It was heaven. They returned tanned, relaxed, and happy. Good times.

Beth sat in her lounge chair and looked at her sandy toes. She remembered more. Sometimes Aunt Ethel used to join them. She would breeze in from some exotic location and still in her diamonds, relax for a few days on the beach. Ethel, Mom, Vicky, and Beth spent hours building intricate sandcastles. They worked like beavers on heroic works of engineering using found objects on the beach. Dad offered advice, but only when asked. This was *their* project. Girls only!

Different-sized plastic cups replicated turrets made of sand: small Dixie cups for the very tippy top, red Solo cups for the sturdy bases. Gum wrappers were stuck to plastic straws and repurposed as flags for the top. Popsicle sticks made drawbridges. Bottle caps decorated windows. Old cigarette butts lined upright as fences. Endless buckets of water filled the moats.

"Mary," Ethel had said to her sister, hand on a popped hip. She peered out from a humongous straw hat, the size of a Mexican sombrero. "Do you think it's big enough? I think it needs a balcony."

Beth's mom laughed. "Nothing's too grand for you. Okay girls, let's build a balcony, how about one overlooking the sea?"

Vicky and Beth eagerly scooped up more sand.

And after it was built to everyone's satisfaction, all four would finally brush the sand off their knees, circle the castle, and exclaim, "It's the best one yet!" and, "Fantastic!"

"Hey Dad, look what we made!"

"Ladies, it's terrific. Give yourselves a hand." He raised his Budweiser in a toast, while watching from a folding beach chair, a sun-bleached bucket hat covered his thinning hair.

"Yay for us!" Vicky and Beth clapped and jumped up and down. Ethel and Mary clapped too. "Yay for us!"

Eventually the sea would claim their creation. But the next day brought new prospects to make another castle, bigger and better than yesterday's. The girls, undaunted, fell back to work. At the end of her visit, Aunt Ethel brushed the sand out of her rings (Dad called them her "knuckle dusters") and she'd exclaim, "This was the best trip ever!" and kissed everyone before she departed in a private car which seemed to magically arrive for her.

"Hey, Elizabeth-Beth," Miguel called from his shack. "You wanna beer?"

"Uh, no thanks," she said. "Hey, Miguel, are there any sandcastles around?"

"Si, there's one by the lifeguard. Big one." He pointed further down the beach. Beth followed his finger and saw a mound of sand off in the distance. Thank goodness for her contacts. Amazing what new vision can do.

She put on her sunglasses and walked toward it. The lifeguard station stood in between her and the pile of sand. Up close it was a castle, a gigantic one standing at least five feet tall. As Beth approached, she could see more of its architectural elements. With many intricate details, it was a work of art. A drawbridge, several watchtowers and even flying buttresses ... all crafted from sand. Amazing. The castle was indeed grand.

"Hi there." She shaded her eyes looking up to the lifeguard. "Did you build this?"

"Hola. No, a man builds it in the morning. Comes every morning."

"He comes every day?"

"Sí."

Beth circled it and looked at it from every angle. On the highest turret, in the center, a single red flag flew.

"Do you know the man's name?" she asked.

"Sí, Miguel."

"Uh-huh."

"But he likes to be called Mike."

Bingo! "And he was here today?"

"Sí, he's here every day."

"Thanks." Beth circled the sandcastle again. The clue had to be in there. Beach. Sandcastle. Mike. This was it! Plus, the red flag gave it away.

Even though Mike rebuilt it daily, Beth hated to ruin his work. She walked around it a few times to find the most logical place to enter. It was inevitable; she would have to wreck part of the castle to get to the red flag in the middle. She grimaced as she destroyed the drawbridge, pulverized the moat, and obliterated the outer ring. Just like Godzilla, she squashed it to rubble with her size nines. Tourists looked at her in dismay. Some children playing at the water's edge shrieked, "Mamá, mira!" while pointing at Beth. The lifeguard just shrugged his shoulders and readjusted his sunglasses.

Beth bent over a parapet, plucked the red flag off the center turret and stuck it between her teeth. With both hands, she carefully lifted the turret off its base as sand crumbled in between her fingers. She filtered through the sand until a flash of color appeared. She shook free the red satin bag and untied the strings. Inside was a piece of paper and another charm, this time a sandcastle in silver. She tucked it all back inside the bag and replaced the flag on the mound of disrupted sand. She backtracked out of the castle, trying to retrace her steps.

She tilted her head up to the lifeguard. "Can you tell Mike thanks?"

As excited as Beth was to have found the clue, a chill of sadness ran through her. She wasn't ready to leave quite yet. She walked slowly back to her chair and unenthusiastically packed up her things. She looked at her watch and found moisture inside the dial. It wasn't even three o'clock yet. She couldn't be late again, just couldn't. But, maybe, just a little while longer. The small sleep hangover persisted from last night. She yawned. Again.

She sat back on her lounge chair. She put her feet back up and looked at the ocean. The waves crashed loudly on the beach. The sun made radiances on the water, twinkling and sparkling just like Aunt Ethel's diamonds. The salt in the sea breeze drifted over the water and into her nose. Her lip balm and the remainder of sangria on her tongue made for an interesting combination. Grains of sand stuck between her toes, which provided a pleasing friction when she wiggled them. Her senses were open. Alive. She could see.

Memories refused to leave. She couldn't help but think of her absent family. She reached over to her tote bag and grabbed her wallet. Inside, behind an expired New York State driver's license, was a faded 3x2 photo. She wedged her finger inside to unstick it. Edges worn. Faces discolored. Yet, she could still recognize the people. She and Vicky had it taken at the shopping mall when they were teenagers. They had found a five-dollar bill by the food court and in celebration, used it at the photo machine. A strip of three popped out, each shot goofier than the last. At home they cut them apart, kept one each, and gave the last one to Mom. It was the last photo Beth had of them together. She hadn't looked at it in years. Yet ... today ... it made her smile.

She spent another hour just remembering the past. And it wasn't all bad.

CHAPTER 22

"Hola! Elizabeth-Beth?" Miguel tapped her gently on the shoulder. "I need my chair back."

"Huh?" Beth shook her head, trying to clear the fogginess of a deep beach sleep.

"It's five o'clock. Time for me to go home." He shut the umbrella and abruptly pulled it out of the sand.

"It's not five! It can't be!" Her watch said 3:20. "What time is it?" She grabbed Miguel's wrist and saw 5:05. Beth looked wildly for her tote bag, shoes, hat ... anything she could grab.

Miguel pointed with his cigar. "You need a taxi? There."

Beth took off and attempted to run on the sand, which was always harder than it looks. She got to the boardwalk and stuffed her belongings inside the tote while putting on her sundress at the same time.

"Taxi!" she yelled. "*Taxi!*" A yellow cab pulled up. She grabbed the door and shrieked, "Take me to the *Queen Elizabeth* at the dock."

The taxi driver drove as quickly as he could without mowing down pedestrians, which at times was close. After a few minutes, the taxi pulled up to the pier. Beth paid the cab driver and sighed with relief. As she collected herself (untwisted her dress back toward the front and buckled her sandals) she walked toward the gangplank.

The ship was the wrong color. It was pure white. The *Queen Elizabeth* had a black hull. *Am I at the wrong ship?* She looked up and down the pier. There were no other ships. A port agent walked by with a walkie-talkie.

"Where's the *Queen Elizabeth*?"

"She sailed at five." He pointed off toward the sea. In the distance, Beth could see a receding ship and a plume of smoke drifting from the red smokestack.

"Oh, my God." Her skin felt clammy. Small beads of perspiration sprouted quickly on her forehead. Her tote bag dropped to the ground. She felt dizzy. Wobbly. Shaky. The port agent caught her before she fell to the cement pavement.

———

Hot and sticky, her legs adhered to a white vinyl chair, Beth held an icepack to the back of her neck and tried to breathe. *In and out. In and out. Easy now.* The ceiling fan helped a little. It circulated the moist air and blew around unweighted papers and empty Styrofoam coffee cups on the front counter. An officer smiled sympathetically at her from the desk. The port agent's office was located in a small building on the dock. Beth sat in the reception area, a space large enough for two chairs.

Rapid and unintelligible Spanish was being spoken on the phone. At times, it seemed angry, followed by long pauses of silence. She couldn't follow the conversation. Just when she thought it was over, the heated discussion started again. This went on for quite some time. Resigned, Beth sat and focused on what she could control, namely her breathing. A small victory in a big sea of failure.

Yes, she failed. The ship was gone and she wasn't on it. Her passport, clothes, everything she had except what was shoved in her tote bag remained inside her cabin. She would miss the next clue and task. She wouldn't find the will. Max would get all the money. She failed Aunt Ethel. If she wasn't so mad at herself, Beth would have burst into hysterical tears. Her heart started to pound again, so she readjusted the ice bag and closed her eyes. *In and out.*

The officer hung up the phone with a bang and walked around the counter to Beth. He squatted down in front of her.

"Senóra Schiff, are you okay now?"

"Yes, I think so."

"You have big problem." His face wrinkled in a compassionate grimace.

"I know. How do I solve it?"

"You go to Lisbon and the ship will pick you up there."

"I don't have my passport."

"Ah, not good."

"There must be another way."

"Yes, but it's expensive." He grimaced again. "Helicopter."

"A helicopter? Do you have one?" A glimmer of hope. Suddenly a way forward. Maybe.

"We, no. But I can hire you one." He went back to the counter, rifled through some papers and came back with a brochure. He pointed to *Hugo's Heavenly Helos*. "He's good and can get you there. But you need to go now."

"Could you call him? Can I land on the ship? How much?" Beth sputtered questions at him.

After making a quick call to Hugo, the officer came back with a plan. Beth would get picked up at the helicopter pad on the pier and would fly out to meet the ship. Apparently, the earlier phone conversation in Spanish was with the *Queen Elizabeth's* bridge. They were not happy. Yes, they had a helipad landing on the top deck, but it was only for emergencies. This was not considered an emergency. But after the Commodore was consulted, he finally granted permission for them to land. Apparently, Aunt Ethel had Cunard friends in important positions.

Hugo agreed to fly her. But it would cost one thousand US dollars.

"Does he take VISA?" She felt the small feeling of hope return. It grew larger when ten minutes later, the *thump thump* of whirring blades cut the air above the office.

"He's here!" the officer said, pointing toward the door. They scurried from the office and ran toward the end of the pier. When they passed the docked ship, *Diablo* was written on her port side. About a hundred feet away, a painted circle on the dock displayed the heli-pad. As they ran toward it the *thump thump* got louder. It got windier. Beth held onto her bag with one hand and clutched her sundress with the other.

Suddenly, like a huge bird, the golden helicopter descended, hitting the yellow circle's interior white H precisely. *At least he knows what he's doing.* She gave the officer an awkward hug, mouthed *thanks*, and climbed clumsily into the cockpit next to Hugo. He handed her a headset and mimicked pushing a button on the side for when she wanted to talk. Beth nodded. As soon as she adjusted it on her head, a *whoosh* issued from below, and with a sudden tilt they were airborne. Floating. But with purpose.

"I can't believe I'm doing this." She spoke into the microphone attached to the headset.

"I do this all the time, Miss," Hugo said without turning his head from the water in front of them. His large sunglasses masked his face. The ship sailed in the distance.

"You fly passengers to their ships?"

"No. I give tours of the island."

"Oh. But have you ever done *this* before?" Beth chewed her bottom lip as she clutched her bag.

"No."

"Oh. How far are we?"

"Maybe two miles, not far. We'll catch her." Beth caught a slight New York accent.

The chopper tilted again, this time more abruptly and she grabbed her seat with her free hand.

"Is there a seat belt?"

"You don't need one, we're almost there." He smiled.

Still, she felt uncomfortable. Hugo held the throttle loosely with experienced confidence. *He's flown a million times*, Beth chided herself.

Instead of watching the sea tilt back and forth on the horizon, which made her nervous, she focused on Hugo. He was older, in his 50s. His silver hair gleamed and he wore an expensive navy cashmere sweater. *What's he doing wearing cashmere? In the Canaries?* He wore a heavy gold watch on his wrist and a sapphire ring on his right pinky finger.

What? Before Beth could say a word, he turned toward her and took off his sunglasses.

It was Max Birnbaum.

He grinned as he maneuvered the chopper to list quickly. Beth grabbed her seat and groped for a handhold as balance eluded her. He laughed at her fumblings. The chopper descended suddenly and tilted sharply again to the right. The ocean met the sky in a fuzzy line as if drawn with an old blue marker. *Oh, my God, he's trying to kill me.* She slid toward the open doorway, a hole to nowhere. Her hands grasped for anything, but she couldn't bend her fingers.

"Goodbye, Beth. You lost."

She fell. Fierce wind scraped over her skin as she gritted her teeth for the water's impact.

Soft sand cushioned the blow.

"Wha?" Beth looked around. The waves lapped at the shoreline. The sun had moved significantly to the west. It had grown cooler with practically a chill in the air. The beach was almost empty.

What happened? She sat up in the sand next to the lounge chair. Her heart pounded wildly in her chest. She looked around her. There was a lifeguard stand and the ruined sandcastle off in the distance. Miguel's beach shack sat behind her. She tried to wipe the drool off her chin, which now had sand stuck to it. Miguel waved his cigar to her from his chair. She waved back and looked at her watch ... 3:20. Strange. And still horrifying.

"Hey, Miguel. What time is it?"

"Almost four. You want that beer now after your nap?"

"No, thanks." Beth stood up and dusted herself free of sand. "I need to go." She packed up, shaking sand out of her items as she placed them in her tote bag.

The red bag was gone.

She emptied the entire tote bag. It wasn't stuck in the map or wedged in a sandal. It was nowhere to be found. How could she lose it? She glanced around the beach.

"Miguel, did you see a small red bag?" Maybe it flew out in the wind.

"Sí. Your grandmama took it," he replied, walking over to remove the umbrella from the sand.

"My grandma?"

"Sí. She didn't wanna wake you. Said you were tired." He folded up the umbrella and put it under his arm.

"What did she look like?"

"Like a grandmama."

"Think, Miguel. It's really important."

Miguel glanced up toward the heavens for divine inspiration. He crossed his arms over his chest. His face twisted hard.

After a few seconds he said, "She was black and had sparkly eyes."

"What?"

"She wore black," he corrected, pulling on his T-shirt. "Black like this."

"Oh, she wore black clothes?"

"Sí."

"Did she have glasses, with little diamonds in them?"

"Sí, sparkly."

Mabel? Mabel! That sweet little lady ... a thief! Why would she do that? How did she even know about the red bags? In addition to being shocked, anger bubbled up inside Beth. Someone stole something from her. *How dare she!*

"She's not very nice. Called me 'Beaner.' I don't know that word, but it doesn't sound nice," Miguel stated for the record.

"I'm sorry, Miguel. She's *not* my grandmother. And, no, she's not very nice."

Beth packed up her remaining items and marched back into town. As she got closer and closer to the ship, she kept repeating in her head, "Not very nice at all."

———————

Within thirty minutes of placing her order, room service delivered a humongous cheeseburger with extra fries and an ice-cold Heineken. Famished, Beth devoured everything in a matter of moments. Beth popped the last remnant of fries in her mouth. As she licked ketchup off the plate, she tried to puzzle the pieces together. It was one thing to traipse around the Canary Islands having a grand ol' time, but now someone was trying to stop her from finding the next clue. Was this the passenger Mr. Watkins warned her about? Who knew it would be a little old lady named Mabel?

But it all made sense. Beth remembered back to the previous night at Café Carinthia and how after meeting Mabel she got tired. So tired she couldn't open her eyes. Did Mabel slip something into her drink when she wasn't looking? Was it when Beth picked up her cane? Maybe it's why she had those weird dreams. Then she fell asleep *again* at the beach today.

Yesterday, Beth would have scoffed at the very idea, but now things were adding up. Getting a nasty note. The whole Covid incident. Tripping at the pool. Oversleeping. These were incidents she could have brushed off as circumstantial—or just Beth being Beth. But the stolen red bag? There was only one explanation for it. Plus, Miguel described Mabel perfectly—well, almost.

She swigged the last of the Heineken. The worst part, the absolute worst part of all, was she had never read the last clue. She needed it to find the next. If Mabel had it, then she could find the next red bag before Beth. Which meant she could find the will before her. Filled with anger and frustration, Beth used her remaining energy to scheme how to get the red bag back and how to get even with Mabel. But most importantly, who was she?

She stayed up past midnight, used her writing skills and plotted. Who knew they would come in handy? It was after midnight before Beth finally felt confident with her plan, however there was one thing left unaccounted for ... the expected anxiety which would nonetheless raise its ugly head and thwart her. However, with millions of dollars on the line, the possibility of losing out on revenge for Max, and getting some sense of justice for Aunt Ethel, the sum totaled larger than Beth's pride.

So ...

After years of ignoring Dr. Joan's pleading, she finally did the unthinkable. Beth decided to take her medication on a daily basis, as prescribed.

CHAPTER 23

A day at sea. Thank God. Originally, Beth had scheduled herself a day to sleep in, have a leisurely breakfast at the Lido Buffet, and catch up on emails. Just chill. That was the *intended* plan. Now Mabel shot her agenda to hell. Also, at eight o'clock sharp, the phone rang and woke her up.

"Good morning, Madame Schiff. This is Raul, the purser."

"'lo," Beth murmured from inside her cocoon of bedsheets where she lay half-asleep.

"I just wanted to inform you we conducted a thorough search in our Lost & Found. There's no record of finding anything in your aunt's cabin."

"Thanks. I appreciate you looking."

"My pleasure."

"Hey Raul, can you tell me how much I have left in ship's credit?"

"Certainly, you have ... $2,750 remaining."

"What happens if I don't spend it all?"

"It disappears, so to speak. You're unable to take it with you. Please enjoy yourself in the next five days."

"One more thing."

"Yes?" He laughed.

"I met this charming woman named Mabel and I wanted to surprise her with a little present, but I forgot her cabin number. I'd hate to leave it at the wrong door. She's on the Club Level."

"Well, I'm not sure ..."

"I know it's probably a security thing, but I really wanted to make her day. She hasn't been well lately. I'd *really* appreciate it," she pleaded.

"What's her last name?" Beth could hear him typing.

"Uh, I'm not sure."

"You're in luck. We only have one Mabel onboard. Mabel Birnbaum has suite #7058."

Silence.

"Madam, are you still there?"

"Yes. Suite #7058. Thanks, Raul," Beth hung up. She sat upright, cross-legged in bed looking at the phone as if it would bite her.

Birnbaum. Incredible. Absolutely, undeniably incredible! Mabel wasn't just some random, crazy kleptomaniac. She was Max's mother. Ezekiel's first wife. How did she know Beth was looking for the will? How did Max know? *Wait a minute* ... it all made sense. If Max loses out on the inheritance, so would Mabel. They're in it together. But still, to send his mom? He must be desperate. Beth didn't know whether to laugh or cry. Still, Mabel *had* tried to kill her. Okay, maybe not *kill*, but definitely hurt her. The stakes just got higher. The action was rising. Beth realized her newly devised plan, the one she came up with late last night, *had* to work. There was no room for error. Not anymore.

First things first—she needed a big breakfast. Then go see Daniel to pick out a new watch. Nothing flashy. Then, if she had time, a visit to the gift shop to find a nice thank you for Frank. Maybe they have a *Queen Elizabeth* hoodie? Afterwards, she would put her plan into play and steal the red bag back. Beth hoped her anger-fueled confidence would provide positive karma over the next few hours.

She defiantly took a pill. So far, so good.

At the Lido Buffet, she opted for a generous stack of pancakes, sausage, and some fruit—hey, she missed lunch yesterday. As she wolfed down her breakfast, she recognized the family with the three kids sitting at the table next to her. No wonder this table was free. Surprisingly, they were quiet. Way too quiet. She glanced at the kids and noticed all three with their heads hanging into their cereal bowls. The little girl had tears sprinkled on her cheeks. Beth eavesdropped.

"If we have to tell you *one more time* to behave, that's it." The dad affirmed behind clenched teeth, his finger waving. "Your mother and I could have left you at Nana's, but we thought you were old enough to behave on the ship. Boy, were we wrong!"

One of them sniffled.

"I am *so* disappointed with you three. People are trying to have a nice meal, so not *another word* out of you. Do you understand?"

All nodded their heads without raising their eyes.

Beth remembered when her dad would lecture both her and Vicky. Fortunately, it was seldom and usually when they went out to eat, which was almost never. She remembered playing the Pinching Game. Ah, the Pinching Game! Each would take turns pinching the other underneath the table, trying to see who would squeal the loudest. It was passable behavior at Pizza Hut, but probably not on Cunard. When their squeaks escalated, they usually got a soft reprimand from Dad, "Girls, now what did I tell you before we left the house?" which would halt the game immediately from going any further. But then there was just the two of them; Beth couldn't imagine having another sibling to get in trouble with. Trouble to the third power.

She felt bad for the kids. The oldest wasn't more than seven and the *Queen Elizabeth* certainly wasn't a Disney cruise. Beth took a teaspoon from her tray and blew on it. Then she balanced it on the end of her nose. As it hovered there, she looked slowly over to the kids and crossed her eyes. They saw her and after quickly glancing at their parents, secretly smiled. Beth waved. The younger boy with vivid blue eyes shyly waved back with a bigger smile. *Okay, my work is done.* She removed the spoon. She finished her coffee and left for Deck 3 and the jewelry store.

"Don't you ever get a day off?" she asked Daniel as he used Windex to clean the display cabinet counters.

"Yes, but only when we're in port and the ship changes out passengers. The shops are closed then."

Beth explained her watch wasn't keeping time well. Daniel tested the battery.

"The battery is fine. I believe water got inside the seal and it's now rusted." He held the old Timex from its discolored strap, like a dead mouse. Its face was scratched and metal flaked from the case. "Is it valuable to you?" he asked respectfully.

"Yes. Kind of. It was my mom's. I'd like to keep it." Beth put it in her pocket. "I guess it's time for a new one."

After looking at several options—too big, too expensive, too fancy—Beth and Daniel found one just right. A two-tone metal band with a plain champagne face, the date placed at the noon marker. A second hand counted seconds. A practical Seiko.

"Is it a good watch?" She admired it on her wrist, turning it to and fro in the light.

"Yes, very nice. It's a classic and will last you a long time." Daniel took her wrist and polished her fingerprints from its crystal with a jeweler's cloth.

"Okay, I'll take it." Beth signed the $250 charge to her room.

The watch stayed on her wrist while he placed the box and warranty card in a red satin bag.

"Can I get an extra bag? A small one? I could use it for my bracelet."

Daniel gave her a second one and also attached her new charms. The bracelet was getting noisy with four charms clinking together. Sometimes they got caught up in her clothing, an unfamiliar accessory hazard. Every so often, Beth caught herself fingering each individual charm, exploring its edges. The shapes were becoming familiar: the ship, wineglass, fish, and fig leaf all had unique contours. Unsure of how many more were to come, she had asked Daniel to space them about an inch apart. Beth admitted she liked it. It was personal, a travel experience on her wrist instead of photos plastered on social media.

Beth found a chair in the Grand Lobby and waited until the main clock chimed ten o'clock, the exact time to execute her 'I'm-stealing-my-clue-back' plan. She took a deep cleansing breath and took stock of any physical issues. No tingling. No sweaty palms. She was good to go. After some quick adjustments, she silently checked off the pre-arranged steps in her head: *put charm bracelet in pocket to prevent jingling, wear squeak-free sandals, be on the lookout for Mabel at every corner, and most importantly, pretend you know what you're doing. Be confident!* She stood and casually swung her red satin bag with the empty watch box.

The cabin stewards were in full maintenance mode. From ten o'clock until noon, passengers could count on their rooms being cleaned and refreshed. Beth had run into Roberto often during this time period, so she tried to stay away to give him some space. She took the staircase to Deck 7 and just as she hoped, laundry carts jammed the passageways and cabin doors stood propped open. She figured the suites probably took longer because they were bigger. But still, she needed to be quick.

At the top of the staircase, Beth turned left and headed aft. As she bypassed carts, cabin stewards stepped out from the passageways and apologized for being in her way.

"Oh, no worries!" she sang. "I forgot my magazine. Just need to get my magazine." She smiled and continued down the passageway noting the cabin numbers ... #7048, #7050, almost there. She swung her red bag nonchalantly. *Just pretend you belong up here.* She peeked into open doorways. *Yikes, these cabins are huge!*

A few more steps brought her to #7058. A cleaning cart sat positioned in front. The door was propped open. *Bingo!* She peeked inside. There was no way to tell if it was Mabel's but Beth had to trust Raul had given her the right cabin number. Breaking into Mabel's cabin was one thing, but a perfect stranger's? That wouldn't be right.

She slipped inside the cabin. It was empty. A separate sitting room, a larger desk, a double-wide balcony ... *okay, focus!* She quickly opened the closet door and found five black dresses hanging inside. *Yep, definitely Mabel's cabin.* Beth figured it must have been a last-minute trip for Mabel too, since she had packed even less clothing than Beth had.

A noise from the passageway made her pause. Two cabin stewards began to argue over whose turn it was to clean a bathroom.

"I did it yesterday," complained one.

"I'll give you five dollars," answered another, "and a beer when we get to Lisbon."

On the other side of the closet, Beth found the small safe bolted to a shelf. It was just like her own. She only kept her passport in hers. *Please let this be right.* Beth entered a four-digit code, the cabin number, and crossed her fingers for luck.

The steward's voice got closer. The cleaning truck rattled outside the door. She quickly jumped inside the closet and tried to close the door behind her from the inside.

Ga! The dead bird hat almost made Beth's heart stop. She slapped her hand across her own mouth. Someone entered the cabin and griped about cleaning Mabel's bathroom in Filipino. Or was it Tagalog?

In any case, Beth leaned up against the back of the closet and waited with the scent of mothballs for company. She tried not to sneeze. This was exciting, in a way. A good way. *What am I doing?* She almost giggled. This caper was straight out of a movie.

After about five minutes, the toilet flushed, someone swore, and the bathroom door slammed closed.

She waited a moment. Stepped out slowly from the closet. No one there but her.

Beth faced the safe and reentered 7-0-5-8, then hit #. She turned the handle. It swung open.

Inside the safe rested a red bag. She pulled it out and looked inside. The clue and a charm were still there. She quickly switched it with a new red bag. *Success!* She buzzed with excitement. She locked the safe, quietly closed the closet door, and stepped outside into the passageway. Her entire operation took less than a minute.

"Can I help you, miss?" a cabin steward asked. He held a toilet plunger in one hand.

"Oh, no—just needed my magazine. I must have left it in the Garden Lounge. Bye!" Beth walked away as fast as her legs could carry her without running.

Since no ports were scheduled for the day, the ship bustled with passengers. Sun worshippers and book readers packed the pool areas. Movies played in the theater. Well-attended dance lessons were scheduled all day in the Queens Room. There was lots of activity in the library. Beth tucked herself in a quiet corner of the Garden Lounge—a peaceful space with potted plants and greenery placed amongst white wicker furniture, like an English garden floating on the high sea.

After the excitement wore off, Beth congratulated herself on a successful caper. Outstanding, if she did say so herself. For someone without a criminal background, she pulled it off quite nicely.

She had rationalized that old people and technology generally didn't mix. Plus, they tended to be forgetful. Her recent experiences at Table 8 taught her that. So, she figured the most logical combination for Mabel's safe was her cabin number. She was right. 7-0-5-8 did the trick. Thank goodness, because if it hadn't, she would still be there punching in arbitrary numbers.

Now she was the proud owner of a new clue and a sandcastle charm. Beth opened her pink bunny notebook. First, she copied the haiku—she wasn't going to make *that* mistake again. Then she wrote about what occurred in the last week. It started with just the facts, what she ate, where she went, who she met, but then it morphed into what she felt. The experience of laughing at Table 8, buying fancy perfume, and wearing an elegant party dress. Dancing like a wild woman at Alex and Mike's wedding reception. Embarrassing herself in front of everyone at Madeira's. And Tenerife, for that matter. Swimming with sharks ...

Who was this person? In the last seven days, Beth had learned a lot, especially about herself. She wasn't pathetic. New food, languages, and foreign locales weren't intimidating. Yes, they were exciting, but in a pleasing way. Meeting new people was fun. Lots of fun. In the past week, she'd met Mike and Alex, Daniel, Roberto, Raul, and all her Table 8 dining mates. Each was a unique individual, but all had dreams, hopes, and fears just like she did. *We aren't so different.*

She tapped her pen to her chin. This was all because of Aunt Ethel's game. A smile crept up at the corners of her mouth. Her pages quickly filled with words. *Her* words ... not someone else's story she got paid to wordsmith. It was Beth. All her.

When was the last time she wrote? Really wrote? And something truly original? It had to be back in college. She missed it. The free-flowing creativity. The more she kept writing, the more words tumbled from her. There was no organization to it, just an emptying of the balloon ... an exercise to dump everything from her head to the page. Enlightening.

Mike and Alex called out, "Hello," as they walked by. She waved back. They held hands. *Good for them.* They looked happy. Madeline followed, walking briskly and with purpose.

"Beth, fancy a judo class?" she asked, all business, "It starts in a few minutes."

"No, but thanks."

Madeline continued walking, never breaking her stride. "Suit your-self." She waggled her fingers goodbye.

Beth dove back into her writing. As she wrote, confidence returned like a long-lost friend she was genuinely happy to see. Her writing emboldened her. After a time, this self-assurance spilled over. She thought about the will and her achievement in finding the clues thus far. Little steps. She was doing it. Maybe not as well as she'd like, but she was making progress. In a way, she was forced to place trust in both Aunt Ethel and herself. Hard to do when only one of you is alive. But so far, they were working successfully in their strange existential partnership.

As Beth became more inspired, she began to plan how to get the will to Mr. Watkins once she found it. Earlier, she had noted that Connexions had a scanner that emailed documents. It would work. Once the ship returned to Southampton, she could overnight the originals to him in New York. Then what? Fly home?

She imagined Mr. Watkins would file the will in New York and see to Aunt Ethel's final wishes. She wondered what, if anything, she would get. A little money would be nice. She didn't want to be greedy, especially since the cruise was paid for and she already got some nice new clothes. What would she do with more money? Get a larger apartment? Hers was just fine. Maybe a car? Why would anyone want a car in New York City? She had no student loans to pay—she was completely debt free. But any extra money would be a nice problem to have, she decided. Maybe travel more … without the anxiety of looking for red bags? Take another cruise? *Hmmm.*

Ian walked past her with a stack of books. He simply nodded, respectful of her writing. He took a table in the sunshine, placed his glasses on his nose, and began to read.

The money didn't matter. It was the principle. Aunt Ethel's money should go to deserving people. Beth considered her parents. Mary and James Schiff were loving, hardworking, and genuinely nice people who died before their time. It wasn't fair. Good guys shouldn't always finish last. Beth's motivation wasn't the money, only that Max didn't get it. It was that simple. Maybe Aunt Ethel knew what she was doing all along.

Saul sat hunched over at a large table across the room working on a puzzle. His tongue stuck out the corner of his mouth as he focused on a fitting a piece. Beth surmised Judy worked on some kind of math problem by the way she used her fingers to count. It wasn't Sudoku, was it?

Bob Gunderson ambled by looking confused.

"Hi Beth, did you see Teresa?" he asked, "I hope she has my wallet."

"No. You didn't lose it again, did you?"

He shrugged and hurried off in search of his wife for answers.

After a time, her hand began to cramp. She massaged her fingers and looked down at her new watch—it's attractive face surprised her. She'd miss her old one, but this one was all hers. It was time for a change. *Ha! That's funny. Thanks, Aunt Ethel.*

Beth spent the rest of the afternoon contentedly writing about anything and everything that came into her head. Which was a lot.

CHAPTER 24

Seventeen Years and Seven Months Ago

The phone trilled from inside Beth's dorm room while she fumbled to unlock the heavy oak door. Her mittens couldn't grasp the keys and she faltered trying to find the correct one to stick inside the tarnished brass keyhole. With luggage at her feet and a heavy backpack falling off her shoulder, she finally unlocked the door and tripped inside the room. She flung the backpack on her twin bed.

Her six-week internship just finished. New York City was exciting, but she was glad to be back at school. *Maybe that's them offering me a job.* She grabbed the phone before it stopped ringing.

"Hello?"

"Hello, Elizabeth Schiff?" a professional-sounding voice on the other end asked.

"Yes. This is she."

Damn it's hot in here. Beth reached toward her desk and turned on a purple plastic fan. The air began to swirl around the small room. The ancient wall radiator pumped out scorching heat. No wonder tuition was so expensive.

"Elizabeth, this is Dr. Williams from Our Lady of Victory Hospital."

"Oh. How's Mom? Is she okay?" Beth sat on the bed, removed her mittens, and tried to peel off her coat.

"I'm sorry, Elizabeth. She passed away this afternoon."

Beth stared at her No Doubt poster taped to the plaster wall. Her eyes moved to a stack of books piled on the linoleum floor, then to a photo of Vicky dressed up like her character, autographed with 'Fiddlesticks!' on her desk. She looked at the afghan on the bed, shades of purple, lilac, and amethyst. Her mom had knitted it. Beth fingered one of the tassels on the end and played with the individual strands of yarn.

"Elizabeth?" Dr. Williams asked.

"Yes."

"I'm so sorry."

"Thanks … can you put my sister on? Victoria?"

"She's not here."

"My sister's not there? She's supposed to visit today."

"No. We haven't seen her." A rustle of papers in the background validated.

"You mean she was alone? My mom died alone?" Beth stood up from the bed, her coat still hung off one arm.

"Your name was listed as first to call. Is there anyone else you'd like us to contact?" Dr. Williams sounded as though she needed to wrap it up.

"No. I'll do it. Can I come down to see her? Is it possible?"

Beth made arrangements with Dr. Williams to be at the hospital within the hour. She would deal with her luggage later. She kicked everything to her side of the room and left a quick note for her roommate, Gwen. *Sorry for the mess. Mom died. Going to hospital. Will call later.*

In the last few months, Beth got to know her way around Our Lady of Victory quite well. Enter through the middle automatic doors. Check-in with the reception desk on the right. Take a piece of hard candy from the glass bowl. Walk to the elevator bank on the left. Press button for UP. Wait. Smell coffee from the cafeteria further down the hall. Press 3. Ride elevator, get out. Turn left, walk twenty-three steps to room number twelve. At the end, she would find her mom. Unconscious, but always present, always there. Now, Beth stood in the doorway and saw an empty bed with a bare mattress and pillow without a case.

She held onto the bed railing. Machines sat silent and dark. No beeps or blips, which made it even more tangible. She was really gone. After all this time, it had happened. Beth's shoulders collapsed as tears arrived. She stood as pain bloomed in her chest. Her heart hurt. First Dad and now Mom. Both gone within a few months of each other. She didn't get a chance to say goodbye to either of them.

Her cell phone rang, startling her.

It was Vicky. "Beth? I just got the call from Dr. Williams. Where are you?"

"I'm at the hospital. Where are *you*?" Beth demanded. "You were supposed to be here. You promised." She wiped her nose with the back of her hand. Her sorrow flipped to anger.

"I'm still on the set. The shoot's going over. I planned to come over tomorrow."

"Well, it's too late now, isn't it? I can't believe you left her alone."

"Beth, she's alone all week. We can't be there all the time," Vicky said matter-of-factly.

"How would you know? You never visit. I came every weekend during my internship. The *one* weekend I'm not here ..."

"Beth, I ..."

"There's always an excuse, Vicky. You're too busy, it's too expensive to fly from L.A. ... I was here *every* weekend. It's not fair."

"Not *fair*?" Vicky responded quickly. "I have a job, Beth. A *job*. Do you know what that's like? No, you wouldn't." She sniffed and blew her nose. "Don't think you're the only one upset because Mom is gone. I loved her, too."

"You have a funny way of showing it. Just because you *happened* to be filming in Philly, now you *manage* to find the time. You said you would ..." Beth's voice became louder as she spoke faster.

"I got it Beth. I *got* it."

"And I *was* working. I just finished my internship, which is why *I* couldn't be here."

A nurse appeared in the doorway and ducked her head inside the room.

"Miss, please. Can you keep it down?" She gave Beth a warning look and closed the door.

Vicky spoke to someone in the background. "Yeah, just give me a few minutes." She said to Beth, "They need me back on set. They only have City Hall for another two hours before they tear down cameras. I've got to go."

"You're kidding, right?" Beth's eyes and mouth fell wide open.

"Beth, she's gone. It really sucks. But there's nothing we can do about it." Vicky paused, "I'm sorry I wasn't there, but ..."

"What about the funeral? I need your help, Vicky. I need you here." Beth couldn't hold back any longer and exploded in a wave of tears. She reached for a tissue on the bedside table. She couldn't do this again, bury another parent. Her fingers started to tingle like they had fallen asleep.

"Can you call Aunt Ethel? I just don't know if I can take the time off."

"I can't believe it. You barely made Dad's and now you're going to miss Mom's? Really?"

"I don't know Beth," Vicky repeated quietly. "I'll call you later. I have to—"

Something in Beth's heart switched off and her head followed. "I know your career is important. Mine will be too, but Vicky ..." She paused. "I don't think I can forgive you if you don't come. I can't do this alone." The tingle in her fingers traveled to her hands, making it difficult to hold the phone.

Silence met her. And before Beth could say anything further, a click reverberated. Vicky had hung up. The conversation was over.

Beth collapsed in an uncomfortable guest chair and wept, for her mom, her dad, but mostly for herself. Her life would never be the same. How could it possibly be?

CHAPTER 25

The martini was tart on her tongue. Icey, but tart. Beth unconsciously made a face with her lips puckered.

"Don't you like it?" Alex asked.

"It's a little sour."

"Maybe that's why they call it a Tartini. We'll try something different next round," Mike said. He raised his glass and they all toasted by clinking.

Earlier that afternoon, when she returned from her epic writing jag, Beth found a note had been slid under her cabin door. At first, she fretted—*oh no, not again*—but it turned out to be an invitation for pre-dinner drinks at the Commodore Club from Alex and Mike.

Now all three were comfortably seated in club chairs around a small cocktail table. A crystal dish of cashews sat in the center. The pianist was in the middle of a Sinatra set.

This is class, Beth decided.

"You look smashing by the way," Mike said. Beth glanced down at her new silver sequined dress from the Cunard boutique. No Spanx needed, as it fell loosely to her knees, kind of like a 1960s shift. She wore her new red lipstick and no more wonky glasses. She felt spunky. Who knows, maybe she'd go dancing later at the Yacht Club. Beth relaxed and joined in the easy conversation; they bantered back and forth like old friends.

"I can't believe you're here alone. Did you leave anyone special back home? Kids? Pets?" Alex asked.

"I have a cat. And lots of books. That's about all my apartment will fit," Beth answered.

Mike's two dimples deepened. "We have cats too! *And* we're thinking of adopting."

"Another cat?" Beth asked. She took another sip of her drink ... still tart.

"No, a child."

"Wow. That's a big change. I can't imagine," she said.

Alex shook his head. "I don't know how we can raise a kid if we can't handle three cats. Let's just say, we're discussing it." He popped some cashews into his mouth. "Plus, you *really* can't forget to feed your kid." He glanced over at Mike with a raised eyebrow.

"I promise. I'll get better." Mike leaned over and kissed Alex on the cheek.

Beth laughed. All three agreed the ship was wonderful, the service exceptional, and opportunities to people-watch, extensive. On the farthest possible young side of old, the thirty-somethings stood out among the passengers.

The pianist started playing Billy Joel and Beth tapped her toes. This reminded her to complement their party.

"Your wedding reception was awesome. I haven't danced like that in forever," she said.

"Thanks," Mike said. "At first we were concerned, you know a gay wedding at sea, but it turned out not to be an issue."

"It shouldn't be," Beth said.

"Surprisingly," Alex said, "the passengers have been welcoming. It's not every day you see a gay, married couple out, loud and proud. Most of their generation would have fallen overboard seeing us hold hands on the ship, let alone get hitched. But hardly anyone's batted an eye."

"Except for that one lady," Mike said.

"Oh, yeah." Alex sipped his drink.

"What happened?" Beth asked.

Alex continued, "This older lady approached us on deck. We were just standing at the railing and looking out at the sea. I may have had my arm around Mike, I honestly don't remember. Anyways, she taps my shoulder and informs us in the most saccharine voice possible, that we're going to hell."

Beth choked on her drink. "What did you say back?" she sputtered.

"I said, 'No problem, see you there.'" He laughed.

"What did she look like?"

"A little elderly lady dressed all in black, like a professional Italian mourner. She had a cane. We're lucky she didn't hit us with it."

Hmmm. Beth wondered if it was possible to hate Mabel even more. Now she knew for sure who had left the nasty note on her cabin door a few days ago. But then she smiled, picturing Mabel's face when she opened the safe and realized the red bags had been exchanged. Beth's grin grew even wider thinking about what she had written on the piece of paper: *Screw you and your little Max, too.* Yes, it was childish, but still ...

"What's so funny?" asked Alex.

"Nothing, just having a great time." She smiled and meant it. The Tartini wasn't so bad.

Even on vacation, work invariably wormed its way into their discussion. Mike was a senior partner in a law firm and Alex a corporate tax accountant on Wall Street. Both successful, they liked to travel when their infrequent vacation time aligned. And, small world, they lived only a few blocks from her apartment in lower Manhattan. They all declared, "Brunch!" at the same time and laughed.

Beth said she was a ghostwriter with several non-fiction books published, all with her name in small letters inside the cover.

"Does it bother you?" Mike asked.

"I'm okay with being a ghost ... but it's recently started to irk me," she said. "So-called 'authors' getting credit for things they never wrote. But it's why I get paid well." She explained that to be a successful novelist, not only did you need to write exceedingly well, but be a business manager, web designer, *and* social media expert. Her college advisor never mentioned that. "Some of my classmates tried self-publishing their novels, but the marketing was too hard. You know business and art is difficult to mix. Now I see Facebook posts of weary women I no longer recognize. Apparently, being married with kids can do that. So, be careful, you two!"

Mike and Alex pounced on her with questions from either side. Who did she write for? Who was the nicest? Who was the bitchiest? Basically, all the dirt. Beth tried to be professional but couldn't help dishing a little.

They compared their favorite restaurants and decided Queens had the most diverse food options. They complained about the high cost of rent. They discussed movies, music, and TV shows. All agreed there was nothing original anymore.

"Same old, same old. If I see one more Marvel superhero movie, I'll lose it entirely," Mike said.

"Or what about remakes? How many times can you reboot *Spiderman*?" Alex asked. "There was nothing wrong with the first one."

"Or sequels and prequels? I loved *Star Wars* as a kid but come on. What are we up to now, nine movies?" Mike shook his head and finished his drink.

Beth added, "What about hospital shows? How many can there be?"

"I can't stand the legal shows," Mike said. "They get so much wrong. What's the one with the ditzy, blond receptionist?"

"*Legal Briefs*?" Beth asked. Her gaze darted into her glass.

"Yeah, *that* one. Talk about terrible. It sets women's rights back a few decades," he said.

Beth finished her Tartini in a single gulp.

"That's why I love New York City. Yes, it's ridiculously expensive, but the theater saves me," Mike said dramatically, putting his hand to his brow.

"When's the last time you went to the theatre?" Alex asked Beth.

She shrugged. "I couldn't tell you. I don't do a lot of things outside my apartment."

Alex and Mike glanced at each other. "Why not?" Mike asked.

"Is it because of your job?" Alex volunteered.

Beth hesitated. She readjusted her dress hem over her knees. "No ... it's just that I ...well ..."

The friendly conversation felt like it came to an uncomfortable stop. Alex patted her shoulder kindly.

"You don't have to tell us."

Beth looked at the men. Their sandy hair almost the same color, Alex's a little darker, showing some gray. Mike's dimples disappeared. Both sets of eyes rested on her. Caring. Understanding. Like Frank's. She decided to share. "I have some anxiety issues. But I've been working on them." It was enough and simply put.

Mike smiled. "That's it? We *all* have issues, some big, some small. And *some* appear more frequently." He looked over at Alex. "Like visits from your mother."

They laughed, breaking the small tension.

Alex looked at their empty glasses, frowned, and motioned the server over. "Okay, Miss Beth, what are we drinking next?"

Beth glanced at the drink menu and pointed to one.

"Manhattans, very appropriate." Alex turned to the server. "We'll take three."

It was eight-fifteen and Beth sashayed her way to dinner feeling no pain. No pain at all. Bobbing and weaving, she smiled at passengers and staff. She waived grandly and said "Hello" to people she didn't know. When she finally arrived at the Britannia Restaurant, she took the arm of the maître'd as he escorted her to Table 8. Her dress glinted in the lights as she swayed toward the table.

"Helloooo, everyone!" she announced while plopping into her chair. Glenn helped her with her napkin.

"Beth, look at you. So sparkly!" Constance said.

Before she could respond, Bob Gunderson stood up and nervously readjusted his bow tie. He cleared his throat in preparation.

"I have an announcement. Now that we're *all* here," he glanced with mock irritation at Beth, "Teresa and I are celebrating our anniversary. Forty years ago, this lovely lady said, 'I do.' To celebrate, I'd like to buy the wine tonight."

Table 8 erupted in enthusiastic applause as Brigitte ceremoniously handed the wine bible to Bob with a small bow.

Beth listed to her left side and decided to test Ian's food knowledge for fun. The menu was full of foreign languages she couldn't place with her fuzzy brain. What is this, United Nations Night?

"What's fromage?" she asked with a hiccup.

"Cheese," Ian responded, "in French."

"Why don't they just say cheese?"

"Fromage sounds classier."

"What's gazpacho?"

"Soup."

"Ceviche? I forgot." She giggled.

"Raw fish."

"Ewww." She hiccupped again.

"Beth, just order." Ian laughed.

Dinner was outstanding. Beth ate smoked Norwegian salmon mousse for an appetizer and the Chinese roasted duck with Croatian wild mushroom pierogies for an entrée. Bob's selection of French-oaked chardonnay was perfect. Rich and buttery, it complemented all her food choices. *How awesome is this!* She ate her way through several international specialties. Everything tasted delicious. *Delicious!* Beth felt pretty fantastic. *Fantastic!*

Conversations around the table ran the gamut.

Madeline and Constance disagreed about port stops on previous cruises.

"Yes, we *did* visit Dubrovnik in 2005," Constance insisted.

"Prove it," Madeline argued, using her steak knife as emphasis, jabbing it towards her.

Constance looked up at the chandelier. "Hmmm. Maybe I'm thinking Talin? Where did you buy that lovely amber necklace? The one I'm eventually going to steal?"

"That was the Dominican Republic ... and an entirely different cruise," Madeline said.

Judy and Teresa exchanged photos of grandchildren, pointing and laughing together.

"Yes, hopefully mine will have hair soon. Oh, those poor bald babies," Judy said.

Saul and Bob discussed the cost of a good whisky.

"Don't you think it comes down to the distillery?" Saul asked, peering into his own glass of amber liquid.

"Absolutely," Bob agreed. "But time-in-the-barrel? That always adds a few zeros. Plus, you can't beat a good Scotch. And that's a whisky *without* an 'e.'"" They laughed and clinked glasses from across the table as if a true kinship had been fostered.

There were no awkward pauses. Everyone had something to discuss and found commonalities with each other. They did not always agree, but politely discoursed. Beth smiled and looked down at her charm bracelet. She had things to talk about now too.

"Did you find another clue?" Constance asked, inclining her head at Beth's wrist.

"Yes." Beth abruptly stuck out her arm and almost punched Constance in the nose to show off the new sandcastle charm she stole back from Mabel.

"Oh, my! Everyone, look! Beth found another clue!" Constance announced loudly for the table to hear. A flood of questions surrounded her from all sides. Her tablemates wanted to hear the entire story from the beginning. Beth relayed how she searched for Mike and found Miguel instead at the beach stand. How she found the sandcastle built by Miguel, aka Mike. Then how she fell asleep and fell off her lounge chair.

"How lucky for you," Madeline said. "You could have missed the ship!"

"I know. I actually had a nightmare about it. But now," Beth held up her other wrist, "I have a new watch that keeps excellent time." She showed off her new Seiko as compliments vocalized around the table.

"Lovely."

"Beautiful."

"A classic."

Feeling emboldened whilst the center of attention, Beth confessed, "I really need your help with the next clue."

It seemed her table mates had traveled to many of these international destinations more than once before. The next stop was Lisbon. Certainly, someone had been there already. Plus, this next clue had her completely stumped. It was written differently. Not really a task, but more of a riddle. Based on her recent misfortune, she not only had it safely written in her notebook but memorized.

Maybe it was the pre-dinner drinks in addition to the wine at dinner, for Beth proceeded to recite it in a sing-song-y voice.

A panicky clown
prepares to die on the stage.
Shot provides relief.

Saul looked at Judy. Madeline looked at Constance. Bob looked at Teresa. Ian looked at Beth. The table sat muted. Saul scratched his head. Glenn approached with the dessert menus and saw Table 8 in silent bewilderment.

"Is there anything wrong?" he asked. He glanced at each passenger looking for some sort of problem. Bob quickly ordered Hungarian Tokaji wine for dessert.

After Glenn left, Ian said, "Read it again."

They brainstormed but came up with nothing tangible. Theories, musings, but nothing concrete. Disappointed, they wished they could have provided better help.

Brigitte returned with two small bottles of the dessert wine and dainty cordial glasses balanced on a tray. As the table watched, she professionally uncorked and poured equal amounts into each. Beth sipped her Tokaji between bites of warm Viennese apple strudel with Mexican brandy sauce. Sweet, but nice with the flaky strudel. Many toasts were made for Bob and Teresa. They both laughed and kissed each other like newlyweds.

Alcohol continued to flow as if prohibition was just around the corner. Constance and Ian exchanged dirty limericks and competed with each other for audience effect. Saul stood up and for no good reason, sang "Sweet Caroline" by Neil Diamond. He had a pleasant-enough voice, which resulted in applause from other diners at surrounding tables. When Teresa lost a false eyelash, Madeline laughed so hard she had to fan herself with a page from the wine bible to catch her breath. Now the reds and whites were mixed up in the wine menu, but when Beth tried to organize the pages by country, she forgot the alphabet. Judy's voice kept raising additional octaves with every drink until she sounded like a parrot getting a colonoscopy. Bob stood up to take everyone's picture but had misplaced his camera again.

When after-dinner coffees were finally served, they unanimously agreed to add Bailey's Irish Cream to complete the evening's international food tour. Glenn politely asked if anyone needed anything further. Looking around, Table 8 noticed they were the last table remaining in the entire restaurant, which precipitated more laughter. They reluctantly finished their dregs of coffee, pushed back their chairs, and said goodnight to the staff. Bob actually hugged Brigitte, and Constance kissed Glenn's cheek while he turned a bright crimson.

Just after eleven o'clock, Table 8 tripped out of the dining room. With arms linked like the Radio City Music Hall Rockettes' kick line, they forced other passengers to move to one side as they bulldozed their way down the passageway. At the end of the hall, a photographer set up for formal portraits spied the troop approaching and a small panic flitted over his eyes. The group took a quick vote. After much frenzied discussion and disorganization (and to the dismay of the photographer) all eight squeezed into a single picture. As the photographer pulled the camera further back to accommodate, the group rearranged themselves. Finally, they assembled into a reasonable tableau.

"Say cheese!" he said, trying to focus the shot.

"Fromage!" Beth yelled. The photo snapped while the group howled with laughter.

Chapter 26

A Google search on keywords 'Lisbon' and 'clown' equaled a single result: The Chapitô Circus School and Restaurant received fair to average reviews according to TripAdvisor. Beth's tour ticket didn't include Chapitô. Maybe it was a good thing. Or not? Beth wondered if the clown school had the next red bag. What if Mabel found it before her?

Beth laid in bed, flummoxed, scrolling on her phone. The clue *had* to be in Lisbon since it was the last scheduled port stop on the cruise. Beth wanted to trust she was booked on the correct tour. But after the Blandy's/Oliveira's debacle in Madeira, she couldn't be so sure.

Unbelievably, the cruise was almost over. For as many incidents and misadventures she had while finding the clues, Beth was enjoying herself. She loved her cabin. She loved the food. She loved her new friends. Were all these wonderful things because of her medication? It was only day number two of taking it regularly. None of it mattered if she couldn't find the will.

Yet after she read Mr. Watkin's last email, she felt some pressure.

Dear Beth,

I know you are trying your utmost best, but a gentle reminder less than ten days remain in which to file Ethel's will. In the meantime, we received correspondence from Max Birnbaum's legal representation notifying us of their intentions to file the existing trust. They are moving forward.

I await your next email with reserved optimism.

Sincerely,

J. J. Watkins

Like she needed to be reminded. Okay, Beth admitted she was having fun. With her headache, maybe a little *too* much fun. This morning, she woke up and found her new silver sequined dress hanging askew from a wall sconce in her cabin. How it got there, who knows? She just remembered sleeping like a big wine-induced baby. It must have been the Tokaji. She blamed Bob.

After popping two aspirins and chowing down on her breakfast delivery of a pot of black coffee, fruit, and yogurt, Beth's synapses began firing. She pulled out the brochure and tour ticket for 'Luscious Lisbon.' Like all major port cities, it was jam-packed with history. She read up on the historical sites, restaurants, and activities and determined it was tragic the ship only stayed in port for a single day. There was just too much to see.

Her booked tour was a walking tour—no bus today. *How thrilling!* Busses were a great way to see many sights in a single day, but she preferred walking. It was the only way to experience the true flavor of a city, or at least that's what Constance said. Beth agreed. It was hard to smell freshly baked bread from inside a bus.

She picked out a bright yellow dress, her most comfortable, broken-in sandals and her straw hat. In a few minutes, her tote bag was packed and she was ready. She met the tour group, a small cozy gathering of twelve, which included the Kippermans, at the bottom of the ship's gangplank.

Beth scoured the dock looking for Mabel. Was she on another bus? A different tour? One including the Chapitô School? She kept an eye out while they grouped together in front of the ship. Unless Mabel had decided to go incognito and change her outfit into something racy, like beige, Beth didn't see her.

"Can you believe we've never been to Lisbon?" Judy admitted to Beth. "After so many cruises, this is our first time. I can't wait to visit the pastry shop—it's world famous!"

Saul fussed with his fanny pack and searched for fresh camera batteries. He looked up and beamed at Judy.

Beth couldn't imagine being married to Saul. He constantly viewed the world from his camera lens, taking pictures instead of experiencing the moment. But still, Beth had to admit he was a kind man. The way he looked into Judy's eyes and held her hand like a schoolboy. No doubt he absolutely, positively, adored her. With his camera bag permanently attached to his hip, he was poised to take photos by the hundreds of Judy, as if she were a supermodel on location. Mom always said, "There's a lid for every pot." Beth reminded herself to buy another postcard to send Frank and Paul.

An outrageously handsome Portuguese man, Alfonso, led the day's itinerary. With his black hair, flashing green eyes, and ridiculously sensuous smile, he had a way of looking at the older women that made them feel decades younger. He wore tight black jeans and a tailored button-down shirt with a few buttons casually undone. He carried a red umbrella and gestured with it like a fencing sword. Beth decided she wouldn't mind a picture of him.

"Yes, ladies and gentlemen, we have a day planned ... such a day like no other. I promise beautiful sights, delectable food, and at the end, you will fall in love with Lisbon, as sailors have for centuries. A beautiful, magnificent city to adore and love ... deep, deep in your heart ..." he went on.

Yikes. He's like a live telenovela.

"But first, a small history of Lisbon, as we stand at the mighty Praça Do Comercio square." He swirled the umbrella toward the archway, as if he were on stage. His exaggerated movements incited drama. Ladies swooned.

Beth learned Lisbon was founded in 1256. Its history was built on trade between many international ports, so ships were its lifeblood. Even the many hand-painted tiles decorating building facades depicted ships. The blue and white tiles looked like intricate wallpaper from afar. Alfonso dutifully pointed these out intricate details one would normally miss traipsing through the city without a guide.

They strolled toward the majestic archway directly north of the square and into the Baixa district. Shops lined either side of the cobblestone streets which gave it a medieval feel. The tour's first stop was an old church, placed high above them as if the street had sunk over time. The church was nothing spectacular, but it did provide a rest-stop away from the sun.

After a hike up a very steep street, the group stopped and panted at a non-descript corner. There they waited for a famous trolley. Alfonso explained it was famous because it was old and still working on the steep slopes. Unbelievably, the modern ones didn't. Even with all the new technologies and energy efficiencies, new trolleys couldn't climb the famous Lisbon hills.

In a few minutes, they heard (before they saw) number 28 rattle up the hill and stop with a screech. The trolley had bright yellow paint and scarred wooden benches. Beth got a window seat, which provided great city views. The trolley clanged, shimmied, and sputtered up another steep hill to the very top of Lisbon, where they all disembarked.

On a broad piazza, they could see the *Queen Elizabeth* docked directly below. The front steps of the Castello de Sao Jorge turned out to be a terrific photo spot. The tour group took pictures of each other standing in front of the seemingly miniature ship. Because of the forced perspective, they pretended to hold the ship in the palm of their hands. The women asked Alfonso to pose with them. When it was Beth's turn, Alfonso wrapped an arm around her waist.

He looked down at her, smiled with a corner of his mouth and said, "Lindeza."

The tops of her ears tingled. Beth gulped. "Hey Alfonso, any chance we're going to the Chapitô Circus School and Restaurant for lunch today?"

"No. That place is shit. Other tours go there. Not me. I take you to a fantástico spot." Alfonso gave her an extra squeeze before releasing her waist. *Great.* She winced.

The piazza was popular with street vendors, who tried to sell hand-painted tiles to tourists. Beth selected one of a ship painted with varying shades of blue. She turned it over and noticed a 'Made in China' sticker before handing it back. Still, for three dollars, it would make someone a nice coaster.

Alfonso swirled his red umbrella to reassemble the group. With great fanfare, he announced the next stop was lunch.

Saul responded with, "Thank goodness. I'm starving," and finally stowed his camera away.

After a few steps down a small incline and around a corner with a stone tower, the group arrived at the Restaurant de Santa Luzia. As though perfectly timed, the owner waited at its arched stone entrance. Two young women with aprons stood on either side of him.

"Oh, this is a great restaurant," Judy gushed. "They have excellent mussels."

"Alfonso!" The proprietor grabbed him in a big hug and smacked kisses on each cheek. The women blushed and shyly bowed their heads, while trying to catch a side eye glimpse of Alfonso.

"This is my tremendous friend. He will feed us like kings," Alfonso said as he ushered the group to a stone patio. The outdoor seating provided spectacular views. While seated in their chairs, the tourists could still view the ship in the distance, lying peacefully on the cerulean sea. The sun glinted off the water, requiring everyone to wear sunglasses.

Beth sat with the Kippermans. Chilled bottles of Vino Verde, a Portuguese white wine, were placed on the table with carafes of water. Still harboring a small but persistent hangover, Beth poured herself a large water instead. There were no menus in sight.

The two young servers brought out platters piled high with food to each table. One dish after another arrived. Seafood paella, lamb shanks, squash soup. Fresh warm bread. Mussels and clams swimming in garlic sauce. As one platter was finished, another magically appeared. Beth wondered about the army of cooks in the kitchen preparing all this food. The guests not only tried it all, but they ate every bit. Lips smacked appreciatively as they ate for almost two hours. In the end, there were no unhappy stomachs. Just tight pants.

From the restaurant, Alfonso brought out a woman with a dish towel tucked in a dirty apron. Her hair tied back in a scarf. He held her hand and kissed it regally, like a devoted servant.

"Here's the cook, everyone. Say hello to Marta."

She blushed and the group applauded while shouting their thanks. She patted Alfonso's cheek.

"Thank you!"

"Obrigado!"

"Delicious!"

After all the wonderful food, Beth didn't mind the walk back down to the city. The group wove slowly down steep cobblestone sidewalks leading back to the Baixa. As they approached a pedestrian street filled with shops, the cobblestones organized themselves into beautiful patterns. Black and white stones laid out in graphic patterns provided direction, just like the yellow brick road to the Emerald City.

"My lovely ladies and gentlemen. Now I have something wonderful to show you." Alfonso's eyes flashed. The group huddled around him in excitement. A large rectangular plaza, two football fields long, showcased alternating black and gray cobblestones in a wave pattern. It went on seemingly for forever.

The group collectively oohed and ahhed at the workmanship. Saul took out his camera and snapped away, angling the lens for more artistic shots.

"Yes, it's nice. But not what I want to show you. Come with me." Alfonso waved for them to follow, while he turned to the right onto a narrower side street. He continued to talk, "I have a fascinating story to tell …"

Beth stopped paying attention. Again, like on the other tours, time wasn't her friend. While the ladies focused on Alfonso, Beth checked her new watch. It was after two o'clock and the tour only had a few stops left. She studied her Lisbon map and searched for anything clown-related. Maybe she should just take a taxi and go to the shitty clown-school-restaurant. Mabel could be there right now getting the next clue.

Panicky clown … stage … shot … did Lisbon have a gun shop? She wanted to interrupt Alfonso and ask, but he was in the middle of his story. She waited for him to pause.

"… and he was Italian but would come to Lisbon to perform at the Coliseu. But, oh Eduardino, he would be so nervous, each time he was afraid to fail. So, he wandered the streets trying not to think of his show. One day he came across a Lisbon favorite …" Alfonso's eyes got theatrically large as he gestured to the left side of the street.

Encased in stone blocks, stood a narrow, green-painted shop, perhaps only five feet wide. An ornate sign with gold lettering said, "Ginja Sem Rival" and featured bright red cherries painted into the corners. Windows spanned the entire front of the store so they could see that inside held glass shelves with bottles. Only two sizes, large and small, were neatly displayed in rows from the ground to the ceiling.

"Here." Alfonso pointed. "Since 1850, this shop makes the famous Lisbon ginja—a cherry liqueur. So, Eduardino goes in and drinks at the counter. He feels so much better; he goes on stage and is his funniest ever. Here, we'll all try it. But we must take turns, as it's very small inside. Only fits two at a time." He led the way with his umbrella.

From the street, Beth could see an elderly man with white Einstein-like hair standing behind a wooden counter inside the shop. He waved and called out, "Alfonso!" His arms stretched wide in greeting.

Beth asked Judy, "I missed the first part. He wasn't talking about a clown, was he?"

"Yes. Wasn't that a terrific story? Saul, we have to buy another bottle." Judy maneuvered into the line leading inside. Saul snapped more pictures of Judy pointing overhead to the famous bar's sign.

Could this be it? *Clown ... shot ...* it had to be. Beth had no other choice but to queue with the rest of the group. Just ahead, inside the shop, the sound of bottles being uncapped and liqueur pouring into small plastic cups provided some optimism. As they waited, Alfonso explained to the group there were two kinds of liqueur, one infused with whole cherries and one without. They could try one of each. The shopkeeper poured several cups. Beth waited patiently for her turn. As the Kippermans exited, Judy held up a small brown paper bag with intricate gold lettering on it.

"Quite a kick, especially the cherry at the bottom. Watch out!" Saul warned.

From inside the doorway, more shelves lined with bottles, an ancient brass cash register and a closed door behind the counter. She listened as the owner asked customers questions.

"Who are you? Where you from?" A smile crossed his face as he poured more ginja into cups. Finally, it was her turn. She approached the wooden bar.

"Who are you? Where you from?" he repeated.

"My name's Beth and I'm from New York City." She took one of the cups and drank the liqueur in one shot. He laughed when she sputtered and coughed. After she got her breath back, she asked, "Did you know my aunt? Ethel Birnbaum?"

His eyes flew wide. His hands raised up in surprise. "Miz Ethel? Ohh, you are *the* Beth? I have something for you. Something special." Before she could respond, he immediately took her hand and dragged her around the counter toward the other door.

Inside, a storeroom held many dusty, dirty boxes. The man pointed to them.

"Uh, all these are for me?"

"No, no," he laughed. "You find a ginja bottle."

Aha! Here's my next clue. Beth looked at him. He continued to smile. His hair twanged in all directions.

"Where is it?"

"In a box."

"Which box?"

"You find." He patted her hand, turned around and went back into the store to serve more customers.

Really? Beth looked at the cardboard boxes, stacked from the floor to the ceiling. Ten rows high and ten boxes across equaled a hundred boxes. They resembled a Jenga puzzle. Or better yet, the cardboard houses she and Vicky had played with before receiving Aunt Ethel's wonderful playhouse. She arbitrarily opened a box on the ground next to her. It was filled with six large bottles of ginja. It wasn't too heavy. She needed to start somewhere, but which one?

Each box had a label with a combination of three letters and four numbers. Probably for inventory, Beth guessed. Or maybe shipping. Yet each label was different and none of them matched. Also, they were organized in no particular order. Box AUA-1854 sat below box ZRH-2001, so alphabetization was out. She glanced back to the shop and wondered how much time she had before the tour got going again. Hopefully, people would keep drinking. A lot.

BUF-1969, LAX-1982, RSW-1946. They weren't license plates. The letters and numbers meant something. She could ask the owner, but already knew he wouldn't help her. This puzzle belonged to her and it had Aunt Ethel's fingerprints all over it. Wait a minute. She remembered back to her British Airways ticket. *Could they be airport codes?*

The sun shone through a small window and highlighted dust particles swirling through the air, which was hot and thick. DEN-1901, CHI-1954 ... they *could* be. Boxes at the very top row were labeled with LGA-2005 and JFK-2010, New York airports. She wondered if the numbers were years. That would make sense. PHI-1986.

She was born in Philadelphia in 1986.

Of course, the box had to be at the top. *And* in the middle.

She sighed and wiped her forehead with the back of her hand. The heat made the room stuffy. The PHI-1986 box must be twenty feet high up there. *Heights ... it figures.* What if she got dizzy climbing? What if she fell? What if the whole stack of carefully balanced boxes crashed on top of her? What if her mouth was open? What if she died due to alcohol poisoning? What if ...

Enough! She grabbed her wrist and felt the charm bracelet. This was just one more step closer to finding the will. She disregarded her nerves (and The List) and got to work figuring out a plan.

She couldn't move the boxes; they were stacked too high over her head. But if she had a ladder ... Beth searched the storeroom. No ladder. In fact, nothing at all except for the wall of boxes. Could she *make* a ladder?

She stood at the far left-side of the wall and kicked off her sandals. At waist-high, she tried pushing a box in front of her, just to see if it would move. It was heavy, having eight more boxes stacked on top of it, but when she pushed really hard, (really, really, hard) she found it moved back just an inch, maybe two. This left an edge to stand on with her toes. She balanced on top of the exposed space on the box below. Her body and hands stretched flat against the boxes, there was nothing else to hold onto.

Beth pushed another box up and to her right. Then she climbed up to its edge, moving up another row. One more up and to the right. Then another. And another until she had a diagonal ladder reaching up to the top row. By this time, she was filthy and exhausted. Her hands hurt and her toes cramped from balancing. She hauled herself to the top and straddled the top row of boxes like a horse.

Geez, it's high! It reminded Beth of the playhouse, years ago, the feeling of being taller than anyone else and seeing a different perspective than from the ground. Powerful. She closed her eyes remembering. Just for good measure, she sang, "I'm fine!" And she was. Then she wiped her forehead leaving a streak of dirt across it. Her new yellow dress was a disastrous sweaty mess. She reached forward and tried to lift the PHI-1986 box up with her fingertips. It was surprisingly light. She took a corner and pulled it up toward her. Instead of trying to haul it back down the way she came, she opened the cardboard flaps. Inside, lay a single, small bottle of ginja with a small red bag secured to its neck. *Jackpot!*

Beth untied the bag and found a piece of folded paper. She read it quickly.

Make joyful music.
Keys are elementary,
just like black and white.

The charm was missing. Beth double-checked the bag. It wasn't there. There was nothing left in the box. *Damn.* She tucked the bottle inside her dress and wrapped her bra strap around its neck. She wedged the red bag in her cleavage. *Now, that's creative.*

Her armpits dripped sweat and her knees were shaky. But she carefully retraced her steps and followed the edges she had already created to get back down the stack of boxes. Step by careful step. Once on solid ground, she grabbed her sandals and ran quickly out of the storeroom. She reached into her dress and untangled the bottle. The proprietor laughed and clapped her on the back.

"Special ... for you!" He took the bottle from Beth's hands, opened it, and poured her a shot. A cherry sat at the bottom of the cup. She looked at him, with an eyebrow raised. This time, she sipped the liqueur slowly. A warm feeling hit the back of her throat and meandered south to her belly. The corners of her eyes smarted. At the bottom of the cup, lay the alcohol-infused cherry.

"Please," the man said, encouraging her with hand motions.

She took the cherry out of the cup and bit it in half. Metal clinked against her front teeth. Instinctively, she spat it out into her palm. A silver charm lay sandwiched inside.

"Oh, ho, ho ..." The older man laughed. He slapped his palm on the counter. Alfonso looked confused. "Miss Ethel, she's so funny. Always funny."

Beth looked into the palm of her hand and pulled out a charm. A silver cherry.

"You have another present. Here. A present." He screwed the cap back on and handed her the bottle with the remainder of the liqueur.

"Thank you!" she said smiling. She excitedly stuffed everything into her tote bag, including the sweaty red bag. Beth leaned over the counter and hugged the old man, transferring cobwebs and dirt onto him. *Oh, what the Hell.* She hugged Alfonso too, leaving dirty handprints on his shirt. Oh, he smelled so nice. But not as nice as pine trees after a Colorado snow. She danced out of the shop. Saul and Judy waited for her in the street.

"Where have you been? You look terrible!" Judy said. Beth showed them the charm and note. They hugged her too. Judy gave her a few wet wipes from her purse to try and clean off her face and hands.

The tour couldn't have ended any better. The last stop on the itinerary was the Confeitaria Nacional Pastry shop. A perfect way to celebrate. Established in 1829, it was a veritable institution of baked confections and sweets. The now familiar intricate blue and white tiles faced the building's exterior and large black lanterns hung above the windows. Inside, on the first floor, glass display cases held a bounty of appealing treasures. Small eclairs fashioned in the shape of mice complete with chocolate tails. Shortbread cups filled with gleaming jellied fruit. Miniature pastry shells with golden custard, lightly caramelized with sugar.

Where to start? Lunch was practically hours ago.

The tour group gawked at the cases while they followed Alfonso up an ornate wooden staircase to the second floor. High ceilings and tall windows afforded unlimited views of the square below. A server, with a white apron up to his armpits, held a small pad and pen at the ready.

Too many choices. The group implored Alfonso for guidance. But before he could answer, Beth suddenly announced they would have one of everything and she was buying. The group looked astonished. However, the server responded with, "Absolutely, madam," as if this happened daily. He turned and headed downstairs to look for a larger tray.

CHAPTER 27

B ack in her cabin onboard the *Queen Elizabeth*, Beth unbuckled her sandals and stretched her cramped toes. Her grimy fingernails and stinky armpits necessitated a quick shower. Now freshly dressed and scented from the fancy bath soap (which she hoarded in her suitcase, requiring Roberto to replenish it each day), she sat at the desk, took out her notebook, and copied down her new haiku. Then she started to doodle.

Another clue—how many more? So far, Beth located them all ... at least the ones she knew about. But on top of finding red bags, she now had to contend with Mabel, an unplanned and unexpected adversary. She wondered if Mabel had actually gone to the Chapitô clown school. Did she buy a 'Bozo' T-shirt for Max as a souvenir? Ha!

This puzzle was challenging her in ways she hadn't expected. As a result, The List was whittling down. Was it the scavenger hunt or the medication? Or both? She doodled some more, making swirls and circles. Who was behind it all? Someone determined the tasks. Someone wrote them out on tiny pieces of paper. Someone packaged them with silver charms. Someone hid them in red bags. Who?

Beth thought about the great mystery novels she had read over her lifetime: classic Agatha Christie, wry Lawrence Sanders, sparkling Dorothy Sayers. How would *they* have written this story? Beth identified herself as the protagonist, but in the end, would she also be the hero? Isn't that what a protagonist is? She tapped her teeth with a pen and wondered how this hero's journey would turn out. The drumming of the pen helped her form new ideas, which she scribbled down in her notebook. She flipped through old pages. She played with some concepts, circled some, crossed out others. Listed names. Arrows connected viable options; big angry X's dismissed most others. She started to see a faint pattern. Nothing exciting, but a glimpse.

Beth decided to write Aunt Ethel another postcard. Silly, but it made her feel connected to her. She found one she purchased at the pastry shop. It had a mouse éclair on it.

Dear Aunt Ethel—
I had a terrific day in Lisbon and wished I could have stayed longer … but I was busy climbing a jungle gym of cardboard boxes. Still, I ate lots of delicious food and learned about ginja. Very funny.
Love, Beth

A quick double knock on the cabin door startled her. She opened it and found Roberto holding a pile of folded towels with more dry cleaning hooked onto his arm.

"Thanks, Roberto," She opened the door, allowing him room to pass inside. He smelled like bleach and lemon-scented cleaning spray.

"Did you have a nice day in Lisbon?" Roberto replenished her towel supply and hung the newly cleaned and pressed clothes in her closet by color.

"Yes, I did. Do you know what ginja is?"

"Sure. It's cherry liquor. Do you want some?"

"No, I have some already." Beth held up her bottle from Sem Rival. "Do you know this place?" She pointed to the gold label with its fancy embossed lettering.

He glanced at the label. "Sure. It's famous in Lisbon." He tidied her desk area, removing old candy wrappers and empty Diet Coke cans. He closed her notebook and left the Cunard pen on top.

"Why is it famous?"

"A clown went there. Did shots. Got drunk. Now, he's famous." He emptied the trashcan full of crumpled papers from her notebook.

"Geez, Roberto ... where were you two days ago?"

He shrugged his shoulders and left the cabin with her dirty towels.

Beth sent Mr. Watkins a brief message, updating him with the recent find. She wanted to sound positive, but most importantly, confident she had everything under control and that she was still alive.

In her inbox, she found the following message:

Dear Beth,

While you're sailing the seas, eating lobster, and popping fine Belgium chocolates into your pie hole, Paul and I have taken quite a shine to Grendel. Fair warning, we're taking pictures for his new scrapbook. If you're not back soon, Paul's costume designer is creating a pilgrim ensemble in time for Thanksgiving. For Grendel, not Paul.

Seriously, I haven't heard from you lately and am starting to worry. I'm hoping all is fine and you're enjoying your adventure. But, if you need a song, let me know.

By the way, when ARE you coming back?

Kisses,

Frank

Attached to the email was a hi-res, professional-looking photo that took forever to download. It was Grendel wedged inside a cornucopia with faux autumn leaves spilling out artistically. The caption read: *Wishing You a Bountiful Harvest.* Grendel looked pissed. How did Frank know she got a chocolate on her pillow every night?

Tired from the Lisbon tour—though just as billed, it *was* Luscious—she got dressed and went to Café Carinthia for a re-energizing coffee. She walked past the beautiful flower arrangement, now changed out with new posies. Dramatic pink gladiolas, white baby's breath, and purple hydrangeas filled the urn on the circular table. Beth couldn't help herself and plunged her nose into the fragrance. *Ahh.*

She slowly climbed the grand staircase to Deck 2 and realized it was only ten days ago that she boarded the ship. She remembered looking down from the balcony for the first time. How many times had she climbed this staircase since? At least the map was no longer needed. Madeline was correct; it took less than two weeks for the ship to become comfortably familiar.

The café was crowded with passengers taking a late afternoon tea or coffee before the ship sailed. Across the room, Ian sat by himself at a table for four. The size of the table highlighted his aloneness even further. He sat polished and spiffy in a powder blue seer sucker suit. A straw boater was poised on his knee. Beth made her way over to him.

"Hi, Ian. Care for some company?"

"Beth, so nice to see you. Please join me." He offered her the chair across from him. On the table, in white Cunard china, a pot of tea steamed and a dainty scone sat slathered in strawberry jam. "What can I offer you?"

"I'll just have some tea. I already had too many pastries in town."

Ian motioned for the server to bring another pot and teacup. "Beth," he said, "I believe you have some blue ink on your lip. Would you care for a handkerchief?" He handed her one from his breast pocket.

Beth dipped it in a glass of water and scrubbed her lip. The fine linen now had a blue stain on it. She clutched it in her lap under the table.

"How's that?" She puckered her lips at him.

"Better. Now, tell me what you did today, young lady." Ian leaned back comfortably with his teacup and saucer balanced across his chest and smiled as Beth described her tour. Ian listened appreciatively, asked insightful questions, and chuckled when he heard about the number of pastries she ate. Beth also gave a good impersonation of Alfonso, which got another laugh. She told him about climbing the boxes and finding the next clue.

As Ian tilted his head down, Beth could just see a small wistful smile. Something she had said must have triggered a memory. She had an impulsive thought and decided to test it out.

"Ian, you've traveled a lot, right? On Cunard?'

"Yes, I'm what they consider a diamond guest." Ian pointed proudly to a small pin on his right lapel.

"How do you get it?"

"After completing fifteen cruises."

"Wow, that's really something. So, you've been on all three Cunard ships?" She took a sip of her mint tea, which helped settle the multiple pastries vying for space in her stomach.

"But of course."

"Which is your favorite?

"Ah, that's like asking which woman is more beautiful, more charming. They're all special in their own way."

"Ian, did you know my aunt?" Beth looked at him squarely in the eye, not giving him an opportunity to look away. Still, he broke her gaze and fiddled with a sugar spoon. He repositioned the tea pot. He wiped some crumbs off the ivory tablecloth. "Ian ... it's okay, you can tell me."

He looked at her, his eyes slightly pained. "Yes, I knew Ethel. She was a great friend of mine for many years," he said softly.

Beth leaned in closer toward him, "Are you involved with all this? This whole game?" Ian had been at every port stop and on most (not all) of her tours. He was the most likely culprit behind it.

"Why? Are you having fun?" His eyes started to twinkle. He tried to hide a smile underneath his mustache, unsuccessfully.

"Ian, I need your help. It's so important I find Ethel's will. Do you know what will happen if I don't? The consequences?"

"Yes, Ethel explained it. We know."

"There's more than you?" She sat back in her chair.

"I meant the royal 'we.' It's a British saying." Ian folded his hands. Beth watched him try to gather his thoughts before speaking again. She was patient. She looked down at the stained handkerchief. It had lovely hand-stitching and a fanciful 'EB' monogram embroidered in one corner. Then she looked out the window.

Seagulls flew by the glass, their shadows making abstract patterns on the cement dock below. Up and down the length of the ship, safety-orange-vested port officials untied heavy ropes from cleats and in preparation for sailing. A hubbub of activity, which would eventually result in a loud toot of the ship's horn, signaling to all onboard the quietness and stillness of the sea would soon be in their near future.

Ian cleared his throat. "I met Ethel when she started sailing on Cunard. Our itineraries crossed more than once. We became close friends ... confidants." He smiled. "She confessed your mother's death just devastated her." Ian paused long enough to take another sip of tea. "Like all siblings they had their differences: lifestyles, income ... but still, they always found common ground. I'm certain it was an effort on each of their part, to stay in touch, to forgive slights, to bury any jealousies. But at their core, they loved each other. They were better together and they knew it."

Beth said nothing.

"After Mary passed, it was years before Ethel could smile again. Traveling helped her regain that spirit ... her zest for life. Making friends helped, too. Without Mary and losing Ezekiel so soon afterwards, she had a lot of vacant space in her heart to fill."

Beth sniffed. "It must have been difficult. Aunt Ethel was always so happy ... at least the Ethel *I* knew." She thought about her own personal challenges. "But why would she do this? Make it so hard to find her will and possibly hand everything over to Max, someone who had been so awful to her? It just doesn't make sense. Why?"

Ian sat and ruminated for a few seconds, as if deciding which avenue to take.

"No, she didn't trust Max, that's for certain. Beth, I don't have all the answers, but it was important to Ethel, very important, you do this on your own. My job was to watch over you—a silent observer. I promised not to do anything else. Please don't make me break my vow to her."

She took a moment. "Remember when I first boarded the ship? You toasted me?"

Ian smiled and nodded.

"You were the first friendly person I met. Since then, I've met so many more." Beth thought about Table 8. After a few more moments sitting in silence, she held up the handkerchief with the monogram face-up. "Would you like her handkerchief back?"

"No, my dear, please keep it. She'd be glad you have it."

———————

The ship was sailing. Beth sat on her balcony and held Aunt Ethel's handkerchief while Lisbon's port slipped by. The fabric was a touch-stone, a connection to her aunt that felt as real as holding her hand. She thought about Ethel and the immense circle of friends she had built. People who cared about her, loved her. Beth's circle was painfully small. Could she change it? If she ever reached eighty years old, would she have as many friends as Aunt Ethel did? Beth already knew the answer and didn't like it.

Ian's words haunted her. It was a glimpse of an Aunt Ethel she hadn't known before. She had always been so cheerful, so full of exuberant life, Beth hadn't imagined Ethel ever in so much pain. *But Mom was her only sister.* Beth closed her eyes. Her only sister. Her only sister. Her only sister. How many times had she heard that before? *Oh, Vicky.*

Seagulls chased the ship. The sun hung heavy in the sky, obstinate to sink further toward the horizon. The late afternoon's familiar pink haze started to creep in. Beth took in a deep breath of the briny air. In two days, she would be back in Southampton. Hopefully with the will in hand. Then what? Once back in New York, what would she do? It would be easy to go back to her old job and apartment it was safe. But perhaps, just perhaps, she should think about doing something different.

She went back inside the cabin and folded the hanky inside the desk drawer with her clues and notebook. Would it function as a memento of her trip, lying in a shoebox with the rest of her memories and old family photos? Along with the years of unopened birthday cards from Vicky? Or would it be a symbol of something more?

CHAPTER 28

Seventeen Years and Six Months Ago

What a nightmare. Two conferences at two separate lawyers' offices for readings of two wills, all within two days of each other. A jumble of family, dwindling in numbers, meeting to discuss the future, with most not speaking to each other.

Yesterday, Aunt Ethel met Beth and Vicky at the Schiff's family lawyer in Allentown. His office was a precursor of the meeting's findings; with plywood paneling, an avocado green shag carpet, and orange-plastic chairs, the décor also matched Beth's sinking expectations. Plus, he used a paperclip to scratch his ear. Aunt Ethel sat in between Vicky and Beth. With one hand, they each held Styrofoam cups of either very strong tea or weak coffee, and with the other, grasped one of Ethel's tightly, her rings digging into their fingers. As always, Ethel was appropriately dressed for the occasion, as she wore a severe black suit and netted cloche hat.

It was a short meeting. The lawyer explained, after the life insurance claim paid off the mortgage balance, the car loan (even though the car was totaled the insurance didn't cover all of it), and some accrued bills, Mary and James Schiff had $574.31 remaining in their joint account. Yet, they still owed for the funerals and hospital bills. It was shocking to hear how little her parents had. Vicky sat stone-faced. At the end, when they stood up to leave, Vicky took the lawyer's paperwork and put it in her own purse.

Afterwards, a private car picked them up and drove them to New York City. This time for Ezekiel Birnbaum's will. He had passed away only a week after Mary, dying in a freak skiing accident on his and Ethel's Swiss honeymoon, which he had insisted they take. He said it would, "Do Ethel some good." Apparently not. Ethel, whose tears continued ad infinitum, had stopped speaking. Even though there wasn't much help they could offer, the young women accompanied Ethel for moral support.

The next morning, at the Apex Bank conference room (it was the largest room they could find), teams of lawyers, bankers, and accountants filled every chair and lined the walls. The three women sat silently in plush tufted leather chairs. The chief lawyer, dressed in a raw silk suit and bow tie, promised it wouldn't take long. But if the number of pages determined the amount of time it would take, they'd be there till next month. His multiple assistants wore similar suits and held reams of more paper while looking efficient yet weary.

Then Max and Bernadette Birnbaum entered with an entourage. Max, still attractive, Bernadette, still glamorous. Bernadette approached Ethel to offer her condolences. She was heartbroken, *just heartbroken*, about the tragedy. But she didn't look heartbroken. Not at all. With her hair perfectly styled and makeup expertly applied, Bernadette Birnbaum wore a pink crepe Gucci suit. Tahitian pearls gleamed at her throat and ears. A large diamond ring, the stone the size of a quail's egg, caught the light as she brought a tissue to her eyes and patted away imaginary tears.

Max Birnbaum didn't say anything but sat down and adjusted his tie. It was hard to decipher his sentiment, since the look on his face was of confused triumph. Did he expect all the money? None of it? In any case, he brought his own lawyers.

"Let's get on with it," Max said looking at his watch.

Beth unconsciously ground her teeth, until Aunt Ethel elbowed her to stop.

Since major life events seemingly tie together, Beth lumped Max being mean to her family at the wedding reception with her parent's accident. Irrational, but the timing was too close to separate. Maybe Mom had been so upset, Dad consoled her and lost control of the car? Maybe Dad was searching for a happier song on the radio and took a hand from the steering wheel? Or maybe, simply, the weather caused the accident, which was what Lieutenant Marvin Bloom's police report and investigations concluded. But Beth had to blame someone for the tragedy, so it might as well be Max. Plus, how evil can someone be at a memorial service? She'd never forgive him.

There were many minutes of low talking and shuffling of papers, which felt like forever. At sporadic intervals, Max would lean over to whisper something to Bernadette, like a bored student at lecture. The lawyer sitting at the head of the conference table cleared his throat and began. Simply put, since the trust was in both Ezekiel's and Ethel's names, it automatically transferred to her. Ezekiel, that dear man (even from the grave he was still a mensch) had the good sense to establish the trust the day they were married. It made sense; Ethel had brought her own financial assets to the marriage, doubling their total net worth.

But there were two caveats:

1. Max Birnbaum would receive an annual salary (ahem ... allowance)
2. Max Birnbaum would be named Director of the Birnbaum Foundation.

Ezekiel was explicit, stating in his own words, as the lawyer read them aloud, "With wealth comes responsibility and it's our obligation to give back. I've spent years developing programs supporting the less fortunate, now it's your turn to lead the Birnbaum Foundation. It should not only succeed but flourish in your care."

To the very the end, Ezekiel still tried to help Max. Ethel wasn't surprised at the caveats, or at least she didn't show it. Her face remained quietly passive, which was certainly out of character. She said nothing.

"How much is there?" Max asked.

An accountant at the lawyer's elbow handed him an Excel spreadsheet, "There is ... just shy of twenty-five million," he said.

Bernadette threw her arms around Max. "Oh, honey!" she squealed. "You'll make your dad so proud!"

Max's face broke into a wide grin. He stood up and shook his lawyer's hand. Max picked up Bernadette and twirled her in the air. Beth and Vicky watched in horrified awe at the tasteless reaction of a windfall and it wasn't even theirs to spend. Money never bought class.

And that was that.

On his way out, Max passed by their chairs and with blue eyes twinkling, bent down to say in Ethel's ear, rather loudly, "You'll have to find another rich husband."

He always liked to exit on a nasty note. The girls, of course, overheard. Was it possible to hate someone even more?

That bastard! Beth silently raged.

Vicky had more gumption. "You son of a bitch!" she called after him.

Aunt Ethel's face collapsed into her hanky, sobbing fresh tears.

The last two days had taken their toll. There was nothing left to say; the shock should have silenced them. But instead, as soon as they were outside the building, the sisters tore into each other. Their misplaced emotions of grief turned into anger and blame. Awful things were said, terrible things. Beth accused Vicky of being unreliable. Vicky called Beth a big baby. They both agreed neither did as much as the other. Each was cloaked in their own martyrdom, safe and comforting, while wrapped in righteous despair.

"I cleaned out the house and you were no help!" accused Beth.

"Try picking out headstones from L.A. Really, Beth?" Vicky said.

"I wrote my parent's obituaries."

"I had to pay for them!"

"You didn't come to Mom's funeral ... your own mother!" Beth cried.

"I couldn't," Vicky said. Her forehead puckered into worry lines.

"Maybe you should have taken off more time from the show! Really, what's more important?"

"Maybe *you* should get a job and move on with your life, Beth."

"Maybe you should think about *other* people."

"Maybe you should *grow up*."

The laundry list of peeves escalated from petty to personal until Aunt Ethel grabbed each girl by the shoulder and shook them as hard as she could.

"Both of you, stop it. Honestly!" Aunt Ethel seethed, her voice raw from weeks of sobs and silence.

Beth glowered at Vicky. Vicky turned away, buttoned her coat, and collected her purse. She sniffed indifferently and smoothed her hair.

Ethel shook with emotion. "I can't believe what I'm hearing. I know you're both upset, but this is uncalled for. Really." Her voice was as stern as they had ever heard.

Beth looked at her shoes.

The truth was Beth had buried two parents within months of each other, which necessitated taking on responsibilities she was neither ready for, nor could emotionally handle. Help came from nowhere. In addition, the Birnbaum family showed no empathy for their loss and dismissed the entire affair as if inconvenient to their schedules. Unfortunately, Aunt Ethel was stuck in between both sides and now Ezekiel's death put her over the top. Vicky wasn't available. Her career came first. When an onlooker approached Vicky for an autograph, Beth almost lost it entirely when she acquiesced with a big toothy smile.

"I know this has been awful ... truly and utterly awful. Terrible tragedies we can never go back and fix. There will never be justice for it. Never. But you both have to concentrate. Now. You are all you have, the two of you." Aunt Ethel pulled out a fresh linen handkerchief from her crocodile handbag, adjusted the netting on her hat, and wiped her nose. She choked, "You only have one sister and mine is gone."

But her plea didn't make a difference. Both Beth and Vicky's anger clouded any rational judgment. Their parents weren't coming back. No one would pay for it. So, in an effort to grasp any sense of it—this unrealistic and unfathomable event—they turned on the only thing left ... each other.

Now outside the bank building, they stood in a small circle. Aunt Ethel continued to cry into her handkerchief. Her shoulders rose and fell in conjunction with her weeping. Always so together, she was now broken. This shook Beth to the core. If Aunt Ethel couldn't handle it ...

As if in response to Beth's silent uncertainties, Vicky gently kissed Ethel on the cheek and whispered, "I'm sorry," stared blankly at Beth, and walked down the steps.

That was the last time Beth saw her sister.

CHAPTER 29

After dinner, Beth returned directly to her cabin. She was not in a celebratory mood, which was unbelievable since she was a huge step closer to solving the mystery. Dancing should have been in order, but memories of her conversation with Ian still gnawed. Once, during her appetizer, Ian had reached over and patted her arm. No words necessary. He let her alone with her thoughts, which were many.

Beth carefully hung up her dress; the black crepe with red flowers had seen its second successful outing. Surprisingly, she didn't trip this time or have to play with her fringe over dinner. She changed into her comfortable Dave Matthews T-shirt and poured a glass of water from the fridge.

She decided to check her email one last time before bed. One from Mr. Watkins slowly materialized, eating away at her precious internet time.

Dear Beth,

Alas, more unfortunate news. In anticipation of probating the trust, Max's lawyers submitted financials on The Birnbaum Foundation. Our firm's accountants (after a diligent review) found a deficit. Simply put, there are no funds remaining. We have many questions for the board and will investigate.

Sincerely,

J. J. Watkins

She fell back against the bed pillows and tried to process.

The money was gone. All of it. Poof!

No more rainbow flags for the Pride Center. No more food for homeless kittens. No more funding for controversial exhibitions of misunderstood artists. Incredible. For someone who still used a BOGO coupon at Antony's Authentic NY-style Pizza, Beth couldn't imagine blowing through millions of dollars. Maybe that's why Mabel was there—Max didn't just *want* more money ... he *needed* more money. He was broke. Beth wondered how far he would go to get it. He wouldn't hurt her, would he? Would Mabel? Beth had lots of questions for Mr. Watkins but needed more time to think them through.

She sat cross-legged on the bed and turned on the TV for a diversion.

She clicked the remote and sitcom reruns appeared. Normally, these would have soothed her. No surprise endings. Familiar plot lines. But already-watched episodes of *Frasier* and *Everyone Loves Raymond* didn't do their job. It was inevitable. Vicky's face appeared on channel 52. Or rather, her boobs. It was *Legal Briefs*, second season. Candy, Vicky's character, had a few additional lines this episode. Beth actually liked this one. It was the first episode where Candy showed some gumption and made someone *else* look foolish.

Beth watched Candy sit at her desk, her breasts resting on the blotter. She twiddled a pen and chomped gum. On the phone with her voice raised to a high-pitched nasal tone, she berated a client who called her 'Sweets', which was actually her character's last name. *Candy Sweets.* "Call me *Miz* Sweets," she had said. Candy got big laughs. So big, the laughs overshadowed another actor's lines. Consequently, the writers gave her more lines in the next episode. It was also the year fans could buy a coffee mug with Candy's face on it, with a text balloon tethered to her mouth saying, "Fiddlesticks!"

She watched Candy's face for some recognition of her sister. The clothes and makeup were one thing, but the mannerisms and facial expressions had changed, too. Vicky was in character a thousand percent. Her blue eyes were more pronounced, as if she bulged them on purpose. She thrust her shoulders back and arched her body like a bow. But for a second, a mere moment during this particular episode, Beth noticed a tell-tale flicker. A small grimace, a facial twitch she made—that was Vicky. But as soon as she recognized it, it disappeared as quickly. Once again, back in character. A real professional.

The show ended. Beth turned off the TV. The piece of angst she so carefully and methodically swept to a back corner of her heart, refused to stay put. She pulled the white Cunard robe from the closet, used it like a blanket on the bed, and pulled it up to her chin. She turned off all the lights and sat in the darkness.

Her earlier conversation with Ian rattled inside her head. Ian's words hurt her. By no means was it intentional; he had simply relayed a story about her aunt. It was obvious he cared for Ethel deeply and knew her well. She had never really considered how *Ethel* felt about her mom's death. At the time, Beth was busy nursing her own broken heart. Of course, she knew Ethel was devastated, but the relationship itself ... the part about being her only family. Ian's words had made an impact on her.

Outside, the waves gently tapped the hull of the ship. The wind whistled through a gap in the balcony door. The sounds poked through the quiet and prodded Beth into deeper thoughts, ones she didn't want to acknowledge.

Beth sighed. *Let's be honest. I need to think about Vicky.*

Over the years, she had recognized her estrangement from her sister was three-fold. First, Beth was angry. Angry that Vicky hadn't kept her promise. Angry that Mom died alone. Yes, Beth felt guilty and some of the guilt translated into blame, which then transferred to her sister. It was much easier to be angry at Vicky than at herself.

Next, Vicky left her high and dry at the worst possible time. When Beth really needed help, Vicky focused on herself instead. She chose her career over helping Beth navigate funerals, packing up personal items, and selling the family house. Beth felt abandoned, not only by her parents, but by her sister, too. This emotion was easy to carry like a torch, always glowing and never extinguished. A perpetual beacon of bitterness Beth could always count on.

Lastly, the hopeless sorrow of losing a parent—or worse *two* parents—was unbearable. The unconditional love of her family, the motivation, and unending encouragement was gone. Forever. No more holidays, no more spontaneous phone calls. *Dad, my car's making that funny noise again. Mom, what's your recipe for meatloaf?* Shattered opportunities. So sudden, so quick, so unplanned. Any sense of stability died the night of her parents' car accident and spun Beth into a role she was unready and unprepared for—an adult.

Beth knew all this. Knew it at every conceivable, cognitive level.

She locked this great sadness inside to deal with later. But later never came. This repressed sorrow began to seep into other areas of her life. Her insecurities, her awkwardness, her fears; she could only blame on herself. So, Beth punished herself again and again in unconscious ways for her immature abilities at the time. An evil, vicious circle of pain with no end in sight. She couldn't move forward while in perpetual limbo, even with Dr. Joan's help.

The ship lurched sideways heavily. She grabbed the side of the bed. Glasses rattled. Something crashed inside the bathroom. Outside, passengers in the hallway exclaimed their surprise. Cabin doors slammed closed. The seas picked up the *Queen Elizabeth* and carried her onward, thrusting her forward. The motion, as sudden as it was, jarred Beth's thinking and a sense of clarity appeared. The ship slowly righted itself and began to sway gently. Then she heard passengers laugh.

Honestly, she screwed up. She should have picked up the phone years ago and said with genuine remorse, "I'm sorry," to Vicky. But she didn't. She couldn't. At a time when she was emotionally vulnerable and needed every ally on her side, she shoved away her most avid supporter, her sister. To admit she, herself, was wrong ... was maddening.

This emotional blockade of sorts had built itself into a barrier. Each year's silence laid another row of stubborn bricks, building the wall higher and more impenetrable. It was so easy to ignore its growth over time. The longer it continued—the silence with Vicky—the more impossible it was to fix. Now Beth viewed it as irreparable.

She recognized what she was doing. For years, she knew it. But tonight, Beth finally owned it. She admitted it all to herself, her harshest critic.

Beth wept. For the injustice of her parents' death, for her own inability to handle it, for her stubbornness. For her only sister, Vicky.

This wasn't anxiety; it was true sorrow.

In the darkness, huddled on her bed like a child, she cried great tears. Once they started, they didn't stop. Her whole physical body, every muscle and tendon, released in great throbbing sobs. She wailed. She bawled. When tears were finally spent, she continued to rock back and forth clasping the mini-Grendel to her chest.

It seemed like hours. Beth collapsed still holding the toy cat. Her nose ran onto the sheets. Spent, she took a deep breath and released it. She took another one. The eternal clamp screwed around her stomach loosened. She felt lighter. She sat up and grabbed the box of tissues on the bedside table and tried to mop up her face. She ran out of tissues.

Through the sheer balcony curtains, Beth could see bright stars. She crept off the bed, slid open the patio door, and walked outside to the balcony. The air was chilly in her T-shirt. In the distance, running parallel to the *Elizabeth* was another cruise ship, its lights twinkled. She looked up to see thousands of stars glittering against the black velvety backdrop of sky. Beth closed her eyes and wished, "I want to move on. Please. Help me."

A booming voice responded in careful measured tones, "Good evening."

Geez, was it God?

"Good evening, this is the Commodore speaking. My apologies for the recent instability. We expect calm seas for the reminder of the evening. Good news—our sister ship, the *Queen Victoria* is sailing alongside us for the next few minutes. Fair warning, we are sounding the ship's horn in salute."

HOOONNNKKK!

Even forewarned, Beth still jumped back in surprise. The *Victoria* honked back. She took it as a good omen and waved back to the passengers braving the cold on *Victoria's* own deck. After a few minutes of shivering, she went back inside the dark cabin. Beth took the toy cat and put it in the closet.

She felt as though she had run a marathon: her lungs hurt and her chest felt empty and hollow. Even her jaw hurt from crying. A hot shower helped. She relaxed standing under the spray. She rested her hands against the stall to stabilize herself as the ship bounced over waves. All her muscles ached. But deep inside, a small feeling of reconciliation with herself. A slackening peace.

Exhausted, her wet head hit the pillow and before she fell into a blameless sleep, Beth wondered, now without regret, how her sister was and where. Suddenly, on a luxury ship in the middle of the ocean, Beth felt closer to Vicky than she had in years.

CHAPTER 30

"Point!"

Beth high-fived Madeline after successfully smacking the ball over the net, far into their competitors' corner.

"Losers buy drinks tonight!" Madeline called over to Constance and Judy. The pair looked at each other in dismay.

"Not fair, you have youth on your side," Judy said pointing to Beth.

"Tough," Madeline responded.

Beth wiped some sweat off her forehead and prepared to serve again. Pickleball was cut-throat.

"Come on Madeline, we have to finish this game. I have shuffleboard with Mike and Alex at two o'clock," Beth reminded her.

"Okay, Miss Popular! Let's finish these old ladies off," Madeline said. As Beth served, her charm bracelet twinkled in the sun. The ball hit the net, stopped and rolled over to the opposite side. Judy scrambled but couldn't reach it in time. It hit the court and lay there like a petrified matzo ball.

Madeline yelled, "Whoopee!"

"Point, set, and match!" Ian announced from his deck chair where he held an iced tea. His straw boater shielded him from the sun on the upper deck of the ship. "Game to Madeline and Beth." After handshakes all around and threats of a rematch the following day, the ladies agreed to pre-dinner drinks at the Commodore Club at half-seven.

"Now don't worm your way out of paying. I'm ordering a large glass of wine, a large, frightfully *expensive* one," Madeline threatened.

The ship sailed methodically, yet almost reluctantly, back to Southampton. Passengers ran in a frenzy, trying to make the most of their final days as home and all its responsibilities loomed. Outside on the games deck, the sun was high in the sky and provided searing heat for passengers involved with athletic activities. The hot air smelled a little like burnt toast spread with SPF 30.

Beth checked her shiny watch, 1:45 p.m. on the nose, and walked from one end of the deck to the other where the shuffleboard tournament would begin. She thought back to the previous night. In the light of the day, she realized as painful as it was, the reconciliation with herself was necessary. It wasn't a pity party, but a 'get-your-shit-together-girl, come-to-Jesus moment.' She needed it and it was long overdue. The only physical evidence of her weep-fest were her swollen red eyes safely hidden behind her sunglasses.

But more importantly, her soul felt free of the oppressive, debilitating weight she'd lugged around for so long. She was ready to move on. After all those years on pause, she needed to hit play. Beth knew Aunt Ethel recognized that. Or why else did she devise the scavenger hunt? Aunt Ethel had her going through the motions, sometimes awkwardly and embarrassingly, but her ultimate goal was to get Beth back out there and reconnecting with Vicky. Ethel would never allow Max to get the rest of the Birnbaum money. Never.

Speaking of Max, Beth hadn't seen Mabel in a few days. Did she fall overboard? Choke on a fish bone? *Maybe she got attacked by her hat.* Still, Beth needed to keep a wary eye out for her. Mabel was sneaky.

The intermittent breeze from across the top deck provided an inconsistent cooling effect. Small gusts of wind lifted Beth's damp bangs off her forehead. She shook the hem of her new bathing suit cover up to get more air circulating underneath. Her sandals squeaked on the wooden deck as she walked. She passed the Play Zone, a kid's camp and/or glorified day care. The three small kids from the Lido Buffet were inside, one finger-painting artwork on an easel, another banging on a tambourine, and the third making something frightening out of clay. They glanced up at Beth. She waved through the window and made a silly face. They waved back.

Only two days left. She would miss the ship.

"I absolutely, positively, refuse to play," Mike announced. "I will watch enthusiastically and cheer with gusto, but my athletic abilities are crap." He sat outside on a deck chair, lounging in white slacks and teal polo shirt. "Plus, I may ruin my new pants."

"You're lucky you can still fit into them," Alex said.

"Very funny, smart ass."

Earlier, Alex had asked Beth to team up with him. Because, "Honestly, how can you go on a cruise and *not* play shuffleboard?" he rationalized.

So, while Mike sat contentedly in the shade and sipped something cool, Beth and Alex joined the tournament.

Click, swish, and *swoosh*. The heavy plastic discs flew across the deck. Some landed in desired spots, most not. Their competition was not very competitive; they were all equally unskilled. Beth and Alex won three games out of five and moved ahead to the final round. After placing second, they congratulated the winning team with more sweaty handshakes.

"Not bad for two young pups," Mike praised them.

"How about some pre-dinner drinks tonight, Beth?" asked Alex.

"Can't. I'm already booked," she said with a smug smile.

"Okay, Social Butterfly, fine. How about after dinner?"

Hmmm. I am *kinda popular.* "Sure. Let's meet at the Yacht Club. The daily program said they're playing dance music tonight."

"Thank God. You're on!" Alex said.

After Beth collected her tote bag, she walked down two flights of stairs to the Lido pool. Resigned to not being too choosy about location, she dropped her bag on the first empty lounge chair she found. She grabbed a folded warm towel from an organized stack and removed her sunglasses and cover up. She scanned quickly for Mabel. Nope, nowhere. With her items firmly established in her space, she walked over to the side of the pool and unceremoniously jumped in.

She sank to the bottom. Quietness and coolness surrounded her instantaneously. It was colder than expected, but welcome after the sweaty pickleball and shuffleboard games. Her scalp tingled as her hair floated around her like a veil. As her feet hit the tile floor, she pushed off and came up for air. She shook her hair from her face. She swam over to the side, rested her chin on top of her hands on the deck, and lazily kicked out her legs behind her. She closed her eyes.

"I'd give it eight at best!" Saul Kipperman yelled over from his lounge chair.

Seated next to him, Judy held up a bulb-shaped cocktail glass with a pink parasol. Beth waved from the pool. Over her shoulder, she saw the Gundersons getting into the hot tub. Bob wore a heavy gold chain with an eagle glinting on his large hairy chest. Teresa wore some kind of bathing suit with a skirt attached. She looked like a retired cheerleader.

After eleven days on the ship, it seemed Beth couldn't go anywhere without running into someone she knew. Initially it annoyed her; as a creature of solitude, she didn't like making small talk and self-disclosure wasn't a fun activity. But on a ship of almost two thousand people, wasn't it nice to know someone? It was almost as if they were keeping an eye on her.

Hey, wait a minute. She thought back to her conversation with Ian. He had said, "The royal 'we.'" She reconsidered his response.

Whoever placed the clues, he (or she) must have known Aunt Ethel very well. Not just anyone would do that for her. Plus, it was a lot of work and was more than one person could do. Ian couldn't have done it all himself. Beth's mind went clickity-click, trying to fit the pieces together. She remembered her doodles and sketches in her notebook. More dots connected. She hypothesized a plan. One that would help answer some major questions she'd had since the day she stepped inside Mr. Watkins's office in New York.

Beth floated on her back to the other side of the pool while thinking about the next task. With no more port stops, the next red bag *had* to be on the ship. If it were the case, she had a feeling she knew where it was. *I'll find it. I've found all the others.* Her confidence was a welcome visitor.

Her head bumped into the gutter. She reached out to steady herself and looked down at her empty wrist. Her charm bracelet was gone. Gone! *How can that be?* She submerged underwater to look for it at the bottom of the pool. Nothing. She sputtered and wiped her hair off her face. She got out of the pool. She looked around her chair and in her tote bag.

Oh crap!

How could she lose such a thing? She dried herself off with a towel. As she quickly gathered her items, she decided to retrace her steps. Her wet toes squished inside her sandals and her cover up plastered itself to her wet butt. Back up the staircase to the shuffleboard court. Nothing. Down to the Play Zone. Nada. Over to the ladies' bathroom. Nope. The pickle ball court? Zilch. Hopefully someone had found it and turned it in to Lost & Found. By this time, Beth was sweating again and would have liked to jump back into the pool.

Instead, she hurried to the purser's desk. She hoped Raul would have good news. Once there, a line of about ten guests queued for help. She got in line and noticed a stack of plain white envelopes at the desk. Also, Raul was counting out dollars like a Las Vegas casino cashier, handing wads of cash back to passengers. When it was her turn, she asked about her bracelet. Raul checked and reported no one had turned it in.

"Raul, what's with the money and the envelopes?"

"For tipping. Gratuities are already built into the cruise cost; however, if you want to give staff a little something extra, we have envelopes here," he explained.

"Good to know. Will you call if anyone turns in my bracelet?"

"Absolutely, madam. Oh, you got some mail today."

He pulled out a postcard and handed it to Beth. On the front was the *Queen Victoria* sailing on the ocean. She looked exactly like the *Queen Elizabeth*. Written on the back, *I hope you're having a fabulous time! Love Ethel*. Odd. How did she possibly send it?

Confused, Beth muttered, "Thanks," and sulked her way back to her cabin still lamenting her lost bracelet.

Once there, she found Roberto inside making the bed. This was a surprise, since it was normally done in the morning.

"Busy today?" she asked.

"Yes, a lot to do. Where's the cat?"

"The what?"

"The cat—with the missing paw? I can't find it."

"Oh, I don't need it anymore."

Beth tried to stay out of his way. As he plumped pillows, she asked him about his plans for when they docked in Southampton. It turned out he didn't have time to visit the port, because as soon as the ship docked, the crew went into overdrive, changing out for the next cruise leaving that evening. Sheets, towels, pillows, mattress covers, toiletries, robes ... everything that wasn't nailed down in the cabin had to be exchanged for new. The quick turnaround made the crew a little on-edge.

"When is your contract over, Roberto?"

"December. I get a month off to go home."

"That's soon. You must be excited to see family."

"Oh, yes. All my family comes to visit—aunts, uncles, cousins. We have a big party, with lots of good food and beer. Lots of talking too. My mama, she won't shut up for the first week. Then, I take her shopping."

"It's nice you're so close to your family." Beth stood in the doorway of the bathroom watching as he removed dried toothpaste from the sink. "Here's a question, if you had extra money to spend, what would you buy?" Beth thought of her onboard credit. It still was over two thousand dollars and she had no idea what to do with it.

"Hmmm." He stood with an armful of toilet paper rolls, deep in thought. "I would buy my mama a car, she takes the bus to work. Yes, I would buy her a car. A shiny red car."

"You know, Roberto, you're a nice guy."

He blushed and said goodbye while closing the door behind him. Beth sat back at her desk, opened her notebook, and transferred her sketchy ideas from the pool to the page. Then she moved bits and pieces until they fell into a semi-logical pattern.

Tonight, it's time for some answers.

CHAPTER 31

When Glenn brought the menus around that evening at dinner, Beth chose the Royal Spa selection, supposedly a lower-calorie dining option. Still, she couldn't call it diet food because the sautéed shrimp and spinach appetizer and lobster with jasmine rice main course was a far cry from frozen Lean Cuisines. According to the menu, it was about five hundred calories. *Fine, it leaves me room for dessert*, she rationalized and resolutely handed the menu to Glenn.

With her hands calmly in her lap, Beth waited for her wine selection, a 2015 Les Clos Chablis Brigitte swore by at only thirty-five dollars a bottle.

"It's a grand-cru," she had whispered, almost conspiratorially. "It'll go beautifully with your fish." She was right. It tasted great alone in the glass, but even better in between mouthfuls of garlic shrimp for which Glenn offered fresh lemon. He took a fork and stabbed a lemon wedge, then braced a teaspoon alongside. As he squeezed the two utensils together, the lemon juice squirted perfectly on Beth's dinner. *Impressive.*

"Have you ever taken out someone's eye?" Beth asked.

He laughed. "No. I've had years of practice and never lost a guest yet."

During dinner, Beth made a concerted point of speaking to her table-mates. She had to admit the shared travel experiences made it easier to do so than on day one.

"How was the pool today, Judy?"

"Oh, I think I may have overdone it. I look like a crustacean." Judy pulled back a cap sleeve to show an angry red line. Plus, her nose was glowing. "I hope the shop has some aloe."

"I have some if you need it," Beth offered.

"Thanks, love."

"Beth, are you reading anything fun?" asked Ian.

She turned towards him. "I got a book from the library I've never read before. It's a memoir by Mary Carr called *Lit*. It's been on my list for years."

"Outstanding! Excellent taste."

Beth smiled to herself. *I've come a long way in a short time. But it's time to solve some pieces of this puzzle.*

Between forkfuls, she looked up and saw Brigitte pour Bob's last glass of wine from his bottle. After quickly scanning the wine bible, he ordered another. While Brigitte uncorked his second bottle, a 2006 Mendoza Malbec, Bob glanced at the cork and set it on the silver dish in front of him. He swirled the small pour and stuck his nose in deep to inhale. Then he swished the red wine in his mouth. His cheeks ballooned. He swallowed.

"Fine, fine," he declared.

"Bob, how's the wine been on the ship?" Beth inquired with feigned curiosity. "I'm not much of an expert." Even with Brigitte's tutelage, she still couldn't tell the difference between an Italian Chianti and French Burgundy, something she vowed to work on back home.

"What a selection! Every bottle has been exceptional. Plus, Brigitte is spot on. I've been testing her and she sure knows her stuff," he exclaimed.

"You must know a lot about wine."

"After thirty years in the biz, I should know a thing or two."

"Oh, I thought you were in oil and gas."

"Whatever gave you that idea? I own Big Texas Imports. I buy lots of wine," he said, "Over a million bottles a year."

Beth replied, "I'm probably confused."

Her main course arrived—lobster! Sweet and succulent, it tasted like candy in her mouth.

She turned towards Constance.

"I remember you said you managed an art gallery. Have you ever been to New York City? Have you visited the museums there?"

"Certainly. New York has many world class museums. However, since I favor the classics, I prefer the Met over the MoMA. Especially for works in bronze. It was my specialty. Bronze can live forever; it provides such a wonderful glimpse into history. I dealt mostly in statues from the Greco-Roman period." Constance adjusted a diamond hair clip in her curls.

"Wow, I didn't know that." Beth checked another box in her head.

She watched Constance cut her halibut with the appropriate fish fork. Her hands were spotted, with crepey skin and swollen knuckles which looked painful. As if to compensate for their age, she dressed them up. Each finger sported a ring and her nails were perfectly manicured. Beth looked down at her own hands. Smooth, except for a small scar on her right thumb. A bagel battled a knife and lost. But overall, her skin had consistent color and now a little tan. While comparing her hands to Constance's, Beth wondered when hers would look that old.

Constance noticed Beth staring. She smiled and patted Beth's hand. "It's not so bad ... getting old." Beth, embarrassed, opened her mouth to say something, but Constance quickly patted her hand again as if to end the necessity of a reply. Beth squeezed it in silent thanks.

"Do you ever get scared?" Beth asked her quietly.

"No. Just more thankful. For my experiences, for my opportunities. I'm very fortunate. 'Life is a banquet and most poor suckers are starving to death.'" Her eyes shone.

"Funny ... my aunt used to say that."

"Really? She must have been a smart woman," Constance said with quick authority. She released Beth's hand and went back to eating her fish.

Beth, satisfied with her little experiment, finished her dinner and ordered a 'heart-healthy' almond pear torte with a double espresso for dessert. She needed caffeine because her night was far from over.

There were three pianos onboard, Beth knew, because she had called Raul. One in the Queens Room, another in the Commodore Club, and the third located in the Garden Lounge. A piano is where the next clue was.

Make joyful music.
Keys are elementary,
just like black and white.

She solved the haiku easily. *Music ... keys ... black and white ... Bingo!*
It had to be in a piano. Plus, remembering her piano recital debacle years
ago, it made perfect sense. Poor Aunt Ethel was almost as embarrassed as
she was. Another memory. Another shared experience from her past she
needed to address and move on from.

It was just after ten o'clock. Since the Queens Room orchestra played
until eleven, it would be difficult to look inside the piano without people
gawking. In the meantime, she took the elevator—hey, it *was* seven decks
up—to the Commodore Club on Deck 10. She squeezed inside with
other guests. Someone had pushed all the buttons. She waited patiently
until they arrived and by then, she was the only one left.

Across the hall, the dance party thumped at full bass in the Yacht Club.
Crap! And oh, they were playing good music. *Maybe if I find the red bag
fast, I can join Alex and Mike sooner. Okay, focus!*

Inside the Commodore Club, the number of guests remaining was
more than she bargained for. Apparently, passengers couldn't drink
enough while onboard. How much could the average guests' liver take?
On this trip, Beth admitted she did her fair share too. She noted a sign
stating the club closed at two in the morning. There had to be at least
fifty people guzzling cocktails. *Okay, I'll check back later.* Her last option
was in the Garden Lounge.

Down one flight of stairs, the last piano sat tucked in the corner. A
small, white upright with matching bench sat ensconced by the miniature palm trees and potted ferns. Only a handful of people occupied the

lounge. One couple slept soundly on a rattan couch, heads leaned in toward each other, propping the other up. Another man spoke loudly on his cell phone, "I'll take care of it when I get home," he exclaimed, frustrated with whomever he spoke to. An elderly woman sat alone while knitting a long scarf. It collected around her feet in a pool of wool as her needles clicked away.

With so few people, Beth decided to take a chance. She ambled to the piano, opened the top, and peered inside. Just an intricate array of strings and nothing else. She tilted the music rack open and found nothing behind it. She opened the bench lid and discovered some sheet music and a few books of collected arrangements, titled *Showy Showtunes* and *Rousing Ragtime Ditties*. No red satin bag. *Humph*. She sat on the bench and tried to open any other part of the piano which could be opened.

"Miss, can I help you?" A Cunard staff member, wearing a custodial uniform wheeled a large garbage container from around the corner.

"Uh ... no thanks." Beth tried to look as if she knew what she was doing, but unfortunately playing the piano after so many years was beyond her abilities. Instead, she just tinkled the keys a little and tried to act nonchalant. The man raised an eyebrow, nodded, and continued to wheel his garbage can past her, picking up dirty napkins, newspapers, and other odd pieces of trash left over from the day.

Beth checked her watch, 10:45 p.m. One down, two more to go. She went back downstairs to the Queens Room to watch the orchestra finish up their set. The vocalist warbled the last stanza of *Memories*. The pianist gave a final flourish on the keys, ending the song in a big crescendo. The dancers finished waltzing and the sparse audience clapped appreciatively.

"Thank you, ladies and gentlemen, that concludes our show. We'll see you back tomorrow evening for our final performance—don't forget,

Big Band night!" The conductor gave a quick bow. The pianist gathered her music, closed the lid over the keys, and exited behind the curtain. The musicians packed up and dispersed. Beth sat in a chair and waited for more people to leave.

It took about ten minutes. Only a few waitstaff mingled, removing empty glasses and cocktail napkins from the small tables around the dance floor. Beth walked over to the grand piano at the front of the stage and pretended to just look.

Hmmm ... a piano. What a nice piano.

She went through the same drill as before. Nothing underside on the lid. Nothing behind the music rack. Only sheet music found inside the bench; this time it was *Songs to Swing By* and *Hold Me Close Harmonies*.

On her tiptoes, she leaned over to see the far side of the strings and even though she was careful not to bump the lid prop, she did. With a large crash, the top hit her in the backside as she fell forward, her face smushed against the strings.

What a disaster ... being swallowed by a baby grand! She quickly assessed the damage. Her back smarted, yes, but all in all she was okay. Beth imagined how she must have looked, with her feet dangling out like the Wicked Witch when Dorothy's house fell on her.

"Ah ... help! Help!" she cried from inside.

"Miss, what are doing?" a muffled voice asked from behind her.

"Can you get me out?"

"Hold on ..." The top was lifted and Beth quickly scooted backward from the ledge of the piano. "What are you doing?" It was the cleaning man from earlier. He still had his garbage can on wheels with him. He readjusted the lid prop.

"I was just looking at the piano. And I, uh, fell in."

"You must really like pianos," he said.

"Well, not anymore."

"Just be careful, now." He wheeled his garbage can away, looking back at her suspiciously.

Beth told herself to be extra, extra careful. *It could have been the end of me. Can you imagine? Cause of death: piano.* It wasn't even on The List.

She walked out of the Queens Room, trying to determine the fastest route back to the Commodore Club. When she turned a corner, she ran into someone she least expected. Mabel. The other woman's face turned further downwards once she seemed to recognize Beth.

"You!" Mabel spat. "I'll have you arrested." Her sweet, dulcet voice had disappeared along with her angelic disposition.

Beth gulped and replied, "For what?"

"*You* know." Mabel waved her cane at her.

"No, I don't." Beth tried to play it cool. She wondered how long it would last.

Mabel took a step closer toward Beth. She stuck her pointer finger at her, "*You* broke into my cabin. *You* stole something from me."

Up close, Beth noticed Mabel's eyebrows weren't plucked. They looked like two dead caterpillars.

"Mabel, if you want to call the cops—go ahead. I've got an interesting story to tell them myself," Beth responded, taking a step closer to her. *This old lady isn't going to scare me.* Beth got right up to her face. *Ewww.* Mabel had fish tonight and something garlic. The shrimp?

Mabel glared at her. "Once we get back to Southampton, Max is going to be there. And he'll make sure you don't find it."

"Find what?"

"You know, Ethel's will. It's *his* money. All of it. He's a smart boy. He'll figure out a way," she said.

Something snapped inside Beth. Enough. She'd had enough of this. All of it.

"Figure out a way? Figure out a way?" she screeched. "Max *always* figures out a way. He's stolen money for *years*. There's *nothing* left! It's all gone! *Gone!*" Beth shouted. "He spent *it all*. It wasn't even *his* to spend! Did it ever occur to him that Ethel had her *own* money? She didn't *need* Ezekiel's!" She didn't care who heard. "Max is *not* getting any more. Not a damn cent! He's an awful person ... and a thief and ..." Beth simultaneously ran out of both breath and words.

Mabel took an abrupt step backward. Her face froze in a look combining disbelief and fright. A small mew escaped her lips, as if a placeholder for what to say next. Something about it made Beth feel sorry for her and she was immediately embarrassed she yelled so loudly. But it only lasted a moment. Because shortly thereafter, Mabel regained her composure.

"You ..." she said, while she shook her cane again and pointed it at Beth. "Just prove he stole the money."

Beth glowered back at her and didn't respond. It was like a wordless duel. Seconds went by. Beth waited it out.

"I'm warning you."

"Warn all you want. But when you get a chance, tell Max he's an asshole. But then he's *so smart*, he probably already knows." Beth turned to walk away, but then twisted back and said, "And *you* go to hell!"

She stomped off. What a nasty, old biddy. Her heart rate thumped in her throat. But damn. It felt good to yell at her. Really good.

While marching down the hallway, she laughed a little. Then laughed a lot. *Oh, Vicky would've loved that. I wish she could have seen me.* She leaned up against the Cunard display case filled with historical mementos, giggling until tears stung her eyes.

Beth wondered how Max had stolen money over the years without the board knowing. Twenty-five million dollars doesn't just disappear without consequences. Did Aunt Ethel hear whispering from society friends: What was going on with the Foundation? Did the charities contact the board with imploring letters: Where did our funding go? Ethel didn't have the power to stop Max; all she could do was protect herself. Poor Ezekiel—everything he built was tumbling down.

That stopped Beth from giggling. The will was so important. She had to get the next clue. Hopefully she had scared Mabel enough for her not to follow her.

Get back on track. Okay, two out of three pianos searched and nothing. It means, through the process of elimination, the clue *must* be in the piano at the Commodore Club. Completely logical.

Back to Deck 10.

She stepped off the elevator to strains of vintage Depeche Mode. *Oh, man.* The Yacht Club was filled to capacity. She reluctantly ducked into the Commodore Club to see plenty of passengers still with cocktails. It was almost midnight. She couldn't just wait around for them to leave, right? It would take forever. Instead, she scampered back to the Yacht Club to have a quick drink with Alex and Mike. *Maybe that cute bartender is working?* The room pulsated with a full dance floor. *Awesome.* Mike and Alex waved to her. She ran over to hug them both.

CHAPTER 32

Two Weeks Ago

D r. Joan Einhorn sat behind her paper-strewn desk, her ten fingers making a tee-pee over a pile of Hershey's Kisses foils.

"So, Beth ... how do you feel?"

Dr. Joan always started her sessions this way. She never deviated from her shtick. Maybe that's why Beth liked her; she provided routine in a shaky timeline.

Since her parents' deaths, Beth had sunk into a deep depression. At first, she considered it was just a series of bad days, but the days stretched to months and then years. When her fragile psyche had paralyzed to the point of incapacitation and she couldn't leave her apartment for fear of the unknown, Frank begged her to get help. "You're just not yourself, pussycat."

Physical symptoms began to manifest. Pain in her chest, rapid heart-beats, excessive sweating. Was she dying? The third frantic trip to the emergency room changed everything. A first-year resident diagnosed anxiety attacks. Beth was relieved to know it wasn't a stroke or worse, a heart attack. The informational pamphlet provided at discharge illuminated more details, many already recognizable to her: irregular heartbeat, difficulty breathing, tingling in extremities, etcetera. They sounded like warnings on a prescription bottle. And it's what most doctors prescribed: medication.

"Why don't you try it?" Dr. Joan had asked at their first meeting, a decade ago. "I'll start you on a baby dose."

"No. I don't want to take pills." Beth, stubborn in her suffering, was also resolute in her treatment plan. "I'll just stay home."

Their initial appointment hadn't gone well. Beth's expectations were for immediate answers—a solution—not a strung-out process doomed to last months. Or, gulp, years. *And* it required her leaving the apartment.

"Okay. Just know medication is an option. Do you want to talk?" Dr. Joan asked.

Beth shrugged.

So, it began. The first year with Dr. Joan consisted of Beth shrugging and head shaking. Maybe an occasional nod. The second year produced mumbling. The third, actual words. But after Beth calculated the cost of health insurance copays for basically miming her therapy, she decided to make it more cost-effective. The last three years produced better results and lots of tears. But Dr. Joan was patient.

Together, they unpacked unresolved issues: Her parent's tragic death, estrangement from Vicky, her irrational correlation of Max being responsible for everything bad in her life (Dr. Joan called this association and attribution), poor self-image, anxiety ... but no actual phobias, only fears induced by anxiety which added to Beth's List. Both she and Dr. Joan were intent on checking each one off, but it was a slow process.

In the meantime, they developed positive self-talk, which seemed to be helping. They met bi-weekly.

"So, how do you feel?" Dr. Joan repeated. She unwrapped another Hershey's Kiss from an old glass fishbowl acting as a candy dish. "I hate dead things," she had mentioned when Beth asked about it years ago. On her messy desk also sat a plastic bust of psychologist Albert Bandura (Beth had to look him up), an Etch-a-Sketch (Dr. Joan said it was for younger clients, but Beth had a sneaking suspicion she actually played with it), and a collection of coffee cups from her travels. Bad motivational art from the 90s hung askew on the walls. Her office looked like a garage sale.

"I feel okay," Beth answered. "I went out to eat last night. I liked it, especially because I don't like to cook. Plus, it gave me an opportunity to people-watch. I didn't have to talk to anyone, just observe. It's good for my writing." She sipped some lukewarm coffee from a Bisbee, Arizona mug. It had a cowgirl on it.

"Where'd you go?"

"Wong Fu's. I've always ordered in ... never been inside the place. Did you know, there's an *actual* Wong Fu?"

"Really?" Dr. Joan popped another Kiss in her mouth.

"He's a nice man. Gave me an extra fortune cookie once he found out I was one of his best customers."

"What did it say?"

Beth opened her purse and pulled out a small bit of paper.

"*Life is either a daring adventure or nothing.*"

"That sounds promising. Was it the first or second fortune?"

"Does it matter?"

"It does."

Beth made a grimace. "It was the second one."

"What happened to the first?"

"I threw it away."

"What'd it say, Beth?"

She sighed before reciting, "*All things are difficult before they are easy.*"

Dr. Joan laughed. "Why'd you throw it away?"

"Because I didn't want to be reminded of *difficult* things. I'm trying to be more optimistic."

"Good for you! That's real progress."

"Wong Fu's was enough of an adventure. I still had to do my breathing exercises."

"It's why you have them … just in case. Now, let's take a look at The List."

Beth removed the folded piece of paper from her wallet. The paper was dirty and creased like ancient origami. Once opened, it was riddled in ink. Words and phrases covered the entire page. Only a few (very few) were crossed off.

"I can cross off 'eating in public' now, right?"

"Can you?" Dr. Joan unwrapped another Kiss. Beth wondered how much candy she ate in a day. Or was it only during her session? Maybe she really wanted a cocktail and this was the next best option at ten a.m.

"Well, I did it."

"Yes, but will you do it *again*?"

Beth sat back in the Ikea Poang chair. "Okay, I get it. I need to feel *comfortable* doing it." She looked up at a framed print. A pair of hands played on a piano keyboard with *Practice Makes Perfect* underneath in a large font. "I'm thinking about going to Athena's tonight for Greek food."

"Terrific! You'll be back in the world in no time." Dr. Joan smiled. She pulled out a hand mirror and faced it toward Beth. "So, how do you feel ... right now?"

Beth stared into it. "I'm fine."

"Yes, you are." Dr. Joan checked her watch. "Time's up, Beth."

CHAPTER 33

Beth stood with her tray at the Lido Buffet and looked wistfully at the monumental display of food. It wasn't because the choices overwhelmed her, but because she was hungover. The bacon was mocking her and especially the eggs Benedict. Her stomach did an unfamiliar lurch, bordering on a heave.

A muffin couldn't hurt. Plus, after tomorrow, these eating opportunities would end. Which was a good thing, because her linen pants already felt tight in the waist and she only bought them a few days ago. She sighed and selected a lemon poppy seed muffin. And a blueberry. So far, so good. She took her pill (day number four!) and some aspirin with freshly-squeezed orange juice. She slurped, cautiously, a cup of coffee.

Last night was *too* much fun. Alex had ordered them every cocktail on the menu while Mike insisted on dancing to every song, even the guitar ballads. They danced and sang until the DJ unplugged his equipment. Beth didn't remember stumbling back to her cabin, but it's where she woke up. Thankfully. She awoke with rings like dark pencil smudges under her eyes and it wasn't makeup. Her breath smelled like she had chewed on an ashtray. Her head continued to bang to an imaginary electronic baseline. She wondered how Alex and Mike were feeling this morning.

After a second cup of coffee and checking her stomach's willingness to settle, it was time to get back to work. Beth left the Lido and lumbered to the Commodore Club, which was empty. Finally! She walked over to the lounge area to the piano. She peered inside the baby grand. Nothing but piano strings. She investigated inside the bench. Also, nothing. No sheet music. Not even a scrap. She crawled underneath to see if anything was underside. Only a rogue spider web.

She got up, head pounding. How could she have missed it? She had checked each of the other pianos thoroughly, one even intimately.

That was it. All there was. No more pianos. She had blown it.

She waited for the anxiety to arrive. Anxiety which usually made her armpits awash in sweat. It never came. Just a loud beating of her heart. Was she upset? *Absolutely.* In control? *Yes.* But just in case, Beth sat down on the piano bench. *Breathe in and out. In and out.*

She had been so cocky last night—so sure she'd find it this morning. The one drink with the guys turned into many. With each one, she rationalized she could continue her search in the morning. But now ... what a disaster. Tears burned in the corners of her eyes. *No. No.* She couldn't give up. She must have missed it somewhere. She'd recheck all the pianos.

Beth pulled the haiku from her pocket and re-read it.

> Make joyful music.
> Keys are elementary,
> just like black and white.

Music ... keys... elementary ... where did she go wrong? Elementary. Maybe it didn't mean simple ... maybe it referred to school. Like elementary school. Kids. The Kids' Club? What was it called?

Beth raced back to her cabin to find her torn, worn-out map. Some of it was hard to read now but it was worth a try. Her head continued to pound. She took off running, bumping into Roberto holding a cleaning bucket and rag.

"Sorry!" she yelled, running down the passageway.

The Play Zone's door was locked, either to protect the kids from being snatched by evil pirates, or more so from escaping. From the window, Beth saw the three kids inside. One worked on a puzzle, another stacked blocks, and the third drove a truck over a carefully constructed city of Legos. A Play Zone staff member sat dazed and shell-shocked in the middle of the room, looking as if she wanted to throw herself overboard. It wasn't even noon yet. The attendant practically pounced after Beth knocked on the door.

Beth came up with a quick lie. "My friend was interested in sailing with her kids, so I told her I would check out the Kids' Club."

The staff member smiled and eager for a distraction, went out to get a brochure. Which left Beth alone with the three kids ... exactly her plan.

The older boy maneuvered a truck back and forth over the Legos and the younger one cried, "Hey, that's not fair—I'm telling Mom!"

The older boy ignored him. He looked up at Beth, "What's your name?"

"Beth. What's yours?"

"Jimmy. That's Michelle and Greg. I'm the oldest."

"Of course you are. Hey kids, is there a piano around, like a toy you can play with?" The three looked at each other and one actually scratched his head. Greg took the initiative, ran to the toy cabinet and dug around, tossing toys to the floor in his search.

"Is this it?" He brought over a small guitar.

"No, that's a ukulele," Beth said quickly, looking over her shoulder before the assistant came back. "A piano has keys you press with your fingers. Like this," she made the motion. All three kids were interested. "Can you help me find one, fast? Who can find it first?" Now it was a competition. The kids jostled each other while they searched the toy bin. All of a sudden, Greg squealed in excitement and abruptly stopped after Jimmy pulled something out of his hands.

"Not fair, doo-doo head!" Greg cried. Jimmy triumphantly brought Beth a Fisher Price keyboard. It was ancient - like from the 1970s. It was also sticky; Beth didn't want to know with what. She took it carefully by the corners. Black and white keys. She pushed on the keys but no sound came out.

"It's broken," Michelle stated matter-of-factly.

The assistant in the office opened file drawers and banged them closed. Beth didn't have a lot of time. She turned over the piano and saw a space for batteries. She unclipped the plastic latch. A small red bag. She quickly jammed it into her pants pocket just as the assistant returned.

"Here you go." She gave Beth a stack of brochures. "In case you have more friends."

"Thanks. Oh, I noticed this toy needs new batteries; the kids were showing me." She handed her the keyboard. "Nice talking to you, kids!"

Beth waved to them as she quickly exited. She sat on a staircase around the corner and took a soul-cleansing breath.

Oh, please let this be the last one! She untied the bag quickly. A silver heart charm fell into her lap. It was three dimensional and heavier than her others. Also, a piece of paper had been rolled into a scroll and tied with a thin red ribbon, just like a roll of sheet music. She unrolled the paper and read:

Here's the final clue.
Beth, good for you! Don't be late.
Your fate is at eight.

This is it! Oh, thank God. *I'm really going to do this.* She was giddy with glee. She sat on the stairs and hugged herself. Finally, for the first time in two weeks, Beth not only hoped success was in reach, she knew it.

She returned to her cabin to change her shoes—why *do* they keep squeaking? —and found a note on her desk written in neat block letters which looked vaguely familiar.

Someone turned in your bracelet to lost & found.
–Roberto

Resting on top of the note was her charm bracelet. Cleaned, of course.

Oh, happy day! Today's turning out to be great! Beth, thrilled to get her only piece of jewelry back, clipped the bracelet on her right wrist and headed back out. Her hangover quickly faded.

The last day at sea precipitated all kinds of onboard events. The photography studio slashed prices for a fire sale on all remaining photos. Please (we beg you) take these, we really don't want them. A sous-chef demonstrated intricate vegetable carving in the grand foyer. Passengers hung over the second-floor balcony and watched him create Mickey Mouse from a watermelon, papaya, and coconut. The gift shop sold discounted posters, pens, and bookmarks emblazoned with *Queen Elizabeth* in gold. At twenty percent off, the stores were making room for new merchandise. Beth finally succumbed and purchased a red hoodie with an embroidered Cunard logo. *Classy.*

"Daniel, I need to spend some money," she announced as she entered the jewelry store.

"I can definitely help." He immediately stopped polishing the glass cases.

"Do you have anything for cats?"

"Unfortunately, no. But if you are looking for something cat-themed, I have these." Daniel walked over to a showcase filled with diamonds and stood behind it. He unlocked and slid the door open. Each piece winked seductively at Beth, trying to catch her eye. Daniel placed a velvet pad on the counter and presented two identical paw prints in diamonds. "Fourteen-carat, white gold, about ten points of diamonds. Not very large stones, but still, nice color."

"Oh, those are nice earrings."

"Beth, they're cuff links," he corrected her.

"Oh ... oh! Then, they're perfect! I need a gift for my friend Frank. He's been watching my cat. How much are they?" She tilted them back and forth on the pad with her fingernail to watch them glitter.

"$950 US dollars."

"Do you have another pair?"

Daniel checked in the back stockroom and found a second set in yellow gold. Beth purchased them both. Now she had gifts for both Frank and Paul. Daniel cleaned and assembled them in Cunard presentation boxes and placed each in its own red satin bag.

Beth pulled out the last charm from her pocket. The puffed heart had some lint on it, which she tried to pick off. Daniel attached it to her bracelet.

"It's the last one," she said. A tinge of satisfaction inflicted her voice.

"Your bracelet looks far better than it did at the start of the cruise."

"I agree."

Her cabin door clicked shut. Beth sat at the desk and pulled her notebook from the drawer. First, she double-checked her onboard credit. Based on her last call to Raul, and after accounting for her recent jewelry purchases, she figured her balance was just under a thousand dollars. She could buy some wine tonight for the table and maybe blow the rest in the casino. She'd seen a slot machine called *Glitter Kitty*, which sounded hilarious.

But in the remaining time she had before dinner, Beth sat at her desk and found the pages covered with her doodles. The puzzle of arrows and circles materialized into an organized, methodical pattern. Her myriad questions now had answers. The most obvious answers were, well, the most obvious. Now, Beth felt confident she knew most of them.

She tapped her pen and strategized. She planned carefully what she would say and the order she would say it. This would be important. She couldn't help but feel some excitement for the last dinner on the ship. To celebrate, she'd wear her favorite dress, the silver sequined number purchased at the ship's boutique.

Beth showered, did her hair, and applied the red Harlot lipstick. Looking at herself in the mirror, she decided, *I look all right. Better than all right.* She smiled at herself, then wiped some lipstick off her teeth. Her luggage, now tightly packed with her new wardrobe and souvenirs, sat outside her cabin door. Cunard staff would pick it up after midnight and bring it down to customs. She had her tote bag to fill with any last remaining items, her dress, some toiletries, and any Cunard stationary left in the desk drawer. And the Cunard pens. And the hand lotion.

While taking the elevator to Deck 3, she chatted with some of the guests about the trip. They all agreed the weather had been fine, food outstanding, and they would miss it all. She stopped at the Midships bar and treated herself to a glass of champagne. Seated at the bar, she sipped her Veuve Clicquot and felt empowered. Excited about the future. Feelings she hadn't had in a very long time. *I hope it lasts. I feel ... confident.*

Beth unsnapped her evening bag and removed a piece of paper that was old and torn at the edges. She didn't bother unfolding it. She stared at it for a moment, then held it out to a votive candle on the bar. She quickly realized it was electronic, not an actual flame, which kind of robbed her of the transcendental moment. So instead of burning it, she tore it into pieces. She dropped it inside the crystal candle holder.

No more list of things I can't do. From now on they'll be things I want to do. She toasted Aunt Ethel silently. A man sitting next to her wearing a white dinner jacket whistled at her. Actually whistled. She laughed out loud in surprise.

When she entered the Britannia Restaurant, she studied her table-mates from afar. Their grayed heads were bowed over menus reviewing their dining options. A collective wealth of information and experiences. Such genuinely nice people. Honestly, she admitted, she wouldn't mind keeping in touch with all of them. But now, on the last night, she hoped she wouldn't piss them off.

Glenn seated Beth at her usual spot. After she greeted everyone at the table, Beth announced she would buy the wine this evening, as she had something to celebrate. Claps and murmurs, with a touch of incredulity thrown in, were vocalized around the table.

Constance asked, "What are we celebrating?"

"Yes, what's the occasion?" Ian inquired.

"Let's wait until the wine comes."

"How mysterious!" Madeline said. The other diners looked intrigued. Brigitte arrived with the wine bible and helped Beth select two whites and two reds.

Typical dinner conversations began. Constance and Madeline sold the merits of skydiving to Saul. Ian explained a menu item to Teresa. Bob and Judy politely argued about British politics. The wines arrived and were promptly uncorked. Beth sampled each and concluded them fine. Brigitte poured out.

Beth waited for conversations to find their natural lull before she stood up and cleared her throat. She was a little nervous. Just a little. The group quieted down and looked at her in polite anticipation. Whoever purchased the wine got to make speeches. It was almost expected.

"I'd like to propose a toast. To Table 8—a bunch of liars," Beth announced.

CHAPTER 34

Silverware clanked. Glasses tinkled. Music played from below. Conversation and laughter surrounded them from all sides. But Table 8 sat in awkward silence, their wine goblets suspended in the air.

"You must have forgotten that I'm a ghost writer, so I have experience wading through exaggerations and lies," Beth explained "In fact, I'm rather good at it." Any nervousness she had earlier was long gone. This was fun.

Her tablemates looked at each other, some with guilty faces, others in surprise. Their glasses, still raised high, trembled.

"You're all terrible liars, but I have to say ... you're still pretty terrific." Beth glanced down at her charm bracelet. "You've been helping me, or at least *most* of you." She smiled. "So, I thank you for that. Cheers." Beth raised her glass even higher and drank before she sat back down. A red lipstick stain marked her glass. The others tentatively sipped and waited to hear what came next.

"It's obvious my Aunt Ethel couldn't write the clues since she's dead. So, someone, or *lots of someones*, had to have helped," she explained. "Ian."

Ian looked up from gazing at his empty plate.

"You were a literary professor, so you know books. And the classics. You must have written the first clue and hid it in *The Odyssey*, right?"

Ian looked at the rest of the group, as if for permission. Then he shrugged a shoulder and said, "The jig is up. Ethel and I discussed literature for hours, as she adored books. Yes, I was the one. The most logical one to write it."

Beth nodded. Okay, this was going to be easy. Glenn arrived to take their dinner orders. Beth, liking her new-found authority, requested he return in a few minutes. She looked over accusingly at Bob Gunderson.

"Bob, nice try."

Bob crossed his arms across his big chest, narrowed his eyes at her, and tried to look mean. It didn't work.

"Early on, you said you were in oil and gas, then yesterday you imported wine. The best way to be caught in a lie is to forget what you lied about."

Bob bowed his head. "Yeah, I'm not very good at that. Plus, I forgot what wine bar in Madeira you needed to be at. I almost ruined the whole thing. I'm sorry. Boy, was I ever glad to see you running for the ship. I would've never forgiven myself if you didn't make it." He looked at her with his forehead wrinkled and creased.

"You're not a master of deception. You forget your wallet, your camera ..." Beth said. "But still, I think someone else helped with changing the venue." She remembered Mabel talking to the tour guide earlier that day. She probably paid Constancia to change the itinerary.

"Madeline ..." Beth turned toward her. "I know you love adventure. Sometimes it's hard keeping up with you."

Madeline smiled. "Life is short ..."

"Yeah, and 'most poor suckers are starving to death.' I've heard that a few times, too. You've dived at La Palma before, haven't you?" Beth asked.

"Yes." She patted her hair.

"You've actually dived with Maria before?"

"Yes." She touched her earrings.

"You seemed to know the gift shop didn't have much but sweatshirts."

"Damn, I thought I was being awfully deceptive, I guess not," Madeline said. "But I'm so glad you enjoyed yourself. Scuba diving is such an exciting sport."

"Constance."

Constance choked on her wine as she swallowed. "Yes, dear?"

"You have such a wicked sense of humor. Only *you* could have written the clue for Tenerife. You knew about the bronze statues. It was you, right?"

"It *was* me and thank you for the compliment." Constance's eyes danced merrily.

Beth looked around the table for her next victim.

"Judy, you've been to Lisbon before, correct?" Beth asked.

Judy fidgeted with her silverware. "I have no idea what you're talking about."

"Oh, come on Judy, you're a bloody terrible liar." Saul laughed.

"Okay, yes, we've been to Lisbon many times. But how did you know? I thought I was being frightfully clever," she said.

"You went out of your way to mention how you've never been there. Plus, how Restaurant de Santa Luzia was your favorite. How you loved their mussels. And how the cherry ginja was terrific ..."

"Okay, okay," Judy conceded. "I mucked it up."

"Who's next?" Beth looked around the table. Teresa, silent as usual, gave a little wave of her hand.

"Okay, Teresa. You taught piano lessons to kids, so you must have been the one to write the last clue. *And* I finally found it, by the way. Today."

Teresa smiled.

Beth continued, "So ... who *placed* the clues? In some cases, there just wasn't enough time. Especially on the tours, you were with me the whole day. This leaves me one more mystery to figure out."

"Details, details," remarked Madeline, as she waved her hand in a dismissive action. "But, Beth ... the most important thing of all ... did you find Ethel's will? Isn't that what we're celebrating?"

"Almost, there's still Saul," Beth said.

The tips of his ears grew pink.

"You're the last one at the table," She explained. "But the first one I suspected. On the second day of the cruise, I noticed something. Judy doesn't wear earrings. But you were looking for her missing earring under the table."

Saul hung his head. The rest of the table burst out laughing.

"You got me there. Beth, you're a corker," he said.

"Constance, can I borrow your flashlight?" Beth asked. Constance rummaged through her evening bag and handed it to Beth. Beth pushed back her chair and got on her knees before anyone could say a thing. She rested her chin on the tabletop and repeated, "My fate is at eight," the last line of the last clue.

She hitched up her dress and crawled underneath among the shoes and handbags. She noticed Bob wore white socks with his dress shoes. She looked up and tried not to hit her head on the underside of the table.

Directly in the middle, taped underneath with at least a full roll of packing tape, was a fat legal-sized envelope. *Jackpot!* Beth crawled to the center. She picked at the edges of the tape and unpeeled it from the underside of the table. She crawled out backward. She smoothed her hair and dress with one hand, as she held up the envelope with the other in triumph.

All seven faces beamed, genuinely happy for her. Beth sat down and used a butter knife to saw through the tape. Constance squeezed her arm in encouragement. She pulled out a sheath of papers from the envelope.

This is the last will and testament of Ethel Papadopoulos Lorenzo Birnbaum. Being of sound mind and body...

"Mr. Watkins, Mr. Watkins, I found it!" Beth screeched from the phone at the purser's desk.

"Easy, Beth. I can hear you," the lawyer said.

"I found it, I found the will," she said for a third time.

"Terrific! I knew you could do it. Great work. Now scan and email the complete document to me tonight. When you get to Southampton, overnight the originals."

"Will do. How's that for timing?"

"Yes, it helps tremendously. We can file it immediately and stop Max from proceeding with the old trust. Ethel would be very proud of you.

Now, please hang up and send me those pages!" He immediately clicked off.

Beth went across the hall to Connexions and scanned the document. All twenty-nine pages. While it processed through the machine, she read the pages as they fell into the tray. The majority of the text was complicated legalese. But most importantly, she wanted to see who got what. The bequests began on page eighteen. The SPCA, AIDs & the Arts, the New York Public Library, and the Metropolitan Art Museum were all receiving substantial sums. A long list of more charities continued for the next few pages. She didn't see Max's name listed anywhere. Yippee! But Beth also didn't see hers or Vicky's. It didn't entirely surprise her. Ethel had promised Mary she'd never give the girls money. She had kept her promise to the very end.

The machine saved the document as an electronic PDF which she emailed to Mr. Watkins, cc'ing herself for good measure. She waited until her copy hit her email's inbox. Beth put the original pages back in the envelope.

"There." She sighed. *Done.*

She made her way back to the dining room. *Max Birnbaum, you're in for a surprise. No more money for you, jackass.* Down below, guests at the commodore's table ate dessert. Mabel sat next to Commodore Pederson. Beth held on to the railing and peered down at her. Mabel, who must have sensed Beth's stare, raised her head. Even though it was totally and completely childish, Beth held up the will with one hand and gave Mabel the middle finger with the other.

Table 8 was just finishing their late dinner, so she sat and ordered dessert for herself. Actually, she ordered all three desserts listed on the menu. *Hey, I missed dinner*, she rationalized. Glenn served her coconut

ice cream, strawberry cheesecake, and a caramel torte covered in chocolate ganache, all on one plate.

She deserved it. She took big forkfuls and savored each bite. She did,
however, remember to use her dessert fork.

There was much to talk about. As each diner compared notes about
their haikus and specific clues, a competition started as to whose was
funnier, whose most clever.

"Thank goodness for Ian," Saul said. "I wouldn't have known a haiku
if it bit me in the bottom."

Ian chuckled and informed them all they were excellent students.

"Some of the haikus actually rhymed," Beth noted.

She acknowledged fondling statues in Tenerife was the most embarrassing, although singing in Madeira was a close second. The scuba trip
was the most fun. She counted herself lucky to find the clue in the sandcastle. Even luckier that she could steal it back from Mabel. Rescuing the
ginja bottle was difficult. Beth confessed the last clue, the piano, created
the most panic. Laughter reigned as Table 8 rehashed the entire cruise.

As much as they wanted to take credit for their parts, Beth knew
someone else had masterminded the entire affair, executed the plan, and
managed all the details. Orchestrating the diners at Table 8 didn't just
happen on its own. It must have been like herding cats. Also, how did
Aunt Ethel know about The List? She would figure it out later. In
the meantime, she let them revel. Beth sat back, crossed her legs, and
sipped her wine. Though elated to have solved the puzzle, she felt a little
melancholy knowing this was their final evening together.

"How did you all know Aunt Ethel?" she asked when the conversation
died down a bit.

Ian volunteered, "We've been on several cruises with her. This very one last year. She sat in your seat, that very seat." He pointed to Beth's chair. "Ethel had everything organized. She asked us to help when she needed to put her plan into play. When we were notified of her passing, it only left us a short time to get on the ship. But we had a little inside help." He fingered the diamond Cunard pin on his lapel. "Plus, we are retired and fancy-free, so to speak, and can move fast."

"What a wonderful lady," Saul said.

"Do you remember Lisbon?" asked Bob.

"Oh, we drank so much ginja, I didn't think I'd ever look at a cherry again," Constance roared.

Judy laughed. "And the beach at Las Canteras? Remember how Ethel lost her bikini bottom when we went parasailing?" she hooted.

Oh, what Beth wouldn't have given to cruise with Aunt Ethel. As much fun as she had by herself, it would've been hilarious with Aunt Ethel.

"Lots of great memories," Saul said.

"We were the three musketeers, Constance, Ethel, and I. We miss her terribly," Madeline said. "But we're so happy to have met you, Beth."

"Thanks," Beth said. "Now, I'd like to propose another toast, a proper toast to my Aunt Ethel." She stood up. "Thanks for introducing me to this cast of characters, devising a most interesting plot, and especially for this happy ending."

Glasses raised and clinked again. They all sipped.

A small voice piped up, "You should write a book."

The table fell silent. Teresa Gunderson had finally spoken. After twelve days, she finally had something to say.

"What?" Beth asked.

"You should write a book. You're a writer, aren't you?" Teresa blinked like an apprehensive owl.

"Yes." Beth gulped and said faintly, "Maybe I should," with more conviction than she realized possible.

Everyone agreed with Teresa.

"It'll be a bestseller."

"An original!"

"I'd buy at least three copies."

Beth blushed from their avid support and encouragement. *Hmmm. Maybe it wasn't a bad idea.* She had lots of great characters ... an engaging story with plenty of intrigue and plot ... Beth decided to run it past Frank when she got back to New York.

They brainstormed possible book titles, "Table for Eight," "The Great Eight," they got raunchier as the evening wore on.

Bob requested Beth make him thinner in her book. Madeline wanted younger.

"Now, that wouldn't be who you are," Beth said with some authority. "All your flaws make you infinitely more interesting as a character."

"That's right, we all should be thankful for who we are." Constance said. She glanced at Beth. Beth nodded back.

As the clock crawled to eleven o'clock, the wait staff hovered patiently in the corners of the dining room. Most other diners had said their final goodbyes and departed. Now an empty cavern filled with dirty plates and glasses, white napkins tossed here and there, the Britannia Restaurant had finished her service for the voyage. Beth gave each of her dining mates a hug and thanked them for their help.

She shook Glenn's hand. "I'll always know my salad fork from my dinner fork, thanks to you," she said. She signed her bar bill. *Eeek!* Five-hundred dollars on wine. It was worth it.

Satisfaction filled Beth. It cleaned all the empty cob-webby corners of her soul. The balloon of sorrow she had been lugging for years and apprehensive about the consequences of breaking ... well, it finally popped. *She* had made something happen. Now Max had to suffer consequences. A small revenge, even if misplaced. Yet, it felt so good, Beth went with it. She wondered what Dr. Joan would have to say about all these new revelations. Beth felt so light, she skipped out of the dining room in her kitten heels. And didn't trip.

But she took her time returning to her cabin. It was her last night onboard and she wanted to spend as much time as possible taking her leave of the *Elizabeth*. Goodbye Golden Lion—best pub lunch ever! Goodbye flower arrangement—you smell marvelous! Goodbye library—great book selection! Goodbye Queens Room—never danced there, but maybe someday! The casino looked empty, except for a handful of die-hard gamblers slouched at the roulette wheel. Mabel was nowhere to be found. Maybe she really *was* out of money. Beth stopped. *Oh, what the hell.*

She took out her ship's card and used onboard credit to buy a hundred-dollar chip. She placed it on her new lucky number, eight.

The croupier raised an eyebrow and asked, "Madam, are you sure you want to place the bet on a single number? The odds aren't in your favor."

They never used to be. But, "Yes, I'm sure."

The croupier looked over to the pit boss for approval, who inclined his head and nodded consent.

The dealer spun the wheel and announced, "No more bets," as the tiny ball started to circle round in the track. He waved his hand across the table for emphasis. The wheel went clackety-clack ... clackety-clack. The ball bounced into 36, then jumped into 9, then 29, and back to 36. The wheel slowed to clickety ... clickety ... click. Beth clutched the back of the chair in front of her as the ball finally stopped and rested in ... 8. The table of gamblers burst out in surprised applause.

The croupier winced as he said, "Congratulations."

The winning number paid out thirty-five to one ... which meant Beth now had thirty-six hundred more dollars in her account. At the payment cage, she handed over her ship's ID for the credit. What could she possibly spend the money on? All the shops were closed. No more alcohol to buy. Then an image clicked in her head. A shiny red car. After a somewhat heated discussion with Raul at the purser's desk, which took longer than she planned, they eventually came up with a solution. Satisfied, Beth went back to her cabin.

She undressed and brushed her teeth. She slept soundly in the big comfortable bed with a wide smile on her face. Ah, sweet justice. Finally.

CHAPTER 35

B eth stood on her balcony for the last time. The *Queen Elizabeth* had company in the Southampton port: a similar-looking ship was docked on her left. She could make out *Queen Mary 2* on its hull. She looked bigger, but from Beth's angle, it was too difficult to tell. Another cruise ship—a gigantic monstrosity with three-story waterslides and a rock-climbing wall—was docked further down. Yikes, it was huge.

The *Elizabeth* had to be turned around in just a few hours for her next voyage. Beth watched industrial-sized cranes and forklifts transport supplies between the dock and the ship via a car-sized hole in her hull. Dock workers scurried about, almost a blur, as they quickly exchanged garbage and recycling for fresh vegetables. There were foodstuffs, bottled water, and a ginormous pallet of shrink-wrapped toilet paper swinging precariously toward the ship.

That's a lot of toilet paper ... the magic is gone. She sighed.

Commercial dollies wheeled passengers' luggage into the terminal. Packed with crumpled and wrinkled finery, the baggage held evening gowns, dress shirts, and bowties all destined for dry cleaning. Thousands of black bags were stacked on top of each other. Some bags had scarfs or bright yarn tied to handles so their owners could identify them. Good Luck.

How will I ever find mine? Maybe she should've bought an orange suitcase.

After a hasty shower, Beth shoved the remaining bath products into her tote bag. The Cunard slippers, too. She looked in all the drawers and double-checked the closet. Everything was packed and the cabin looked very empty. The last red gladiola stem sat lonesome in the vase. It tipped to one side, its head bowed, crumpled, and faded. When Beth touched the petals, they fell to the table.

How poetic ... it must be my cue.

Oh, she would miss the comfy bed, generous pile of pillows, and sheets with thread-counts so high she couldn't count them. She said goodbye to her luxurious cabin and shut the door for the final time. Slightly depressed, Beth dragged her feet upstairs to Deck 10 for breakfast.

The Lido Buffet! Food always makes things better. A final opportunity to shove as much food in her maw as she could, since tomorrow it would be back to lackluster frozen dinners. Unfortunately, her hopes for a genteel breakfast were soon dashed as she walked through the automatic double doors. Inside, it resembled a clearance sale at Macy's.

Passengers frenzied, almost manic, searched for their waffles, eggs, and breakfast meats. They jostled and elbowed. They ran, not walked. Recognizing their normal, humdrum lives awaited in only a few hours, it was every person for themselves. Cunard civility ... now in danger of immediate extinction. Beth grimaced. During the entire cruise, she had never witnessed the buffet run out of anything. Not even parsley garnish. The noise was deafening.

Beth looked for a seat and wound up sharing a table with other passengers, since it was the only way to sit, eat, and hopefully not get hurt. She tried to tune it out. She didn't want this to be her last memory of Cunard. Instead, she wanted to enjoy her remaining few hours thinking back on the positive aspects of her trip. Somehow, Beth and the *Queen Elizabeth* had finally become friends. How did that happen?

A ship-wide announcement reminded all guests to assemble in the Queens Room to wait until their scheduled disembarkation time. It made sense. Otherwise, the gangplanks would be awash with the canes and wheelchairs of anxious passengers exiting simultaneously. Beth's assigned time was 10:30 a.m. Not in any rush, she sat and drank a third cup of coffee as the Lido cleared out.

A passenger slipped a muffin into her bag. *Now that's a good idea.* Waiting in Gatwick airport for the next scheduled flight back to New York could take a while. *I may need a muffin too.* But by the time Beth got to the bakery station, alas, the muffins were gone except for a few crumbs even she could resist.

Over by the coffee machines, Mabel, dressed in her traditional black, poured coffee into a cup and fussed with cream and sugar packets. Her tray, piled high with food, sat off to one side. Her back was turned toward Beth, who noted condiments arranged nearby. She considered sprinkling tabasco onto Mabel's plate of scrambled eggs. No, she couldn't. It would be too mean, even for Mabel. But still ... Beth exited fast before changing her mind. Goodbye, Lido!

In the Queens Room, the pandemonium continued. It looked like Grand Central Station ... at Thanksgiving ... during a snowstorm. Purses, shopping bags, and small carry-on luggage scattered around passengers like an obstacle course. All seats were occupied, so people perched on their luggage. Again, uncharacteristic chaos unsettled everyone. After last evening's grandeur waltzing to a live orchestra, sipping cocktails, and using fish forks, it all seemed ... unseemly.

The lucky ones, those who had found a chair, didn't dare leave their sacred spots. They hunkered down with the day's newspapers (thoughtfully brought onboard by the staff) and got caught-up on news they hadn't really missed for the past twelve days. Smartphones appeared; texts, emails, and social media posts swirled across the virtual atmosphere. Switched on, their musical beeps, rings, and tones sounded throughout the room.

Beth spied a chair in the far corner and took off running. Her age won over experience, as she quickly maneuvered herself toward the vacancy and outgained a number of nimble octogenarians to get it. *Ha*!

She plopped down and crossed her legs. Where did these calf muscles come from? A nice souvenir from hours of walking. She arranged her red, polka-dot dress which coordinated nicely with her hat. Now tan with sunglasses perched confidently on her head, she looked like a well-seasoned traveler. Her bracelet gave her look just a little more shine ... a twinkle. She wondered if Frank would even recognize her. This cruise was like a makeover both inside and out. Maybe she would go to her publisher's party.

Then she noticed something interesting. On their final day, passengers wore jeans, T-shirts, and sneakers. Basic, everyday clothing. Clothing she wore all the time at home. For some reason, she took great comfort in that. The show was over, the costumes put away, and the passengers onboard one of the most luxurious ships in the world would have to go home and clean out lint traps in the dryer. There was always next year to pretend again. A man next to her removed his shoes and had a hole in his sock. She quickly placed a hand over her mouth to prevent her laughing out loud.

From her tote bag, she pulled out a small blue folder embossed with gold edging she had found slipped underneath her cabin door that morning. Inside was a glossy 5 x 7 photograph taken by the ship's photographer on the last formal night. All of Table 8 squeezed in laughing. Lots of teeth. Beth had her mouth open, yelling something. She looked good. Her new hairstyle, contacts, red lipstick. But most importantly, her smile ... wide, happy, and confident. She compared it to the photo she bought while arriving on the first day. Geez.

She flipped to the back of the group photo and read:

Dear Beth,
Don't forget us when you become famous! Our addresses for autographed copies
of your book ...
With Fondness,
Table 8

All their names and addresses were neatly spelled out.

While she sat among the frenetic noise and hubbub, Beth couldn't *help* but smile. So many good things were happening ... okay not just good, but fantastic. Terrific. In addition to the wonderful port stops, she made new friends and had a book idea to propose to Frank. Would he go for it? He always said when she was ready to write ... in any case, she was ready to try.

Also, her bracelet jangled with new improved memories.

Plus, she would see Grendel soon. Hopefully, he would forgive her.

And, The List was confetti. Torn to bits. What would she and Dr. Joan talk about now?

But most importantly, she had accomplished her goal: the will was safely in Mr. Watkin's hands. Things were really looking up. She was pretty-darned pleased with herself. She sat and gloated.

Beth realized the trip was about her. Not about the money, nor to get even with Max (though it was a great motivator) but to start living. She'd spent too much time focused on the dead when there's living to be had. Yes, it meant she needed to make amends with Vicky.

Without pausing, she pulled out her cell phone and switched it on. She scrolled down her contact list and found her sister's info. She took a deep breath and called. The phone immediately went to voicemail; Vicky's voice asked her to leave a message. Beth said, "Hi, it's your sister. Call me?" and hung up. She did it. Now the ball was in Vicky's court.

Beth picked up a discarded newspaper and tried to read. But she couldn't. She giggled. If all those weren't enough reasons to smile, there was one more thing. And this one was a goodie. Before she left her cabin that morning, she left a big fat envelope on her desk.

Dear Roberto,
Nice job. You were very sneaky.
Here's a little thank you for successfully managing this entire affair.
I need you to do one more thing—the next time you're in New York City,
please contact Paul Patronis. He's a musical producer and a good friend of mine.
His info is below. Please do, because you have great talent. You see, life is a
banquet.
But no matter what, let's keep the whole Spanx incident to ourselves, okay?
Best,
Elizabeth Schiff

Included with the letter was a crisp stack of forty hundred-dollar bills. Beth imagined the expression on his face when he read it. She hoped, really hoped, he would take a chance.

Last night in her cabin, Beth had arrived at the conclusion that Table 8's roles were small. Valuable, but minor in the grand scheme of the scavenger hunt. Yes, they wrote the haikus, but that was about it.

Someone delivered Aunt Ethel's letter and flowers to her cabin the first day. *Someone* packaged the haikus and charms together in red satin bags from the jewelry store. *Someone* had legible and recognizable handwriting. *Someone* hid the clues, especially in the sandcastle in Las Palmas. It was the only spot she didn't have a likely candidate ... everyone at Table 8 had been accounted for. Plus, she had seen him there. Only *someone* with intimate knowledge of the ship and the ports could do it. Plus, they had to be young, smart, and have lots of energy ... Roberto.

What a guy. He must have worked his tail off during this cruise. Not only did he fix her glasses, unstick her from a dress, and get stains out of her clothes, but he did his normal everyday work and planted all the clues. Where did he find the time? *He must be so happy I'm leaving.* She had put some money aside to tip him, but after thinking about all he did and winning last night at roulette, Beth figured he deserved it all.

Still, she had a few unanswered questions. Not all the lines had connected in her notebook. Who initially contacted Roberto? Had Aunt Ethel known him? Who masterminded the nitty-gritty details? Another mystery to solve later. She had done plenty on this trip and was looking forward to reading with Grendel on the old velvet couch in her apartment. *And* writing a book. Her own.

"Paging passenger Elizabeth Schiff? Elizabeth Schiff? Please see the purser's desk." A voice over the ship's announcement system shook her back to the present. She put down the newspaper she hadn't been reading, grabbed her hat and tote bag. She gave up her coveted chair and walked down the grand staircase to Deck 1.

When she arrived at the purser's desk, a man in a wrinkled suit smiled at her. Then he waved. Wildly. With his whole body, like he was ecstatic to see her. He looked vaguely familiar, yet misplaced. She'd seen the man before, but in a different setting—one far removed from the ship. As she got closer, Beth smelled his cologne. Pine trees in Colorado. *I've never been to Colorado,* she reminded herself.

Then Beth saw the chipped front tooth. The handsome, yet quirky face from her apartment hallway all those days ago when he delivered the letter which started this entire thing. His eyeglasses had tape on the corner.

"Hi, Beth!" he said. "Did you like the flowers?"

Beth stood with her hat in her hands. All she could manage was, "Huh?"

"The flowers. In your cabin. You got them, right?"

"The gladiolas? *You* sent them?"

"You had a bunch at your apartment. So, I figured ..."

"Oh ... yes. Thanks, they were very nice." What does this guy want? She gave him a questioning face, with a wrinkled brow and pursed lips.

"Anyways, my dad wants to talk to you."

"Who *are* you?" Beth burst out. Her reaction must have startled him, because he nervously rubbed a shoe on the back of his trouser leg.

He swallowed. "I'm J.J. Jr. I'm the '& Son.'"

"You're kidding."

"No."

"You're Mr. Watkins's son?"

"Yes."

"Have you been onboard the whole time?" Beth asked.

"No, I just got on to see you."

"Oh."

They continued looking at each other. Passengers streamed around them like water around a steadfast boulder in a raging river. Nonetheless, carry-ons, shopping bags, and duty-free liquor boxes bumped up against them. He took Beth by the elbow and they relocated to a safer spot behind a column with a potted palm.

She wondered if he liked cats, but instead asked, "What does J.J. stand for?"

"Jay-Jay."

"What?"

"J-A-Y. J-A-Y," he spelled out.

"Seriously?"

"Yeah."

"Your family's hilarious."

"Tell me about it. But you can call me John. Anyway, he *does* want to talk to you." John handed Beth his cell phone. It was warm from his hand.

She cleared her throat, "This is Elizabeth."

"Beth, it's J.J. Watkins."

"Mr. Watkins. You scared me. Is everything okay? Did you get the email last night? The attachment?" She pulled out her lipstick from the tote bag as she slid the phone between her ear and shoulder.

"Yes, yes. We got it just fine."

"Oh, thank God. You had me worried." She turned around to make sure John wasn't looking and applied another coat. "I'll overnight the originals once I leave the ship, just like we planned." She smacked her lips together.

"I have something for you ... that is if you want it," he replied.

"What?"

"While going through your aunt's personal effects, we found something which may be of interest to you. It seems there's some documentation."

"Documentation?" She put the lipstick back in her bag. She hoped she got none of it on her teeth.

"Detailed financials from the Birnbaum Foundation."

"So?"

"It's evidence of Max stealing from the Foundation ... just as we suspected. This could put him away, Beth. But we need your help to get it."

She reached out for the trunk of the potted palm to steady herself. "Are you kidding me?"

"No."

"Is this a joke? Come on, Mr. Watkins ..."

"Justice will not be served until those who are unaffected are as outraged as those who are. Benjamin Franklin."

Beth dropped her hat on the floor. Her tote bag slid off her shoulder. If this were true, it could change everything. No, Max wasn't responsible for her parents' death or estrangement from Vicky, but in some strange existential way, by nailing him, she'd get justice for others. Mr. Watkins was right. Max was still a bad man. A rush of heat enveloped her; was it excitement?

"Beth, are you there?"

"Yes."

"It's your choice. Are you up for it?"

Beth considered it for a moment, a *mere* moment, before saying, with a confident and unequivocal "Yes."

"Excellent, my dear! Ask John if he has something for you."

She turned toward John.

"John, do you have something for me?" she repeated.

He grinned and his chipped tooth looked even more comical. Not in a bad way. John handed her a white envelope from inside his jacket pocket embossed with the Cunard logo. Beth put the phone back up to her ear.

"Now Beth," continued Mr. Watkins, "you're going on a trip. Here's your ticket. The *Queen Mary 2* sails in four hours."

Beth froze. "Oh, crap."

THE END

Author's Note

I know.

Really, I do.

There are errors and general mistruths, but this is a work of fiction and I daresay, some were intentional. So, dear reader, before you contact me about: the safety drill happening the day *after* embarkation, the Midships Bar's *turquoise* velvet furniture, and cabin #7058 being a *suite*, I already know they're incorrect. But I love you for caring about the accuracy of such a gorgeous cruise ship ... I mean *ocean liner*. In this, my debut novel, I get to play pretend and revise details to help the story sing. Or at least hum along to a familiar tune.

I've had the extreme good fortune to travel on all three Cunard ships: the *Queen Mary 2*, the *Queen Victoria*, and the *Queen Elizabeth* (don't worry *Anne*, I'm looking at you next!). They're an inspiration for stories, characters, and plot twists. Onboard I can't help but feel inspired to write. I started this novel seven years ago, and it's been a voyage with both rocky waves and calm seas. But in the end, the destination was worth it.

Surprise! There may (or may not) be clues in actual places written about - just don't ask me which. If you are lucky enough to find one (or two), please post a snap to #elizabethsails on social media and leave for fellow travelers to do the same.

For readers who travel by car, ship, train, plane, escalator, elevator, or armchair, I wish you safe and memorable journeys. For those who haven't, what are you waiting for? "The world is a banquet," my friends. Eat and drink up.

Acknowledgments and Oodles of Thanks

For my professional team: literary agent Madelyn Burt, Rising Action Publishing Co. editors Alexandria Brown and Tina Beier, copy editor Marthese Fenech, marketing specialist Miruna Cucu, cover designer Miss Nat Mack, and Simon & Schuster for distribution.

For Cunard support: Jackie Chase, US Public Relations; Andrea Lenihan, UK Public Relations; and the ship librarians.

For subject matter expertise: Suzie Germany, JD; Edward Lacy, DDS; Farouk Parker, MD, Cunard Chief Medical Officer; Sally Sagoe, Cunard Entertainment Director; and Teresa Smith, MS.

For the fearless Prestigious Rigden Writers group, both current and past members: Donna Bevans, Louise Frager, Anne Hunsinger, Jack Matthews, and Kathy Mendt

For early eyes: Kim Dinan and Rachel Weaver

For beta readers: Kevin Finucane, Jeanmarie & Tom Muldoon, Joel Sanda, and Riki Urban

For craft education: Aspen Words 2019, Lighthouse Writers, Northern Colorado Writers, Rocky Mountain Fiction Writers, and the Women's Fiction Writers Association.

For initial professional validation: Alicia Clancy, Angie Hodapp, Paula Munier, and Janet Ried.

For cheerleading authors: Rumaan Alam, Erin Bartels, Lainey Cameron, Kerrie Flanagan, Alison Hammer, J.C. Lynne, Laura Mahal, April Moore, Amy Rivers, Ronda Simmons, Paulette Stout, Jessica Strawser, Chuck Wendig, and Tracey Enerson Wood.

For my writing retreat roommate extraordinaire: Eleanor Shelton

For offering unwavering encouragement: neighbors, friends, and family too numerous to mention

For courage: my Owens family

For all the above and everything else: Greg Soukup

About the Author

Kristin Owens, Ph.D. is a full-time writer based in the United States. She has over a hundred bylines with celebrated magazines such as Writer's Digest, Wine Enthusiast, and 5280. Her personal essays have won Honorable Mention for the 2018 New Millennium Writing Awards, awarded finalist for the 2019 New Letters' award in nonfiction, and are included in RISE! Colorado's 2020 Book of the Year. She holds certifications with the Court of Master Sommeliers and Cicerone, and travels the world writing about wonderful wines, beautiful beers, and surprising spirits. You can find her working and playing on cruise ships. Elizabeth Sails is her debut novel.